# Diva

Also by Daisy Goodwin

*The American Heiress*
*The Fortune Hunter*
*Victoria*

# Diva

Daisy Goodwin

ST. MARTIN'S PRESS
NEW YORK

First published in the United States by St. Martin's Press, an imprint of St. Martin's Publishing Group

DIVA. Copyright © 2023 by Daisy Goodwin. All rights reserved. Printed in the United States of America. For information, address St. Martin's Publishing Group, 120 Broadway, New York, NY 10271.

www.stmartins.com

Designed by Jen Edwards

Library of Congress Cataloging-in-Publication Data

Names: Goodwin, Daisy, author.
Title: Diva / Daisy Goodwin.
Description: First edition. | New York : St. Martin's Press, 2024. |
Identifiers: LCCN 2023036026 | ISBN 9781250279927 (hardcover) |
    ISBN 9781250279934 (ebook)
Subjects: LCSH: Callas, Maria, 1923–1977—Fiction. | Onassis, Aristotle
    Socrates, 1906–1975—Fiction. | LCGFT: Biographical fiction. |
    Novels.
Classification: LCC PR6107.O6625 D58 2024 | DDC 823/.92—dc23/
    eng/20230817
LC record available at https://lccn.loc.gov/2023036026

Our books may be purchased in bulk for promotional, educational, or business use. Please contact your local bookseller or the Macmillan Corporate and Premium Sales Department at 1-800-221-7945, extension 5442, or by email at MacmillanSpecialMarkets@macmillan.com.

First Edition: 2024

10  9  8  7  6  5  4  3  2  1

*In memory of Hope Dellon—a great editor and a beloved friend.*

# AUTHOR'S NOTE

This is a novel about Maria Callas, not a biography, so while I have stuck to the facts as far as possible, I have taken a few liberties when it comes to dates. I am sure there will be many keen Callas fans who will spot these liberties, but I hope they will allow me some dramatic license. I wanted to tell a story as compelling as its subject.

# Overture

# PROLOGUE

## *The Treasure*

It had snowed the night before and for once, the sixteen-year-old Maria Kalogeropoulou felt grateful for the clumpy men's brogues that were the only shoes in Athens large enough for her size nine feet. She hadn't seen snow since leaving New York, three years ago. The night before, she had been listening to the radio and Milton, her sister's boyfriend, had turned to Maria and said that maybe she should think about going back to America. "Everyone thinks that the Italians are going to invade. You would be safer there."

A year earlier, Maria would have been delighted at the idea of going back to the States and her father. But not now. She couldn't possibly leave her singing teacher, the great Spanish soprano Elvira de Hidalgo.

It usually took Maria twenty minutes to walk from the apartment on Patission Street to the Conservatoire, but today the snow was slowing her down. As she turned the corner into Syntagma Square, she saw a familiar figure come out of an apartment building.

"Madame," she cried, slipping and sliding on the snow as she tried to catch up with her teacher.

Elvira de Hidalgo turned to smile at the eager face in front of her.

"Madame! I have mastered it. The trill." Standing in the middle of the road, Maria started to sing the trill from the mad scene in the second act of *Lucia di Lammermoor*, her voice so urgent and full of emotion that it shook the snow-muffled silence of the street.

Elvira put up a hand to silence her.

Maria looked mortified. "Did I make a mistake? I was so sure I got it right this time."

Elvira sighed. "That is not why I stopped you. Maria, you should not be singing at the top of your voice in the street."

Maria looked back at her in surprise. It had clearly not occurred to her that there was anything strange about her behavior. Of all Elvira's pupils, Maria was always the first to arrive and the last to leave; even if her own lesson had finished she would sit through all of Elvira's classes, hoping to learn something. She wanted to be the best singer that Elvira had ever taught.

Now she looked crestfallen, "Did I embarrass you?"

Elvira shook her head. "My concern is for you, Maria. A voice like yours must be looked after. It is a precious gift. Don't waste it singing in the snow. Right now, you are young, and you think that your voice will always do anything you want. I used to think that too. But it won't be like that forever. The more you protect it now, the longer it will last."

Elvira took the girl's arm as they walked along Patission Street.

"You think you are invincible, and that I am making a stupid fuss, but I know what I am talking about. You must have patience, Maria."

Maria nodded obediently, but Elvira could see she was not convinced and she tried to think of a way to convince her. A display in the window of an antiques shop caught her eye.

"Imagine an amphora like the ones in the Acropolis museum filled with those gold coins." She pointed at the tray in the shop window. Maria turned her head to look.

"That is your voice now. Every time you sing you are giving away one of those coins. So spend them wisely, my dear, because once they are gone, there won't be any more."

Maria looked so solemn that Elvira almost laughed.

"One day, I am sure, you will be a great diva, one of the greatest sopranos the world has ever known, and you will think you are immortal.

4

But when you are taking your curtain call at La Scala and the crowd is throwing roses at your feet, remember the coins, Maria. Hold on to your treasure for as long as you can."

They walked along in silence for a minute, and then Elvira said, "You sang the trill quite brilliantly by the way, light and dark at the same time. Just the way it should be done."

The solemn face of her pupil broke into a beaming smile.

The Conservatoire loomed in front of them. Elvira touched her pupil on the arm.

"Right, Maria. Time for class."

# Act One

# CHAPTER ONE

# *In Performance*

PARIS, OCTOBER 20, 1968

In her apartment on Avenue Georges Mandel, Maria drew the brush across her eyelid into an italic flick. Her hand was surprisingly steady. It was always like this before a performance: there would be nerves before, but once she sat down in front of her dressing room mirror, she would become completely absorbed in her task and the terrors would recede as she painted her face.

The door opened and Bruna, her maid, came in carrying a white fox stole.

"I brought you this, madame, from the *cave*—it is chilly tonight."

Maria nodded her thanks. She didn't ask Bruna why she had gone all the way to the *cave* when there was a cupboard full of furs just across the hall. She knew why her maid had made the extra journey. This fur had been a gift from the director Luchino Visconti after their first *Traviata* at La Scala. The other, more convenient furs, had all been given to her by her lover of the last nine years, Aristotle Onassis.

"Will madame wear the ruby earrings tonight?"

Maria nodded. The bodice of her white satin gown was embroidered with red and gold crystal beads. The rubies would bring a little color to her face, which was pale despite her makeup. She would wear no other jewelry, no bracelets, no rings. Definitely no rings.

She heard the sound of her poodle, Toy, barking; that must mean that Franco was already here. Franco Zeffirelli, her favorite director and the closest thing she had to a best friend, was always punctual. She picked up a lipstick that matched the red beads on her dress and began to paint a sweep of color. Up close the shade looked alarming, as if her mouth were full of blood, but Maria knew that from a distance it would give her smile conviction.

Franco was playing with the dog when she made her entrance. When he saw her, his eyes flicked up and down, inspecting, and then he nodded.

"I approve. Dignified but also spectacular. Did I tell you that we are sitting next to the Burtons?" Franco Zeffirelli had just directed Elizabeth Taylor alongside her latest husband, Richard Burton, in *The Taming of the Shrew*.

Maria was surprised. "But do they speak French?"

"I doubt it, but they like drama." Franco smiled.

Maria looked at the boulle clock on the mantelpiece. It was seven thirty. The ceremony would just be beginning in the church on Skorpios, the sickle-shaped island in the Ionian Sea that Onassis had bought just after their affair began and where she had spent every summer until this one. Then she remembered that Greece was an hour ahead. The wedding that Maria had first learned about from the newspapers two days before would already be over.

The most famous widow in the world, Jacqueline Kennedy, would now be Mrs. Aristotle Onassis.

"Maria?"

Franco was holding out his hand to her. It was cool and dry and he smelled faintly of limes. Maria hesitated and then crossed herself. In answer to Franco's look she said, "Always, before a performance." There was no other word to describe what she was doing tonight. She would not be singing, but she would be performing the role of a woman without a care in the world, just as intensely as if she were standing on the stage of La Scala.

Franco nodded and said, "I guarantee that you will upstage everybody, even Liz Taylor."

For a moment Maria hesitated. "I hope I can do this."

Franco raised an elegant eyebrow. "Most women would find it impossible, but Maria Callas?"

Looking at his watch he took her by the arm. "*Andiamo*. We don't want the photographers to use up all their film on the battling Burtons."

The play, at the Comédie-Française, was a Feydeau farce, and Maria's cheeks were aching with the effort of smiling. She was not wearing her glasses so the action on the stage was just a blur, but Elizabeth Taylor's delighted cackle in the seat next to hers made it easy to know when to laugh.

She had met the Burtons before. They were the sort of shiny people that Ari adored. He had asked them to come on the *Christina* many times, but it had never worked out. The Burtons had their own yacht.

Maria could see a huge diamond glittering on Liz's hand, which at that moment was squeezing her husband's thigh. It was a gesture that spoke of ownership. Maria tried to remember which husband Burton was—the fourth or the fifth? An image of Elizabeth in a lace mantilla flashed into her mind. Was that the wedding with Burton or the one before? But that reminded her of that other wedding on a Greek island far away, and she had to breathe from the pit of her stomach to stop herself from screaming. For a moment she felt a surge of rage corroding her stomach and scalding her throat. If she were onstage now, she would be Medea, singing a vow of vengeance against Jason, her faithless lover who has set her aside to marry another woman.

The sigh of fury was loud enough to make Franco turn his elegant profile toward her and touch her arm. She knew what that touch meant. She was forgetting to give a performance of a woman having the time of her life. She fixed her eyes on the stage.

When the curtain fell, a couple of photographers came rushing down the aisle to capture the audience. Maria was about to turn her head away when Elizabeth Taylor grabbed her arm and leaned over to her, whispering, "Act like I am telling you the funniest thing you have ever heard."

Maria complied, throwing her head back with feigned glee. Elizabeth's astonishing violet eyes sparkled.

"That should make the front page. Maria Callas without a care in the world enjoying a joke with her old pal Liz Taylor."

She patted Maria's hand. "We divas need to stick together. Next time, don't trust a man till there's a ring on your finger."

"I will try to remember that, Mrs. Burton."

⇌

It had been Franco's idea to go to Maxim's. Maria wanted to go back to her apartment, but she had been persuaded that dinner at the restaurant, the one she had eaten at so many times with Ari, would send an unmistakable message. As the car pulled up outside the restaurant's red-and-gold exterior on the rue Royale, Maria took a deep breath. Holding Franco's hand, she stopped in front of the coven of photographers and gave them her best first-night smile. She pretended not to hear the shouted questions—"Do you have a message for Mr. Onassis, Madame Callas?" "Is that your new man, Maria?"—and kept her head up and her eyes bright until she was safely inside the red plush interior.

"What a pleasure to see you tonight, Madame Callas. An honor, in fact." The maître d', Girardoux, gave a little bow that acknowledged both her bravery in coming and his gratitude that once again she had chosen to put his restaurant on the front page.

"Your usual table is ready, unless, of course," Girardoux continued smoothly, "you would prefer to sit somewhere else."

"Now why on earth would I do that, Gaston?"

Adjusting her stole, Maria made her entrance into the main room of the restaurant. She headed for the table in the corner under the art nouveau painting of a bathing nymph. It was Ari's favorite table because he thought it gave him the best view of his fellow diners, and vice versa.

"You'll have to tell me who's here, Franco. You know how blind I am."

Maria had been nearsighted since childhood, and in private she wore glasses. But tonight was a public occasion. She did not want to see the expressions on people's faces as they spotted her. It was bad enough hearing the whispers of recognition—Yes, it's her, Maria Callas, the opera singer. The one who was with Onassis before Jackie Kennedy. I wonder how she is feeling now.

Maria thought of all the times that she had stood on a stage as Norma, singing of the pain her lover had caused her by his desire to marry another woman. Audiences had wept as she brought out all the magnificent pathos of Bellini's score. No one had ever sung it better. But now she understood how inadequate her performance had been, because now she knew what it felt like to be abandoned by the man you loved.

Franco surveyed the room. "The Windsors are in the far corner with Marie-Hélène de Rothschild. The duchess is waving at you."

Maria lifted a hand to wave back.

Franco continued. "And in the other corner I can see Noël Coward having dinner with Marlene Dietrich and a very pretty boy."

The waiter put two coupes of champagne in front of Maria and Franco, and he lifted his to toast her. "Your health, Maria."

"To the new man in my life." They touched glasses and smiled at each other. To anyone who didn't know Franco's predilection for porters from Les Halles, they looked like an ideal couple. Franco Zeffirelli had directed Maria in some of her greatest roles and was one of her closest friends. They had seen less of each other during the nine years that Maria had spent with Onassis, as Franco had refused to set foot on Onassis's yacht. "I cannot wake up to gold taps, darling, not even for you." He had disapproved when Maria had cut her hair short at Ari's suggestion: "Very suitable for your new career in news reading, Maria."

The hair had grown back, and now it was piled on top of her head, giving her an extra inch over her five foot nine.

She had found the first gray strands earlier that spring. She had shown them to Onassis, laughing. "Look what you have done to me, Ari."

In retrospect it seemed that her body already knew what was to come.

Girardoux was back to take their order.

"I'll have the usual," Maria said.

Girardoux nodded. "Perhaps with some cèpes to start, madame? The chef picked them himself this morning."

Girardoux's tone was coaxing.

"He prepares them with shallots and a whisper of cream, a little tarragon . . . nothing heavy, I assure you."

Maria knew that he would not have made the suggestion if Ari had been there; with him she always had the same thing—steak tartare with a green salad—but she could feel that Girardoux was trying to bring her some pleasure on this night of all nights.

She nodded. "If you insist."

She was rewarded by the man's smile of delight.

"You won't regret it, madame."

He moved away and Franco gave her a smile of encouragement. "I am glad you are eating again, Maria. You really can be too rich and too thin, whatever the Duchess of Windsor says."

The champagne was beginning to do its work, and Maria was able to laugh as Franco kept up an amusing monologue about the other people in the restaurant, who Marie-Hélène's latest lover was, and how the Duke of Windsor had asked his niece Queen Elizabeth for a state funeral and she had refused. He deftly avoided mentioning anything that might cause Maria pain, without ever appearing to do so.

The cèpes appeared in small copper chafing dishes, the plump fungi glistening under the coating of cream flecked with green. She speared a morsel and put it in her mouth. It was as delicious as Girardoux had promised, the savory richness of the mushroom and the cream spiked by the tartness of the tarragon. Maybe this was the way forward, to lose herself in these other pleasures of the flesh, the ones that she had denied herself so long. She thought of the flaky croissants from the boulangerie around the corner, coffee ice cream in Sirmione, spanakopita just out of the oven in Athens. She could eat as much as she wanted; after all, who would care now if she lost her figure. But even as the thought crossed her mind, she put down her fork and pushed away the dish of mushrooms still two thirds full. She still wanted to look like Maria Callas, la Divina, not Maria Kalogeropoulou, the fat teenager who knew no other way to feed her hunger.

"*Avez-vous terminé*, Madame Callas?" She looked up and saw Girardoux's disappointment as he took in the unfinished dish of cèpes.

"They were delicious, but at my age you have to be careful."

Franco was in the middle of an anecdote about the Black and White Ball that Truman Capote had held at the Plaza when he stopped in mid-flow and put his hand on Maria's wrist.

"Keep smiling," he whispered.

She heard a familiar voice behind her.

"Well, if it isn't my old friend Madame Callas. I have to say I didn't think I would find you here on this particular evening, but good for you!"

Maria turned to face the small glittering eyes and resolute mouth of Elsa Maxwell, the veteran party giver and society gadfly who eleven years ago had introduced her to Ari. "Elsa! What a surprise! I thought you lived in New York now."

Maria leaned in to kiss the other woman's cheek, carefully avoiding the whiskery mole at her jaw.

"Marie-Hélène insisted that I come and help her with the party, and I couldn't refuse. She has always been such a loyal friend." Maria knew that comment was directed at her. But pretending not to notice, she gestured to her companion.

"Elsa, do you know Franco Zeffirelli?"

"Know him, why I practically invented him!"

Franco was kissing Elsa's hand with its stumpy, beringed fingers.

Elsa Maxwell smiled, showing her unnaturally white teeth. She was dressed in swathes of gold brocade that contained her bulk, but only just.

"I must say, Maria, the years have been very kind to you. You were so wise not to have children—that is why you and the Duchess of Windsor look so remarkably youthful—none of the cares of motherhood to crease that pearly brow."

She raised her cigarette holder to her mouth and inhaled.

Franco, who could see Maria's nostrils flaring, spoke. "Won't you sit down, Elsa?"

"No thank you, dear Franco. I mustn't keep the duke waiting, not to mention the duchess, who I declare is even more royal than he is these days, and as for Marie-Hélène . . ." But Elsa showed no sign of moving on. She let out a sigh and put her pudgy hand to her heart.

"I just wanted to say how . . . responsible I feel, Maria. I mean if I hadn't introduced you to Ari all those years ago, you wouldn't be here, putting such a brave face on it all. Of course now I regret it deeply, but then . . . Well, I thought it was only right that the two most famous Greeks in the world should meet each other."

Elsa pushed out her lips to show just how sorry she felt.

Maria was silent. She felt petrified, an attitude she had taken so many times onstage, but this was the first time she understood what it was like to be unable to prevent a catastrophe unfolding.

"I mean, if I hadn't gathered you up, so to speak, you would still be with that husband of yours. Signor Meneghini. What did you call him? Tita, wasn't it? Quite a small man, I remember, but then you have never minded being with men who only come up to your shoulder."

Elsa blew out a cloud of smoke.

"But you can't say that I didn't warn you, Maria. I feel like a character in a Greek tragedy, the one that nobody listens to. What's her name?"

She paused to exhale another plume of smoke. "Cassandra, the one who predicts the tragedy to come but is destined always to be ignored, and in my case rejected."

The veneer of apology on Elsa's face had gone.

Maria tried to smile. "Elsa, so lovely to catch up, but here I am having a dinner à deux with my dear friend Franco in my favorite restaurant, and I see nothing tragic about that. But I am worried that you will be guilty of lèse-majesté if you stay here any longer. The duke keeps looking over. It would be a real tragedy if you caused offense to such valuable friends on my account."

But Elsa didn't even glance back at the Windsors; she kept her eyes on Maria.

"If only you had listened to me, Maria. You know that all I ever wanted was your happiness."

Maria heard the note of self-pity in Elsa's voice and shuddered inwardly. It was a note that had been played for her since childhood. Her mother weeping in the kitchen in Patission Street, saying, "I have sacrificed everything for you, Maria"; her husband, Battista Meneghini, in their villa on Lake Garda insisting, "I have devoted my life to you."

She had learned early that no one cared what was best for Maria, just for Callas, the diva. Only one man had seen her as a woman, not simply a vessel for a God-given voice, and now that man was the husband of another woman, a woman whose only talent appeared to be the annexing of rich and powerful men.

She stood up and, leaning down, whispered in Elsa's ear, "If you really want me to be happy, Elsa, you will leave me alone. And, by the way, you don't even have to pretend to feel guilty about introducing us. Ari and

I were always going to meet. It was Fate that brought us together, not Elsa Maxwell."

She turned her back on Elsa and, sitting down, she smiled at Franco. "Now, where were we?"

Franco started to chatter about his latest project, a film about Saint Francis of Assisi, until Maria felt it was safe to ask him, "Has she gone?"

Franco nodded.

"I had forgotten that Elsa has a nasty habit of turning up just when you least expect it like the wicked fairy ," said Maria, draining her glass.

Franco laughed. "Well, don't let her spoil your evening. Remember we are having fun!"

He lifted his glass. "No more wicked fairies."

Maria touched his glass with her own. "Elsa has no power over me now"—her face sagged—"because the worst has already happened."

# CHAPTER TWO

## *"Casta Diva"*

NEW YORK, SEPTEMBER 1956

I

As the airplane circled around before coming into land, Maria saw the familiar skyline and she felt herself smiling. Italy was now her home, but there was something about New York that she found nowhere else. This was the place where she had first realized the power of her voice, this was the place where Mary Anne Kalogeropoulou had understood that one day she would be Maria Callas.

Clutching a protesting toy poodle in her right hand, she waved to the photographers from the door of the plane. Behind her, Tita was grumbling about the heat. "How can it still be so hot in late September." Ignoring him, Maria walked down the steps in her Dior-inspired suit with a shawl-collared jacket, hobble skirt, and black-and-white straw hat.

She had ordered the outfit specially from Madame Biki in Milan, who as the grand daughter of Puccini understood how a diva should be dressed. Greeting the American press on her first trip to New York since she had become the world's most famous soprano was, Maria knew, as much of a performance as anything she would be giving onstage.

"How does it feel to be back in New York, Madame Callas?"

The reporters' questions started as soon as she started to walk down the steps.

"It is wonderful to be back in the city of my birth." Maria smiled at the press pack.

A reporter in a seersucker suit leaned forward. "Madame Callas, you were born here in New York, moved to Greece when you were thirteen, and now live in Italy. That's three languages right there. I wonder what language you think in?"

The diva put her head to one side as if to better consider the request.

"What language do I think in? What an interesting question, but not one I can answer. All I can tell you is that I count in English."

There was an appreciative chuckle from the press. Then the questions started coming from all directions.

"Is it true that you insisted on being paid more than the conductor Herbert von Karajan at the Staatsoper in Vienna?"

"Maria, is it true you eat steak tartare for breakfast to stay slim?"

"Would you like to comment on the report you are going to Hollywood to play Cleopatra?"

Toy the poodle barked at the idea that her mistress might be going to Hollywood, but Maria's smile didn't waver. She saw the tall figure of Rudolf Bing, the general manager of the Met, over the heads of the reporters.

"Gentlemen, please, Madame Callas will answer questions later." His English was a mixture of the clipped consonants of his Viennese childhood and the looser vowels of his adopted country.

She offered him her hand and he kissed it slowly, so that the press would have time to take the picture.

"I have a surprise for you, Madame Callas."

Bing stepped aside and behind him stood her father, George Callas (formerly Kalogeropoulos), wearing a cream linen suit, still sporting his Clark Gable mustache.

"Papa!"

She stepped toward him, and he opened his arms to enfold her. For a moment, and it was only a moment, she felt safe. Her father emerged from the embrace to be dazzled by flashbulbs.

"Mr. Callas, what's it like to be the father of Maria Callas?"

"Does she get her voice from you?"

"How long since you last saw each other?"

"Where is your mother, Madame Callas?"

Bing led the way to the limousine parked by the terminal building, and soon they were driving through Queens. Maria spent the journey speaking English to Bing; Italian to her husband, Tita, who spoke almost no English; and Greek to her father. As she looked at George, who was sitting next to Tita, she thought that, although they were almost the same age, it was her father who looked younger. He had kept his figure and still had all his hair. Being separated from Maria's mother clearly agreed with him.

Bing was boasting about how they could have sold all the tickets to the season twice over. "And the press interest has been extraordinary. Everybody wants to put you on the cover, even *Time* magazine."

Maria grimaced. "I hope you said no, Mr. Bing. If, as you say, you have sold all the tickets, then you clearly do not need the publicity, and I would prefer not to waste my time with journalists. They can write about me after they have heard me sing."

Bing looked shocked. "To be on the cover of *Time* is a great honor. It is on every newsstand in the country and they have never featured an opera singer before."

Bing sounded as if she had refused the Légion d'honneur.

"Do you really imagine," Maria said as she focused her gaze on Bing, "that *Time* wants me on the cover because of my singing? You heard what sort of questions the press were asking me out there—they weren't about my music."

Bing didn't blink.

"They want you because you are the greatest diva alive today. *Time* gives covers only to the most prominent people in their field. Albert Schweitzer, Salvador Dalí, Eleanor Roosevelt."

Meneghini asked her in Italian what Bing was saying. Maria replied that Bing had arranged for her to be on the cover of *Time* magazine without asking her. Tita looked impressed at the mention of *Time*.

"How much will they pay you?"

Bing, who was fluent in Italian, suppressed a smile and noted the impatient expression on Maria's face, as she said, "They don't pay for these interviews, Tita. In America they think they are doing you a favor if they use you to sell more copies."

George, who had been sampling the contents of the decanter he had found in the arm well of the limousine, looked up and said in Greek, "Are you really going to be on the cover of *Time* magazine, Maria? Everybody reads it, you know. They have it at the barbers I go to. The whole neighborhood will be so proud."

Bing couldn't understand what Callas père was saying in his spiky language, but he saw that it was persuading Maria, who after a while nodded to Bing.

"Very well. I agree to be interviewed by *Time* magazine."

II

The trees in Central Park were just beginning to catch fire. Green was being replaced by yellow, orange, and in some places red. Fall, that particularly American season: Maria remembered her father taking her to buy hot dogs from the street vendor around the block from their apartment. They stood on the sidewalk and devoured the sweet pink sausages in the cake-like buns, dripping with the primary colors of yellow mustard and red ketchup. Maria had known better than to mention this outing to her mother, who regarded such American food as the devil's work. At the time it had been one of the most delicious things she had ever tasted. Would it still taste the same? she wondered. Not that she was going to find out. Hot dogs were not on the menu for her now.

She turned back into the suite, which although luxurious enough and boasting the grand piano that she needed to practice, was not, she suspected, the most lavish accommodation that the hotel had to offer. Tita had made the booking, and he hated to spend more than was necessary.

The last time she had been in New York, she had slept on the sofa in her father's apartment in Washington Heights. It had been twelve years ago, just after the end of the war. She had come straight from Athens, convinced that the Met would recognize her talent immediately. She had sung impeccably at the audition, but the musical director had offered her only a second-tier contract, singing maids and ladies-in-waiting. Maria had turned it down without hesitation. In Athens, she told him, she had been singing leading roles for three years. The musical director had pointed out that most twenty-three-year-old singers from an obscure European opera company would be overjoyed at any opportunity to sing at the Met.

Maria had walked out, telling the director that one day the Met would be begging Maria Callas to perform on its stage. It gave her some satisfaction now to know that she had been right.

The telephone rang.

"Madame Callas, we have a gentleman here who says he is from *Time* magazine."

Maria was tempted for a moment to deny that such a person existed, but she had promised her father, and she did keep her promises.

After a quick look at herself in the mirror to check that she was in what she called "Callas mode"—hair done, makeup perfect, and no glasses—she went to open the door.

The slight man in glasses introduced himself as Robert DeGerasimo.

He was carrying a large reel-to-reel tape recorder which caused him to list to one side.

Maria looked at the recorder in alarm. "I hope you aren't planning to record me singing."

DeGerasimo shook his head. "Oh no, this is just to record our conversation."

Maria raised an eyebrow. "How American. In Europe they use shorthand."

DeGerasimo patted his machine. "Well, the advantage of this baby is that we know exactly what was said."

"In case I decide to sue?" Maria asked.

"It means I can't misquote you, Madame Callas."

DeGerasimo smiled and she gestured for him to sit down on the sofa opposite, the giant tape recorder between them.

The interview began with all the usual questions about her childhood in New York. Was her family musical? What was the first song she remembered singing, and so forth. She had been asked and had answered these questions many times before. She began to relax.

"Would you like something to drink, Mr. DeGerasimo?"

DeGerasimo shook his head. "Never drink when I'm on duty and I am guessing that you don't encourage smoking." He smiled at her.

"No, I do not. Smoke is my enemy."

"Your only enemy, Madame Callas?" DeGerasimo leaned toward her.

"The only one that I am really scared of. Anything that threatens my voice threatens me." She clutched at her neck to illustrate her point.

"You don't view critics or unappreciative audiences as the enemy, then?"

Maria gave a practiced smile. "Every performance is a battle, Mr. DeGerasimo. I must fight every single second that I am on the stage. Usually I win, but there are times when I lose, and that is painful. But I do not blame the audience if I have failed to win them over."

This too was an answer she had given before.

"But what about other singers? There are rumors that you have had difficult relationships with rival sopranos—Renata Tebaldi, for example."

Tebaldi was Callas's main rival at La Scala and had a following almost as devoted as Callas's own.

Maria's laugh covered a full octave. "I assure you that Renata and I are the best of friends. It may be that some of our more loyal fans may amuse themselves by inventing an enmity between us, but that is simply invention."

DeGerasimo looked back at his notes. "You were born here in New York and when you were thirteen your mother took you back to Greece. You lived in Athens during its occupation by the Italian and German armies during the war. That must have been a time of great hardship. . . ."

Maria nodded. "You can't imagine. . . ."

"I wonder how you managed to continue with your studies in the middle of a war." DeGerasimo paused. "I suppose your mother's support must have been crucial."

Maria looked at him in disbelief, her Callas mask cracking.

"My mother? My mother was worse than the Nazis, Mr. DeGerasimo. She used to make me sing in the street for food. The only reason that I was able to keep singing during the war was because I had learned from an early age that the only person I could rely on was myself. You see, I never had a childhood. Once my mother realized how talented I was, she was determined to exploit me for her own ends."

DeGerasimo watched the spool of tape wind its way through the machine and resisted a smile of satisfaction. Everybody had a button somewhere and the secret of a good interview was to find it. His investigations into Maria's background had revealed that she had not seen her mother for six years, which had been a red flag. His background was Italian, and he could not believe that the Greeks were so different—a WASP parent might see their child once a decade, but it was unthinkable in an Italian or Greek mother. He suspected that there had been a rift, and as Maria's voice lost its practiced poise, he knew he was right. There was always one question that the subject felt compelled by their inner torments to answer honestly, and now he had found it.

"And despite everything I did for her, I was never her favorite. She always preferred my sister, Jackie."

### III

#### WASHINGTON HEIGHTS, 1931

*The apartment was on the second floor, so that even on the brightest day it was always dark. Maria was sitting under the kitchen table where her mother couldn't see her. She was playing with one of Jackie's old dolls. It had long golden hair and blue eyes like her older sister. Every Christmas she hoped that Santa Claus would bring her a doll of her own, one with black hair and brown eyes like hers. But her mother said that she was lucky to have any toys at all, because times were hard in this terrible country.*

*Hidden from view under the tablecloth, she could hear Jackie playing the piano and her mother making the soft cooing noise she always made when Jackie played. Her mother liked to say that Jackie would one day play at Carnegie Hall, and then she would buy her mother a mink coat. Maria did not know what mink was, but she knew that it must be very nice because Mama always hugged herself when she said "mink" and smiled with her eyes closed.*

*Maria could see Jackie's feet working the piano pedals. Her sister was wearing her new shoes, which were of gray polished kid with a double strap across the instep that fastened with two small pearl buttons. Mama had taken them both to buy shoes the day before. She was cross because Maria could no longer fit into Jackie's old shoes. "You take after the women on your father's side*

*of the family, Maria. Giantesses! All of them with feet the size of pumpkins. Thank God that Jackie has small and dainty feet like me."*

*Maria looked at the dark brown shoes with laces that had been the only shoes in her size and wished, not for the first time, that she too took after her mother.*

*The front door opened, and Maria heard her father's footsteps as he walked over to the wireless and turned it on. The piano playing was replaced by what Mama called "American music." The springs of the armchair complained as her father sat down heavily. He called to his wife to bring him a beer. Maria knew they would start fighting now, and she wished that she was in the bedroom she shared with Jackie so she wouldn't have to hear them.*

*She concentrated on brushing the doll's hair with an old toothbrush. Maria liked it when her mother brushed her hair sometimes before bed, even though she grumbled that Maria's hair was so thick that it could stuff a mattress.*

*Her mother was talking about how they must get a better piano teacher for Jackie; and when her father answered, he sounded sad, saying he didn't know if he would have a job next week. Maria hated it when her father sounded sad.*

*Her mother's heels made a clicking noise as she walked over to the radio. Maria recognized the tune that was being played. It was one she had learned at school. She began to sing along, and as her mother turned the radio down, Maria felt the power of her own voice echoing under the table.*

> *"But come ye back*
> *When summer's in the meadow,*
> *Or when the valley's hushed*
> *And white with snow,*
> *And I'll be here*
> *In sunshine or in shadow*
> *Oh, Danny boy, oh Danny boy, I love you so!"*

*Suddenly the tablecloth was pulled back and Maria's mother was kneeling opposite her with a look in her eyes that Maria didn't recognize.*

*"I had no idea that you could sing like that, Maria. Why didn't you tell me before?" Maria wasn't sure how to reply. It hadn't occurred to her that her mother would be interested. Maria had been told at school that she was good*

*at singing, but it had not seemed worth telling her mother because all the songs she knew were in English and she did not want her mother to frown because she did not understand the words.*

*"I'm sorry, Mama."*

*Litza bared her teeth in a smile that was alarming in its intensity.*

*"You should never apologize for being given a gift by God. It is something very special to have a voice like that. And if, God willing, you make something of that precious gift, you must thank him every day for his goodness."*

*"Yes, Mama."*

*"No more of these American songs. From now on you must sing real music. You are not Shirley Temple with her lollipops. You are going to sing opera,* agapi mou.*"*

*Maria felt a warmth creep over her. Her mother had never called her* agapi mou *(my love) before.*

*Litza went over to their gramophone and took out one of the five or so records that constituted their music library. She put it on the turntable and as she wound the handle she said, "This is what you should be singing, Maria, and one day the whole world will listen." Maria heard a high pure voice, clear despite the scratchiness of the recording, singing in a language that she didn't know. But although she didn't recognize the words, she understood from the music that the song was about wanting something very much.*

*Maria had always wanted her mother to look at her sometimes the way that she looked at Jackie, with dreamy eyes and a soft mouth. She heard that longing in the music, and she knew exactly how she would sing it.*

IV

The sidewalk outside the Metropolitan Opera House was already packed when Maria's car pulled up. She took off her ordinary spectacles and put on her prescription sunglasses.

That way she could look like the diva the fans were expecting and still find her way to the stage door. It was surprising that there should be so many people here on a rehearsal day. This would not happen in Milan. How many of the eager faces she saw through the window had heard her sing? But in America, she remembered, fame had nothing to do with

talent. She smiled and signed autographs as she walked from the curb to the stage door.

As she waited for the door to open, a pale young man held out a single red rose to her.

"I can die happy now that I have seen you in the flesh, Madame Callas," he said with tears in his eyes.

"Perhaps you should hear me sing first," said Maria crisply as she disappeared into the opera house, handing the flower to Tita who, as always, was two steps behind.

Maria was early, as usual. She knew Mario del Monaco, the tenor, would be late—he was always late—but she liked to be the first to arrive and the last to leave. This *Norma* was going to be perfect.

On the second day of rehearsal, Maria was blocking the second act with Mario, who was playing her beloved, Pollione. The director asked them to get closer to each other as the duet progressed and Mario, who as usual was unshaven and smelling strongly of sweat, pulled her against him.

"Like this?" he said to the director, as his hand deliberately grazed Maria's right breast. She pulled away from him as if she had been stung and slapped him on the cheek.

"No, absolutely not like that, *testa di cazzo!*" said Maria, her nostrils flaring with anger, calling him a prick in Italian.

Mario stepped back, rubbing his cheek. "Maybe if you weren't so uptight, you might hit that top C instead of wobbling around like a dying cat."

Maria drew her hand back for another slap, but then she glimpsed DeGerasimo sitting in the corner of the rehearsal room and thought better of it. Anyway, she wanted to get this bit right, and fighting with Mario was not going to achieve that. All the tenors she had ever sung with believed that she found them irresistible. They simply couldn't understand that what she felt for them onstage did not transfer into real life.

The director put his hands up. "Okay, everybody, let's have a ten-minute break to cool off."

Maria was on her way back to the dressing room when Mimi, the young mezzo who was playing Adalgisa, Norma's rival for Pollione's affections, caught up with her.

"Mario is such a pig. He is always pawing me in our duet. Thank you for putting him in his place."

Maria smiled and put her hand on Mimi's arm. "Don't let him get away with it, Mimi. It's all a game for him. He once did it onstage with me, to put me off, because he was jealous that I was getting more curtain calls."

Mimi looked at her in admiration. "He should count himself lucky to be singing with you. You make everybody better. Every time I hear you sing, I learn something new."

Maria nodded. "That's because you are an artist. We can all learn from each other. But Mario is only a performer. He thinks he is in command of the music; but we know, don't we, that we serve our voices, not the other way round."

She leaned down and put her arms around Mimi, who said, "You're not at all like I thought you would be. Everyone said you were terrifying."

Maria laughed. "Oh, I can be, Mimi."

Back in her dressing room, Maria heard a knock at the door, and Bing entered, a frown on his cadaverous face.

"I heard about what happened earlier in rehearsal. That kind of behavior may be condoned at La Scala, but not here."

He looked at her accusingly, and Maria gasped as she understood his meaning.

"There is no opera house on earth where I will allow myself to be manhandled, Mr. Bing. If Mario del Monaco behaves like a jerk, I will treat him like one."

"But to slap him in front of the whole company . . ." Bing almost wagged a finger at her.

"He put his hand on my breast in an improper manner."

Bing shrugged. "He says that was a mistake. You could at least have given him the benefit of the doubt before resorting to violence."

Maria's voice rose a semitone. "Possibly, if this had been the first time it had happened. But Mario has made these 'mistakes' before and I will not tolerate it."

Bing sighed. "He wants an apology."

"And so do I."

They stared at each other. Maria did not look away. Finally, she said, "I will shake his hand if he offers it. I don't want to waste any more time."

Bing left the room, and Maria looked around for something to break.

s

The dress rehearsal had gone better than Maria had expected. She had not performed on the stage before without her glasses, but it seemed that her mental calculations had been right. If the conductor paced the music as he had today, she knew exactly how long it would take her to get from one side of the stage to the other without falling off. And Mario, for all his many failings, was the best Pollione she had ever sung with.

She touched the image of the Madonna that she always kept in her dressing room—it was bad luck to start thinking that things were going well. The ancient Greeks had invented the idea of hubris for a reason.

Tita came in. He had been watching from the auditorium, which would be the last time that he would see it from a seat, as during the actual performances he always watched from the wings.

"Well?"

"One of your best, *tesoro*. 'Casta diva' brought tears to my eyes." Tita put his hands on her shoulders and kissed the side of her neck.

"I am so lucky to have you, Tita." Maria clasped the hand nearest to her. "I know that you are always there, watching out for me."

"Always, *carissima*."

They smiled at each other in the mirror. They were always at their closest in the lead-up to a performance. Battista knew exactly how to soothe her fears; and because he had seen every performance she had given since they had first met in Verona, she could trust him when he said that this was one of her best.

"Will you send some flowers from me to Mimi, for opening night?"

"Of course. And to Mario?"

Maria shrugged. "Whatever you like."

"Remember that you are being paid much more than him, Maria."

"I should think so too! It is me they have come to see."

Battista always liked to remind Maria of the success of his negotiations on her behalf, which, as Maria always needed to remind Battista, was only getting her what she deserved.

There was a knock at the door that Maria recognized as Bing's. Every manager had his own way of announcing his arrival at an artist's dressing room. At La Scala Antonio Ghiringhelli, the manager, almost battered the door down before he stormed in. Bing, on the other hand, was gentle but somehow reproachful.

He was carrying something brightly colored in his hand. Maria put on her glasses to see what it was.

"I have brought you an advance copy of *Time* magazine. It will be on the newsstands tomorrow." Maria noticed that Bing's tone was carefully neutral.

She looked at the painting of her on the cover. It had been copied from a photograph and to her it looked almost unrecognizable. In the lower right-hand corner, it said SOPRANO CALLAS.

She flicked open the magazine to the cover article, which Bing had marked for her with a slip of paper. Her eyes fell upon the words: "A diva more widely hated by her colleagues and more wildly acclaimed by her public than any other living singer." Maria looked at Bing, who was examining the ceiling, then she snorted. "Well, I wouldn't be here if it was the other way around, would I?"

Meneghini, who was expert at understanding his wife's mood, even if he couldn't understand the words, braced himself.

Maria read on, her eyes widening in horror. Her hands were shaking so much that she could hardly read the page in front of her.

"Mrs. Callas had moved back to Athens, was living there with Jackie, and very little money. In 1951 she wrote Maria to ask for $100, 'for my daily bread.' Answered Maria: 'Don't come to us with your troubles. I had to work for my money, and you are young enough to work, too. If you can't make enough money to live on, you can jump out of the window or drown yourself.'"

Maria threw the magazine at Bing. "I never ever wrote that. She is a lying bitch, and this is all your fault, Mr. Rudolf Bing."

Bing blinked but otherwise showed no sign of emotion. "The article also says that you are the greatest singer of your generation."

"And how is that supposed to make me feel better? I *am* the greatest singer of my generation. This article is full of lies—I shall sue."

Bing shook his head. "I really would advise against it. If any of these . . . allegations could be proved, then you would be in an uncomfortable situation. And as to this being my fault, I still contend that to be the subject of a *Time* cover is an honor and an artist of your stature must expect some degree of criticism."

"But they aren't attacking me as an artist but as a woman."

Bing coughed. "I am sure when you have had time to reflect, you will see that this article is not as bad as you think. Your performance tomorrow will be a triumph and everything else will be forgotten."

Maria shook her head. "Do you really think that I can perform tomorrow knowing that every member of the audience hates me? My voice comes from my heart, Mr. Bing. I am not a machine. You will have to cancel."

Bing did not flinch; this was not the first time that an artist had threatened to cancel a performance. "I always think that these decisions are best made in the morning." He looked at Tita, saying in Italian to be quite sure that he understood, "Your wife must be exhausted. I will call you tomorrow."

With his hand on the doorknob, Bing added, "The other thing it says in the article, Madame Callas, is that you have never walked away from a fight. I feel sure that part is accurate at least."

᠊᠊

In the car on the way back to the Plaza, Maria took her husband's hand and clutched it tightly.

"I want you to take me home, Tita."

"That's where we are going, *tesoro*."

"I mean Milan. I can't stay here."

Tita sighed. "Bing will sue, Maria."

Maria tossed her head. "I have been sued before."

Tita sighed again. He was almost certain that Maria was not serious, but he also knew that the scene would have to play out.

"If you walk out on the Met, you will never sing there again, and that would be a disaster for your career. Bing will do everything he can to ruin you."

"So what? Nothing would give me greater pleasure that to give it all up and go back to Milan with you and be Signora Meneghini and wear an apron like your mother."

Tita did not bother to reply. Maria had threatened to become Signora Meneghini many times before.

The car drew up outside the hotel, and the conversation was interrupted by the fans who kept a vigil by the entrance. As Maria walked into the hotel, sunglasses on, they surged forward, one woman succeeding in pushing past the commissionaire and shoving her autograph book in Maria's face.

"I am so sorry to do this, but it would mean so much to me, Madame Callas. Every time I listen to one of your records, I feel that I can do anything." The woman was about her mother's age, but she had a soft face and dreamy eyes, and she looked so hopeful that Maria fought back the impulse to let her anger propel her into the hotel; she stopped and signed the proffered page.

The woman gasped with delight. "Oh, thank you so much. And good luck for tomorrow," she called after her.

But Maria had already disappeared through the revolving door.

In the suite, Bruna was waiting for her. Although she hadn't seen the *Time* article, she instinctively knew what was needed from looking at Maria's face.

"I will run your bath, madame, and bring you some hot milk with cinnamon the way you like it."

Maria nodded submissively and Tita hoped that the storm had passed. But then Bruna added, "And your father called, madame."

At once Maria's face changed.

"Bruna, we are going home tomorrow, so you will need to start packing."

Bruna's face did not flicker. She nodded and padded into the other room, leaving Maria and Tita alone. Tita resigned himself to the battle ahead.

"Really, Maria? You want to give it all up, everything you have worked for, because your mother has lied to a journalist?"

Maria took a step toward him. She was a good five inches taller, and he had to look up to meet her eyes.

"What's the matter, Tita? Don't you want to settle down with me and live a normal life in Sirmione as Signor and Signora Meneghini, pillars of the community?"

Tita took her hands. "I am only trying to help you, Maria. We both know that if you walk out now, you will regret it."

But Maria's hands were still trembling.

"I think you just want to protect your investment," she said, taking her hands away.

Tita was hurt. Even though she had said this before, it never failed to wound him, which of course she knew.

"Maria, I have given up everything—my home, my family, my work, my friends—to be the husband of Maria Callas."

Maria sat down on the sofa and her poodle jumped onto her lap. This was a good sign, Tita knew. Toy could soothe Maria like no one else.

"And what happens when I can't sing anymore, Tita? Will you still want to be the husband of Maria Callas then?"

Tita sat down next to her. "Oh, Maria, I will always be proud to be your husband. But I will be disappointed if you go back to Milan tomorrow."

Maria stood up, holding Toy in her arms, and started to pace.

"But how can I sing when I know that everyone thinks I am a monster?"

Tita did not say that he thought she sang better when she knew she had to win the audience over.

"*Carissima*, the moment you start to sing, they won't be able to think about anything else."

Maria stopped in mid-pace, her eyes wide with fright, Toy wriggling in her arms because she was clutching him so tightly.

"But what if this is the moment when it all goes wrong, when I just can't do it?"

Tita stood up and gripped her shoulders. They were so bony now. He remembered the soft flesh that had enveloped the Maria he had married in Verona nine years earlier. Sometimes he wished that she was still that large, badly dressed girl who could always be soothed with pasta and ice cream. He had loved to watch her eat, gobbling her food as if someone were going to take it away from her. She had been a simpler creature then, her Italian strangely emphatic and full of antiquated emotional declarations that she had learned from operas. That girl had known twenty different words for love but didn't know how to ask for the bathroom.

He spoke in his most soothing voice. "But Norma is your part, Maria. You will win over the New Yorkers, just as Norma wins over her people. Perhaps it will be a little harder than usual, but you will fight and you will win. You always do."

Maria looked down at him. He could see that her face was beginning to relax. He carried on. "Remember that night in La Scala when the Tebaldi claque started to boo and how you stopped and faced them down . . . and then at the end you took twenty-four curtain calls?"

Maria smiled like a child who is being told a well-known story about her early life.

"Twenty-five curtain calls."

Tita wondered if he should ring Bing and tell him that the crisis had been averted. Better to wait until morning. There was an English expression about not counting your chickens until they are hatched, but he thought with Maria it was more like not picking up your tiger cub until its claws had been removed, and even then, it paid to be cautious.

v

Bruna looked around the dressing room for somewhere to put the latest bouquet. The gladioli were almost as tall as she was. She took out the envelope and gave it to her mistress, who was sitting in front of the mirror putting on her makeup. Maria opened it, read the contents, and then went back to applying the white pancake on her olive skin.

Tita looked inquiringly at her in the mirror. "From the mayor, saying, 'Welcome home.'"

Maria laughed. "It's funny how easy it is to be an American once you are famous."

There was the familiar tap at the door, and Bing came in, carrying an attaché case.

"I have come to wish you good luck, Madame Callas."

Maria looked up, and her look suggested that luck would be super-fluous.

Bing continued. "Such a distinguished audience. Everyone in New York is here—the mayor, Mrs. Astor, Elsa Maxwell, even Marlene Dietrich. People talk about 'glittering occasions,' but this is the first time that I have actually been dazzled by the jewels in the stalls." He permitted himself a smile.

"And I just wanted to remind you, Madame Callas, the custom at the Met is to take the curtain calls as a company. I know that they do these things differently in Europe, but here we like to celebrate our collective achievement. And now, Signor Meneghini, perhaps we could go outside for a moment?"

Maria picked up a brush and started to outline her eyes in kohl. She knew that the briefcase that Bing was carrying was full of dollar bills. Meneghini always insisted in being paid in cash before each performance. Maria found his insistence on cash embarrassing, but it made Tita happy to make powerful opera managers wait while he counted their money.

The bell went for the half, that meant thirty-five minutes till curtain up. She touched the Madonna icon and closed her eyes for a second, praying that when she opened her mouth onstage the sound would come.

When she opened her eyes, her father was standing behind her, wearing a tuxedo and holding a copy of *Time*.

"Get that dreadful thing out of here," Maria shouted.

George looked bewildered. "What thing?"

"That magazine!" Maria snatched it out of his hands and threw it in the wastepaper basket.

"But, Maria, you should be proud. Mrs. Zombonakis says it is the first time they have ever put a Greek on the cover. Everyone in the neighborhood is talking about it."

Maria shook her head. "Have you actually read it, Papa?" And she knew from the way his eyes flicked upward that he hadn't got further than the pictures.

"Well, when you do, you will see that Mama has said that I refused to support her and told her to jump out of a window."

George looked at her in admiration. "Did you really say that?"

"Of course not! Although right now I wish she would jump off the Empire State Building. The whole world thinks that I am a terrible daughter."

Her father flicked a speck of powder from his sleeve. "Well, *Time* magazine should have talked to me. I could have told them that your mother is impossible. It doesn't matter how much you give her, she will never be satisfied. Do you know how happy I was when she told me she was going back to Greece?"

Maria felt a surge of anger. "You let her take me away to Athens, Papa. Why didn't you keep me with you?"

George shrugged. "But if I had, then she wouldn't have gone."

↬

### NEW YORK DOCK, FEBRUARY 2, 1937

*Maria waved until she thought her hand would drop off. She held a pink handkerchief that she hoped might make it easier for her father to spot her as she clung to the rail of the steerage deck. Litza had already gone down to the cabin, which they were sharing with two other women, to make sure that she had enough closet space. Her farewell to her husband of twenty-one years had been a brief peck on the cheek.*

*Maria had been distraught when her mother announced her plan to go back to Greece. Maria was looking forward to going to high school, and then perhaps to Juilliard, which she knew offered scholarships. But no matter how often she pointed this out to her mother, Litza wouldn't listen.*

*Maria prayed for her father to intervene. But when his wife had an-nounced that she had decided to go back to Athens so that Maria could have the musical opportunities that she would not find in New York, George had fallen over himself to help. He bought their tickets and promised to send them a hun-dred dollars a month. He never questioned the wisdom of his wife's judgment, or even objected to being separated from his daughters. It was clear that he did not expect to be lonely in his family's absence.*

*The boat's whistle blared behind her. Maria tried to catch one last glimpse of her father, but she could not make him out in the blur of people on the quay.*

In the dressing room Maria turned to her icon and touched it. "You don't know what it was like for me. She never loved me the way a mother should."

George spread his hands wide with the ease of a man who has never willingly taken responsibility for anything.

"Maybe. But, *agapi mou*, here you are."

George gestured to the mountains of flowers that surrounded them.

Before Maria could answer, the announcement for beginners came over the public-address system.

"You should go, Papa," she said, pushing him out of the dressing room.

In the moment of silence that followed she looked at herself in the mirror and tried to summon Norma, the high priestess of the Druids, a woman torn between her duty to her people and her love for Pollione, the Roman soldier by whom she has two children. Norma was a woman of passion, but she was also a politician who could soothe her people's anger with the right words.

But at this moment she felt like the little girl in Washington Heights who had wanted her mother to be like other mothers who crouched down to embrace their children as they came out of school. She remembered once running out of school and putting up her arms for a hug, but Litza had ignored the gesture and had set off down the sidewalk for home in quick, impatient steps, leaving Maria to trail, disappointed, in her wake.

Battista was waiting for her in the wings. She clutched his arm and whispered in his ear, "I can't do it, Tita. My voice . . . it's not going to come."

Tita lifted the briefcase in his other hand. "There are ten thousand reasons in here why you will go on, and you will triumph. You always have and you always will."

Maria was shaking with fear. "But this time is different, Tita. I know that they hate me."

Tita could see the stage manager behind Maria, the cue for her entrance was less than a minute away.

"Give me your glasses, Maria." He took the heavy spectacles off her face. "Now make your crosses."

Obediently, her hands still trembling, she began to trace the sign of the cross on her chest, once, twice, three times. On the last cross, her hand was a little steadier.

The long note from the trumpets that signaled Norma's entrance began. Maria stood as still as a statue. The stage manager stepped forward. Tita's hand hovered, waiting to push, but then Maria lifted her shoulders and stepped out of the wings and onto the stage. She could hear applause, but there was also something else: a sibilance, a rumble that she recognized as the enemy's artillery in the distance. The auditorium was a dark chasm, the audience a pale blur. Even the conductor was just a blob at her feet. The chorus was all around her, asking for her as their priestess to tell them what to do.

The strings started to play the ghostly arpeggios that heralded the start of her great aria, and then on the eighth bar Maria lifted her head and it was Norma who sang the opening bars of "Casta diva," her voice soaring over the orchestra and reaching right to the back of the auditorium. Norma implored the goddess to bring peace to her people. The voice was filling her body; it was pouring out like the silvery beams of the moon she was worshipping; and it floated out over the listeners who, as the voice reached the high notes at the end of the aria, understood what it was to have faith.

At the end of the aria, she paused, and for a moment there was silence. Maria bowed her head waiting for the return of fire, but then a voice from the gods shouted "*Brava!*" and a storm of clapping surged through the theater. Maria felt the warmth of the applause run through her, burning away her fear. She was no longer Maria, the vulnerable woman, but Callas, la Divina, who could bring a hostile audience to its feet.

In the interval, Battista sat in the corner of the dressing room clutching the briefcase, looking at her in the mirror, smiling.

"You have won them over, *tesoro*, as I knew you would."

But Maria said nothing; she never spoke in the interval.

At the end of the opera, Norma took Pollione's hand and together they walked toward the funeral pyre that was to consume them both. As the curtain came down, Mario dropped Maria's hand as if it were a burning coal.

There were shouts of "Maria" and "Callas" from the audience, clearly audible through the curtain. As the cast lined up to take their communal curtain call, Mimi whispered to Maria, "Go out, Maria—they want you."

As she stepped out from behind the curtain the crowd exploded with delight. A wave rippled through the audience as one by one they stood up, clapping all the while. A rose fell at her feet and then another one. Maria stretched out her arms, and let the applause lift her up and fill the darkness inside her.

Bing was at their suite the next morning with a pile of newspapers. "You couldn't hope for better press! The *Times*, the *Post* are raves. The *Financial Times* calls it the operatic event of the century."

As he spoke, he dropped the papers in question onto the piano.

But Maria noticed that there was one paper that he did not throw down. She pointed to it.

"Oh, this isn't a review—it's just Elsa Maxwell, the gossip columnist. She fancies herself an opera critic, but she is the only one who thinks she has anything valuable to say."

"So what does this Maxwell say." Maria's voice was sharp.

"Nothing of interest. She is a Tebaldi devotee, so she is bound to be biased."

Maria reached out her hand in the same imperious gesture that Norma used to raise her sword against Pollione, and Bing yielded up the paper. Maria brought the print up to her face and read aloud.

"'Her "Casta diva" was a great disappointment. Perhaps she was nervous, or maybe through dieting, she has lost some of the magnificent voice we have heard so much about. The one I heard last night was hollow.'" The paper fell to the floor.

Bing shrugged. "As I said, Maxwell is part of the Tebaldi claque. Renata sings at Maxwell's parties, and in return, Elsa will support her in print."

Maria snorted. "That is totally corrupt. I would not have thought that even Tebaldi would stoop so low."

Bing said nothing.

Maria lifted her chin. It was always the same: there could be a hundred reviews calling hers the voice of the century, but it took only one negative comment to puncture the soufflé of praise. It was as if she were eleven again with her mother ridiculing her for wearing the wristwatch that was the second prize in the radio talent contest: "You should have come first, Maria."

"I think I should like to speak to this Maxwell?" Maria said.

Bing looked wary. "Well, that could be arranged—tonight in fact. She is coming to the gala."

Maria looked shocked. "You would really allow her to come to the gala, after she has written these vile things about me. Do you see here she calls me the 'devious diva.'"

The manager of the Metropolitan Opera did not even blink at the inconsistency.

"Madame Callas—Maria, if I may—she may know nothing about music, she is frequently rude, and delights in her own power; but just as no opera house will be content until they have secured the services of Maria Callas, I am afraid that no party in New York is complete without Elsa Maxwell."

VI

Maria checked her outfit against the sketch that Alain, Madame Biki's son-in-law, had given her. She had a folder of such sketches that showed her exactly how to wear all the outfits he had created. Tonight, she was wearing the white sheath, made of a heavy silk crepe that was draped in a majestic swathe across her right shoulder. She had the evening sandals from Ferragamo, made with a middling heel so that she did not tower too much over her husband. Her minaudière in the shape of an elephant had been a present from Franco Zeffirelli after the first night of *Lucia* at La Scala. The shape was a reference to her extraordinary weight loss. As Franco had said, "When we started working together you sang like a goddess, but now, *cara mia*, you look like one too." There was something missing; but before she could ask for it, Bruna handed her the long black evening gloves that made the outfit utterly chic.

The diamonds lay in a case from Harry Winston. They had been loaned to her for the event, and a security man was even now standing outside the door of the suite waiting to accompany her to the party. Bruna took the glittering necklace out and fastened it around Maria's throat. This, Maria thought, is how you get the world's attention if you can't sing.

Maria and Tita stood together hand in hand at the top of the staircase that swept down to the ballroom, the burly security guard standing discreetly six feet behind.

The words of the emcee came booming across the room. "And now, Mr. Mayor, ladies and gentleman, put your hands together to welcome Manhattan's very own diva, Maria Callas."

The band played the march of the toreadors, and Maria walked slowly down the staircase, the faces of the guests a blur as she concentrated on not falling over. At last, she reached the bottom and Bing was there with a woman whose diamonds made her own borrowed finery look insubstantial.

"May I introduce you to Mrs. Vanderbilt, who is on the Metropolitan board." Bing made the Metropolitan board sound like Mount Olympus.

Maria looked at the hawklike face in front of her. The thin lips were a slash of coral in the weathered face.

"A remarkable performance, Madame Callas. Truly remarkable. I had the privilege of hearing Adelina Patti's Norma, which was, of course, sublime. But I think you are rightfully her successor."

Maria stretched her face into a smile. It was remarkable how many people liked to compliment her in a way that revealed their own knowledge.

She nodded and said that her teacher in Athens had been taught by Patti. This did not interest Mrs. Vanderbilt at all, and she drifted away, aware that she claimed her right as the grande dame of New York society to speak first to the guest of honor.

A waiter offered her a glass of champagne and Maria waved it away, asking for a glass of water at room temperature. Bing introduced her to more of the Met patrons, with surnames like Whitney and Houghton. The women were mostly tall with lean arms that spoke of afternoons playing tennis. They were followed by their husbands, who held tumblers of whiskey and smiled eagerly when their wives explained that "Only you, Madame Callas, could have persuaded Buffy/Charlton/Winston to come to the opera. You really should be flattered."

At last Bing had run out of board members to introduce her to, and Maria asked him, "So where is the famous Elsa Maxwell, Mr. Bing?"

Bing pretended to look around him, but then he pointed to a corner. "She is over there talking to Marlene Dietrich." He pointed to where the elegant German star sat, her famous legs crossed languidly.

"Well? Are you going to introduce us?"

Bing hesitated, but after a look from Maria he led the way to where the film star was laughing at something Maxwell had said.

Maxwell was small, and almost spherical in shape. She was dressed in a brocade frock trimmed with sable that appeared to be upholstered to her ample frame. Maria saw at once that although Maxwell was neither shapely nor beautiful, she had a confidence that defied anyone to define her as ugly or fat. Her bright, intelligent eyes danced in her wrinkled face, calibrating everything around her.

Maxwell looked surprised when Maria loomed over her.

"Fräulein Dietrich, Elsa, may I present Madame Callas." Bing almost clicked his heels.

Dietrich smiled warmly and took Maria's hand. "I was so lucky to hear you sing last night. You had that tough audience at your feet, and I salute you. But you mustn't stay too long here—it is not good for your voice. Too much smoking and talking is dangerous. I shall make you some of my chicken broth and send it over tomorrow. It is an elixir for the throat."

"How kind of you," said Maria, surprised that such an exalted person should be so down-to-earth.

"A singer must look after her voice; it must always come first."

She leaned over to kiss Maria on the cheek. "And don't tell Elsa here any secrets that you don't want to see in print tomorrow." Dietrich gave her trademark slow sideways smile and glided away.

Maria looked down at Elsa Maxwell. "I thought when I read your words about me in the newspaper, Miss Maxwell, that you would be taller."

Elsa grinned. "But I have to look up to you. I would say that puts you at an advantage."

"Do I need an advantage?" Maria asked.

"Everyone needs an advantage when they go into battle," said Elsa, her small black eyes glittering.

Maria looked at the sturdy little figure in front of her and suddenly her anger subsided. She understood that this woman was not a critic but a fellow performer wanting to be noticed.

"I think it was brave of you to contradict all the other opera critics when you wrote about my performance." Maria raised an eyebrow.

Elsa swelled a little as she replied, "I could only write what I thought was true."

Maria leaned in and said, "Then you know nothing about opera. My performance that night was one of my best. But perhaps you wanted to be the exception."

Elsa frowned, and then her face creased into a smile of admiration. "Do you know, Madame Callas, a woman brave enough to confront a critic must be right. I never have liked being one of the crowd. Perhaps there was more to your performance than I realized at the time."

She put a cigarette in her lacquered holder, lit it, and took a long drag before she spoke again. "I believe, Madame Callas, that you may be about to join the very select company of those that I call my friends."

Maria acknowledged this distinction with a brief nod. "I really must be going."

Elsa looked at her watch. "But it's only eleven thirty."

"I am singing tomorrow."

"If this were one of my parties, you wouldn't be so ready to leave."

"Maybe, but I haven't had that pleasure."

"Oh, well, that can be put right." Elsa smiled wickedly. "Will you be bringing your husband?"

Maria opened her eyes wide. "But of course."

She gestured to the waiter. "Could you find Signor Meneghini, and tell him I want to go."

The waiter nodded.

Elsa tapped her on the shoulder. "I'll see you for lunch on Thursday," she said, and walked away before Maria could answer.

## VII

Lunch was at the Colony, the women's club that Elsa wrote about frequently in her columns as the place to see and be seen. Ambrose, the maître d', recognized Maria at once and led her over to the corner table where Elsa liked to hold court.

Maria was glad that she had worn the blue linen suit and the hat with the veil. Although her vision was blurry, she could see that the women around her were impeccably chic.

Elsa had a martini in one hand and the inevitable cigarette holder in the other. As Maria sat down, Elsa made a great display of putting out the cigarette.

"I don't want to poison that golden voice of yours."

"I thought you said it was hollow," Maria said.

Elsa smiled. "And I thought we'd established that you can't believe anything you read in the papers."

Maria laughed.

Ambrose brought over the menus, but Maria waved hers away.

"I'll have steak tartare and a green salad."

"And to drink, madame? A martini, perhaps, or glass of champagne."

"Just an iced tea."

Elsa raised her eyebrows. "My, my, how abstemious you are. You know what they say: all work and no play makes for a dull diva."

Her eyes twinkled and she laughed delightedly at her own joke.

"Well, I would rather be dull than ruin my voice," said Maria.

Elsa patted Maria's hand. "Don't mind me. I know how you singers need to look after yourselves. My friend Dickie, who I always go and stay with in France, is a singer—in fact Dickie was a pupil of Toscanini no less and we were both there at the famous performance of *Turandot* when the maestro put down his baton halfway through the third act and said there is no more. I would love to hear you sing *Turandot*, Maria."

Maria sipped her iced tea. "Well, I shall be sure to invite you next time."

Elsa gulped down her martini. "Of course I have seen Renata Tebaldi sing it many times, but she doesn't look the part in the same way that you do." She looked at Maria and added, "I am very cross with Renata, as I said in my column, for what she said about you."

Maria tried not to show her surprise. "I didn't know she had said anything."

Elsa tutted and patted her hand again. "Oh, Maria, Maria, you naughty girl. Though I say it myself, my column is considered essential reading."

Maria moved her hand back a fraction. "I don't have time to read papers. Every morning I get up and practice and then I am either rehearsing or performing, and at night I like to read scores."

The food arrived. Lobster thermidor for Elsa and steak tartare for Maria. Elsa picked up her napkin and tucked it under her many chins, and speared a piece of lobster meat onto her fork as she said, "I forgive you, especially when you look so enchanting in that little veil. Renata told a reporter in Milan that she had the one thing that you didn't have and that was a heart." She popped the lobster into her mouth and chewed with evident pleasure.

"So delicious; they make it specially for me, you know. I like the sauce to be extra creamy."

She looked at Maria, who was piercing the egg yolk and mashing it into the circle of red minced beef on her plate with her fork.

"But then I stopped watching my figure years ago, not that I ever really had one. You know the secret of my success?" Another gulp of martini. "That no woman has ever been jealous of me."

Maria put a small amount of steak tartare on her fork. "Then you are lucky. I am surrounded by jealousy."

"Oh, you mustn't mind Renata. She is just piqued that you have made such a success here in New York."

Then her gaze flicked upward as a tall, handsome man, whose profile looked familiar to Maria, blew Elsa a kiss as he walked by.

"Darling Cary, always such a gentleman. I must get the two of you together, perhaps a little dinner party."

Maria looked at Cary's Grant's elegant back. "You clearly know every-body."

"Well, that is my job, darling: to know everybody worth knowing. And I always say that they don't have to be rich or famous, so long as they aren't dull. Bores are the vacuum cleaner of society; they suck in everything but give nothing back."

Elsa leaned back with the expression of someone who had delivered the punch line and was waiting for the laugh.

Maria duly obliged.

By the end of the meal Maria was exhausted. Elsa did most of the talking, but she expected total engagement in return.

Maria's cheek muscles ached from the effort of finding the appro-priate expression. Thank goodness it wasn't a performance day. She was intrigued as to the status of Dickie, whom Elsa referred to constantly. Was he her lover? Elsa wasn't wearing a wedding ring.

As Maria leaned forward to kiss Elsa goodbye, the gossip columnist clasped both her hands and said, "Oh, Dickie will be livid not to have met you."

"I am singing in Paris next year; you must both come. And if Dickie speaks French, he can talk to Tita, who gets so bored when everything is in English."

Elsa let go of Maria's hands. "Dickie does speak perfect French and Italian, but I suspect that she would much rather talk to you than your husband."

"Dickie is a woman?"

Elsa smiled at Maria's astonishment. "Well, yes, even though she only wears suits from Savile Row."

Maria tried to conceal her confusion.

"I don't suppose you have ever been to the Isle of Lesbos, have you, Maria"—Elsa smiled—"where burning Sappho loved and sang?"

Maria shook her head. "I have hardly been to any of the Greek is-lands. It's a great shame."

"Oh, but you have plenty of time," said Elsa.

# CHAPTER THREE

## *La Sonnambula*

### JULY–AUGUST 1957

From that point on, Elsa went from being the lone critic to Maria's greatest supporter. In her column, in her syndicated radio show, on her weekly spot on the *Tonight* show, Elsa would rhapsodize about Maria's voice and stage presence. Tebaldi was cast into the outer darkness and Maria became, in Maxwell's words, la Divina. Elsa not only wrote about Maria constantly, she came to every performance that Maria gave in New York, Milan, or London. And while Elsa's devotion could be oppressive, the parties and events she organized broke up the monotony of practice and performance, airplanes and hotel suites, the onstage bouquets and the offstage suitcases of cash. After years of thinking of nothing but her voice, Maria found it was pleasant to walk into a room full of beautiful people who were dying to meet her.

Battista was polite to Elsa in public, but inwardly he was suspicious of Maxwell and her entourage of European royalty, Hollywood film stars, and millionaires looking to give their lucre some cachet. He would sit mute while Elsa gave intimate little dinners for Maria with Cole Porter, Tallulah Bankhead, and "the dear Windsors."

As her offstage life became more interesting, Maria was beginning to complain about the number of performances that Meneghini had committed her to. She was exhausted after her season at the Met and was looking forward to spending the summer at their villa in Sirmione overlooking Lake Garda. But Tita had already agreed to an engagement in August at the Edinburgh Festival with the La Scala company. When she objected, he told her, as he always did, "that I just want us to make hay while the sun shines, Maria."

In the past Maria had always complied with his wishes, but since she had met Elsa, she had begun to question his decisions, declaring that she needed more time to rest. Meneghini pointed out that if she needed rest, maybe she should spend less time going to parties with Elsa.

The new tension between them flared up over the La Scala engagement. Maria was defiant. "I don't care what you have agreed. I need time to recover, and I won't go to Edinburgh." Tita cajoled, threatened, and pleaded, but Maria was adamant. Tita knew that he needed reinforcement, so he invited Ghiringhelli, the manager of La Scala, to lunch at the villa.

Battista announced that Ghiringhelli was coming while Maria was having a fitting for the gown she was going wear to the costume ball that Elsa was throwing for her in Venice. Maria had declared that she was not going to come in character, as she spent quite enough time pretending to be somebody else. Alain had come up with a very simple design, a square-necked black bodice above a full white satin skirt sprinkled with black polka dots. The skirt would be full-length so that she wouldn't have to worry about her ankles that, despite all her dieting, had never lost their sturdiness.

Alain was just pinning the toile to show off Maria's waist when Battista made his announcement.

"Did he say why he wanted to talk to me so urgently?" Maria asked.

Tita shrugged.

"Did you tell him that the doctor said that I must have complete rest?"

Tita shrugged again. "He reads the articles of your friend Elsa. He knows that she is giving a ball for you."

"A ball is not a performance!" Maria threw out her hands and winced as the pins in the shoulder straps pricked her skin.

She felt a familiar flush of anger—her husband was using her just as her mother had done in Athens—when she had sent her out to sing for Italian soldiers in return for food. She had told her mother that it was not good for her to sing in the open air, but Litza had ignored her then just as Tita was ignoring her now. The doctor had been very clear: her blood pressure was too low and her heartbeat was irregular. "You need three months of complete rest, Madame Callas." Tita had been there too, and yet here he was letting Ghiringhelli into the house.

"He is going to ask me to do the Edinburgh Festival after I have already said no."

She saw Tita's gaze shift to the view of Lake Garda. The house was only a few years old and had picture windows that looked out over the lake. Maria had been thrilled with the villa until Zeffirelli had visited her there one day. When she had taken him into the sitting room, which she had filled with antiques, she noticed him wince as he looked around the room. "Do you like it, Franco," she had asked, her voice a little plaintive, and he had smiled and told her that it was magnificent. But she had seen the wince and since then she had looked around at her Empire sofas and ormolu clocks and wondered what invisible rule she had broken.

One of the ormolu clocks was chiming midday, which meant that Ghiringhelli would be here any minute. After Alain had unpinned the toile, she went upstairs and put on her most severe suit.

Ghiringhelli made polite conversation about the terrible traffic in Milan and the new restaurant that had opened opposite the opera house, until Bruna brought in the coffee. This was his cue. "You cannot imagine the excitement there is about the La Scala season at the Edinburgh Festival. Normally I would think twice about taking the company to a festival in Scotland, but when we announced the lineup—the tickets sold out in minutes."

Maria said nothing, just looked at him with a gaze that would have shriveled a lesser man. But Ghiringhelli was not a lesser man, he was the savior of La Scala—the man who had rescued it from postwar chaos and brought it back into magnificent life. He continued unabashed. "But although La Scala is undoubtedly the greatest opera company in the world, it is nothing without its greatest star, the incomparable Maria Callas."

He held out his hand as if he were onstage, pledging his undying love. Ghiringhelli was a handsome man with his silver mane and blue eyes, and he liked to audition all the new sopranos in private. But Maria had not been one of the young women who had been used by Ghiringhelli. He told himself that she had been too heavy in those days to be worth the effort, but the truth was that Callas had always made him a little nervous.

Maria ignored the gesture. "If you are selling tickets on the strength of my name, then, Antonio, you should have made sure that I was going to appear. As Tita must have told you, I am taking a break from performing, on medical advice. So there is no question of me coming to Edinburgh."

Ghiringhelli looked at Meneghini, who had indeed told him about the doctor's recommendation but had not ruled out the possibility that Maria might be "persuaded" to perform.

"She likes to say no at first; like all women, she needs some persuasion, and after that she enjoys it." Meneghini had then asked for a ridiculously high fee.

Battista put his hand on Maria's. "*Carissima*, your health must come first, of course, but what Antonio is proposing is a concert performance, not a full opera."

Maria took her hand away. "I still have to sing, Tita."

Ghiringhelli leaned forward. "I was hoping that you would sing *La sonnambula*. There hasn't been a production in Britain since its premiere in 1831. You have done so much to change the repertoire, Maria—all these great operas that you have revived. You are not just a voice; you are a pioneer. In the future, every soprano will have to acknowledge their debt to you."

Ghiringhelli wondered if he had gone too far with that last comment, as he had never met a soprano who didn't want to scratch Maria's eyes out; but she had stopped glaring at him.

"Yes, I have made Amina my own. But I think even Bellini himself would not want me to sacrifice my voice for his opera." As she spoke the word "sacrifice," Maria put her hand on her heart and lowered her eyes.

"Of course not, but it is your role and no one can sing it better. And the Edinburgh audience will be so grateful to have the opportunity to listen to you," Ghiringhelli replied.

It was true that there was nothing like singing to an audience that had been starved of opera. Perhaps they were less discerning than the patrons of La Scala, but they responded so enthusiastically in places like Dallas or Mexico City that she never regretted those engagements.

Tita put four spoons of sugar in his coffee and stirred vigorously. "You seem so much better now than when you got here, *tesoro*, I am sure Dr. Lanini would say the same."

Ghiringhelli started to drum his fingers on the table. It was time to wrap this up.

"La Scala has been good to you in the past, Maria. Now is the time to repay the debt."

He realized his mistake the moment the words had left his mouth. The softening he had detected earlier disappeared and Maria came back, eyes blazing.

"I seem to remember that you rejected me when I first came to Italy, and it was only after I had made a success at La Fenice that you understood what a blunder you had made. Yes, I have been in some excellent productions at La Scala, but do not imagine for a moment that my career has depended on your patronage, Signor Ghiringhelli. I have made my career through my own talent and dedication, and I owe you nothing."

She put her coffee cup down with a rattle and stood up. "I am going upstairs to rest now. Goodbye."

Both men got to their feet.

Ghiringhelli spoke. "You are quite right, of course. You did not need La Scala to become the greatest singer in the world, but, Maria, La Scala needs you desperately. Without you we will have to cancel the Edinburgh season, which will cost us a fortune and will make it impossible to put on a new production next year. I know how much you want to sing *Anna Bolena*. Please, Maria, I beg you to reconsider—if you come to Edinburgh, I promise you the undying gratitude of La Scala."

Maria gave a little nod. "You have made yourself very clear. I will think about it."

When she left the room, Meneghini said, "She will do it, Antonio, I am sure. Especially when I tell her the terms on which we have agreed."

"You are truly rapacious, Meneghini."

The smaller man smiled. "But as you yourself said, think of what it will cost you if my wife doesn't sing."

Maria lay down on her bed and closed her eyes. She knew that at this moment Tita would be negotiating her fee with Ghiringhelli. She had known from the moment that Tita had told her about Ghiringhelli's visit that her husband had set it up. To refuse now would damage Tita's standing as her manager and, although she was furious with him for not consulting her, she did not want the world to think that he was no longer to be trusted.

It had worked so well at the beginning. Tita was thirty years older than her, and it had been such a relief to let him handle everything. He had given up his brick factory and had become her manager, choosing her engagements, calming her fears, and encouraging her to take on the most difficult roles. He had told her the first time they met that he thought she could be the greatest diva in the world. At the time she had been two hundred pounds, with legs like tree trunks, but Battista had never doubted that she was prima donna material. In the first year of their marriage, she had been so happy: at last she had found someone she could rely on, someone who wanted only the best for her. For a wedding present he had bought her a mink stole, and as she wrapped it round her bare shoulders the velvety softness had made her feel protected for the first time in her life.

Tita had not been her first lover, but he was the first man that she had felt relaxed with in bed. He was not urgent or overpowering, and Maria had found his gentleness a relief.

Tita never sulked if she was tired after a performance or wanted to go to bed early before one. Their lovemaking, which had never been frequent, had dwindled to almost nothing. But Maria was happy to have him in bed beside her, sleeping while she read through scores late at night.

She had once imagined that they might have a family. But Battista had been careful at the beginning not to make her pregnant, and at the time she had hardly noticed. All she wanted then was to sing at La Scala. She had once asked Elvira if she had ever wanted children, and her teacher had looked at her as if she were mad. "I already had a gift from God," she said, pointing to her throat. "To have a child too would be greedy."

When they bought the Villa Sirmione, Maria had put a swing in the garden as a gesture to a future child, to indicate that her offspring would have the kind of carefree existence that she had been denied. But the only occupant of that swing had been Maria herself, and then only for photoshoots that were designed to show what a happy domestic life the great diva enjoyed in "her charming villa on the shores of Lake Garda." In these interviews Maria always declared that she would be perfectly happy to give up singing to settle down to a life of cooking, cleaning, and childcare. "All I have wanted," she would say to the interviewer, her eyes often wet, "is to be a wife and mother."

The journalists, the male ones, had nodded in sympathy. No one had ever wondered, aloud at least, why in that case she didn't give up her career and have a baby. They had been happy to accept the assumption that Maria Callas had put aside her own personal fulfillment in the service of her art, a vestal virgin at the shrine of Opera. And if some tactless reporter, usually female or at least American, asked whether she planned to have children in the future, Maria would lower her gaze and talk about fertility treatment.

There had been moments recently though when, from the windows of her limousine or on airplanes, she had seen women with babies and she had wondered whether she really would one day become a mother. But then she imagined Battista sleeping next to her, his remaining hair confined to a hairnet, and she pushed the thought away. Battista never talked about having a child, he was too busy filling her diary.

She decided to make herself feel better by buying the diamond and emerald necklace that Alain had shown her in the jeweler's next to La Scala. He had suggested that she should wear it in her hair at Elsa's ball.

When she mentioned the necklace to Tita at dinner, he surprised her by agreeing immediately. "After the fee I have extracted from Ghiringhelli, you can buy two necklaces if that's what you want, Maria." He looked very pleased with himself.

"Antonio protested, of course, said that La Scala couldn't afford to pay so much, that it went against all precedent, etcetera, etcetera. But he had lost his negotiating position because he had already admitted that the tickets would not sell without you taking part. And, as I know how much he is charging for the tickets, there is no danger of La Scala going bankrupt."

⟝

A few weeks later, just before she was due to leave for Edinburgh, Maria was coming from Madame Biki's, where she had been having her final fittings for the outfits she would be wearing during her visit to Venice, when she saw Tommaso Rossi, their accountant, drinking an espresso in a café in the cathedral piazza. She stopped and greeted him. He was delighted to be recognized by the famous Madame Callas in front of all his cronies, and even more excited when she agreed to sit down with him. He ordered her an affogato and watched in delight as she poured the black coffee over the yellow scoop of ice cream. She would have only one tiny bite, of course, but she would make it look so delicious that Signor Rossi would feel like a god. After surrendering to the ice cream, she looked up at the accountant and said that she longed to be like him and sit in a café in the sunshine, instead of toiling around the opera houses of Europe.

"Oh, but, madame, think how much pleasure you are giving to the world."

"I don't know for how much longer, Signor Rossi."

A shadow crossed the accountant's round face. "But, Madame Callas, tell me that you are not planning to retire any time soon. It would be a tragedy for the world of music."

"Sadly, Signor Rossi, the decision may not be mine—a singer's career can end in an instant, a vocal injury, an inflamed node—these things happen and when they do, I hope that I or rather we will be comfortable in our retirement. But of course I know that you and Tita have been working together to make sure of that."

The accountant shifted in his seat. "Well, since you mention it, madame, I do have a concern on that score. Your husband is a very generous man, as you know, a family man, but I sometimes think he is a little too generous. Recently I have said to him that maybe it is time to let the family fend for themselves and to put more money aside for your future as a couple. As you yourself have so gracefully pointed out, a singer's career is not forever, and it is sensible to have savings for all eventualities."

"He must have been very grateful for such prudent advice. I hope he followed it," Maria said.

There was something in her voice that made Signor Rossi dab his forehead with his handkerchief. "In the end, it is always the client's decision, Madame Callas."

Maria got up.

"But aren't you going to finish your affogato?"

"No, Signor Rossi. I find that I have lost my appetite."

Maria wanted to confront Tita immediately. But she had a performance the day after she arrived in Edinburgh, and she needed to conserve her energy. She decided to wait until the four performances were over, and they were on their way to Venice. She could hardly believe that Tita could have been spending her money on his worthless family in Verona. How often had he told her that she was all the family he needed? How dare he use the money that she had earned to support his grasping relations, who had never made the slightest effort to be nice to her?

ɔ

The suite at the Balmoral Hotel had a splendid view of Arthur's Seat, the volcanic outcrop that dominated the city, but it boasted a tartan carpet so lurid that it gave Maria a headache just to look at it. While Meneghini went to the barber's, Maria rang the front desk and asked if they had another suite with a grand piano.

"Certainly, Madame Callas. There is the Royal Suite, which I am sure you will find very comfortable. Madame Tebaldi stayed there for the festival last year, and she was kind enough to say how much she enjoyed it."

The Royal Suite had an even more splendid view of Arthur's Seat, and while the carpet was still tartan, the pattern was a whisper rather than a shriek.

When her husband returned, Maria forestalled any protests about the change by telling him that this was where Tebaldi had stayed, adding, "As you are always telling me how much money I am making by coming here to sing, I thought it was only right that I should be as comfortable as Renata. I don't want the world to think that she is earning more than I am."

⊇

The first three performances were a pleasure. The Edinburgh audience was rapturous in its appreciation of her Amina. But on the morning of her last performance, she woke up with a tightness in her throat. She tried her usual warm-up exercises, but she could not shake the constriction. She told Bruna to make the usual tea with honey and went to bed, leaving a note for Tita to warn Ghiringhelli to have a replacement ready just in case she couldn't sing.

When it was time to leave for the theater, her throat was feeling looser. Maria thought that it was tight rather than damaged and that if she sang carefully, she would be able to get through what would be her last performance without injury.

But halfway through her most difficult aria, where Amina is sleepwalking through the moonlit glade and the melody is ornamented by the kind of cadenzas and trills that are the hallmark of bel canto, she reached for the high B and she felt her voice falter.

She told herself that she had to think beyond the note. She started on another trill and this time the note was there—and for the rest of the aria she concentrated on being Amina, the sleepwalker. The audience appeared not to notice her faltering. Thank God, she thought, that this was Edinburgh and not Milan, where she would have been booed and cabbages thrown onstage.

Between acts Bruna and the dresser changed her costume behind a makeshift screen in the wings. She was telling Bruna how relieved she was to have got through the aria when one of the young sopranos from the chorus stopped to speak to her. "I just wanted to say, Madame Callas, that you are an inspiration to me. It was your recording of *Norma* that made me decide to be a singer."

Maria nodded and gave the younger woman a brief smile, hoping that she would get the hint to leave her in peace. But the girl, who had large blue eyes, was still gazing at her.

"I just wanted to ask your advice for a young singer like me, just starting out."

Maria winced as the dresser pulled the laces of her corset.

"I have two things to say. First listen to the music, but I mean really listen—it will tell you everything you need to know. The composer has left you instructions; it is your job to follow them."

The girl nodded vehemently. "And the second piece of advice?"

"Never bother a singer in the middle of a costume change. Concentration is everything."

The girl flushed. "I am sorry, Madame Callas. But I was so hoping that you would put in a good word for me with Signor Ghiringhelli. My name is Flavia Leith."

"If you have the voice and the belief, you will succeed. Nothing I can say will make any difference. Now please go away."

Flavia left, and Maria tried to get back into the mind of Amina, sleepwalking her way into disaster. She prayed that she could get through the reconciliation scene and then she would be done.

⸚

As the curtain came down, she saw Tita waiting for her in the wings. Maria grabbed his arm.

"Did you hear how I missed a B in the cadenza? Thank God this is the last performance."

The clapping from the audience showed no sign of diminishing, and she could hear them shouting her name. The stage manager beckoned her onstage again. When she came back, Tita was looking nervous. "But, *tesoro*, this is not your last performance."

Maria stared at him, but she was being beckoned onstage again.

When she came back, she said, "What do you mean?"

"You have another show on Tuesday."

The applause was getting even louder—she would have to go back out again. She strode onto the stage and made a gracious curtsy to the audience. They yelled in delight as she gestured to the cast, to the orchestra, and finally to the audience with outstretched arms. She curtsied again, but as she came offstage, her eyes were blazing.

"I agreed to four performances! How can there be another one?"

Meneghini shrugged. "I don't know. There must have been a mistake somewhere."

Maria felt the anger surging through her; she wanted to break something. But the audience were still calling for her, and she could see the stage manager beckoning to her from the wings opposite. She took a deep breath and went onstage. On her return, she hissed in Tita's ear, "I agreed to four performances. And I have sung four. Basta!"

"But they have sold the tickets, Maria."

"That is not my problem," she said as she went onstage again.

There were nineteen curtain calls for Maria that night, and the audience would have called for more, but Maria signaled to the stage manager that she had had enough.

When she finally came offstage, Tita had vanished. Maria started to walk back to her dressing room but then decided that she would speak to Ghiringhelli at once and tell him about the mistake. She pointed at the stage manager, a slender young man with red hair.

"Where is Ghiringhelli?"

The young man went a painful scarlet. "I don't know, Madame Callas. Shall I go and look for him?"

Maria shook her head. "I don't have time. Take me to his office."

The young man gulped. "His office is miles away. Let me bring him to your dressing room."

Maria shook her head again and waited until the stage manager, who looked as though he might cry, began to lead the way. She followed him through a corridor onto a landing where he stopped in front of a door and made a tentative knock. Maria did not wait for an answer and pushed the door open.

The first thing she saw was Ghiringhelli's back. Then she looked down and saw the large blue eyes of Flavia, the soprano from the chorus. The young woman was scrambling to her feet.

"Am I disturbing you?" Maria said.

Ghiringhelli wheeled round, his fingers fumbling with his trouser buttons.

"I came to say goodbye, as this is my last performance, but clearly I picked an inopportune moment."

She moved her gaze to Flavia. "It's the music you should be listening to, not bastards like him." Maria pointed at Ghiringhelli.

Flavia looked as if she had been slapped and then ran past Maria, bumping into the stage manager in her hurry to get away.

"Well, now that you have made a scene of truly operatic proportions, Maria," said Ghiringhelli, who had brushed off his initial embarrassment, "perhaps we can talk in private."

The stage manager scurried away, and the corridor emptied of the various stagehands and chorus members who had followed the diva as she stormed upstairs.

"Your dramatic farewell is premature, Maria. You have another performance on Tuesday—surely you haven't forgotten." He gave her a rictus smile.

"How could I forget something that I didn't know about?" Maria cried. "I agreed to four performances of *La sonnambula*, and tonight is the fourth."

Ghiringhelli put out a pacifying hand. "Shall we find your husband, Maria. I am sure he can help us resolve this . . . situation."

"But there is no situation. I am leaving in the morning for Venice."

She turned away from him and walked back to her dressing room.

Ten minutes later she was taking off her makeup when Tita came in followed by Ghiringhelli.

Tita's face had faded from its usual olive to parchment.

"Where have you been, Tita? I need you to tell Antonio that he has made a mistake and that he will have to find someone else to sing on Tuesday. I am sure there will be no shortage of candidates. Indeed, I believe I interrupted him in the middle of an audition." Maria smiled nastily at Ghiringhelli.

Ghiringhelli looked at Tita, waiting for him to speak.

Tita opened his mouth silently like a fish gasping for air before saying, "Maria, I think perhaps you have misremembered. We agreed to five performances."

Maria looked at him in disbelief. "No, we didn't. Do you really think that I would make a mistake about a thing like that, Tita?"

Her husband shrugged, and again he and Ghiringhelli exchanged glances.

Maria wanted to scream, but she managed to control her voice. "I said I would do four performances when you begged me, Antonio. Even though it was against my doctor's advice. I missed a note tonight because I have overtaxed my voice, and now I must rest."

Ghiringhelli made a face that attempted to look sorrowful, but it was clear that he was just as furious as she was. "I am sorry to hear that, Maria, but the house is entirely sold out for Tuesday. Even if the performance is not up to your usual standards, it will not matter. How many curtain calls did you have tonight, fifteen?"

"Nineteen," said Maria automatically.

"Nineteen. Do you think that anybody out there even noticed your stumble? You are adored here. Surely you don't want to disappoint all those fans."

It was the only argument, as Ghiringhelli knew, that was likely to change her mind; and for a second Maria wavered. There was something in the applause that gave her strength; it was a feeling impossible to find elsewhere; it was the strongest love she had ever known. But she was not foolish enough to think that the love was unconditional—she would not sing if she could not fulfill the audience's expectations. Antonio might think that they would not know the difference, but he would not be the one standing on the stage, putting his reputation at risk.

She started to rub the cold cream on her face and then wipe it off with savage strokes.

Tita broke the silence. "Why don't you have a day of silence tomorrow and then see how you are on Tuesday?"

Maria caught Bruna's eye in the mirror. "Are we packed, Bruna?"

"Yes, madame."

Ghiringhelli shook his head. "Have you forgotten how when that *Time* magazine article came out, I stood up for you. Told everyone that asked how unfair it was, and how easy you were to work with?"

"I remember that you said I was always punctual for rehearsals and that you had no cause for complaint on that score." Maria took off her false eyelashes.

"It would be unfortunate if I had to revise my opinion publicly and tell the world how unreliable you are." Ghiringhelli cracked his knuckles.

"So that is how you demonstrate the undying gratitude of La Scala? By threatening me? When it is your mistake, not mine," cried Maria.

Ghiringhelli opened the door. "I just want you to be aware of the consequences of your actions. I will leave you now to talk it over with your husband. I am sure that together you will make the right decision."

After the door closed the silence was broken only by the sound of Maria screwing on the lid of the cold cream jar.

Battista opened his mouth to speak, but Maria silenced him with a hand. "Don't even try. I am not going to change my mind."

Battista came to stand right behind her. "No, you must do exactly what you please even if it means humiliating me in front of a man like Ghiringhelli."

Maria turned round to look him in the face. "You think that's humiliating? What about standing in front of an audience of a thousand people and being unable to sing? That is real humiliation."

Lowering her voice a little, she said, "You should have told them I wouldn't do it when you discovered their mistake. That is your job, after all."

Her tone was soft, but Tita looked as though she had slapped him. "My job?" he said almost in a whisper.

"Yes! And one for which you are paid handsomely." She stood up, looming over him, bending her face to his. "You think I don't know about all the money you are squirreling away in secret accounts."

"I don't know what you are talking about," he protested.

"It's no use pretending, Tita. Rossi has told me all about your little arrangements for your family. And I decided that I would think of the money you have stashed away secretly as your wages, not a man stealing from his wife." She jabbed him in the chest with her finger, and he rocked back a little.

"So I may have helped my family out a little. That's what normal families do—they help each other. I didn't tell you because I knew you wouldn't understand."

The injustice of this made Maria close her eyes momentarily. Tita, of all people, knew how badly her mother had treated her.

"Perhaps I don't know how normal families behave, but that is not my fault. You know how it was. My mother used me for her own ends—she always preferred my sister—and even my father has never stood up for me. Why should I help them? They never loved me. All they do is exploit me."

But Tita did not soften. He said quietly, "So you say, Maria."

"What does that mean?"

"Maybe there was fault on both sides. You are not always an easy person to love, Maria."

Maria remembered her mother, in the kitchen in the Patission Street apartment in Athens, saying the same thing. Then she had not known how to answer, but now she had found the words.

"But I don't think you have ever loved me, Tita, only my voice."

# CHAPTER FOUR

## *Un Ballo in Maschera*

Elsa was waiting for them at the airport, surrounded by a pack of reporters. She rushed toward Maria and embraced her side-on so that the photographers would get the best shot.

"Now that you are here, darling, the party can start!"

But her words were lost in the clamor of the reporters' questions.

"Is it true you canceled a performance in Edinburgh because you didn't want to miss Elsa Maxwell's party?"

"What is your message to the people who paid to hear you sing in Edinburgh?"

"Will you ever go back to La Scala?"

Maria opened her mouth to explain that she was the one who had been wronged, but in that moment, she understood that it would do no good. Ghiringhelli had been bad-mouthing her, and the press only wanted to print a story where she was the villain.

Elsa, on the other hand, had never heard a question she couldn't answer, so she batted away the reporters with her own version of events. "Of course Madame Callas wants to come to the party I am giving for her. But I am flattered that it is so important to her. To have the greatest singer in the world turn down an engagement so that she can come to my little shindig is a great honor."

Maria could hear Elsa feeding the story, but she walked on, her poodle under her arm, her husband following in her wake.

Elsa trotted over to the launch that was waiting for them at the end of the jetty. Maria sat in the stern, and Elsa immediately sat next to her, leaving Meneghini with no choice but to help Bruna check that all sixteen pieces of monogrammed luggage had arrived safely.

"Do I detect a rift in the marital lute, Maria?" asked Elsa, the beetle eyes glittering.

"He thinks that I should have stayed in Edinburgh and given the fifth performance. He thinks that pleasing Ghiringhelli is more important than my health."

"Or happiness? Think how miserable you would be to miss the ball," said Elsa.

"Oh, Tita doesn't care about that. All he cares about is the money."

Elsa patted Maria's hand with her liver-spotted diamond-encrusted paw.

"My poor darling. What you need is someone who will really take care of you."

Maria said nothing. As the campanile of St. Mark's Square came into view, she stood up and gazed across the lagoon at the city where she had had her first great triumph in the jewel-like opera house, La Fenice. How happy she had been, working day and night so that she could sing two operas in a week. Tita had been her right hand then, telling her that she could perform miracles; bringing her the zeppole filled with zabaglione that she had loved so much. They had worked together so well then, but now? She looked over to where he was sitting in the forward cabin, his eyes closed because, as she knew, he felt seasick even on the calm waters of the Venetian lagoon. The beauty of the scene in front of her made her irritation seem petty. When the boat pulled up outside the Gritti palace, and Tita opened his eyes, he saw her smiling at him.

The hotel manager was waiting for them on the jetty. He bowed as Maria stepped off the boat.

"Welcome to the Gritti, Madame Callas. May I say how honored we are here at the hotel to have you as a guest."

He led her up the grand staircase to the piano nobile where he opened a door set in a gilt portico. Maria followed him into a long room that had three double windows looking out onto the glittering water of the Grand Canal. Between the windows, on scagliola side tables, were two enormous flower arrangements whose heady fragrance masked the muddy aroma of the canal as the manager flung open the windows.

"I hope everything is to your satisfaction, Madame Callas." He opened an adjoining door onto a bedroom with an elaborate frescoed ceiling.

"Yes, indeed," said Maria with enthusiasm. She spent most of her life in hotels, and they had begun to merge into one another, but this was exceptional. She clutched Tita's arm, signaling to him that their quarrel was over.

"Tita, isn't this wonderful."

Her husband looked around the room, mentally estimating its cost. "I don't see a piano."

Maria had noticed that too. Normally that would have made her nervous but today she decided that nothing would spoil her mood.

The manager looked anxious. But Maria shrugged. "Oh, I am not here to work, Tita. I am here to have fun!"

The manager slipped away.

Maria went up to one of the flower arrangements and smelled a cushion-like white rose. "Such beautiful flowers, Elsa. Thank you."

"I can't take the credit—they are from Onassis. Although, I confess, I did tell him to send them. It's time the world's two most famous Greeks got to know each other."

Tita sat down heavily on one of the gilt chairs.

"This must be one of the most expensive hotel rooms in Venice."

He glared at Elsa, who stared back unperturbed and said in slow, distinct English so that he could understand, "The best thing about this magnificent hotel suite, my dear Meneghini, is that it isn't costing you a cent. I persuaded the manager to give you the suite for free—he understood the value to the hotel of having you stay here instead of the Cipriani or the Daniele."

Maria impulsively kissed her on the cheek. "Oh, Elsa, you are wonderful. Isn't she, Tita?"

Tita nodded without enthusiasm.

"And wait till you see where the ball is being held. I have persuaded la contessa di Castelbarco to open her piano nobile. The Tiepolo ceilings are simply divine."

Meneghini pursed his lips. "And I suppose you got the Tiepolos for free by threatening to use Veronese instead?"

Elsa did not laugh. "Oh no, Venetian aristocrats never give anything away, but let us say that I have backing. Because when I give a party for Maria Callas, everybody wants to be invited."

⸺

It was obvious which of the palazzos lining the Grand Canal belonged to the Castelbarco family because a fleet of gondolas was lining up to disgorge their cargo of the rich and famous under the red-and-white-striped awning. Elsa had restricted the guest list to one hundred and fifty. "Normally, darling," she explained to Maria, "I would invite three hundred if I wanted a good showing, but as the party is for you, I know that every single person will come unless they are on their deathbeds, and even then, I am sure you could revive a corpse. So, this is a select party: Noël; Cole; Princess Grace; the Agnellis; Ari and Tina Onassis; the Ruspolis; Peggy Guggenheim, of course; the Devonshires; and Prince Ali Khan, because all the women want to sleep with him and all the men want to know the name of his tailor."

In the gondola in front of her, Maria could see a couple who were clearly going to the party—the woman was wearing what appeared to be a galleon in full rig on her head, and her husband wore a silver helmet with the visor down. Maria watched the couple get out of the boat, the woman's galleon shaking as she stepped onto the jetty. Maria didn't recognize the woman's face, but she had a profile that suggested that costume parties in Venetian palazzos were nothing new.

The reporters and photographers had their own boats, and they were bobbing around the jetty when Maria's craft drew level with the landing stage. Tita, who was wearing a gondolier's straw hat, got out first and stretched down to help his wife. As she stepped on the jetty, the flash-bulbs exploded, and Maria turned, giving the cameras her most dazzling smile.

She ignored the questions that were being shouted across the water.

"Is it true that you have given up singing?"

"Are you going to record a duet with Elvis Presley?"

"Is there going to be a film of *La traviata*?"

"Will you ever return to La Scala after Ghiringhelli's comments today?"

"What is the secret of your slim figure?"

Elsa—wearing a gold lace gown and her *corno ducale*, or doge's hat, which she claimed was from the fourteenth century—rushed toward Maria, arms open. As Maria bent down to kiss her, Elsa whispered, "Gianni Agnelli owes me a favor, so I have asked him to keep an eye on your husband tonight because I want you to enjoy yourself. Gianni is very good company and knows all the prettiest women, your precious Tita will be quite safe."

"You think of everything, Elsa."

"That's my job, darling—soaking up surplus spouses." She winked at Maria.

"Oh, but Tita isn't surplus."

Elsa put her finger to her lips. "Don't worry, darling, your secret is safe with me."

She turned to Meneghini. "Make sure you take a good look at the Tiepolo frescoes—they are gloriously pornographic."

Despite the "tiny" guest list, the salon was packed. When Elsa appeared at the door with Maria, there was a hum of recognition and excitement and the crowd parted to allow the diva and her hostess to walk to the center of the room.

"Maria, darling, this kitten is the Princess Ruspoli." A tall woman wearing a furry white cat mask with long whiskers made a faux feline swipe toward her with her black gloved hand, equipped, Maria noticed, with real claws. Maria smiled and the princess purred.

"And this is my dear friend Noël." Noël Coward, who sported a Chaplinesque bowler hat, bent to kiss her hand.

"This is a great honor, Madame Callas. I heard your *Traviata* and I confess that even a stonyhearted creature such as I was misty-eyed when you coughed your last." He brandished an imaginary handkerchief, then he asked, "But tell me, who have you come as?"

"As Maria Callas, the diabolical diva," replied Maria.

Coward laughed. "The diabolical diva, very droll, my dear. I can see that you have been learning from darling Elsa. Everyone may think she looks like a natterjack toad, but she is always the first to point it out, bless her."

A glass of champagne was pressed into her hand and Maria was led by Elsa to "say hello to your old friend Marlene."

Maria remembered to thank Dietrich for the chicken broth that she had sent to the Met every week during the season.

Marlene batted her thanks away. "No thanks needed. I like to look after people. And there isn't a singer in the world who doesn't need chicken soup."

Over Marlene's shoulder Maria could see Tita talking to a man with a tanned face who was wearing an admiral's tricorne. Her husband was rapt, listening so intently he looked as though he might fall over. Maria understood why Elsa had such a reputation as a hostess—she really did think of everything. Of course, her husband would be captivated by the richest man in Italy. The one thing that Tita cared for more than opera was money.

Elsa moved Maria round the room ruthlessly. "Now, Noël, you have monopolized Maria long enough. I have promised to introduce her to the Devonshires—wearing their ducal coronets, bless them."

And five minutes later: "Darling Debo, if you want more time with Maria, you must ask her to Chatsworth. Grace of Monaco is dying to talk to her, and as she is in the family way again, I really think we must put her out of her misery." In this way Maria met everybody, but in the most cursory manner, which was a relief, as Maria was as good at small talk as most of the guests were at singing Tosca. But with Elsa at her side, there would never be a repetition of the terrible moment at a gala dinner, where her neighbor had told her she must see Pompeii, and Maria had asked what sort of painter he was.

After two or three circuits of the salon, stopping off for refreshment at the buffet, which was topped by replicas of Arcimboldo's heads made of fruit and vegetables, Elsa sat down at the piano. She played a few chords which resolved into the blues ballad "Stormy Weather." Maria started to back away from the piano before she could be asked to sing.

But Elsa was too quick for her. "Madame Callas," she called, her eyes rapt in adoration, "won't you make this old broad very happy, and join me?"

The chatter in the room suddenly dimmed as if a volume control had been turned down. Maria felt the eyes of all her new acquaintances upon her. It was her rule never to sing in these situations, but as Elsa gazed up at her, she knew that she was not able to refuse.

> *Don't know why*
> *There's no sun up in the sky . . .*

Maria's voice broke through any chatter in the room and bounced against the walls. She loved to sing jazz standards at home for fun, and Elsa had once called on her when she was singing "Stormy Weather," a fact that the party giver for the stars had obviously filed away.

As she inhaled, ready to start on the next verse, there was a noise as the door opened and a couple walked in.

The man was short and stocky and wore the cap of a Greek sea captain; the woman, who held herself like a dancer, wore a picture hat with a blue satin ribbon tied under her chin, like a Fragonard painting. The man was talking as they walked in, and he did not stop, even when Maria started to sing the second verse.

> *Can't go on*
> *Everything I have is gone*
> *Stormy weather*

Maria pushed from the core of her being so that her voice overwhelmed the chattering latecomer. He looked up at last and caught Maria's eyes. His face was a blur, but she could feel the heat of his gaze. She put one hand on the piano and brought the other to her throat.

There was a moment of silence, and then delighted applause. Elsa climbed on top of the piano stool and, catching Maria's hand, she kissed it and held it aloft as she declaimed, "I never thought that when I was pounding the piano in the nickelodeons of Manhattan that one day I would be accompanying the greatest singer in the world, not to mention the most glamorous. Princes and princesses, millionaires and millionairesses, ladies and gentlemen, I give you the incomparable Maria Callas."

Then Elsa climbed down and, still holding Maria's hand, pulled her toward the latecomers. Panting with excitement, she said, "Maria, may I present the other most famous living Greek, Aristotle Onassis, and his beautiful wife, Tina."

Maria looked down at her compatriot and gave him a chilly smile, saying in English, "I believe I must thank you for the flowers, Mr. Onassis."

Oblivious to her tone, Onassis grinned. He answered her in Greek, "I am glad I got to hear the famous Maria Callas sing."

"You might have done if you had stopped talking to listen," Maria said in the same language.

Onassis laughed, his gold back teeth catching the light.

Tita appeared at her elbow. He couldn't understand what they were saying, but, like a dog, he knew from her intonation that his mistress was not happy.

"Battista, this is Mr. Onassis. He is partial to 'background' music."

Maria spoke in Italian, which Onassis clearly understood. He turned to Elsa, who had been talking to his wife.

"Elsa, I have offended your guest of honor. What can I do to make amends?"

Maria waved her hand. "Please don't mention it."

Onassis settled his warm gaze on her, and said in Greek, "I know nothing about music, but I hate to make a beautiful woman frown."

Maria felt a lurch in her stomach.

Onassis turned toward his elegant little wife, who was talking animatedly to a young man who was wearing a hat with a curving ostrich feather.

"Tina!"

Tina looked round.

"Please invite Madame Callas and her husband to lunch tomorrow."

Tina's voice was the product of an expensive English education. "Madame Callas, Aristo and I would be delighted if you and your husband would join us tomorrow. And I hope you will come too, Elsa."

Elsa beamed. Onassis turned back to Maria and gave her the

buccaneering smile of a man who always got his own way. Taking Tina's arm, he said as he walked off, "I'll send a boat at noon." Maria replied that she didn't remember accepting his invitation. But she was talking to Onassis's back—he was already heading for Princess Grace, cutting through the crowds like a barracuda. What an arrogant man, thought Maria. It didn't make any difference how rich he was—he couldn't just assume that she, Maria Callas, would do what he wanted.

Sensing her defiance, Elsa took her by the elbow. "Remember what I said about all work and no play making Maria a very dull diva. Come on, darling, we will eat Ari's caviar, which is the very best and not fattening at all, and we will teach him the difference between Wagner and Verdi. It will be a hoot."

The button eyes were pleading. "Ari is quite charming when he wants to be, and he is so generous. . . . I shouldn't tell you this"—she lowered her voice to a whisper—"but he paid for this party."

Maria stiffened. "Whatever arrangements you made do not concern me, Elsa. I will not sing for my supper."

"Heaven forfend, Madame Callas." Elsa mimicked Maria's operatic sweep of the arm, and then gave her a no-nonsense look. "But it never hurts to have rich and powerful friends. Powerful enemies are more amusing, of course, but when you have that monster Ghiringhelli bad-mouthing you to the press, then a man with a yacht and all the money in the world is a useful creature to have in your back pocket."

On her other side, Tita was saying in Italian, "But it's impossible, Maria. Don't you remember what the doctor said—you have to rest before flying to New York: those long journeys are so bad for your voice. I will go and tell this Onassis not to bother with his boat."

Maria had been about to tell Onassis the same thing, but Tita invoking the doctor's advice annoyed her, and she decided that she would go for lunch with the rich Greek and his doll of a wife.

"No, leave it, Tita."

Elsa clapped her hands and her chins wobbled with glee. "Oh goody, we are going to have such fun."

⹁

The picture of Maria smiling radiantly as she stepped onto the jetty of the Palazzo Castelbarco was on all the front pages on the hotel's newspaper rack the next morning. Tita, who had gone out to walk Toy and to buy the doughnuts filled with zabaglione that he knew his wife loved, took up a selection to their suite.

Maria was still in bed, her eye mask on. But the sound of Toy's paws clattering on the marble floor woke her up. She threw on a silk peignoir and, picking up the dog, she went to join her husband. She could smell the doughnuts, and her mouth started to water. They were so delicious; one bite wouldn't hurt surely? But then she made herself remember how large she had been in Venice ten years ago, how the tops of her thighs would chafe against each other in summer, and how awkward it had been to move onstage. She did not want to be that Maria again, the one who dwarfed nearly every tenor she sang with, the one compared by one critic to a praying mantis who mated and then gobbled up her spouse. Her voice was a gift from God, but her figure was the fruit of her own self-denial. Of course, Tita had never wanted her to lose weight. He was intimidated by her new chicness. When she had been heavy, he had helped her choose her clothes when she went shopping, facing down the skeptical vendeuses with his checkbook and his limitless belief in her talent. Now she went to Madame Biki's alone. As the house's most famous customer she was quite sure of her welcome.

Out of the corner of her eye, she saw newspapers spread out on the marble table.

"Tita! I thought I told you that I didn't want to even smell a newspaper while I was here."

Tita shrugged. "I thought you should see this."

He held up the front page of the *Daily Express*. Under the picture of Maria looking like a goddess outside the Palazzo Castelbarco was a banner headline: TOO SICK TO SING?

Maria rolled her eyes.

Tita persisted. "Inside there is a quote from Ghiringhelli saying how disappointed he is that after all the support that La Scala has given you through the years you would let the company down. And your friend Elsa has only made it worse by telling a journalist that she is wildly flattered that you chose her party over a performance."

"But I only agreed to four shows!" Maria said.

"That is not what Ghiringhelli is saying."

Maria was about to berate Tita for allowing this situation to develop when she saw the morning sunlight dancing on the water of the canal, and suddenly she no longer cared.

"Oh, what does it matter anyway, Tita? What's done is done."

Tita looked back at her with concern. His wife never let things go. She was still suing a pasta manufacturer who had claimed six years ago that her remarkable weight loss was the result of eating his spaghetti. Every lawyer in Milan had advised her against taking the matter to court, but Maria had insisted, because she said her honor was at stake. But here she was, shrugging and saying it didn't matter instead of fighting back. He wondered if he should call the doctor; perhaps it was something to do with her blood pressure.

"I also got a telegram from Bing. He wants to pull rehearsals forward by a week, which means really that we should leave tonight."

Maria shook her head, "But we have a lunch date, Tita."

"Cancel it."

"That would be rude."

"Maria, you don't want to make an enemy of Bing as well as Ghiringhelli. People respect you for your professionalism. What will they say when they find out you were late for rehearsals because you wanted to spend the afternoon on a millionaire's yacht?"

"Oh, he's more than a millionaire, Tita. Elsa says he is the richest man in the world. And frankly the press will hate me whatever I do, so I might as well do what I want."

She made a gesture with her chin, which her husband knew meant that she was now fixed in her course.

Maria went into the bedroom and pulled out her costume sketches. She settled on a white linen dress with a wide red belt and matching shoes. She would put her hair up into the French twist that Franco had once told her was chic, and she would wear the tortoiseshell sunglasses. She rang for Bruna, who started to look for the outfit among the many trunks.

"Do you think that will work, Bruna?"

Bruna looked at the sketch, and then asked Maria, "You are having lunch with rich people?"

Maria nodded.

"Then this is perfect: you do not want to appear as if you are trying too hard."

Bruna never offered an opinion, but if asked for one, she always said something worth listening to.

Maria finished dressing and was just about to put some diamonds in her ears when she saw Bruna shake her head. Maria understood and picked up some pearl studs instead.

⸎

Onassis was smoking a cigar on the Gritti jetty as Maria made her appearance, flanked by Elsa and Tita. When he saw her, he gave Maria a frank top-to-toe appraisal. Elsa nudged her friend and muttered, "I would say you have made a conquest, Madame C."

Maria ignored her. She made a hand gesture to wave away the cigar smoke as Onassis reached out his hand. He instantly threw the cigar into the canal.

"Terrible habit, I know, but blame Winston Churchill. He smokes them all the time, and I have to keep him company."

Maria looked back at him coolly. "I am afraid that smoke is my enemy, Mr. Onassis. For me it's the difference between a top C and disaster."

"Oh, please call me Ari, or even Aristotle, like Elsa here. And there will be no more smoke, I promise you."

He put out his hand to help her into the launch, and she was surprised at how warm and dry it was. Tita's palms were always so clammy. Onassis kept eye contact all the time, until she broke away to greet Tina. She was with a handsome young man in his twenties, who was introduced as Reinaldo and whose beautifully cut shirt was unbuttoned enough to reveal the smooth bronze chest beneath. Onassis was wearing a dark blue short-sleeved polo shirt, chinos, and deck shoes. Tina, like Maria, was wearing a cotton frock. Elsa was wearing what could only be described as a slipcover.

In this company, Meneghini in his dark blue linen suit looked like a solicitor who had come to read the will.

Onassis turned to Maria. "I thought we would go across the lagoon to Torcello and have lunch there."

He took over the controls of the Riva from the uniformed crewman; and once they were out of the Grand Canal, he let out the throttle and they started to bounce across the water of the lagoon. Maria saw Tita turn green, then go into the cabin. There he sat for the rest of the trip, rigid with nausea. She glanced at Onassis to see if he had noticed, but his eyes were on the horizon.

But he had seen more than she thought because he said in Greek, "You should have married a Greek; they never get seasick."

Maria replied crossly in the same language, "At least Italians understand music."

"You think I'm a Philistine. Maybe. But I know how to surround myself with beautiful things." And he gave her another appraising look.

Maria turned to look out across the lagoon. She spent her life being looked at, but there was something unsettling about Onassis's gaze; she hadn't felt that kind of scrutiny for a long time. She felt that he wasn't looking at the diva but at the woman beneath. It was uncomfortable, but she could not deny that it was also exciting.

Onassis had taken over the restaurant for lunch and had, as Elsa predicted, ordered a great mound of caviar.

He arranged them around the table. "Now, Madame Callas—May I call you Maria?—you come sit next to me; and before you get jealous, Elsa, you come on the other side; and, Signor Meneghini, you sit next to my wife; and, Reinaldo, you can squeeze in here between Tina and Maria."

Maria took her place, and Onassis leaned over. "Do you like caviar, Maria? This is straight from the Caspian Sea. Let me give you some."

Onassis put a spoonful of caviar on a sliver of melba toast and held it out so that Maria had no option but to open her mouth.

"That's the way to eat really good caviar—no adornments, no egg or sour cream or any of that stuff. This to me is the taste of the sea."

Maria crushed the eggs against the roof of her mouth with her tongue. She felt the salty richness of their juices flood her mouth. She had forgotten that anything could taste so delicious.

Onassis was wearing sunglasses, but Maria knew that he was watching her. Sensing his impatience, she made him wait, slowly savoring each bite, until he finally broke in. "Well?"

Maria paused—a couple of bars, and then she smiled. "Oh, it's the most wonderful thing I have ever eaten."

Onassis clapped his hands in triumph, and said in Greek, "You have a beautiful smile."

Elsa and Meneghini could not understand Greek, and Tina, who did, was too involved in an intense discussion with Reinaldo to overhear.

"But rare, like a favorable wind in the Strait of Messina."

Maria replied in the same language. "I do enough acting onstage."

Onassis laughed at this, and Elsa, who could sense a frisson in any language, interrupted. "I am going to help myself to some more of this deliciousness. I hope you don't mind, Aristotle, but if you put an old broad like me in front of the most delicious caviar on the planet, you must expect gluttony."

"My dear Elsa, surely you know me well enough to know that I take it as a compliment that you are enjoying my hospitality."

Onassis turned to Meneghini and said in serviceable Italian, "Please do help yourself, Signor Meneghini, and don't be shy—take as much as you want."

Meneghini took a great spoonful on his plate and Maria couldn't help noticing a few eggs falling onto the lapel of his jacket.

Elsa clapped her hands for attention. "I want to ask you all a question that Noël put to me last night. 'Elsa,' he said"—she put on a theatrical English Noël Coward voice—"'Elsa, what is the secret of your success?' And I said, 'Well, Noël, I have never given any woman cause to be jealous.'"

She paused and got her laugh. Then she turned her gaze to Maria. "And what is the secret to the great diva's success? I wonder."

Maria lifted her chin. "Hard work, plenty of it. And high standards. I don't let anything obstruct my pursuit of excellence."

"You sound like a general," said Onassis, licking the caviar from his lips.

Maria looked directly at him. "Great art is domination. It's making people believe for that precise moment in time there is only one way, one voice. Mine."

There was silence around the table. Then Elsa pointed at Onassis. "And you, Mr. Aristotle Onassis, what is your secret?"

Onassis rocked back on his chair, still gazing at Maria. "I have learned that it's pointless to wait for the sea to rest: you have to learn to sail in high winds."

Tina suppressed a yawn. "Well, the secret of my success is never wear diamonds in the daytime—you want to save the sparkle for later."

Maria inwardly thanked Bruna for vetoing the diamond studs.

Elsa pointed at Meneghini, who said in English, "I married the correct woman." Maria didn't bother to point out that he meant the right woman, she was too busy trying to ignore the way that Onassis was gazing at her profile.

Elsa's finger moved to Reinaldo, who answered in his slushy South American English, "Silk socks. That way, whatever you are doing, your feet are always comfortable." Reinaldo smiled like a child who has made the adults laugh.

≒

On the way back across the lagoon, Maria found herself constantly aware of Onassis. When he stood next to her at the rail of the launch, she could feel the heat radiating from his forearm an inch or so away from hers. She could smell the lime of his cologne; the woodiness of the cigars; and something else that she could not recognize, dark and strong. His arms and the inch or two of chest revealed by his polo shirt were covered by dark hair.

Onassis must have felt her gaze because he turned and gave her his piratical smile. "This is the best time of day, I think," he said in Greek, "when the day and the evening meet."

Maria looked at the familiar skyline that seemed to hover in the warm evening haze. "You know, I had never really thought about it. But then this is the first time I have been to Venice when I haven't been working."

Onassis edged a fraction closer. "How did you start in the singing business?"

She raised an eyebrow at the word "business," but she answered him in Greek. "I was born with a voice, and it became my destiny. And you, how did you get into your business?"

Onassis's smile faded. "Like you, I had no choice. I was sixteen when the Turks came to Smyrna, and I had to find a way to survive."

Maria lowered her eyes; she knew of course about the terrible atrocities the Turks inflicted on the Greeks living in Asia Minor just after the First World War.

"I managed to escape to Argentina, where I dabbled in cigarette smuggling and realized that I had a talent for business. I had dreamed of a different life, of course, but in the end, it hasn't turned out so badly."

Maria nodded. "You speak very good Greek for a—" She stopped abruptly.

"For a *Tourkospouros*, you mean," said Onassis, using the word that was often applied by peninsula Greeks to their countrymen living in Asia Minor. That had indeed been the word that Maria had been about to use unthinkingly, but had stopped herself, realizing that its literal meaning, "sperm of a Turk," was an insult.

"And you, Maria, speak passable Greek for an American."

He had taken off his sunglasses and for a moment Maria saw something behind the self-assurance. It made her think of that church in Rome where you walked down some steps from a serene Renaissance building to the remains of a pagan temple. Onassis had all the outward signs of civilization—the expensive watch, the fashion plate wife, the lightness of manner that made him float easily in polite society—but it was only a surface. Underneath there was something that did not belong in the world of silk socks.

They were both silent for a moment. Both had gone further than intended. Maria knew that when she spoke Greek, she had less of the polite defenses she had acquired in other languages—Greek was the language of her tempestuous adolescence, a tongue in which she had never learned to hold back.

Onassis was the first to speak. "I hope you and your husband will come out with us again."

Maria shook her head. "I have to fly back to New York tomorrow. I start rehearsing at the Met for a new season as soon as I get there. You should come and hear me sing in an opera. Although I warn you that the audience will not be happy if you talk during the performance."

Onassis laughed. Then he said in Greek, "I would sit through the whole of the Ring cycle if it meant that I could see you again."

Maria was about to reply, noticing that Onassis knew enough about opera to mention one that took four days to watch, when Elsa popped up between them. "I thought you two might be getting lonely without me."

The little black eyes flickered.

"Oh, *excusez-moi*. Was I interrupting something?"

Onassis put his hand on Elsa's shoulder. "I was just saying what a pity it was that Maria has to leave tomorrow."

Elsa nodded. "It's really too bad, but we can't all be messing about on boats, Ari. Some of us have livings to earn."

Maria nodded. "And I have been given a very hard time by the press for canceling an engagement I never contracted to sing, so imagine the scandal if I stayed in Venice instead of going to New York."

Onassis shrugged. "You must not let the press worry you—they need you more than you need them. And if you get too many bad stories, you should fire Elsa for not doing her job properly."

Elsa laughed. "Maria can't fire me: we are connected only by the bonds of friendship and, as we know, they are unbreakable." She looked up at Maria with puppy dog eyes.

When the launch pulled up at the Gritti, Onassis leaped onto the jetty with the agility of a much younger man and held out his hand to Maria. His hand was larger than Maria's; and as she stood on the jetty next to him, he did not immediately let go.

"I wonder when I will see you again," said Onassis in Greek.

"I will be at the Met for the autumn season, then Rome, then back to Milan, and so on," said Maria in English. She could feel Elsa and Tita watching them and she felt the need to pull back from the duet that Onassis was playing with her.

She kissed him goodbye on both cheeks in the Greek fashion and felt his stubble graze her cheek.

The launch pulled away and Onassis gave her a wave before turning back to the wheel.

"So what did he say to you in that strange language of yours?" asked Elsa.

Maria was about to tell her, and then she remembered Onassis's joking warning about Elsa, so she shook her head and said, "Oh, the Greek equivalent of 'safe travels.'"

Elsa cocked her head on one side. "Take a tip from the most famous person ever to have been born in Keokuk, Iowa. Aristotle Onassis likes fame—he has quite the collection of celebrities. But, like Madame Tussauds, when their day is done, he melts 'em down."

Maria didn't reply. She was watching the launch as it headed down the Grand Canal, following its progress until it disappeared behind Santa Maria della Salute, to where the Onassis yacht was moored. Only then did she turn back to Elsa. "If that is a warning of some kind, Elsa, then it is quite unnecessary. I have no intention of being added to anybody's collection."

"Of course you don't, but you should know something else about Onassis: he always gets what he wants."

Maria laughed. "You make him sound like a diva, Elsa! Surely that is my role."

Meneghini coughed and the two women looked around. They had forgotten that he was still there. He looked at his watch.

Elsa pouted. "Don't let your big bad husband take you away from me already. One last drink, Maria. I haven't had a chance to talk to you all day."

Maria looked down at her friend—who was swinging their linked hands to and fro like a child.

"Please." The line between the doyenne of the café society and the ugly little girl from Keokuk, Iowa, was razor-thin.

"I am sorry, Elsa, but I must have an early night. I fly tomorrow and I go straight into rehearsals. I have had such a lovely time, thanks to you, but now I must go back to work."

As she spoke, Maria realized that it was a relief to know that the day after tomorrow she would be back in a rehearsal studio. The last few days had been exhilarating, but now she wanted to sit at the piano and work on her scales until she could feel her voice running clear within her. She stooped to kiss Elsa, who shot her arms up like a child and put them round Maria's neck so that their lips touched.

## Diva

"Goodbye, darling diva," called Elsa as Maria walked into the hotel hand in hand with Tita. For a moment Elsa was alone on the terrace and then she heard a man exclaim, "Why, if it isn't Elsa Maxwell," and she turned round, ready to begin again.

# Act Two

# CHAPTER FIVE

## *Two Concerts*

AUTUMN, NEW YORK, 1958

I

The feel of Onassis's skin against hers stayed with Maria on the flight back to New York. Compared to the warm, dry vitality of Onassis's grasp, her husband's hand felt like a wet fish. But once in rehearsal all thoughts of Onassis receded. This season she was singing in *Tosca*, a role she had been singing since Athens, and *Lucia di Lammermoor*, one of the bel canto operas that she had made fashionable again. Both Floria Tosca and Lucia were women who killed the men who had betrayed them, but each night as Maria pierced the pouch under Scarpia's shirt containing the stage blood she thought only of her mother.

Elsa danced attendance on her that season, coming to every performance and talking constantly about her friend—the divine Maria Callas—on her regular spot on the *Tonight* show. After every performance Maria's dressing room at the Met was crammed with Elsa's celebrity friends, air-kissing and opening bottles of champagne as they gossiped about Jackie Kennedy, the glamorous wife of the senator from Massachusetts, and Truman Capote, the diminutive writer who had become the darling of society ladies like Babe Paley, or the best time to go to Palm Beach. Maria was happy to be entertained when she came offstage, still floating on the adoration of the audience. But after thirty minutes or so of glittering chat, she would stand up and Meneghini, who had been sitting mute in a corner, would spring to attention; and Maria would kiss Elsa firmly on the cheek and make her way through the stage-door aficionados to find her waiting car.

If she did think about Onassis, it was in the long baths that she took before bed; relaxing in the warm, scented water, she would remember the darkness behind his gaze and the thought would make her shiver.

One night after a particularly successful performance, Maria came into her dressing room to find Elsa already there, jumping up and down in excitement like an excited child.

"Oh, do I have news for you, Maria. You will never guess—not in a million years."

Maria lifted her hair so that Bruna could undo the fastenings of her costume.

"So why don't you tell me, Elsa? After singing for two hours, I don't think I have the energy to play your games."

She looked across at Tita to see if he had any idea what Elsa was so worked up about, but he just shrugged. Tita did not enjoy the constant presence of Elsa in the dressing room.

"Don't be mean, Maria—have a teeny-weeny little guess. Think of the most bizarre thing in the world and then multiply it by a hundred."

"Don't tell me that my mother is still selling those awful dolls," Maria said, referring to the Callas dolls dressed as opera heroines like Floria Tosca that her mother had made to sell to her daughter's fans. When she found out, Maria was furious, a fury heightened by the memory of the little girl in Washington Heights who had so wanted a doll of her own but was always fobbed off with her sister's discarded playthings.

Elsa shook her head. "But you are getting closer."

Maria was getting impatient. "If it has something to do with my mother, it will certainly annoy me, so if you want to be the bearer of bad news, please go ahead."

"Honestly, Maria. You really need to put it all behind you now. I never think of Keokuk, Iowa, so why you sit in your dressing room in the Met and fret about your mother not reading you a bedtime story is beyond me."

Maria turned to face Elsa. "Your mother never betrayed you to the newspapers, Elsa!"

Elsa put her hands up in surrender. "All right, I will let you bear your grudges. So, the thing I wanted to show you is this."

She held out a newspaper. Maria took it and held it up to her face so that she could read it.

Elsa snatched it back. "Let me read it to you. 'A concert will be given by the Greek soprano, Jakinthe Callas, sister of the famous Maria, at the Fetzner Hall on the third of April. The program includes pieces by Verdi, Puccini, and Bizet.'"

Maria sat quite still.

"Interesting, don't you think? I had no idea that your sister could sing, Maria," Elsa said. "You never mentioned it."

"This must be my mother's doing," Maria said. "She failed to hold on to me, so now she is trying to get Jackie to take my place. But the whole thing is ridiculous. Jackie is six years older—she must be forty now. Much too late to start singing."

She repeated all this in Italian to Tita, who shook his head as if nothing Maria's family could do would surprise him.

"You won't mind if I mention this in my column," said Elsa quickly. "I mean, it's too delicious. The older sister trying to get in on the act."

Maria shook her head. "I forbid you to write about it, Elsa. They are only doing this to annoy me, and I don't want to give them that pleasure. In fact, I feel sorry for Jackie, who is bound to be humiliated. The less publicity this sorry episode gets the better."

Elsa stuck her bottom lip out. "And there was I thinking we might go together. You know how much I want to meet the whole family."

Maria stood up, nostrils flaring and eyes flashing as much as they were a couple of hours ago in the second act of *Tosca*.

"If you want to stay my friend, Elsa, I forbid you to go."

"Yes, ma'am." Elsa did a mock salute. "I'm sorry I mentioned it."

‿

Later, in the car going back to the hotel, Tita was running through the list of engagements coming up.

"You are recording *Traviata* in Paris, and then there is the concert in Cologne, the gala in Rome, and then Madrid in April and on to Paris for the Légion d'honneur."

Maria interrupted him. "Wasn't there an offer to sing in Athens in April?"

Meneghini sighed. "Yes, but I turned it down."

"Without asking me?" Maria said.

"You told me you never wanted to go back to Greece."

"Well, I have changed my mind."

"But, Maria, there is no point in your going. The money is nothing, and Athens is hardly on the opera circuit."

"Why does it always have to be about the money," Maria snapped. "Maybe I just want to go because, after all, I am Greek."

Meneghini shrugged. "Whatever you say, Maria."

Elsa was thrilled when she heard that Maria had decided to sing in Athens. But Elsa's face drooped when she heard the dates. "Oh darn it, that's exactly when I promised to go to Madrid with the Duchess of Alba. I so wanted to see you visiting your teenage haunts."

"I didn't have any haunts," said Maria sourly. "I was always working."

"I wonder if Onassis will be in Athens?" said Elsa slyly.

Maria looked straight ahead. "As he does not care for music, it hardly signifies."

Elsa patted her knee. "Of course I know why you are going to Athens then." She put her face close to Maria's. "Because you know that your mother and sister will be in New York! Am I right?"

"What nonsense you talk, Elsa."

But Elsa had guessed correctly. Maria could not imagine going to Athens if there was the possibility of being ambushed by her mother. But Jackie's concert gave her a perfect opportunity to return in safety. And ever since her encounter with Onassis, there was a part of her that longed to be in Greece again.

Meneghini continued to grumble about Athens being a waste of time and money, but Maria ignored him. Ever since that argument in Edinburgh the power balance between them had shifted.

11

Maria could see the hills of Athens from her airplane window. She could just make out the Acropolis and the amphitheater where she would be performing. It was strange to see the streets of her youth laid out before her. When she had left the city fourteen years earlier, it had been by boat. Her father had sent her a hundred dollars and she had seized the chance to get away: from the poverty of Greece, the spite her talent provoked in the opera company, and above all from her mother.

Maria applied her makeup with special care. It was one of the rigors of her job that she could never get off a plane looking as she felt—exhausted and desperate to sleep. Instead, she had to step out camera ready, smiling and waving.

There was a red carpet at the bottom of the airplane steps and as Maria picked her way elegantly to the bottom, she began to make out the welcoming party. There were a number of officials she didn't know; next to them were two singers who had been unpleasant to her in her days at the Athens Opera; and then a much more welcome sight, the chiffon-clad figure of Elvira de Hidalgo. She rushed over, hands outstretched. "Maestra!" air-kissing her so that the press could get the shot of the two of them. Maria put her hand under Elvira's elbow and walked with her toward the airport building, so that there could be no question of stopping to talk with her old enemies.

"How kind of you to come and meet me, Madame de Hidalgo. You were the only person I wanted to see in Athens."

Elvira smiled. "I think, Maria, now you have made your debut at La Scala, you may call me Elvira."

Maria beckoned Tita. "Elvira, this is my husband, Battista."

Meneghini bowed low over the older woman's hand. "It is an honor to meet you, *signora*. I know that Maria owes you so much."

Elvira inclined her head. "That is true. I taught her how to sing bel canto."

"And was I a good pupil?" asked Maria coyly.

"The best I ever had," said Elvira gravely. Then she said, "But you don't need me to tell you that. That is why you stood out from the very beginning: you have always known how gifted you are."

⇒

### ATHENS, FEBRUARY 1938

*Maria walked up the steps of the conservatory auditorium. She was sixteen years old, wearing an old black dress so tight under the arms that she could not move them properly. She had begged her mother for a new dress, something soft and pretty like the ones that Jackie wore, but her mother had said that Maria did not have Jackie's figure. Worse still, there was a spot on her chin that no amount of makeup could hide.*

*She had taken her glasses off to sing, so she could not see the faces of the judges sitting in front of her in the conservatory's auditorium. But she could hear the sigh that Madame de Hidalgo, the great soprano, made when Maria had announced that she was going to sing "'Ocean! thou mighty monster,' from Weber's Oberon."*

*"An unusual choice. It is extremely difficult," Hidalgo said skeptically.*

*"But I can sing it," Maria replied. And it was true: she could. From the moment she opened her mouth and sang, she was no longer an unfortunate teenager but a shipwrecked princess praying for her lover to return. The words were in English, so Maria knew exactly how to match them to the music. She trembled with the sinister embrace of the "green serpent round about the world," and when she sang about the dawn breaking, there was a shine of hope in her eyes.*

*Elvira told her later that she had known from the second line of the aria that Maria was the pupil she had been waiting for. But the director of the conservatory disagreed because Maria had not passed her music theory exams. "A typical bureaucrat," said Elvira. But no bureaucrat could prevail against a diva like Hidalgo. The director had fallen into line and offered the awkward-looking girl a full scholarship. When Hidalgo announced the decision, Maria cried with joy. She felt as if her life was beginning.*

⇒

As the car drew up outside the Grande Bretagne, the stately belle époque hotel in Syntagma Square that Maria had walked past so many times as a teenager on her way to the conservatory, she took a deep breath as if preparing to sing a high note. Even when she had been singing title roles at the Athens Opera, she had never dared to walk into the Grande Bretagne. She remembered once on her way from a dress rehearsal seeing an Italian officer walking down the steps talking and laughing with the woman at his side who, as they came closer, turned out to be her mother. Maria had been surprised to see her perpetually dissatisfied mother so happy and carefree, looking up at the soldier at her side with uncritical adoration. Maria had stepped back into the shadows, not wanting to be recognized. Her mother would either be angry at being discovered or else she would make Maria do something terrible like sing in the street.

Now fifteen years later Maria was being welcomed by the manager and being taken up to the Olympus Suite, where "Sir Winston Churchill stayed when he came to Athens in 1944."

But first she had to negotiate the reporters.

"How do you feel being back in Greece, Madame Callas?"

Maria smiled. "Like Odysseus reaching Ithaka at the end of his travels."

"And will you be seeing your family while you are here?"

Maria's smile remained in place. "That won't be possible, as they are in New York."

"Can you comment on why you left Athens after the war? Is it true that you were accused of collaborating with the enemy?"

Maria took a deep breath. "I went back to America to see my father and to pursue my singing career. I received a wonderful musical education here in Athens with my teacher, Elvira de Hidalgo, but we Greeks need to see the world before we come home."

The reporter who had asked about the collaboration was about to follow up, but Maria forestalled him. "No more questions. I need to rest my voice for the performance."

She turned to the manager, and he held open the brass cage door of the lift. As it rose, she could still see the upturned faces of the press, like fledglings in a nest—hungry for more.

The hotel suite had ceiling frescoes of Mount Olympus. Maria noticed that Zeus, the king of the gods, bore a disconcerting resemblance to Onassis. She had not thought of him in a while, and the saturnine figure with the thunderbolt reminded her of the frisson that had passed between them on the jetty of the Gritti hotel. The way he had looked at her had made her feel uncomfortable and excited in equal measure. There had been admiration there, but it was not the look she received from so many people that was a product of her fame and talent; rather he had been admiring her not as Callas the great diva but as Maria the woman. She remembered the touch of his skin against hers and the dark hair on his arms; and for a moment she thought of lying in the sun and feeling nothing but the heat and the nearness of this man, but then she saw the piano in the corner of the suite and, opening the lid, she sat down to practice.

That evening she took Meneghini on a stroll around the Plaka, the maze of winding streets and traditional Greek houses at the foot of the Acropolis. The Greek color palette of white walls, blue shutters, and vivid purple bougainvillea was dazzling. But Tita picked his way fastidiously through the narrow alleys in his cream linen suit; Maria could see that he found the piles of donkey droppings, and the suspicion of drains under the smell of jasmine, unsettling.

He was a typical northern Italian, who felt truly comfortable only in his own country. He would tolerate cities like New York and Paris, because they were full of money, but Athens was beneath his notice.

They passed a pastry shop and Maria stopped to gaze in the window at the trays of glistening baklava; bougatsa, the almond-flavored triangles; and galaktoboureko, where the custard was drenched in lemon syrup. Everything in the window had been out of reach when she was a student because she had no money, and now she was rich she still could not afford to eat one. For a moment she considered eating just one custard pastry, but there was no stopping at one. Better just to walk on.

That night Maria lay in bed, listening to the noises of the streets below. She looked up at the shadowy face of the Olympians and felt the knowing gaze of Zeus falling upon her.

III

Maria had not sung in the open air since her first season in the Roman amphitheater in Verona. Every opera house had its own acoustics, but at least it was a constant one. In the open air everything could change. Depending on the weather, a wind could blow the voice off course; rain would muffle the sound; and the air before a thunderstorm could make the notes thicken. Standing in the makeshift wings of the amphitheater with the Acropolis behind her, Maria looked up at the packed semicircle of seats in front. It was a still night—only the very faintest suggestion of a breeze—but Maria suddenly felt a constriction in her throat as she tried to imagine her voice floating out across the night air. They were all out there in the audience: those bitches from the National Opera; her friends from the conservatory; the minister of culture; and of course, Elvira.

The program that night had been chosen with her maestra in mind: the arias were ones that Elvira had taught her—"Vissi d'arte" from *Tosca* and "Casta diva" from *Norma* and others that she had added to her repertoire since: "Divinités du Styx" from the Gluck opera *Alceste* and the trial aria from *Anna Bolena*. It was almost an audition, Maria thought, a star pupil showing off her talents. She was determined that Elvira should be proud of her.

"Callas, Callas," the audience shouted, and Maria gave them a graceful bow. She deliberately stood in front of the culture minister, who had been making a long-winded introduction, and he scuttled offstage.

Maria looked down to where the conductor stood and nodded. He lifted his baton and went into the bright opening bars of "Divinités du Styx," the brass section sounding like a call to arms, in French she sang "Ye gods of endless night, that wait on death below . . ." She was Alcestis challenging the gods to give her back her husband and no god of endless night would defy her. Her voice soared across the audience, and they sat up suddenly alert, as Maria went into battle. At the end of the aria, she stood still, her arms aloft as the audience thundered its appreciation. At last, she put her finger to her lips to silence the crowd and said, "*Kallospera*, Athens. I cannot tell you how happy I am to be home."

She waited for the applause to die down, before continuing in Greek. "I am now going to sing an aria that I first learned here at the Athens Conservatoire, from the teacher to whom I owe everything, Elvira de Hidalgo. This is for you, maestra!" And she bowed toward the front row where she knew Elvira would be sitting.

As the strings played the broken chords that heralded the beginning of Norma's prayer to the moon goddess, Maria heard the gasp of recognition from the crowd—thanks to the recordings she had made, this aria had become world-famous. Taking in a breath of the still, warm, night air she began to sing to the virgin goddess in the sky.

⸚

Afterward, in the makeshift dressing room, she waited for Elvira. Everyone else was there: the hags from the National Opera, the teacher who had tried to stop her joining the conservatory because she hadn't passed her theory exams, and the minister of culture who was pretending that Callas's surprise entrance had been his idea all along. They were lining up to tell her how marvelous her performance had been, what tone, what line, what expression—everyone was gushing in their praise, but Maria was not really listening. The only person whose opinion she wanted to hear was not there. And then she saw Elvira standing in the doorway, looking hesitant, as she saw the crowd in front of her.

Maria raised her hand and beckoned her over. "Elvira, please come and sit down next to me."

She turned to Tita. "Some champagne for Elvira."

Elvira smiled as she sat down on the tiny sofa next to her former pupil. "In the old days, Maria, I don't think that we could have both fitted on this sofa. But now you are so svelte and chic. You even walk differently."

Maria looked down at her slender hips. "I was singing at La Scala and one night Franco Zeffirelli took me to see *Roman Holiday*. I saw how elegant Audrey Hepburn was on screen and how expressive, and I decided I wanted to look like that. I was about to play Violetta and I wanted the audience to believe that I was a frail consumptive, which is harder when you are two hundred and twenty pounds. It wasn't easy—you remember how much I love my food—but it was worth it, don't you think? I remember you telling me that I needed to dress the part."

Elvira smiled. "And you have most certainly succeeded, Maria. You are the most glamorous diva alive."

"Apart from you," said Maria.

The older woman tapped Maria on the hand with her fan. "Stop it."

There was a pause as Maria gazed intently at her former teacher, looking for an answer to the question that she did not dare ask. Finally, she put her head to one side and said in an approximation of her teenage voice, "So, Madame de Hidalgo, how did I do?"

Elvira hesitated for a moment. "Your phrasing is exquisite, Maria, and the smoothness of the line is extraordinary. I don't think I have ever heard better."

Maria did not smile. She leaned forward and said, "But?"

The older woman paused then. "But you are pushing your voice all the time, especially in your middle register, and I can hear how much those B-flats are costing you. It was a wonderful concert, and I am sure that no one else noticed . . . but I will never stop being your teacher."

Maria bit her lip. "How long do you think I have left?" she said.

"Oh, my dear child, I couldn't possibly say. I stopped singing when I was forty-five. I could have gone on, I was still getting work, but I knew that I could no longer be what I was. It was the hardest decision of my life. But then I started to teach and one day I met an awkward girl with terrible clothes and a miraculous voice, and I was able to pass my gift on." She laid her hand on Maria's and squeezed it.

"If only Mother hadn't made me sing so much in the war," Maria said bitterly. "I kept telling her what you said about the golden coins, but she would never listen. She made me spend them, when I did not know what they were worth, and I will never forgive her, never."

The older woman sighed. She remembered the pushiness of Maria's mother, but she also remembered the girl who had been so eager to stand in the center of the stage. It had not been Maria's mother who had made Maria sing Wagner and Bellini in the same week at La Fenice. No voice, not even Maria's, could survive intact under that kind of pressure. If Maria had asked her advice, she would have told her to wait, but Maria had not asked her; in fact, apart from a few letters, they had had no contact since Maria left Greece.

"No voice is immortal. Men are fortunate that they can go on a few years longer, but in the end we all fall silent."

Maria was staring blankly ahead of her.

Elvira attempted to console her. "But you have a husband, a home, plenty of money, and the music will always be there, even if you are not onstage."

The blank gaze settled now on Meneghini, who was talking to an Italian journalist.

"I think my husband is more interested in Callas than in Maria."

Elvira laughed. "Then, my dear, you will find someone else."

"But I am married, Elvira."

"So was I, but I married to protect my voice, and when that was no longer the most important thing, I found someone else."

"I don't remember you being so cynical."

"You were a child then, but now you are ready for the truth. Make the most of what you have left, and when it is gone, find pleasure somewhere else." Elvira looked at the gold watch on her wrist and stood up to leave. She took Maria's hand and leaned in to kiss her.

"Goodbye, my dear, and remember what I said." She walked away, and Maria's eyes followed her as she left the room.

⸗

Maria was silent on the way back to the Grande Bretagne, and when the reporters appeared out of the shadows with their cameras and notebooks, she put her head down and hurried into the hotel without looking right or left.

In the suite Maria rang room service and ordered spanakopita and two fried eggs, much to the surprise of the voice on the other end. When the food arrived, Maria bit into the pastry recklessly, hoping that the forbidden food would soften the terrible whirlwind of disaster in her head. The sharpness of the cheese and the earthy taste of the spinach brought her straight back to the kitchen of Patission Street; but instead of bringing her the comfort she craved, she remembered how miserable that existence had been. The food had not filled her up then: it had just made her fat. The truth was that the only thing that could sustain her was the love she found onstage, and that would be gone all too soon.

# CHAPTER SIX

# *Il Circolo*

ROME, NEW YEAR'S EVE, 1957

I

The TV lights were hotter than she was used to and by the time Maria had finished singing "Casta diva," she was drenched in sweat. It was strange singing in a studio in full evening dress with no audience to perform to, just a camera. But, as the producers kept telling her, the performance was being transmitted live into millions of homes all over Europe. Countries that had once been divided by war were now united by the Greek American Maria Callas and the nineteenth-century Italian Vincenzo Bellini. As she bowed and blew a kiss to the camera, Maria longed to wipe the perspiration that was beginning to trickle past her eyebrows, but she could not do anything so vulgar on camera. At last, the stage manager called, "Cut," and Maria felt the sting of sweat as a drop rolled into her eye.

On the way back from the studio to the hotel, Maria saw people hurrying through the streets on their way to dinners and parties. All she wanted to do now was to sleep. The New Year meant nothing; her focus was on the performance she would be giving the next evening at the opera house for the president of Italy. She would be singing Norma, which was one of the most vocally demanding parts in her repertoire, and she needed to rest if she was going to perform at her best. Ever since her encounter with Elvira, Maria had felt the cold wind of doubt creep into her performances. Every time she reached the high point of an aria without incident, she wondered if she would ever be able to do it again. Tonight's performance had been relatively easy, only one song, but the gala was the full opera. Maria crossed herself three times, to fend off bad luck.

Tita noticed. "What are you praying for?"

"That my voice will hold up for the gala."

"You sang beautifully tonight."

"But that is no guarantee that I will be able to do it again."

Meneghini patted her hand. "Don't worry so much, *tesoro*. You will sing like an angel, as always, and then we will go to Sirmione and relax."

Maria nodded. Although she always knew what Tita would say, his very predictability was reassuring. Sometimes all she wanted was to voice her fears and for Tita to dismiss them as groundless. But tonight, she felt a little shiver of unease that even Tita's placid confidence could not settle.

"Will you check that they have an understudy just in case."

Tita sighed. "Of course I will check, *carissima*, but you know as well as I do that there is no one in the world capable of replacing Maria Callas."

She knew he would say this—it was his stock response—but she hoped that he would talk to the management nonetheless.

~

Maria was lying in the bath when she heard a commotion in the corridor outside. The door burst open and there, wearing what appeared to be a military uniform of some kind, complete with bandolier and high boots, was Elsa. Maria froze even though the water was steaming. She did not want to be naked in front of Elsa. She grabbed the sponge and tried to cover her breasts.

"I know, I know, I should have rung first, but I thought you would give me the bum's rush, so I just decided to come on over. You were wonderful on the television tonight, darling." Elsa was looking at Maria hungrily.

"If you will leave me for a moment to get dry, I will come and talk to you, Elsa."

"Oh, don't worry about little old me. I've been in the dressing room at the Folies Bergère and with the Rockettes at Radio City and I have seen everything. Do you know that in Paris they put jewels in the most intimate places—"

"Elsa!" Maria's volume matched her outrage, and the glass lights rattled in their fittings.

Elsa backed out of the door reluctantly. "I'll wait here, shall I?"

"Shut the door!"

The door was closed, and Maria got out of the bath and wrapped herself in a towel. She took a deep breath before turning the doorknob.

"What are you doing here, Elsa, and why are you dressed like that?"

Elsa did a twirl to show off her costume. "In case you haven't noticed, it is New Year's Eve, a night where traditionally there is revelry and merriment, and sometimes the jesters of this world dress up in costumes to resemble the founding father of their great country in order to provide additional entertainment. So tonight, I am George Washington, because there is a very chic party on the Via Veneto and I want you to come with me. What is the point of New Year's Eve if you can't spend it with the people you love?" Elsa looked up at Maria like a spaniel hoping for a treat.

"I'm sorry, Elsa, but I have a performance tomorrow and I need to rest."

"But it's New Year's Eve! Everybody should let their hair down tonight, even the most dutiful diva." Elsa attempted to flutter eyelashes that had long ago fallen out.

"It is out of the question. You know how important this performance is. Going to parties is your job, not mine."

Ignoring her, Elsa opened the wardrobe and cooed with excitement as she ran her fingers over the dresses hanging inside.

"Such beautiful things. What is this?" She pulled an oyster satin dress with a fur-trimmed train. "Sable?" Elsa laid it down on the bed and then went back for a dress with a black velvet bodice and a full white tulle skirt.

"Imagine having the waist to wear something like this." Elsa's hands in their eighteenth-century lace cuffs stroked the tulle. "A whole wardrobe full of the most beautiful clothes flowering unseen upon the desert air. What a pity."

Maria said nothing. She was longing to wear the oyster satin. It was a dress that she felt particularly elegant in, a dress that was sophisticated, flattering, and had the added advantage of being something that she knew would make her mother green with envy. One of the great pleasures of dressing well was imagining Litza's face as she flicked through newspapers and magazines, looking for images of her daughter.

"Just come for half an hour, Maria. Il Circolo is just a moment away in the Via Veneto. I can't begin to tell you how chic it is. You know, the other night there was a black-and-white party and Laura Pamphili arrived on a zebra! I thought all that kind of thing had gone after the war but not in Rome. Anyway, darling, it will be tremendous fun. Just come—see and be seen, and then you can be tucked up in bed with Tita by one thirty."

Maria shook her head.

Elsa stroked the sable. "Do you know, if I had a dress like this, I don't think I would ever take it off." She picked it up and waltzed around the room with it until Maria, concerned that she would step on it, reached to take it away from her.

Just then Tita appeared in the doorway. *"Ma cosa fai, Maria?"* Tita looked tired and old. "You said you were exhausted and just wanted to go to bed." He looked at Elsa with dislike. "You know how much you need to rest."

Maria felt a spike of defiance. Tita was a fine one to talk about her needing rest. He was always making her do things against her better judgment when it suited him. Tonight was New Year's Eve—why shouldn't she go out and enjoy herself?

"You know how long it takes me to come down to earth after a performance," she said. "I won't be able to sleep now anyway. I can drop in on Elsa's party at Il Circolo for thirty minutes and then come back and have a delicious dreamless sleep. And, if you are tired, why don't you stay here, and I will go with George Washington?"

Elsa put on her tricorne hat and saluted. Maria couldn't help laughing, but Meneghini turned away saying, "Of course I am coming with you. One of us needs to be sensible."

When the car drew up outside Il Circolo, Maria stepped out into a blaze of flashbulbs. There were photographers everywhere, running behind her, in front of her, squeezing between her and Tita, shouting her name and blowing her kisses. She could just see the door to the club on the other side of the pavement and she moved toward it as if wading through a school of minnows. Once she was safely inside, she leaned back against the wall to catch her breath and then turned to Elsa accusingly. "How did they know I was coming?"

Elsa opened her eyes wide. "As I said, Il Circolo is *the* place in Rome at the moment. Everybody comes here, and where the celebrities go, so sadly do the press. It's horrible, I know, but fortunately you look like a million dollars, thanks to your founding father here."

Maria accepted the explanation, although she still suspected that her friend had something to do with the swarm of photographers. They did seem to cluster wherever she went with Elsa. Clutching Tita's arm and gathering up her sable-trimmed train, she walked down the curving staircase into the club.

Il Circolo was full of mirrors and bronze metal, the circular room lined with leather banquettes dramatically lit by classical-looking sconces. It was both luxurious and uncomfortable in that uniquely Italian way. The booths faced a small stage where three Thai girls in traditional costume were performing a dance involving live snakes. Most of the audience, though, were more interested in looking at one another; and when the people at the door caught sight of Maria, a wave of applause started to ripple across the room. Maria gave a regal wave, and Elsa saluted.

Maria followed the maître d' to a booth at the back of the room, where some of Elsa's friends were already sitting. It was only when Maria sat down that she saw that two of the friends were Onassis and Tina.

She turned to Elsa. "You really are wicked not to tell me that the Onassises would be here."

Elsa gave her another butter-wouldn't-melt-in-her-mouth look. "Oh, but I wanted it to be a lovely surprise. And you know that as George Washington I can never tell a lie."

Onassis covered Maria with his assessing gaze, and speaking in Greek he said, "Do you think you might be in danger? I am flattered."

Maria replied in English. "How nice to see you again, Aristo." She leaned in to exchange kisses with him, and felt a shiver as she caught a whiff of his cigar and a something-more smell. He touched her elbow as he leaned in to kiss her and she felt the heat of his fingers on her skin.

Pulling away, she took Tita's hand, and pulled him toward the dance floor. Tita looked surprised.

"Oh, come on, Tita, it's been ages since we danced together," Maria said.

Tita was a surprisingly good dancer, but Maria found it hard to relax into the rhythm. Although she couldn't see him, she was conscious of Onassis looking at her from the other side of the room. She stepped on Tita's foot, and he winced with pain.

"Sorry."

"It's because you are tired, Maria. I still don't understand what we are doing here," Tita complained.

Maria saw that Tina Onassis was dancing with Reinaldo, the young Venezuelan with the silk socks. She saw the young man lean in and almost imperceptibly brush Tina's neck with his lips. It was the gesture of a lover. Maria was amazed that Onassis seemed to tolerate his wife's behavior. In the Athens of her youth, women who were unfaithful were treated very severely. Perhaps the rich were different.

"We'll leave after they do the countdown—it can't be long now," she said to Tita.

The bandleader came to the microphone and announced in every language he could think of, "Ladies and gentleman, the New Year is on its way. Let us count it in. . . . *Dieci, nove, otto, sette, sei, cinque, quattro, tre, due, uno. FELICE ANNO NUOVO!*"

Maria was almost knocked over by Elsa crying, "Happy New Year, darling Maria, the lodestar of my life." Elsa leaned in to kiss Maria on the lips, but a flash from a camera made Maria turn her head just in time, and she found herself nose to nose with Onassis.

"Madame Callas, may I say how honored I am to be bringing in the New Year with you."

"I thought you called me Maria now."

Onassis showed his teeth. "I haven't seen you in so long that I feel that would be a liberty. You have been very elusive."

"Then I don't think much of your detective skills," replied Maria tartly. "I was in New York for the autumn season, then Athens and in Germany for a series of concerts. I sang at La Scala, and now I am doing a gala here. But maybe you don't read the newspapers, Mr. Onassis, or do you only pick up the financial section?"

Onassis's smile didn't waver. "I heard that your sister gave a concert in New York and that you couldn't go because you were giving a concert in Athens. Or was it the other way round? I forget."

Maria stepped back. "You seem to know an awful lot about me, and yet you haven't come to hear me sing. I think you can afford the price of a ticket."

Onassis made a little bow and put out his hand to lead her onto the dance floor. She was about to pull back, but then she saw Elsa looking at her, flushed with excitement, the pink tongue evident, and she decided that Onassis was the lesser of two evils.

"But I don't want to hear you sing . . . Maria," Onassis said in Greek, his lips close to her ear.

"Why not? Everybody else does." Maria felt the pressure of his hand on the small of her back and the solid muscle of his shoulder.

Onassis looked at her. "I am not everybody else. But I think you know that."

Maria said nothing; she was concentrating hard on keeping her body at a distance from his.

"I don't really care for opera," he continued.

She pulled back from him. "That is because you have never heard me sing. The stage is my kingdom."

Onassis laughed, and at that moment a flashbulb went off in their faces. One of the photographers from the street had managed to get inside and could not believe his luck at finding the two most famous Greeks in the world dancing together.

But the luck was short-lived. Before Maria realized what was happening, Onassis snatched the camera and pulled it open so that the film was exposed. Then he handed it back to the photographer with a smile.

"I believe this is yours."

He turned back to Maria. "When you come on the *Christina*, you will be quite safe from these vermin."

Maria looked straight into his eyes. "When I come? I don't remember being invited or, indeed, accepting."

Onassis didn't blink. "Then I invite you now, and of course you will accept."

"What makes you so sure?" Maria replied, breathless at his arrogance.

Ari stared back at her. Then he said, "Because the *Christina* is my kingdom, Maria."

She wanted to slap him. How could he compare a stupid boat to the magic she created onstage? But instead, she drew back and gave him the look she reserved for the odious Scarpia in the second act of *Tosca*.

"How intriguing. But I am afraid I must leave you now, Mr. Onassis, as I have a very important performance to prepare for."

Onassis shrugged. "It's too bad that I have to fly to Washington in the morning. But I look forward to seeing you and your husband on the *Christina* this summer."

Maria looked around for Tita. "My dear Mr. Onassis, you obviously know nothing about the life of a singer. I don't have a few weeks to spare to cruise around the Med, delightful though it sounds. Every moment of my year is accounted for. If I am not performing, I am rehearsing or recording. But thank you for the invitation. I appreciate the thought."

Onassis did not flinch under Maria's gaze. "Just remember that, when you change your mind, the invitation will still be open." He smiled and, leaning forward, either by accident or by design, he kissed not her cheek but the side of her neck. A jolt ran through her, as his lips grazed the skin just under her ear.

"Happy New Year, Maria," he murmured in Greek, and then he was gone.

Maria took a deep breath, and then had another look for Tita, who seemed to have disappeared. Suddenly it was the most important thing in the world to get out of the nightclub.

She needed to go back to the hotel room and prepare for her performance. How could she have let Elsa persuade her to come out? Her voice was a sacred gift and yet she was squandering it in this tawdry place.

There was a tug at her elbow, and she looked round, hoping to see Tita, but instead it was Elsa, her face blurry with emotion.

"Did you have a nice dance with Ari?" Elsa asked. "The two of you looked very cozy together."

"No, I did not have a nice dance—and, as to being cozy, your eyes must have deceived you. Have you seen Tita anywhere? I want to go home."

"Home already? But you only just got here. The night is still young, and you are so beautiful."

Maria felt Elsa's fingers stroking the sable trim of her train, and in a fury of impatience she twitched the skirt out of Elsa's grasp. "I shouldn't be here. I need to go home and rest."

Elsa's lips formed a pout. "But there are so many people I want you to meet."

"I am not here to entertain your friends, Elsa"—Maria bent down to speak directly into her ear—"whatever you have promised them."

Then mercifully Tita appeared, and she lifted her chin and started to walk toward the staircase, the crowds shrinking away from the force of her progress.

11

When she woke up the next morning, Maria knew immediately that something was wrong. Opening her mouth, she tried to call Bruna, but nothing happened. Her voice felt as if it were caught in a vise. This, she knew, was her punishment for putting her own pleasure—no, vanity—before her duty to her art. A great wave of shame came over her. How could she have allowed Elsa to persuade her to go out to that stupid club? Remembering the confident way that Onassis had assumed that she would accept his invitation, she pushed her palms into her eyelids to make the mocking face go away. A philistine who didn't even pretend to like opera, a man who said he found her attractive but who didn't understand her special gift. She was not one of the women in his crowd, who did nothing but lunch and give intimate little dinners for thirty. She was an artist, a woman who was famous because of her own extraordinary talent, not because she had married the right man or inherited a fortune from her father.

There was a knock at the door and Bruna came in with coffee. Maria pointed to her throat and the maid left immediately to get Tita.

Maria wrote on a piece of paper: "They will have to call the understudy."

Tita went white. "But, Maria, you have to go on tonight. The president of the republic has come specially to hear *you* sing, not some understudy. Let me call the doctor and see what he says; meanwhile you should rest and see if things improve. You know that sometimes the voice does come back."

Maria shook her head. Tita left the room to phone the doctor and Maria drank the tea laced with honey that Bruna had brought her. It was true—sometimes her voice did come back, but if this was her punishment, why should she be spared?

A few hours later her doctor arrived. He looked at her throat and took her blood pressure. He looked grave.

"You know what I am going to say, Madame Callas." Maria nodded.

"But I am going to say it nonetheless. Your blood pressure is worryingly low. Your body is under considerable strain and the condition of your throat is reflecting this. What you need is complete rest."

Tita leaned over. "But she is singing tonight for the president!"

"I don't think the president would want her to faint onstage."

Tita looked taken aback. "Do you think that is likely?"

The doctor shrugged. "I would not take the chance."

Maria wrote on the pad in front of her: "Call the manager and say they must find a replacement."

The doctor pressed her hand. "A wise decision, Madame Callas."

Maria could hear Tita on the phone in the next room. "But the doctor has said there is a risk of her fainting onstage."

There was a pause as Tita waited for the torrent of anguished protest at the other end of the phone to abate.

"I know the gravity of the occasion, and I would not be saying this if my wife was not seriously ill." Another pause. "If you think that is necessary."

Then he shut the door, and Maria could hear no more. She closed her eyes and tried to sleep but every time she dozed off, she felt the scrape of Onassis's lips against her neck, and she squirmed with shame.

⇉

Elsa arrived after lunch. Maria could hear Tita unsuccessfully trying to get rid of her, but within seconds Elsa had stormed into the room and was now sitting on the bed, clutching Maria's hand.

"Oh my poor little diva, it's all my fault, for letting you go out last night. I should have listened to my own instincts and insisted that you stay home in bed. But I know how much you want to have fun, and it just seemed cruel that the world's most beautiful woman should be all by herself on New Year's Eve."

Maria took her hand out of Elsa's reach.

"But I think you are going to start feeling better very soon. You cannot imagine the crowd that is going to be there tonight. The Colonnas; the Doria Pamphili; Gina Lollobrigida, no less; and the Duchess of Alba has flown in from Madrid."

Maria scribbled something on her pad.

Elsa put on her glasses to read it and frowned. "Those are hardly the words of a Valkyrie, Madame Callas. Are you really going to throw in the towel because you have a sore throat? When I think of all the times I carried on playing in those movie houses, even though my fingers were bleeding, because I didn't want to let my audience down."

There was another scribble from Maria. When Elsa had read it, she said, "Well now, darling, I know perfectly well that my humble efforts at the piano were not the same as a gala performance at the Rome Opera House, but my point remains the same. The show must go on. Do you think that I want to be the life and soul of every party? There are plenty of times when I too would like to be tucked up in bed with my toy poodle. But I know how disappointed the crowd will be if I don't show up; and in your case, we can magnify that disappointment a thousand times."

Elsa peered at Maria from beneath her hooded eyelids, trying to decide if her monologue was having an effect.

"Of course if you really think it is impossible, I could try calling Renata Tebaldi. I know she has sung Norma in the past, not like you, obviously, but she is the only singer in Italy who could possibly take your place. The opera house management will be too scared to ask, but if I made the request as a personal favor, I am sure she would agree. But I would have to make that call now. What do you think?"

One glance at Maria's face made it clear that this suggestion was not a welcome one.

"Norma is my role," she whispered.

Elsa nodded. "Of course it is—no one else can do it justice. I just thought that at least Renata would make the audience think that they were getting something for their money."

Elsa knew that Renata Tebaldi was currently in San Francisco and there was no possibility of her being able to fill in for Maria, but she had gambled on Maria's not knowing the whereabouts of her greatest rival, and she had been right. The prospect of being replaced had kindled something in Maria.

At five o'clock, Maria was dressed with a silk scarf around her throat and a cashmere muffler on top of that.

"Are you sure they have an understudy standing by, Tita?"

Tita nodded. He knew nothing of the sort, but he was prepared to lie if it meant that Maria would get into the car. He was confident from experience that once she was in her dressing room with the excitement of an approaching performance invigorating her, she would stop worrying about losing her voice. He knew that it was her greatest fear, but he also knew that it was groundless: she always found the notes in the end.

Among her other ills Maria had been aware for the last hour of a dull ache in her groin, and when she went to the bathroom her fears were confirmed: her period had started five days early. This was the worst day of the month to be singing, and opera houses were careful not to schedule her on the first day of the cycle, but this time her body had let her down. She found some aspirin in the bathroom cupboard and knocked them back. Looking at her reflection in the mirror, she wondered if she really could perform tonight. What if there were no golden coins left?

Bruna was waiting for her by the door. She was carrying a thermos of the special throat-relieving tea and a cashmere robe for Maria to wear between the acts.

She looked at her mistress and said, "Shall I bring a hot water bottle?"

Maria nodded, marveling at the way that Bruna always knew everything.

In the car she told Tita that he must promise to make sure both that the understudy was standing by and that the stage manager would make an announcement before the show to say that Madame Callas was recovering from an illness and not in her best voice.

⸗

As she waited in the wings for her entrance, Maria vowed that she would never, ever allow herself to stray from her vocation again. Singing was her destiny, not hanging around in nightclubs with people who did not understand or appreciate her special gift. How fitting it was that she was singing Norma tonight, a woman who betrayed her sacred duty to her people for the affections of a faithless man. But she was a less noble version of the Druid priestess, one who had broken her vows to go to a party. The hot flush of shame rose again and, crossing herself three times, she stepped out onto the stage.

To sing "Casta diva" she had to project loudly enough to float her voice above the chorus. As she listened to the orchestra play the introduction, Maria tried to picture herself singing it as effortlessly as she had so many times before. She clenched her aching stomach muscles as she drew breath into her lungs. The first lines in her midrange were testing enough, but to soar convincingly above the staff was the real feat. It could sound breathy or even forced if she didn't calibrate it properly.

She managed the first verse and the second and she hit the high note—her voice soaring over the orchestra to the royal box where the president and his wife sat. But as she reached the downward glissando of notes that preceded the final flourish, she felt a dry click at the back of her throat. It didn't stop her finishing the phrase, but she knew it was an omen. In the rapturous applause that followed, Maria tried to forget the click and to bask in the adoration of the audience.

But as the act went on, the click caught and turned into a rasp; and in the great duet with Pollione she found herself reaching for a note and finding nothing but a husk of a sound. The surprise in the tenor's eyes made it clear that this was not her imagination. She tried again and this time what came out was not a note but a shriek.

She could not see the audience, but she could hear the collective gasp of horror at the sound she had produced. She was standing at the edge of a cliff; the merest gust of wind would push her over the edge. Suppressing her panic, she breathed in through her nose, trying to fill herself with air and relax her larynx so that she could launch herself through the high notes ahead. But even when she pushed out all the air, she could not produce a note, just that terrible, tuneless shriek.

The gasp in the audience had turned to a hiss. Maria thought she heard a man shouting, "Go back to Milan, you witch."

She forced herself to continue, clutching the tenor's hand as he sung to her, and then they finished the aria singing together. When they came to the end there was applause, rapturous applause, but there was also a drumbeat of boos and hisses. As soon as the curtain came down, Maria scuttled into the wings, looking for Tita, but he was not there. She moved fast, her head down, back to her dressing room, where she collapsed into Bruna's already outstretched arms.

Tita came in a moment later, beaming, followed by Elsa. They were both smiling.

"You were magnificent, *tesoro*."

"If I wore makeup, you would have ruined it," said Elsa, wiping away imaginary tears.

Maria looked at them with dead eyes. "Either you are deaf or you were doing something else. Get the manager and tell him they must put the understudy on in the second act."

Tita didn't move. "Maria, I think you are being oversensitive."

"Nobody called you a witch, Tita. Just do what I tell you."

Tita backed away, as if he had been slapped.

Elsa tried to put her hand on Maria's shoulder, but the singer started violently at her touch as if she had been stung.

Bruna brought some hot flannels and started to wrap them around Maria's neck.

The manager of the opera house, Sanpaolo, came in smiling. "Madame Callas, may I just say how magnificent that was and how lucky we are to have you here to start our season."

Maria looked at Sanpaolo just as she had looked at Pollione onstage ten minutes ago when he had announced he wanted to marry someone else.

"Then you did not hear my voice break in the last duet? Perhaps I was the only one listening. I should never have agreed to sing when I knew that my voice was weak. But I did not want to let you and the audience down. But now I am finished. You must send on the understudy."

Sanpaolo's ebullience was visibly punctured as he took in what she was saying. "Perhaps if we delay the start of the second act that will give you time to recover."

Maria shook her head. "That won't work. You must replace me."

The manager was silent.

Maria pointed at Tita. "You told me there was an understudy."

Tita shrugged. "I thought there was."

Sanpaolo was beginning to go from white to red. "It would be the height of disrespect to leave a performance when the president is attending."

Maria put up a hand to silence him. "Signor Gronchi will understand and the announcement you made before the show will have warned the audience that this was a possibility."

There was another silence.

"No announcement and no understudy." Maria picked up the first thing she could find, which happened to be a jar of cold cream, and hurled it at her husband. The dramatic impact was lessened by Meneghini catching the missile deftly in one hand.

Another silence, and then Elsa stepped forward.

"The thing that makes you unique, Maria," she said tentatively, "is not just your voice but your stage presence. I think that if you were to go onstage and simply speak your lines, the audience would still be enthralled. Only an artist of your caliber could carry it off. But you are such a great actress I really think it could work."

Sanpaolo beamed with relief. "Now that is a splendid notion: far better to continue with the performance, even if it is, um, a little impaired, than to cancel now. Everyone will understand and appreciate your efforts on behalf of the work and the other performers. . . . Roman audiences are not like the Milanese; they understand human frailty. . . ." He stopped when he saw the Medusa-like mask of scorn turned in his direction.

A call went out over the loudspeaker, announcing that the curtain for the second act would be going up in three minutes.

Sanpaolo turned to Maria in supplication, swaying slightly as if wondering whether he should fall to his knees in front of her. But Maria did not look at him. She put her hands over her face with her fingers spread, a gesture she had used as Butterfly when hearing of Pinkerton's betrayal. It had worked to show Butterfly's refusal to accept the truth, but here she was trying to stop herself from screaming.

How could they be talking about her going back onstage? Didn't they understand that she had just been humiliated, that she felt as if she had been flayed alive? She would happily have murdered them all—Tita who had lied to her, Elsa who had tempted her from her place of safety, and this cheapskate opera manager who did not understand that what remained of her voice could not be sacrificed to save his gala.

There was a knock at the door and Giuseppe Di Stefano, the tenor playing Pollione, put his head round the door but retreated when he saw the tableau inside.

But Maria had seen him through her fingers, and beckoned to him to come in. "You heard how I struggled with the last aria, Giuseppe. Tell them what it is like for a singer to lose command of their voice."

The tenor spread his beautiful hands in front of him. "Oh, Maria, my heart was breaking for you. To sing with such expression and then to miss that note. Another opera it would not be such a problem, but Norma, well, it is your role now and the audience expects perfection. If such a thing, God forbid, happened to me, I do not know how I would be able to face going back onstage."

Maria opened her eyes wide. "Do you hear what he says—that the audience expects perfection? I cannot go back on that stage to give them a travesty of my talent. They are expecting Maria Callas."

And she walked past them into the small bathroom at the back of the room and slammed the door.

The small group in the dressing room looked at one another. Giuseppe opened the door behind him and vanished, Elsa sat down heavily in Maria's chair, and Tita motioned to the manager to follow him into the corridor. Bruna tapped on the bathroom door and went inside.

As Elsa sat in the dressing room she began to make out a noise from the auditorium: it was the rhythmic beat of a slow handclap punctuated by whistling and booing.

She moved along the corridor leading to the stage. Maria's tantrums were nothing new, but a gala audience in revolt was well worth seeing. On the way she passed Tita and Sanpaolo. "Don't you think you should go out there and say something?" she said. "Sounds like the folks are getting mighty impatient." Looking at the manager's blank face, she tried again in basic Italian: *"Devi parlare al pubblico."*

But the man seemed unable to comprehend what she was saying. For a moment Elsa thought what a good story it would be if she were to go onstage and tell the audience what had happened, it would make a great anecdote for her next spot on the *Tonight* show. But when she got to the wings and heard the timbre of the commotion in the auditorium, Elsa backed away to find the steps down to the stalls. No story was worth risking her life for.

A great groan went up from the crowd as President Gronchi and his wife were spotted leaving their box. Afterward Elsa swore that she spotted Gina Lollobrigida shaking her fist at the stage and the Princess Doria Pamphili using her cigarette lighter to set fire to her program. And later she realized that the crowd was chanting *"Callas, la strega, a Milano ritorna"* (Callas, you witch, go back to Milan). It sounded better in Italian, she would later tell Jack Paar on the *Tonight* studio couch, because it rhymed: "The Italians do everything elegantly, Jack."

The spectators in the cheap seats were now streaming out of the theater and were gathering in a huge crowd in the piazza outside the opera house, clamoring for Callas, *"la strega."*

Maria could hear the shouting as she walked down the corridor, and she started to tremble. Bruna took her elbow and looked back over her shoulder for Meneghini, who was still talking to the manager.

"Signor Meneghini!" Bruna never raised her voice, so the unfamiliar sound made Tita start.

"Madame needs you." Bruna jerked her head to indicate the clamor outside.

Meneghini hurried toward them and went up to the stage door and opened it a crack. The blast of sound that burst through was terrifying, and the little man shut the door as if trying to stop a hurricane.

Maria was trembling in Bruna's arms. "I can't go out there—they will tear me to pieces."

Bruna did not know the manager's name, but she pointed to him and said, "How are you going to get Madame Callas out of here?"

Sanpaolo looked at her blankly, but the elderly stage doorkeeper came out of his cubicle and beckoned them to follow him. He led them to a locked door that, after much fumbling to find the right key, he managed to open.

Inside was darkness.

The man scrabbled for the light switch and a naked light bulb revealed a long corridor hung with cobwebs.

The commissionaire said, "This leads to the Quirinale hotel."

He bowed to Maria and extended his hand with a courtly flourish. "You are not the first artist to make use of it, Madame Callas. Patti, Malibran, even Caruso have had to leave the theater incognito." His rheumy eyes were full of compassion. He gestured to the manager. "I think Signor Sanpaolo here should go first and make sure that the coast is clear at the other end."

Sanpaolo obeyed his employee's command without hesitation and scuttled down the corridor like a cockroach.

Bruna looked after him and then at the doorman; and they exchanged a glance that showed they were in complete accord about the competence of Signor Sanpaolo.

III

Maria woke up with a start. The luminous hands of her travel clock said that it was two a.m. For a moment she thought that she was back in Milan, and then the horror of last night began to unfurl before her. She stumbled out of bed and made for the bathroom and found her sleeping pills. She shook out two of the blue pills into her hand and swallowed them.

In the bedroom she could hear Meneghini snoring. She felt like shaking him awake, but she knew that he would annoy her by underestimating the terror she had felt that evening. She went into their sitting room. The room was dark, the red velvet curtains were drawn, but she could still hear the chants of *"Callas, la strega"* from the square below. Without turning on the light, she went to the window and peered down.

There were about fifty people milling around outside the hotel, young men mainly, who seemed to be enjoying themselves as they linked arms and bellowed about the witch from Milan. If only one of these heedless young men could step into her shoes and know the nightmare of facing two thousand people when you had nothing to give them. Perhaps some of them had faced heartbreak—a girl who had cheated, a parent who had died—but did they know how painful it was to feel the current of an audience's love pull away from you, perhaps forever? And how could they understand the shame of knowing that you had squandered something infinitely precious for a moment of vanity? She looked back at her snoring husband and wondered how they would manage when all the golden coins were spent. She had told the press so many times about her longing to settle down and have a family, but now that this mirage seemed not just possible but inevitable, she felt herself recoil. A life of listening to those snores every night, without the memory of applause to drown them out, was not appealing. And as for children, like her namesake, the Virgin Mary, any child at this stage would have to be an immaculate conception.

For a moment Maria imagined herself going out onto the balcony and, like Tosca, stepping out into thin air. She had done it so many times onstage, believing in the moment that there was nothing but oblivion below and discovering almost with surprise the softness of the mattress below the cardboard battlements of the Castel Sant'Angelo. But she was not ready for the bloody mess of body on stone.

Her hand itched to shake Tita out of his complacent slumber. To tell him how he had failed her in so many ways. Why hadn't he listened to her when she told him to cancel the performance, how could he lie to her about the understudy and the preperformance announcement? In the past he had been her rock, but now he was a pillar of sand: she had only to lean on him a little bit and he would crumble into nothing. She remembered Onassis's hand on her waist as they were dancing and his smoky smell and the boldness with which he had snatched the camera from the photographer's hand and exposed the film. At least Aristo had not seen her humiliation onstage. It would be worse even than disappointing President Gronchi. For Onassis she wanted to be Norma, walking proudly to her own death, not Butterfly humiliated and alone. And as for Elsa saying that she could go onstage and speak her lines; if she hadn't persuaded her to go that accursed nightclub, none of this would have happened. She would never be forgiven.

A heaviness was building behind her eyelids and she walked slowly back to her bedroom, put on an eye mask and earplugs so that she could retreat into a dark cocoon. As she drifted into welcome sleep, she vowed to the deity that had given her the supernatural gift that she would guard it from now on with her life. The holy flame that burned inside her would be nourished and protected so long as it still cast light. She repented for her sins against her destiny, and she would never forget who had made her. . . .

When she opened her eyes the next day, Bruna was sitting by the bed, the sweet wide face lighting up as she greeted her mistress.

"What time is it?"

"Just past noon, madame, I thought it would be better to let you sleep. So many flowers have come, and calls, but I told everybody that Madame is not well, and she must have her rest."

The newspapers were laid out in the sitting room. Every front page carried the same picture of Maria and Elsa drinking champagne at Il Circolo on New Year's Eve. Through some accident of lighting, the whites of her eyes were flaring, making Maria look like a bacchante. All the papers condemned her for going to parties instead of preserving her voice to sing for the president of the republic.

Maria told Bruna to take the papers away and sat down heavily on the sofa. Tita came and sat down next to her.

"It's all over, Tita," Maria said. "I will never sing again."

Tita squeezed her hand. "Of course you will, *tesoro.*"

"I knew this would happen. You should have listened to me, Tita. But no, you persuaded me to go on."

Tita shrank from the fury that was building in her. "I have arranged a car to take us home."

"Home? But I have four more performances." Tita shook his head.

"Sanpaolo has found another Norma."

"Another Norma! But if I tell him I am willing to perform . . ."

Tita spread his hands carefully on his knees. "I think that it would be better for us to return to Milan. You need to rest."

"Yesterday was when I needed to rest—now I must recover my reputation."

Maria stood up and looked down at him in contempt.

"Two minutes ago, you said you would never sing again," said Tita looking at the floor.

Maria started to pace up and down.

"Ring Sanpaolo now and tell him I will fulfill my obligations."

Tita sighed. "Maria, he has told the press that you will not be allowed back in the opera house, because of the disrespect you showed the president by walking out of a performance halfway through."

Bruna came in carrying a huge basket of red roses, which she put on the table. "There is a note, madame."

Maria tore it open; the message was in Greek.

"We are the only two Greeks in the world who understand the price of fame."

The dark glasses almost covered her face, but she was still almost blinded by the flashbulbs exploding as she came out of the hotel. The crowds of angry opera fans of the night before had been replaced by battalions of the world's press.

"How do you react to the Italian parliament calling your failure to sing before the president an act of treason?"

Maria held her head up, her mouth set. She appeared not to hear the questions that were being shouted at her from every side and in every language.

"What do you say to the accusation that you are neglecting your art for your social life, Madame Callas?"

"Darcy Greenfield, *New York Times*. Is your career over?"

At last, the car was in front of her, the door opened, and still with her head erect she sat in the back seat, looking at the road ahead.

It was dark when they reached Milan. As the car stopped outside the building in the Via Michelangelo Buonarotti, Bruna got out first to open the door. Maria was just finding her handbag when she heard a scream.

"Madame, do not get out of the car, I beg you." Bruna was almost sobbing.

But it was too late. Under the unforgiving light of the streetlamp Maria saw the words "Death to the Bitch" in red paint on the wall. And below the slogan, a dead dog had been arranged carefully on the doorstep.

Meneghini got to her side just in time to catch his wife before she collapsed onto the pavement.

# CHAPTER SEVEN

## *Yellow Diamonds*

PARIS, APRIL 1959

I

After one last check in the mirror to make sure that her makeup was perfect—this was Paris, after all—Maria picked up Toy and stood at the top of the airplane steps. Her suit was, in a compliment to the city in which she was making her debut, by Dior. The nipped-in waist of the jacket and the slimness of the hobble skirt made it difficult to walk down the steps or indeed to breathe, but she had the consolation of knowing that the line was perfect. She raised a white-gloved hand to wave in the way that she had seen the queen do and smiled without showing her teeth.

As soon as her feet touched the ground, the questions began.

"How does it feel to be making your debut in Paris, Madame Callas?"

Maria swiveled to face the reporter and, with her most gracious smile, she said in her excellent French, "It is a great honor to be here. I shouldn't have waited so long."

"Is your suit from Dior, madame?"

"But of course! When in Rome, or rather Paris . . ."

The French press laughed, and there was another round of flashbulbs exploding. Maria put her hand on her waist and gave them the poses of a catwalk model.

She had nearly made it to the safety of the airport building when an American voice came out of the crowd: "How confident are you that you will actually sing, Madame Callas?"

She knew that the best thing was to let it go, to walk into the terminal, and she was almost there when the American spoke again. "Are you going to disappoint the Parisians like you did the Romans?"

Keep walking, she told herself, but as if pulled by an invisible string she turned her head and glared at the American journalist. "The only thing that would disappoint the Parisians would be if I did them the discourtesy of singing badly."

"But what do you say to the audiences who have paid for tickets to see Callas and then you cancel?"

"That I am a real nightingale, not a mechanical one."

Meneghini had caught up with her and, seeing the expression in his wife's eyes, he took her by the elbow and ushered her into the terminal, giving her no chance to reply to any more questions.


II


"Ve, ve, ve, ve." Maria pushed the air through her teeth as she warmed up her voice. As she breathed deep into her stomach and pushed her voice further and further up the scale, she felt her muscles relaxing and the notes becoming longer and smoother. She imagined each phrase as a line of ink she was drawing on the page in front of her that needed to start and end without a mark. She had once talked to a ballet teacher about how she got her pupils ready to dance for the day.

"I tell them to imagine that their muscles are made of toffee: when it is cold, you can snap it in two, but when you warm it up, it stretches, becomes pliable, and is impossible to break."

The same was true for the muscles that supported Maria's voice: they had to be warm and supple so that the notes would flow like water. The vocal cords themselves, tiny folds of skin the size of a thumbnail, had to be well lubricated otherwise they could not blossom. Careful warm-ups and constant practice were the only ways to keep everything in working order, but no amount of diligence could defend against the rogue virus or the weariness of muscles that had been worked too hard for too long. Every time she pulled the air up from her belly to sing, Maria wondered how many coins were left down there. Just as women were born with all the eggs they would ever have to conceive a child, singers were born with a reservoir of performances, and at the bottom of the pool those performances would lose their resonance and vigor.

When Maria thought now of the miraculous month in Venice right at the beginning of her career where she had sung Wagner and Bellini in the same week, she shuddered at that vainglorious waste of energy.

The soprano who had been engaged for *I puritani* had been taken sick and Maestro Serafin's wife had heard Maria singing an aria from *Norma* and suggested to her husband that the singer who had been engaged to sing Brünnhilde in Wagner's *La Valkyrie* could sing Elvira in *I puritani*. The maestro had thought his wife's suggestion was absurd—it was like asking a cart horse to win the Derby—but his wife had insisted. Maria was summoned to his office, sight-read the part perfectly, and the conductor had to admit his wife was right.

Maria had been thrilled when Serafin had offered her the part. It had been hard to learn a whole new score while performing Brünnhilde but she had blossomed under Serafin's confidence in her ability and the almost magical way in which they communicated musically. Here was a world-famous conductor who believed in her and was helping her to become everything she had ever dreamed of.

She had trusted him totally. He had been an ideal musical father, supportive and admiring and able to bring out her talent. Whenever she had asked him about some nuance of a role, he had looked up at her—she was about three inches taller—and, narrowing his eyes, had said, "When one wants to find a gesture, when you want to find how to act onstage, all you have to do is listen to the music." Serafin had taught her to submerge herself in a score.

But—and this was hard to admit—Serafin, her maestro, had not given a thought to what he was doing to her voice.

He had never warned her about the consequences of singing so much so young. He had encouraged her to sing everything because she could, but he had never wondered whether she should. She realized now that the genial white-haired old man, who had studied under Toscanini, had been thinking not of her but of himself. Discovering la Divina had given him something that he could set against the critics who said he was but an echo of his teacher. She was his miracle. And as he encouraged Maria to sing Lucia, Amina from *La sonnambula*, Norma, all the great bel canto parts in her twenties, he had never once hinted to her that there was a price to be paid for her precocity.

The tragedy was that she was a much greater performer now than she had been ten years ago. If only Serafin, or Tita, had told her to wait a few years until her mind had caught up with her body. But all they had cared about was the miracle of Callas. The only person who had tried to warn her was Elvira; and how could Maria be expected to remember the parable of the golden coins when Maestro Serafin, a god of the opera pantheon, was urging her to sing every role in the repertoire.

"Zh, zh, she." The voice was warm now and she was ready to sing. Her debut in Paris was a gala in aid of the Légion d'honneur, at the opera house, with a dinner afterward in the foyer. The president of France would be in the audience, and Elsa assured her that *le tout* Paris would be there: "There will be so many diamonds you won't need stage lights."

In the first act Maria had decided to sing some of her favorite arias; in the second part she would perform the whole of act two of *Tosca* with the baritone Tito Gobbi singing Scarpia, that was without question the most dramatic scene in her repertoire.

She was working her way through the mad scene in *Lucia*, stopping every now and then to practice the trills that are the vocal manifestation of Lucia's madness, when Meneghini came in. He leaned against the doorjamb and listened to her sing for a moment, and then he walked over and put his hand on her shoulder.

"You have never sounded better. There is really nothing to worry about."

Maria looked up at him, annoyed. "After what happened in Rome, of course there is."

Meneghini sighed. "In Rome you had taken some risks the night before, but here of course that will not happen."

Maria slammed the piano lid down. "You sound like a journalist, trying to blame me for something that you know perfectly well was not my fault. I had bronchitis, which is not uncommon in the middle of winter."

Tita stood a step back. "I was thinking that perhaps you shouldn't sing Lucia in the first half."

"Why?" Maria's voice was low and menacing.

"Because it is one of the most difficult parts in your repertoire. Why not something from *Carmen*. Think what a sensation if you sang the Habanera. No one has heard you sing that, and I know how well you can do it."

Maria's eyes began to glitter. "Are you saying that I am not good enough to sing Lucia?"

Meneghini shook his head vehemently. "Of course not! But as this is a concert where you can sing anything you want, I thought perhaps you could show off a different part of your repertoire."

"Carmen is a mezzo part."

"Which makes it all the more remarkable that you can sing it so well."

Maria shook her head. "No, no, no. To sing Carmen would be an admission of defeat. I must sing Lucia to prove that I am still Callas."

Meneghini took a tentative step toward her. "You will always be Callas."

Maria shook her head sadly, her long slender hand at the base of her neck. "No, this is Callas"—she clutched her throat—"without it I am only Maria."

Tita did not react to this; he had heard this statement or something like it many times before.

Bruna came in carrying a bouquet that was almost as big as she was. Maria looked at her in surprise. "Another one?"

There were two equally large arrangements at the other end of the room.

"A secret admirer?" Meneghini asked.

"They have been coming all day. Oh, but this one has a note."

She opened the tiny envelope, and read the Greek script on the card, which said, "From the other Greek."

"Onassis."

Meneghini pursed his lips in disapproval. "Do think about Carmen. It is just a gala and now that you have so"—he winced—"generously waived your fee, why take the risk with Lucia? After all"—he looked pointedly at the flowers—"*we* are not millionaires."

Maria stopped smelling the roses and turned to her husband with something like a snarl. "I don't sing for the money, Tita."

## III

Maria had refused to attend all the little dinners, amusing cocktail parties, and spontaneous picnics in the Bois that Elsa had tried to tempt her with. Lunch at the Ritz was as far as she was prepared to go.

Walking into the dining room there, she sensed the wave of recognition that rippled around her. She pulled her chin a little higher and thanked God for Dior. There was no scrutiny more terrifying in civilian life than walking through a room full of Parisians.

La Maxwell, as the Parisian press called her, was sitting on a rose-colored banquette with a coupe of champagne in one hand and a cigarette holder in the other.

She made a great show of extinguishing the cigarette when she caught sight of Maria. "We can't take any risks with that precious throat of yours!"

She summoned the waiter. "Bring another coupe for Madame Callas."

But Maria shook her head firmly. "No thank you. Don't you remember what happened the last time we had a drink together in public, Elsa?"

Elsa waved a beringed paw dismissively. "Oh phooey. You are too sensitive. You are the only singer I know who complains about being on the front page."

She leaned forward. "Do you know that tickets for your gala are going for ten thousand dollars on the black market?"

"Vultures! They just want to feast on my remains."

Elsa knocked back her champagne, and the waiter immediately refilled her glass.

"That is nonsense, Madame C., and you know it. People are paying ridiculous amounts of money because they want to hear the greatest singer in the world."

Maria picked up a piece of melba toast and broke it in two with an audible snap. "I think the Romans would disagree."

"So you lost your voice one night—that doesn't mean you have lost your talent."

Maria narrowed her eyes. "I thought I had to make a choice between my art and my hedonistic lifestyle."

Elsa laughed. "Who would say such a thing?"

"You did. To a reporter in Rome."

A gulp of champagne. "Then I was misquoted. I don't think I even know what 'hedonistic' means."

Maria was silent.

"Darling Maria, you know that I think you are a miracle, and I have no doubt at all that tomorrow will be a triumph."

"Every performance is a battle that I have to win. You saw what happens when I lose."

"Tomorrow night will be a famous victory, I promise you. Even Onassis is coming."

"I thought he didn't like opera."

Elsa laughed throatily. "He doesn't. But he likes you."

Maria took a sip of water. Elsa rattled on. "I can't tell you how much he wants you to come on his yacht. It is beyond glamorous, you know. It even has its own operating theater in case of emergency."

"That doesn't sound very glamorous."

"The swimming pool has mosaics copied from the palace at Knossos."

"I prefer to swim in the sea."

Elsa pouted. "Mary, Mary, quite contrary. Most people would jump at the chance to go."

Maria looked at her.

Elsa waved a hand. "Okay, you are not most people. But I really think you would enjoy it."

Maria nibbled at the melba toast. "Why do you care whether I go or not? Are you on commission?"

Elsa didn't blink. "Aristotle has been very generous to me, and so naturally I do what I can to make him happy."

"So, how much do I have to give you to make me happy?"

Elsa ignored the taunt and patted Maria's hand. "Anything I do for you, I do out of love."

"But you do expect something in return," Maria said.

Elsa blew her a kiss. "All I want is to be in your slipstream, darling.

At my age one has seen too many imitations, but you, Maria Callas, are the real thing."

## IV

The gown was a dark red silk satin, a strapless sheath that revealed her beautiful neck and shoulders, and there was a matching stole that she would use for dramatic effect when she sang the aria from *Trovatore*. It was a bit like a striptease, thought Maria, the play with the stole revealing and hiding her shoulders and chest. But, in fact, it was easier to sing when one had something to cling to.

There was a knock at the door and Bruna was there with a man carrying a large briefcase.

"Monsieur Verdoux from Cartier, madame."

Maria extended her hand and Verdoux kissed it reverently.

He put his briefcase down on the table and opened it with a tiny gold key.

"As you can see, these are yellow diamonds, very special, very rare."

He took the necklace out of its red velvet bed and Maria gasped as the light hit the stones, immediately filling the ceiling with stars.

"Allow me, madame."

Verdoux fastened the necklace around her neck with deft fingers.

"And now the earrings."

Maria looked at herself in the mirror. The diamonds were extraordinary, creating a halo of brilliance around her face. She turned her head this way and that, observing the light that played on her skin.

"There is only one necklace like it in the world," said Monsieur Verdoux. "And it will be Cartier's pleasure to lend it to you for the evening."

Maria nodded. "I am very grateful. The audience tonight won't be fooled by paste."

Verdoux nodded. "Indeed. The Duchess of Windsor and Princess Grace are among our clients."

Maria sighed. "But they can afford to buy, while I can only borrow."

Verdoux made the shrug of a man who makes his living from the fact that there is no justice in this world.

"Cartier is delighted you will be wearing these pieces tonight, and I personally am thrilled because it means that I will be able to hear you sing, which is my dearest wish."

Maria smiled. "I am glad. I hope they have given you a good seat."

"Under the terms of the insurance, I am not allowed to be more than twenty meters away from the diamonds, so I must stand in the wings. But I consider that a great honor."

"Then you will see the effort that goes into a performance, Monsieur Verdoux."

~

The roads leading to the Paris Opera were clogged with limousines as the guests arrived at the gala. News crews were set up around the red carpet, and there was the usual throng of press. Some of the more enterprising journalists had wandered away from the stream of celebrities like Sophia Loren, Charlie Chaplin, and Marlene Dietrich, to interview the people standing in the line for the cheaper seats, a line that stretched from the opera house nearly to the river.

"How long have you been queuing for?" a reporter asked a thin man wearing a tightly belted raincoat and clutching a bunch of beautiful pink roses.

"Oh, for a day and a night. I don't remember. I would have queued for a year if it meant that I would be able to see Maria Callas."

"Are you worried that she might not actually sing? She has a reputation for canceling performances at the last minute."

The fan shrugged. "Whatever happens there will be drama. It is Callas, after all."

~

On the red carpet there was a little frisson as the Duke and Duchess of Windsor arrived at the same time as the president of France, René Coty, and his wife, Germaine. The question of who had precedence, a former king or the current president, was enough to cause a small diplomatic incident, but fortunately the duke was in one of his better moods and graciously held back so that President Coty could walk ahead of him.

Those of the audience who understood the significance of such things felt that this was a good omen for the night ahead.

‿

Maria had told Elsa at lunch that she wanted no visitors in her dressing room before the performance, so when the knock came just after the first call for overture and beginners, she frowned. It would be typical of Elsa to ignore her command, but when Bruna opened the door, it was not the stubby form of the gossip columnist but a man holding a bouquet of roses and carnations that filled the doorway.

Monsieur Verdoux, who was standing in the corridor outside Callas's dressing room, stepped forward to take the flowers from the man and brought them in himself.

"You can't be too careful, madame."

Maria looked at the flowers. She could see a card nestling at the top. She knew without reading it whom the flowers were from. The card read in Greek, "I have entered your kingdom." She smiled.

Meneghini looked up from the accounts he was checking. "Whom are they from?"

Maria said nothing.

"Onassis again? What a show-off. Still, I heard he bought a huge block of tickets for tonight, so I suppose we should be grateful to him, or rather the Légion d'honneur should be grateful."

Meneghini was still annoyed over Maria's decision to waive her fee. But she had been quite firm. It was the right gesture to make, and she knew that it would be a fig leaf if anything happened that meant she could not complete the performance. After the Rome debacle she wanted to protect herself at all costs. She needed to distract Tita, though; otherwise she would feel his mood as she went onstage.

"Go and have a look at the audience for me, Tita."

Tita obeyed and Maria relaxed. She picked up her brush and carefully outlined her eyes in black, flicking the line up in the outer corners with an italic stroke. Close up, her skin was not perfect, and her features were all a little too big for prettiness. But at a distance this was an advantage, as it meant that audiences could catch every facial expression. It was part of the reason for her success. Unlike so many of her contemporaries who would "park and bark," Maria was so completely within the music that every nuance of its emotion could be read on her face. But this could also be her undoing; she thought of the famous photograph that been taken when she had been served with a writ just as she came offstage after singing *Butterfly* at the Chicago opera house. It had caught her snarling in rage at the process server in his ten-gallon hat. That photograph had been one of the things that had cemented her reputation as a diva, and it was constantly being reproduced when articles about her were published. Maria did not believe in regrets, but she wished passionately that the camera had not been there at that moment.

She pulled herself into the present and painted her mouth a deep red to match the shade of her dress. Bruna brought over the Cartier boxes, and she fastened the necklace around Maria's neck, and helped her put in the dangling earrings. Once Maria was ready, she put on her glasses so that she could inspect the general effect. It was pleasing. She reached out to touch the little painting of the Madonna that came with her to every dressing room, and she prayed that tonight she would be in control of her voice.

Making her way through the labyrinthine corridors of the opera to the wings, she was conscious of the discreet patter of Verdoux's footsteps behind her. At least, she thought sourly, Verdoux's interest was transparent: he was there to protect the jewels.

Tita was waiting in the wings, where he was talking with the head of the Légion d'honneur, who was going to introduce the performance. He turned to her, smiling. "Such an audience, Maria. They are so excited!"

As Maria listened to the president of the Légion d'honneur paying homage, she felt that electric charge that had eluded her in Rome. As she stepped on the stage to rapturous applause, she sensed the stars aligning; and as she opened her mouth to sing the opening bars of "Casta diva," her voice poured out like molten gold.

In the wings, Monsieur Verdoux watched, enchanted. He had all the records, but nothing could compare with the magic of seeing Callas perform. In an ideal world, a woman like that should always be wearing millions of dollars' worth of yellow diamonds—she deserved them, unlike the spoiled rich women who would actually own them.

He did not desire Callas, he worshipped her. She was a goddess who demanded reverence. He was standing next to the husband who was shorter and less imposing than Verdoux had imagined. But he too was a worshipper. Verdoux could see him mouthing the words of the aria, completely under the spell that his wife was weaving.

While the audience applauded, Verdoux leaned toward Meneghini and said, "My job is a strange one, but tonight it is a pleasure not to let Madame Callas out of my sight. What a lucky man you are to be married to a woman like that."

Meneghini turned to him. "The greatest pleasure in my life is to hear her sing."

Maria came offstage for a moment to drink a glass of water and to mop her brow. She smiled at Verdoux. "Can you see all right?"

"I have never heard such perfection, Madame Callas."

Maria winked at her husband. "Do you hear that, Tita? Perhaps he can persuade Monsieur Cartier to give us a discount on the necklace."

And she was gone.

The two men looked at each other a little awkwardly. Meneghini decided to treat his wife's remark as a joke. "She spends too much time going to parties with millionaires. I don't think she realizes how much these things cost."

Verdoux nodded. "This piece is not the sort of jewel a man buys for his wife. It is designed for a man to win over a certain kind of woman, if you understand my meaning."

Meneghini laughed. "Even if I had the money, it wouldn't persuade Maria to do anything."

He gestured toward the stage. Verdoux looked at the profile of the diva, her head thrown back on the long neck, her arms outstretched, her beautiful hands with the tapering fingers reaching out to her audience. He knew that he would keep that image in his head forever.

In the second half when Maria sang Tosca's famous second act aria "Vissi d'arte" ("I lived for art, I lived for love"), an aria sung by a diva playing a diva, the audience was swooning with delight. She heard the collective gasp as she stabbed Scarpia, and the applause at the end seemed to go on forever. The spectators were enchanted when she picked up a pink rose that had been thrown onto the stage and kissed it. This was not the arrogant diva they had read so much about. All they saw today was perfection. Even the seasoned operagoers felt that they were hearing each aria for the first time; and the philistines, who were at the opera that night only because it was the place to be, found themselves stirred by emotions they hadn't felt for years, if ever. And, as this was a Parisian audience, they admired the style of la Callas, the impeccable cut of her frock, and the artful way she held her wrap around her shoulders to reveal every so often a glimpse of shoulder or swoop of neck. Even in Paris the opera singers were not always chic—they were there to please the ear not the eye, but la Callas seemed effortlessly to do both.

In his box Onassis looked at the figure on the stage avidly. He borrowed Tina's tiny mother-of-pearl opera glasses to see her face more clearly and prove his feeling that she was in fact singing to him alone.

As he leaned forward, his elbows on the red plush rim of the balustrade, Tina rolled her eyes at Reinaldo, who was sitting in the adjacent box. He winked at her and mouthed the word "later."

⸗

Up in the gods, the young man who had thrown the pink rose was still reverberating from the moment when she had picked up his offering and kissed it. He was prepared to swear that she had been looking at him when she brought the rose to her lips.

After the twenty-first curtain call, the stage manager brought down the safety curtain. Maria walked back to her dressing room, still floating on the adoration of the audience, hardly noticing Verdoux walking exactly two meters behind her.

For the dinner that followed the performance, Maria changed into a peau de soie gown the color of ivory. This too was strapless to better display the necklace with its central stone that was about the size of a newborn's fist. Maria checked her reflection, and decided to paint her lips a slightly more subdued shade of red. What worked from the orchestra seats could be alarming up close.

Bruna handed her the black satin gloves that came up over her elbows. When Maria was ready, she took Meneghini's arm and together they walked through the drab backstage corridors into the glittering splendor of the opera foyer, with its graceful marble staircase. It deserved its reputation as the most glamorous opera house in Europe, Maria thought, as she stood at the top of the stairs looking down on the crème de la crème of Parisian society gathered below. She put on her glasses to have a better look at the crowd, but the glitter of the crystal chandeliers made the floor below a dappled sea of light.

She gave the glasses to Meneghini and began her descent to greet her public. By the time she had reached the third step, the applause started and swelled until she got to ground level, where she was greeted by the president of France, who kissed her hand with great enthusiasm.

"May I congratulate you on behalf of the French Republic."

"It is an honor to sing for such a noble cause," said Maria.

The president moved on, but Maria was hemmed in by famous faces, wanting to congratulate her. She had sung at many such events, but never had there been such a press of celebrity. Here was Chaplin kissing her hand and saying that she had made him cry. Maria retorted that it was only fitting as he had made her laugh so many times. A feline-looking blonde called Brigitte Bardot purred her appreciation, as did her escort, a film director who said that he wanted to make a film with Callas at its center. Then Elsa appeared, determined, it seemed, to immerse her in a claque of French duchesses who expressed their admiration with aristocratic reserve. At one point Maria thought she saw Onassis hovering behind the ancient aristocrats, but when she looked back, he had gone.

Then she heard a familiar voice. "La Divina!"

Franco looked elegant in white tie, with diamond studs the only nod to his usual sartorial extravagance. He flicked his eyes up and down her outfit. "You look wonderful, *carissima. Impeccable*, as the French say."

"I learned from the best." Maria smiled.

Zeffirelli had been part of her transformation from a great singer who weighed two hundred and twenty pounds to her current incarnation as a great singer who was as photogenic as she was talented.

"And how did I sound?"

"Better than ever."

Franco clasped her hands in both of his own. "Tell me, darling, who is the adorable young man on the staircase who is watching you like a hawk. He doesn't look like a guest."

"Oh, you must mean the man from Cartier who is here to keep an eye on these." She pointed to the necklace.

Franco gave her a sideways smile. "Would you like me to distract him for you while you run off with the diamonds?"

"I think Monsieur Verdoux takes his job too seriously to be distracted, even by you, Franco. And I don't think I am really suited to a life of crime."

Franco smiled. "True. You don't exactly fade into the background. But, darling, I should leave you to talk to the rich and famous. I don't think I have ever seen so many stars. Not bad for a girl from the Bronx."

Maria glared at him in mock horror. "I was born in Manhattan, Franco. There is a big difference."

⸗

At the edge of the crowd, Tina was watching her husband's maneuvers to get closer to Maria. Reinaldo caught the direction of her gaze. "I didn't realize your husband was so interested in opera."

Tina laughed. "Ari is like a magpie. He collects new and shiny things. And I suppose that for now Maria Callas is the shiniest. And besides, I collect too." She gave Reinaldo a seductive smile.

Together they watched Onassis circling the crowd. He ended up talking to an oddly intense-looking young man on the stairs.

Whatever Onassis said to him surprised the man very much. He looked at the Greek millionaire as if he could hardly believe his ears, but Onassis nodded vehemently; and after a minute's hesitation, and a longing look at the star of the evening, the intense-looking man walked down the stairs and disappeared into the crowd.

Tina wondered for a moment what Ari was up to, but then Reinaldo put his hand on the small of her back, and she found herself thinking of other things.

Maria was thinking how glad she was that she was wearing gloves, as another scion of the French nobility kissed her hand with lubricious gusto, when she heard a familiar voice in front of her.

"You look magnificent tonight in your kingdom."

The assessing brown eyes were in front of her.

"I am glad you thought so, but a singer really wants to know how she sounds."

"Well, as you know, I am not an expert, but my unprofessional opinion is that you were excellent."

"Luckily for you, I was very good tonight."

There was a pause as they looked at each other. Maria was the first to speak again. "I should really scold you. Three bouquets in a day . . . it's too much."

"But we just agreed that you were excellent."

Maria was about to reply, when Onassis leaned forward and said in Greek, "Three hundred bouquets would not be enough for a woman like you."

Maria inclined her head like a medieval pope. She was no stranger to fulsome compliments. But her poise was interrupted by the next remark.

"Which is why I have bought the necklace you are wearing. As a tribute."

Maria's hands went automatically to her throat.

Onassis looked straight into her eyes, and she could smell his cologne and the other scent it only just masked, and she was speechless. Before she had a chance to reply, to tell him that she could not possibly accept, her husband grasped her elbow, turning her away from Onassis.

"*Cara*, you should not keep royalty waiting." He lifted his chin to indicate the Duke of Windsor, whose boyish face looked incongruous in the frame of his white tie.

Maria made a graceful diva curtsy. "Your Royal Highness."

"That was a spectacular performance."

"You are too kind, sir."

Looking over Maria's shoulder, the duke recognized Onassis.

"You really can perform miracles, Madame Callas, if Onassis has come to hear you sing. His wife is always complaining that he won't take any interest in culture."

Onassis looked serious. "I appreciate greatness, sir, wherever I find it."

The bell that heralded the beginning of the dinner sounded, and the president came to lead Maria in.

Elsa, who had been hobnobbing with Rothschilds, suddenly popped up at the duke's elbow. "What did you think of my dear friend Maria?"

The duke paused and then, as if dispensing a pearl of great wisdom, said, "I daresay Madame Callas and Mr. Onassis are the most famous Greeks in the world."

Elsa nodded enthusiastically. "Without question, sir."

But the duke hadn't finished. "Apart from Plato and Aristotle, of course." He looked at Elsa expectantly and was rewarded by suitable merriment.

"I must remember to say that to Onassis. I think he will find it most amusing, don't you?"

Elsa couldn't have agreed more.

⊃

Maria sat in front of her dressing table while Bruna brushed her hair. This was a regular part of her evening ritual.

Litza used to brush her hair when she was little, and it always made her feel cared for. Tita had brushed her hair in the early days of their marriage, but now it was Bruna's job.

When the maid had finished brushing, she made to unfasten the diamond necklace that was still hanging around Maria's neck, but Maria shook her head.

"But what about Monsieur Verdoux?" asked Bruna.

"His services are no longer required."

Bruna understood at once, and smiled. "Good night then, madame."

Maria was left alone with her glittering reflection. The necklace was breathtaking, a line of graduated yellow diamonds leading to the huge teardrop diamond that hung at the perfect point just above the top of her breasts. She knew that she should have taken the necklace off immediately and given it to Onassis, because now that she was alone with the diamonds, the thrill of ownership was possessing her. Didn't she deserve to have jewels like this? In the back of her mind, floating as it always did, was her mother's face.

She saw Tita behind her in the mirror, wearing a dressing gown and the hairnet that he was convinced stopped his few remaining strands of hair from falling out.

"What an evening, *cara*. Everything was perfect."

"Almost perfect. I missed the top E-flat in 'Sempre libera.'"

"Nobody noticed, *tesoro*. In fact, I don't think I have ever heard you sing it better. And as for Lucia, it was miraculous."

Maria smiled triumphantly. "Better than the Habanera?"

"Much better. Every item in the program was—" Tita broke off. He had just registered that Maria was still wearing the necklace.

"Where is Monsieur Verdoux? I hope you aren't going to make him stand outside in the corridor all night."

Maria shook her head.

Tita began to look anxious. "But, Maria, it must be worth a fortune."

Maria turned round. "Don't you think I deserve it?"

"Of course . . . but I wish that you had . . ."

Maria put him out of his misery. "Don't worry, Tita. I didn't buy it."

The relief on her husband's face was soon overtaken by another thought. "Onassis," he said. It was not a question.

Maria nodded. "I didn't want to make a scene at the gala, but of course I can't keep it." Her voice rose at the end as if it was a question rather than a statement.

Meneghini was silent. He did not care for Onassis, but on the other hand—he tried to calculate the value of the necklace. Onassis would want something in return, but he knew that Maria was not a woman who could be bought. She might act the part of a kept woman to perfection in *La traviata*, but Maria was not a cocotte. In fact, he thought, with a certain amount of satisfaction, Onassis had just made a very expensive mistake.

He stood behind Maria and looked at her in the mirror, lifting the weight of her hair so that he could see the necklace better. "Your neck is made for diamonds," he said, and Maria reached for his hand and squeezed it.

"Thank you, Tita."

Maria took off the necklace and placed it carefully in its red velvet lair.

She told herself that if Tita had objected, she would have sent the diamonds back. But if her husband did not object to the necklace, then surely there was nothing to worry about. For a man as rich as Onassis, such a gift was nothing. Probably a fraction of his daily income. But even as she lay in bed, reassuring herself that the necklace was pocket change to Onassis, the memory of his deep brown eyes hovered in front of her.

The next morning there was a letter on her breakfast tray. The perfect italic hand was unfamiliar, and she opened it to discover that it was from Tina Onassis, inviting her and Tita to come on the *Christina* for a three-week cruise in August.

> *I imagine that your schedule is booked up years in advance, but we would so love to have you. The other guests will be Sir Winston and Lady Churchill, and their daughter and granddaughter, plus Sir Winston's private secretary and his wife. The* Christina *is very relaxed, and it will be a chance for you to rest and relax in complete privacy.*

She put the letter down and took a sip of her black coffee. Onassis had told his wife to write the letter, she thought. But Tina would have refused if she suspected her husband of anything other than hospitality.

When Tita came in, she showed him the letter. To her surprise he smiled.

"You do have some free time in August; if we moved one of the recording dates it might be possible."

Maria stretched her arms out above her head.

"Three weeks floating around the Mediterranean, swimming every day. I think it might be fun, and if we hate it, we can always leave early."

Meneghini nodded. "Onassis thinks that you should make films, Maria, and he has offered to advise me."

"When did he say that?"

"He phoned me this morning—he has lots of ideas, Maria. It could be a new career for you."

"Do I need one?" asked Maria.

"Of course not, but it might be worth considering. There is a lot of money in movies."

Maria wrote a formal letter of acceptance to Tina, saying that they would be delighted to accept her kind invitation. Her next call was to Madame Biki.

"I need clothes for a cruise on the Mediterranean. The hostess is very chic, so I want to look casual but elegant."

She could hear the couturier taking a long drag on her cigarette on the other end of the line. "It will be a pleasure. Can I ask who your hosts are?" Maria told her.

"You're right. Tina Onassis is very chic in a rather American way. But I am sure Alain and I can come up with something suitable."

"I am going for three weeks, so I will need at least ten new outfits, with the usual." The usual meant a collection of sketches that told Maria and Bruna exactly how to wear each outfit and what accessories to wear it with. Biki understood that Callas was putting on a performance and that she needed direction.

As soon she put the receiver down, it started to ring. It was Elsa.

"Are you feeling triumphant, darling? *Le tout* Paris is talking about last night. The Windsors want me to organize a dinner, the Rothschilds want to host their own gala, and Charlie Chaplin wants you to be in his next film. After all your worries, you are back on top again. Renata will be spitting tacks."

"Renata and I are not in competition, Elsa," Maria said primly.

"Because you think you are in a different league. Anyway, I couldn't be more thrilled, even if you rushed off last night without saying goodbye."

Maria sighed. "I was exhausted and I knew perfectly well that you would be calling me now."

"Perhaps I should play harder to get."

Maria didn't reply.

"Has the Golden Greek asked you on his yacht yet?" Elsa laughed.

"The letter arrived this morning."

There was a slight pause, which Maria understood to mean that Elsa had not received a charming handwritten note from Tina.

"And will you go?"

Maria caught the plaintive note in the other woman's voice. "Why not? You made it sound so enticing, Elsa. How could I resist a yacht with its own operating theater."

# CHAPTER EIGHT

## *Costume Fittings*

MILAN, JULY 1959

"For dinners on the yacht, I have designed one dress for you in a fabulous green, the color of the sea before a storm. It is strapless so that the other diners can admire your wonderful neck and, of course, those diamonds you showed me." Alain Reynaud, Madame Biki's son-in-law, had become the curator of Maria's image. There was a mannequin in the atelier that had been made to Callas's measurements; and Alain knew every inch of the diva's body, he understood her worries about the size of her ankles and her pride in the waist that had taken six months of grueling effort to acquire. He also knew that style did not come naturally to Maria, and that left to herself she would embellish to the point of no return, which is why he wrote down every detail of every outfit, including the jewelry.

It had taken time to persuade her that a woman with her strong features, height, and bearing was meant to dress like a goddess in strong, simple shapes. "No frills, no bows, and absolutely no pink." Maria had been an attentive student and had come to regard her offstage wardrobe as equally important to her role as the great Callas as her stage costumes. Only in her choice of nightwear did she give herself free rein to indulge her taste for what Alain called "froufrou," ordering exquisite silk nightgowns and matching peignoirs that dripped with lace and billowed with chiffon frills. This nighttime splendor was for her own satisfaction. Tita was too busy attending to his own nocturnal regime of facial massage and hair preservation to notice what she was wearing, let alone act upon it.

"And for onshore expeditions, something more casual, like this." The Frenchman showed Maria a sketch of a plain top with matching pants. "With sandals and no jewelry, just a headscarf, perhaps."

Maria looked at the sketch anxiously. "Tina Onassis always looks so feminine. Don't you think I need something more"—out of her handbag she pulled a magazine clipping of Tina in Monte Carlo wearing a sleeveless floral top and matching capri pants with a floral headband—"like this?"

Alain looked at the picture and his lip curled. "But, Maria, I am dressing you, the great Callas, not some rich man's doll."

Maria frowned. "I know, Alain, but this is a cruise, not an engagement. Maybe I should look less like a diva and more like an ordinary woman."

"But why would you want to? You are not an ordinary woman, and it would be foolish to pretend otherwise."

Still Maria looked wistfully at the clipping of the petite blond blue-eyed Tina, who reminded her of her sister, Jackie.

"Perhaps I should go blond again. I would look more chic. . . ."

Alain took the picture out of her hand and ripped it in two. "Maria, you must stop this now. Together we have made you into a goddess. I am not prepared to allow you to debase yourself. You are magnificent just as you are."

He picked up one of the gowns he had designed, a white pleated chiffon that draped and folded like the chiton of an ancient Greek statue.

"Put this on and then tell me you want to be a tiny blond doll."

Valerie, the modiste, helped her into the gown; and as Maria stepped out and looked at herself in the mirror, she knew that Alain was right. In this dress she did look like a goddess, Pallas Athene, perhaps, or Artemis, who could reduce any man to ashes with a glance. But sometimes she longed to be another deity—Aphrodite, the goddess of love, who could reduce a man not to carbon but to a puddle of desire.

"How can you talk to me of being an ordinary woman, *chérie*, when you can look like this?"

Alain put his hand on her shoulder in the mirror, and Maria smiled back. The tiny Frenchman was one of the few people she had confided in about her insecurities. To the outside world, since the great transformation, she always had the patina of elegance, but he knew how much it cost her to present that image to the world.

Alain, who could read the nuances of Maria's emotions better than those of his own wife (a fact that Madame Reynaud pointed out not infrequently), saw what was in her mind and made a surrendering gesture with his hands. "*Alors*, if that is what you want, I shall make you the beach pajamas in a charming little floral print, so that you will look like a cocotte and blend in with all the other 'ordinary' women."

Maria laughed. "I know you think I am mad, but sometimes I just want things to be different."

Alain squeezed her shoulder. "I hope, Maria, that whoever he is, is worth it."

Maria wheeled round in shock. "It's nothing like that!"

The couturier raised an eyebrow. "You have lost weight, Maria, even more weight, and you are talking about bleaching your hair blond." He pursed his lips. "I spend my life watching women, *chérie*. I have to know how they feel in order to make them look their best. Perhaps you don't admit it to yourself, but there is definitely someone."

Maria went back into the changing room.

"Don't take it out on the dress, Maria, I implore you."

Maria came out, her lips set. "There is nothing wrong with my marriage."

Alain shrugged. "Even the best marriages can accommodate a little . . . slippage. In France it would be considered strange for a woman as magnificent as you not to have a lover."

The look she gave him could have turned another man to dust, but Alain was not afraid of Maria. "It might be good for your singing too."

"Oh, that is what the tenors who make advances to me always say," said Maria. "'Come to bed with me and I will make you sing like a woman.' As if they could make any difference! I am a woman, I have no other way to sing! And the only way that I can improve is through hard work."

Alain made a graceful gesture with his hand, somewhere between a bow and a flourish. "Forgive me. I am just a Frenchman, who believes that beautiful women deserve every pleasure that life has to offer."

Maria was still standing on her dignity. "But I have all the pleasures that I could want."

"In which case, I am a foolish Frenchman who talks too much."

Once the decision had been made and the wardrobe ordered, Maria found to her surprise that she and Tita were becoming closer than they had been for a long time. Just as in the early days of their marriage, Tita would beg her to sing for him in the evening, not grand opera but the Neapolitan songs that all Italians adore. For the fortnight before they were due to travel to Monte Carlo, Maria lived the kind of simple, peaceful life she had always said she wanted, swimming in the lake every day after her morning's practice and going on walks with the dogs. Sometimes Maria would even cook for Tita. When they were first married, Tita's mother had been horrified that Maria had no idea how to cook, and she had taught her how to make a few of her son's favorite dishes, so that he wouldn't starve. Maria didn't cook very often, mainly because the food Tita liked was fattening. But with the cruise looming in front of her, Maria cooked all the things she knew pleased him: risotto all'Amarone, bollito misto, and zabaglione. Tita could not believe his luck, and for once he stopped nagging Maria to firm up her schedule for the year ahead but let himself enjoy the long fine evenings sitting next to Maria in comfortable silence looking out over Lake Garda. One night he even tried to make love to her; and, although he had drunk too much Amarone for the experience to be entirely successful, he had taken off the hairnet.

# CHAPTER NINE

## *Spats*

Onassis had arranged for Maria and Tita to stay at the Hermitage Hotel before they set out on the *Christina*. The Hermitage was luxurious enough but it was not the Hôtel de Paris, the best hotel in Monaco that was also owned by Onassis. Maria had been surprised and a little put out, since she knew the Churchills were staying at the other hotel. But the reason became clear when she went down to swim in the pool belonging to the Hôtel de Paris.

The two buildings were connected by a tunnel and Maria walked between the two wearing a bathrobe over her new white swimsuit and a huge pair of sunglasses. But the sunglasses were not prescription, so it was only when Maria had swum a few lengths of the pool with her elegant crawl and had stopped to catch her breath that she looked up and saw an unmistakable pair of spats in white kid leather with black buttons. There was only one person she knew who still wore spats.

"Elsa!"

She looked up and saw Elsa squinting down at her.

"Some people say that I put Monte Carlo on the map. It's an

exaggeration, of course, but Ari is very sweet and always gives me the penthouse suite at the Hôtel de Paris."

Maria wondered if she went on swimming how long Elsa would remain and, realizing that she might easily stand there all day, she pulled herself out of the pool. She understood now why Onassis had put her in the Hermitage. Despite engaging Elsa as his intermediary, he had not invited her on the cruise, and with surprising tact he was trying to keep them apart.

Maria turned to find her robe, but Elsa was too quick for her and was already holding it up.

"You don't want to catch cold now," said Elsa in a parody of a motherly voice.

Maria undid the strap of her bathing cap so that her hair fell down over her shoulders. Elsa's eyes gleamed, and Maria quickly put on her sunglasses.

Then she walked over to one of the pool beds, and an attendant appeared immediately with towels and arranged the sunshade for her. Maria lay down on the bed and closed her eyes, hoping that Elsa would take the hint. But she heard the protesting groan of the bed next to hers as Elsa sat down and the click as Elsa lit one of her inevitable cigarettes.

"Of course you know that he asked Garbo first?" Maria heard Elsa inhale through the cigarette holder. "But you know how private Garbo is, and the last time she went on the *Christina* there were hordes of reporters every time they put into shore. So she said never again."

Maria was silent.

"Sir Winston doesn't mind, of course. Ari looks after him so well. Every morning his breakfast is brought down, first a cup of coffee and a glass of orange juice, then half an hour later some toast, and then half an hour after that a bottle of whiskey—or is it champagne? I forget. But literally his every whim is catered to. Churchill is revered as the savior of Europe but he has no money to speak of, so he likes being spoiled by Ari and Tina."

Elsa took another drag of the cigarette.

"The thing you have to understand about Ari is that he always mixes business with pleasure. The *Christina* is like a floating advertisement for Onassis's enterprises. The more he is written about, the more he likes it.

That's why he is so keen to have you aboard: he knows that the whole world will be watching. I just hope you know that you are being used for publicity purposes."

Although she had promised herself that she would not react, Maria could bear it no longer. She lifted her sunglasses and looked at Elsa. "Well, it won't be the first time I have been used in that way," she said.

Elsa pretended not to hear the meaning in Maria's voice, and continued. "Of course I feel rather bad about abandoning you, but I always summer in Nantucket with Dickie. Ari and Tina know that is my one unbreakable rule, so they never embarrass me by asking me at this time of year."

Maria looked over the top of her sunglasses, they both knew that Elsa was lying through her teeth.

"How thoughtful of them."

Painfully Elsa pulled herself to her feet. She looked down at Maria and said, her face for once losing its jauntiness, "I just hope you will be careful."

Maria closed her eyes, hoping that when she opened them, her tormentor would be gone.

"Of your heart, Maria. I know you have one somewhere."

Maria felt the decking shake as Elsa walked heavily away, and she opened her eyes on nothing but sky.

# CHAPTER TEN

## *En Voyage*

THE *CHRISTINA*, MONACO, JULY 30, 1959

I

That night before she went to bed, Maria put on her glasses and stood on her balcony overlooking the harbor and looked at the bright lights of the *Christina* that twinkled in the middle of the bay like a chandelier. It was far and away the biggest boat on the water. Gossip had it that Prince Rainier of Monaco found it irksome that it was so much bigger than his own yacht and he resented the control that Onassis had over his tiny principality. But since it had been Onassis's money that had redeveloped the faded glories of Monaco's once splendid hotels and Onassis's companies that employed so many of the Monegasques, Rainier could not afford to complain.

The *Christina* had started life as a Canadian frigate, but in the early 1950s Onassis had bought her from the Greek navy and had sent her to his favorite shipyard in Hamburg to be fitted out as a luxury yacht.

There were three decks: the lower one for the crew, the stateroom deck for the guests, and on the top deck a cabin for Onassis that communicated directly with the bridge, so that Ari could put any nocturnal navigational whims into practice. Although Ari and Tina had houses all over the world, the *Christina*, named after their daughter, had become their real home, with summers in the Mediterranean and winters in the Caribbean. The couple's marriage, which could be fragile on dry land, was stronger on the water and Tina enjoyed the boat almost as much as Ari did. The crew, who had originally been German, were now mostly Greek, except for the English governess who worked with the children and the Finnish masseuse.

The yacht was the product of the decorating tastes of a man whose idea of splendor had been formed in the bordellos of Buenos Aires and his young wife who had spent most of her childhood in palace hotels. Onassis had decided that the floor of the swimming pool should be covered in mosaics copied from the palace of Knossos in Crete, and Tina had asked Ludwig Bemelmans, the artist who had decorated her favorite room in the Carlyle hotel in New York, to create murals for the dining room. But they chose the gold taps shaped like dolphins together. There was a reception room on the main deck that could hold eighty people and a cover could be extended over the pool to form a dance floor at the flick of a button.

It could also be retracted, a power that Ari was always threatening to use.

A painting that was said to be by El Greco hung in the marital bedroom. It was a gloomy elongated Madonna that the dealer who sold it to him suspected Onassis had bought for the name of the painter rather than for its artistic merit. The master bathroom was another tribute to the classical past, with mosaics copied from a fifth-century Greek vase.

All the staterooms were named after different Greek islands. The most splendid, after Onassis's, was Chios, which was where Churchill slept, with Clementine, his wife, in Santorini next door.

The boat had two chefs, a Frenchman, who had previously been the *chef de partie* at Maxim's, and a Greek who was happy to make whatever Greek snack Ari fancied in the middle of the night. Onassis never slept well, and he liked to pad around the yacht in the small hours, spending hours in the wheelhouse chatting to the crew. At first Tina had protested at the amount of time he spent there, but when she noticed that he came back more relaxed, she realized that it was something of a blessing. Onassis was always in motion, and to be in his orbit could be exhausting. Tina was an excellent hostess and she had tamed some of her husband's uncouth behavior, like picking his teeth in the middle of a meal. Tina was the perfect blond millionaire's wife; but as the child of a very wealthy ship-owning family, she had no idea of the hardships that Onassis had endured as a young man and that he could not help imagining might one day return.

11

The next day Maria dressed carefully for her first appearance on the yacht. Alain had made her a beautifully cut shirtdress in white linen, which she wore with a tan leather belt and matching sandals. There had been a hat to go with the ensemble, but Maria had been observing the women coming on and off the yachts and none of them were wearing hats.

She had prepared for the cruise as she would for a part. She had the costumes that fitted her role as a great diva on holiday—relaxed but not frivolous—she had thought of what she would say to the Churchills when she met them, and she had even made inquiries as to the right kind of presents to buy for the Onassis children, eleven-year-old Alexander and eight-year-old Christina. Maria knew what to say and how to look; the only thing she could not predict were her emotions. When she sang, the music told her exactly what to feel, but on this journey, she didn't know the score.

Tita was humming one of his Neapolitan tunes as he adjusted the handkerchief in the pocket of his linen suit. He was, as usual, a semitone flat, which usually made Maria leave the room, but today she barely noticed it. She was surprised that Tita was in such a good mood. He kept hinting that he and Onassis had business to do, and that this cruise would be a great opportunity for them both. The only shadow for Tita was the presence of the Churchills, as Tita had been an enthusiastic supporter of Mussolini. What would happen if Churchill asked him what he did in the war? Maria laughed and said, "That isn't going to happen, Tita. You hardly speak English and I am quite sure that Churchill doesn't speak Italian."

Tita had been reassured by this for a minute or two, but then he said, "But what if he asks someone to translate?"

"I think he will have other things on his mind."

Maria's extensive cruise wardrobe meant that there were fifteen pieces of luggage to be taken from the hotel to the quay where the tender would meet them to carry them out to the yacht. As she tried to keep track of the suitcases Maria regretted giving Bruna a holiday. There was a panic at the steps of the hotel when she noticed that her jewel case was missing. The manager personally searched the suite until Maria remembered that she had placed it in a lower layer of her Louis Vuitton trunk for safekeeping.

This delay meant that they were more than an hour late when Maria and Tita walked up the gangway lined with saluting sailors.

"I was beginning to wonder if I should send out a search party," Onassis said.

Maria tried to sound apologetic. "I thought I had lost my jewel case."

Onassis said tightly, "You can always buy more jewelry, but time and tide wait for no man."

"Oh, I didn't realize there was a tide in the Mediterranean. But you are the sailor," Maria retorted.

Tina's laugh tinkled. "She's quite right, Ari. You can't possibly expect Madame Callas to travel without her jewels. I certainly wouldn't."

She looked conspiratorially at Maria. "You never know when you might need to make a quick getaway."

The other guests were sitting under the striped awning that covered the main deck, drinking tea, cocktails, and in Churchill's case, Pol Roger champagne.

Maria took a deep breath. The last time she had seen the great man had been in Athens in 1944, when the prime minister had come to lend his support to the provisional government in their fight against the communist insurgents.

Maria had stood among the crowds watching a large black car driving past and had only caught a glimpse of a white face in the back, but she had felt the force of his legend in the enthusiasm of the crowd. Her mother and all her friends called Churchill the savior of Greece. But Maria knew that among her colleagues at the opera, there were some who felt that Churchill and the British army had no business interfering in the battle for the Greek soul.

Maria had her own reason for cheering Churchill. She had spent three weeks holed up with her mother in Patission Street at the height of the battle of Athens surrounded by gun-toting communists, living on canned beans and dried fruit, until they had been eventually rescued by Jackie's boyfriend. For Maria, Churchill was the man who had saved her from killing her mother.

Onassis led Maria and Tita up to where the great man was sitting in a wicker chair, a straw fedora pitched low over the famous features. His wife, Clemmie, crisp in a striped shirtdress, was standing behind him.

"Sir Winston, Lady Churchill, may I present"—Onassis paused for dramatic effect—"Maria Callas and her husband, Signor Meneghini."

Churchill made a perfunctory effort to get to his feet, but then subsided, saying, "Forgive me for not getting up, but my knee is playing silly buggers again."

"Please don't think of getting up, Sir Winston. It is such an honor to meet you."

Maria made a graceful gesture that was halfway to a curtsy, saying, "The last time I saw you, I was twenty-one years old. You came to Athens to bring peace to my poor country. I remember I cheered so loudly that I couldn't sing that night."

Her hand flew to her throat.

Churchill looked at her, puzzled. "So you are a singer, are you, Madame Callas? What kind of thing? Greek songs?"

Maria took a step back, trying to hide her astonishment. The other English guests tried to hide their smiles. Tina failed to hide hers, but Onassis stepped in quickly by laughing very loudly. "Greek songs!" He turned to Maria. "I hope you have come prepared for the British sense of humor."

Maria stretched her mouth into something resembling a smile. Churchill, looking even more puzzled, added, "Well, I hope you will sing for us one evening, dear lady."

Maria stiffened. Did Winston Churchill think she was a cabaret act? She was about to answer that she was not that kind of singer when

Clemmie broke in. "My youngest daughter, Mary, has one of your records, Madame Callas. I believe it is one of her favorites."

Maria made a graceful bow of acknowledgment, as if receiving a bouquet onstage.

"I am delighted to hear that, and I hope that you will bring her to hear me sing if I come to Covent Garden. I can get you the best seats in the house."

Clemmie gave a small smile. "Oh, that really is too kind of you, Madame Callas."

Onassis indicated a younger couple in their thirties who were standing on the other side of the Churchills. The man was tall and amused, the woman bright and observant; they were introduced at Anthony and Nonie Montague Browne, Churchill's personal secretary and his wife. Beyond them were Churchill's daughter Diana Sandys and granddaughter Celia, who was sixteen.

Diana shook Maria's hand limply, and then turned to Meneghini. "How d'you do, Signor Callas?"

There was a pause, and then Meneghini said rather coldly, "*Mi scusi, signora*, but I am Signor Meneghini."

Diana looked at him, surprised. "Oh, I thought you were married."

Maria smiled graciously. "It is the custom on the stage for singers to keep their maiden names."

"How perfectly fascinating," said Diana.

Onassis was fussing over Churchill, whom he treated as a cross between a beloved uncle and the pope. When he sensed that the silence had carried on just a little too long, he summoned Tina. "I think that now all our guests have arrived, we should show them the boat."

He beckoned Maria, Tita, and all the guests, apart from Winston and Clemmie, to follow him.

He ran down the grand staircase, crowned by an enormous chandelier, and took them into a room kitted out as a bar, complete with a white-jacketed barman.

"Everything in this room is inspired by my hero, Odysseus." Ari gestured to the map on the wall that showed the epic hero's travels across the Mediterranean, and then to the bar counter itself, which was inscribed with lines in ancient Greek. Anthony Montague Browne leaned forward and started to spell one out, "*Thalassos oneiros*, the wine-dark sea, if I am not mistaken."

Ari beamed with pleasure. "I congratulate you on your classical education, Anthony. I have all my favorite lines from *The Odyssey* here on the bar."

He looked at Maria. "What will you have to drink?"

Maria shook her head, but Onassis was already clicking his fingers at the barman. "Champagne for everyone, the Pol Roger."

The barman immediately produced a bottle of ice-cold champagne, which suggested that he had been waiting for this moment for some time.

Ari held up his glass. "To the *Christina* and all who sail in her."

The rest of the party dutifully clinked glasses.

Onassis sat down on one of the barstools, which were upholstered in gray leather. He patted the one next to him and beckoned to Maria to sit down.

Then he turned to her with an alarming smile. "Are you comfortable, Maria?"

This was clearly a rhetorical question, because he went on gleefully, "I hope so, because you are sitting on the largest penis in the world."

Maria stood up as if stung, her drink sloshing onto the wine-dark sea.

Laughing heartily at his joke, Ari caressed the stool. "Oh there is nothing to be scared of. . . . The leather is taken from the foreskins of whales. Feel how soft it is." He stroked the stool with a lingering caress.

Tina turned to Maria. "Take no notice. It's Ari's awful party trick. Nobody ever finds it funny, but he will persist. One day I am going to have those bloody stools reupholstered in a nice bright chintz."

Onassis said to Maria in Greek, "I am sorry if my crudeness offends you. But at heart I am still a *Tourkospouros* from Smyrna."

"That is no excuse for bad taste," said Maria in the same language.

Ari laughed again; and when he caught Maria's eye, she felt something spark between them. An understanding that excluded everyone else in the room. Her husband had not heard a word of the exchange, but he sensed that the atmosphere had changed, and he reacted like a mole coming up for air, turning his head to and fro until he caught the scent of danger.

Tina felt it too, and she touched Maria on the elbow. "Let me show you to your cabin, Maria."

Maria followed her down the corridor lined with doors that all bore the names of Greek islands. Tina stopped in front of Ithaki and Maria noticed the slim gold bangle on her arm.

"Oh, what a pretty bracelet."

Surprised, Tina looked down at her arm, as if she were about to brush off a fly. "This thing? Aristo gave me this when we . . ." She hesitated, not sure how to frame the postcoital circumstances of the gift, and then settled on "got engaged."

Maria looked at the diamond initials on the thin gold band. "'TTWLA'? What does that stand for?"

Tina looked over her shoulder at her husband, who had followed them. "I think it says 'To Tina with love Ari.' Is that right?"

Onassis shrugged his powerful shoulders. "What else?"

⸺

Their cabin was as luxurious as everything else on the yacht. But Maria, who was used to impersonal luxury from her years on tour, hardly noticed her surroundings. She was sitting in front of the burled walnut dressing table, drawing on the winged eyeliner that she always wore for an evening performance. In the corner of her eye was the red leather case from Cartier that contained the jewels that Onassis had given her. She opened it, was dazzled by the yellow fire in the stones, but with a sigh she shut the case with a loud snap.

She pressed the bell on the wall, and a uniformed maid arrived seconds later.

Speaking quickly before she could change her mind, Maria said, "Could you take this to Mr. Onassis, please. And tell him I can't accept it."

The maid nodded, her face a professional blank. "Yes, madame."

"Oh, and best if you give it to him when he is alone."

"Of course, madame."

The maid disappeared, and Maria immediately regretted sending the diamonds back. Nothing she had came anywhere close. But there had been something about Onassis's barstool joke that had unsettled her. It had been familiar in a way that she found uncomfortable. She had not given him the right to make a joke at her expense. If that was the price of the necklace, then it was not one she was prepared to pay.

⇌

Dinner was served in the formal dining room with its murals that portrayed Tina and her children frolicking in olive groves and classical temples like lesser gods.

The children had their own dining room, but that evening they came to be introduced to the guests before dinner.

Alexander, the older, had his mother's delicate features and her lightness of manner; his sister, Christina, was the image of her father, with his strong features and hooded eyes, but without his explosive smile. They both had beautiful manners and moved among the guests without shyness until their English governess came to take them away. As they left Ari picked them up and enveloped them in a huge bear hug, kissing them both fiercely. But Tina only gave them a little wave and said, "Sleep tight, darlings."

At dinner Maria was seated between Churchill and Onassis, Meneghini between Nonie Montague Browne and Tina. As Maria sat down, she glanced at Onassis to see whether he had received the necklace, but nothing in his manner gave any sign of it. Unlike the other men who were wearing jackets and, in Tita's case, a tie, Ari was wearing a short-sleeved polo shirt, chinos, and deck shoes. The two top buttons of his shirt were unbuttoned, exposing the hairy chest. Maria found this rather shocking, and it must have shown on her face because Onassis grinned and said in Greek, "You think I should be wearing a tie, like your husband?"

Maria shrugged. "If you want to dress like a peasant, no one can stop you—it's your boat."

Ari laughed. "That's true. And I say everyone should wear what they want."

"How would you like it if I came to dinner wearing shorts?" retorted Maria.

Onassis looked at Maria's white off-the-shoulder evening dress. "I think it would be a pity, as I know that in the twenty or so pieces of luggage that came aboard with you are some very beautiful evening gowns like the one you are wearing now."

After dinner Onassis was helping Churchill to his favorite chair on deck when Diana Churchill said to Meneghini, "I hope that your wife will sing for us while we are here together."

Onassis turned around at this and said, "Yes. It would be an honor for the *Christina* if Maria Callas were to sing for us."

Churchill caught the tail end of this conversation, and said, "Is she going to sing? Splendid—always had a soft spot for Gilbert and Sullivan. Used to hum the 'Modern Major General' from *Pirates of Penzance* in briefings, drove the real generals potty."

Onassis looked at Meneghini and said, "Do you think we could persuade your wife to sing for us?"

Meneghini shook his head. "I am afraid my wife does not do after-dinner entertainment," he said firmly.

Onassis's smile did not falter. "Oh, what a pity."

Maria appeared behind the two men.

Meneghini said to her in Italian, "I was just saying that you don't sing for your supper, Maria."

There was a growl from where Churchill was sitting. "Is she going to sing or not? If she isn't, then I am going to bed."

Onassis looked at Maria and she saw the appeal in his eyes. If she didn't sing, then Onassis would lose face. For a moment she considered refusing as punishment for his uncouth behavior over the barstool, but she did not want to involve Churchill in her revenge. She made one of her graceful hand gestures toward the old man and smiled. "It would be a pleasure to sing for the man who saved my country."

She walked over to the grand piano in the corner of the room. She thought for a moment about what she should sing. Then she turned to the other guests, her eyes resting for a moment on Onassis.

She breathed deep into her diaphragm and began "L'amour est un oiseau rebelle."

Carmen's siren song pierced the still of the Mediterranean night and wove its spell around the passengers and crew of the *Christina*, who could not help but be swept up in the seductive swirl of the voice. One by one the sailors crept up onto the deck to listen. For a moment everyone on the boat was frozen in time, listening to the music.

When the final note had died away, the passengers and crew clapped enthusiastically and Churchill, who had had a pleasurable doze, woke up. Seeing Maria making a gracious bow, he said, "What a fine pair of lungs you have, Madame Callas. My hearing isn't what it was, but with you I didn't miss a note."

Maria gave a delighted smile and placed a slender hand on her collarbone. "I am so happy to hear it, Sir Winston. I wish all my audiences were so attentive."

As Montague Browne helped his boss to his feet, the grand old man muttered in his ear, "Do you think she is going to sing every night?"

### III

At two in the morning Maria was awake, the Habanera still vibrating through her body. Meneghini's snores were increasing in volume and, irritated, Maria decided to go on deck. She pulled on one of her peignoirs and slipped outside.

The warm sea air embraced her. The boat was moving at a steady speed, and she watched the lights of the Côte d'Azur retreating into the distance. The moon had risen and was lighting the waves. For a moment Maria felt quite at peace, as if she could stand here forever looking out over the water.

She noticed the smell first, and then one of the boards creaked behind her. When she looked around Ari was there, a cigar between his lips.

"Oh, did I startle you? I'm sorry." He did not look sorry.

Maria wrapped her arms around her chest, acutely aware that all she was wearing was a very thin layer of silk.

"I can never sleep after a performance," she said. "It takes a long time for me to come back to earth."

Onassis nodded. "Sleep is overrated. Four hours is enough for me. Seeing as we are both wide-awake, can I offer you a drink, something to eat, a cigar?"

Maria shook her head. "I never smoke."

"I am only smoking this because I heard you sing the Habanera." Onassis waved his cigar in front of her.

"Really?" Maria sounded skeptical.

Onassis grinned. "Your singing made me enjoy it even more."

"I'm flattered," she said.

Onassis took a step closer toward her; and at that moment the moon came out from behind a cloud, and she saw the look in his eyes. She put one of her hands down on the rail and gripped it tightly.

Ari took something out of his pocket.

Even in the moonlight, the necklace was breathtaking. "I am sorry you don't want this."

Maria could feel his breath on her face. "I am sure that it would look magnificent on your wife," she said primly.

"But I bought it for you, Maria."

Without taking his eyes off her, Onassis held his hand over the side of the boat and opened his fingers. Maria gasped as she heard the splash the necklace made as it hit the water, but they continued to look at each other.

Finally, Maria could bear it no longer and she said, "Are you trying to impress me?"

"Perhaps." He took another puff of his cigar, "Did I succeed?"

Maria looked back at him. "Perhaps."

Onassis edged closer. "My wants are very simple, Maria."

Maria leaned away from him. "So are mine: I am hungry."

Ari looked at her. "What for? Caviar? Lobster?"

Maria shook her head.

౨

Ten minutes later they were in the *Christina*'s kitchen and Onassis was cracking eggs into a bowl with some feta cheese and oregano. He put a pan on the stove, poured in some olive oil, and when it sizzled, he added the egg and cheese mixture. Then he sliced up a couple of ripe tomatoes and arranged them on the edge of a plate onto which he slid the eggs.

"Strapatsada. My mother used to make this for me for breakfast. It's so great to eat it again." Maria started to eat like the greedy teenager she had once been.

Ari smiled ruefully. "Really, Maria, if I had known you were this easy to please I would have saved myself a lot of money."

Maria caught his eye and started to laugh, and after a moment Ari joined in.

"That necklace was the most beautiful thing I have ever seen," Maria said between gulps of laughter.

"Perhaps a lucky fisherman will find it and he will start his own shipping empire. And then one day he will come across a beautiful woman who makes him do something very stupid."

Maria touched his hand very briefly. "If it makes you feel better, I was impressed."

He laughed. "Of course you were. Even I was impressed."

Ari sprang up and started to rummage about in the cupboards until he found the coffeepot called a briki, and he started to go through the ritual of making Greek coffee, his tongue between his lips as he concentrated on getting just the right amount of coffee grounds. Then while the coffee was steeping, he took a box out of a drawer, found a plate, and arranged some sweetmeats on it.

As he poured the coffee he said, "This briki was the only thing I managed to bring with me from Smyrna." He tapped the battered copper. "We came through the fire together."

He put the briki down, and said, "I was holding this when I heard the Turks had shot my uncles."

Maria crossed herself, and she was about to speak, but Onassis continued. "I'm biased, but I think this makes the best coffee in the world." He pushed one of the tiny cups toward Maria.

She took a sip and nodded.

Onassis picked up one of the sugar-coated sweetmeats. "And you must try it with a piece of loukoumi. The contrast between the bitterness of the coffee and this melting sweetness is very . . ."

"Greek?" supplied Maria.

"Exactly." He put the sweetmeat in his mouth; chewed it; and then, noticing that his fingers were covered in sugar, he put them one by one in his mouth.

"But," he said, "it has to be eaten with care."

Gravely Maria took a piece, put it in her mouth, and, copying Onassis, she licked the excess sugar from her fingers.

"Great care," she said.

"But it's worth it, don't you think?" asked Onassis.

"I do," answered Maria.

They were silent for a moment, their eyes locked on each other.

"The briki belonged to my mother," said Onassis.

"Is she— Did she die in the massacre . . ." faltered Maria.

"No, she died of cancer when I was nine. After that my grandmother took over. She looked after me and my sisters, until the Turks came." His face darkened.

"That was a terrible time, Maria. I still have nightmares about it."

Maria crossed herself again, and she touched his hand in sympathy. "How old were you?"

"Fifteen. I was in the middle of doing my exams when they came. Suddenly everything I knew was gone."

Maria nodded in sympathy. "I have some idea of how that feels. My mother took me back to Athens from the States when I was thirteen. I was a little American girl. I hardly spoke Greek and I didn't want to leave my father. But she thought it would be better for my voice if I studied in Athens. That was nonsense—I could have gone to Juilliard which is the best conservatory in the world probably, but Mama wanted to be in control and she couldn't be in America as she didn't speak English. So we moved back in thirty-seven."

"Bad timing," said Onassis.

"The worst." Maria gave a bitter laugh. "We lived through so much— the Germans, the civil war—but the worst thing was that my mother never cared about me, only my voice. I kept thinking if I became famous she would love me as much as she loved my sister. And then one day, a week after my thirtieth birthday, I suddenly understood that whatever I did, it would never be enough."

Her eyes pricked with tears. They always came when she thought about her mother.

"And I haven't spoken to her since."

Onassis touched her hand, his eyes on hers. "We have both had to struggle, you and I. It's one of the things that makes you so interesting."

Maria was about to reply when she heard a step behind her and looked round to see her husband in his dressing gown, blinking like a baby owl. Maria stood up, moving away from Onassis.

Tita regarded her with reproach. "I have been looking for you everywhere, Maria. I can't find my seasickness pills."

Onassis looked surprised. "But the sea is perfectly calm."

Maria sighed as she took Tita's arm. "Poor Battista is not a good sailor. He feels every disturbance."

Onassis looked at her. "Then I hope we don't sail into choppy waters," and he grinned, his meaning unmistakable.

Later Maria lay in the dark and ran through her encounter with Onassis in her head. She knew that she was on the cusp of something but what it was exactly and how much she wanted it she didn't know. It felt strange to be with a man whose will was as strong if not stronger than her own, and she was not sure that she liked it. She remembered his smile as he dropped the necklace into the sea, and the image made her shiver.

IV

The boat had dropped anchor in the bay at Portofino early that morning, and the plan was for Tina to take a party onshore while Ari stayed behind to entertain Churchill.

Tina, the three Churchill women, and the Montague Brownes were standing on deck. Clemmie Churchill looked at her watch pointedly and, noticing this, Tina beckoned to one of the crew members. "Stavros, can you tell Madame Callas that we are ready to go."

When she heard the knock on the door, Maria was just looking at herself in the floral cruise pajamas and wondering if they really were the right outfit. But there was no time to change again so she grabbed her sunglasses and the straw bag that Alain had said was suitable for port expeditions and hurried to join the others.

As soon as she saw the party assembled on deck, Maria knew that she had made a mistake. Tina was wearing a stripy Breton top with pedal pushers, and the other women were all wearing cotton shirtwaist dresses in pastel colors, apart from sixteen-year-old Celia, who was wearing shorts. Maria, in her brightly colored floral pajamas, felt like an exotic tropical interloper in a cottage garden. She knew from the imperceptible flick of Tina's eyes and the glances exchanged between the Churchill women that they felt it too. Still, there was no going back, so she held her head high and walked toward the others as if she were Norma walking to her funeral pyre.

As the tender approached the port Tina spotted a small crowd waiting on the stone jetty.

"Oh, what a bore. It looks like we have a reception committee."

As the boat drew alongside, Maria could see a line of paparazzi and reporters clustering around the steps. The sailor, who leaped ashore to tie up the boat, had to bat the men out of the way.

Maria stood up. "Let me go first. Once they have their pictures of me, then perhaps they will leave the rest of you alone."

As she stepped onto the jetty she was surrounded by cries of, "This way, Madame Callas."

"Smile, Maria."

Maria stood and posed for a moment and then a voice asked, "Have you given up singing, Madame Callas?"

Maria turned round and snarled at them. "Will you just lay off. Can't you see I'm on holiday."

Lady Churchill, whose motto was "never complain, never explain," was visibly shocked by Maria's outburst, but she had to admit that the press did retreat when faced by her fury.

Maria sighed heavily. "They are the bane of my existence. I am sure you feel the same, Lady Churchill."

The other woman nodded noncommittally.

Tina and Maria led the way up the narrow winding street of medieval houses crammed with shops selling lace and trinkets designed to attract the well-heeled tourists who had been coming to this picturesque little port with multicolored houses nestling among green hills since the end of the nineteenth century.

In one of dark little lace shops, Tina, Maria, and Lady Churchill were admiring the ever more intricate pieces of lace being brought out by the perspiring shopkeeper.

Maria held up a lace mantilla and wrapped it round her head with a graceful gesture. "Such beautiful work."

"Did your husband not want to come ashore with us, Madame Callas," asked Lady Churchill, who found the lace a little too Roman Catholic for her taste.

"No, poor Tita is feeling unwell. He is not really a sailor."

"Then he is not going to enjoy this cruise, I'm afraid. The sea can be quite choppy in the Med. I hope you don't have to cut short your holiday."

Tina broke in. "I think you should definitely get the mantilla, Maria—so useful for visiting churches. And I am sure that Signor Meneghini will get his sea legs soon."

"Winston thinks it is all in the mind. He says that no sailor ever feels seasick when there is a gun pointed at them," said Lady Churchill.

Maria laughed. "I wonder if I brought my revolver." She turned to the shopkeeper and paid for the mantilla.

Tina ushered them out of the shop. "Aristo absolutely loves the sea. I think he would live on the boat all year round if he could," she said.

"I can see why—it's magnificent," said Maria.

"But even Aristo can't spend his whole time at sea. He must come back to earth eventually," Tina said, looking at Maria. There was an undertone that Maria caught. Was Tina giving her a warning?

That night the dinner was on deck. Tina placed Maria next to Churchill, and Aristo at the other end next to Clemmie.

Maria, who was wearing a red silk column gown with a matching chiffon wrap, made great use of the scarf as she set out to fascinate Churchill, using it to punctuate her conversation just as she did onstage.

Churchill had asked her something about wartime Athens and Maria was telling him a story that she felt must endear her to the statesman, who she sensed was not entirely aware of her significance.

"The RAF pilot spoke no Greek, and he had blond hair and blue eyes, like Mr. Montague Browne. He could not walk around the streets of Athens like that—the Italians would have picked him up at once—so we hid him in our apartment in Patission Street. We dyed his hair brown and stained his skin with walnut juice and pretended he was our cousin Stavros, who had come from the Peloponnese, while we waited for the NKD, the Resistance, to arrange his escape. Unfortunately, not everyone in those days was on the side of the British and one of our neighbors betrayed us." Maria made a dramatic gesture with her hand, bringing it down on the table, which made the cutlery rattle and roused Churchill from his torpor sufficiently to make him drain his glass of champagne and call for another one.

"There was a knock on the door, a hammering, and I knew that the enemy was on the other side. We were in mortal danger. The price of harboring the enemy was death." Maria's eyes opened wide. "But I would not give Jimmy up. I had to think of something that would give him enough time to escape through the window and climb onto the roof; from there he might be able to find his way to one of the Resistance safe houses. I wanted to give him a chance."

By now the whole table had gone silent, and Maria was giving a full performance.

"So I tell my mother, who was shaking with fear, to answer the door. And there on the threshold were five Italian soldiers with guns, looking for Jimmy. I had to act quickly. I wonder if you can guess what I did?"

Her eyes swept the table.

"Remember that in those days I was just a plump teenager with glasses and spots, not glamorous like my sister, Jackie. I knew that they would not be interested in me as a woman. So I sat down at the piano, and I started to sing."

Maria paused and then, seeing the whole table was listening, she opened her mouth and sang the first lines of Tosca's great aria, "Vissi d'arte, vissi d'amore," at full volume.

The stewards, who were coming in to serve the main course, stopped dead.

The notes hung in the air as the whole table wondered if she would continue, and then Maria smiled. "My audience was enemy soldiers, but they were also Italians and they had opera in their souls. When I started to sing, they stood motionless until I had finished, and, because of Jimmy, I can tell you that I did not hurry. And when they finally came to their senses and searched the apartment, Jimmy had escaped. As they left, they thanked me for the music and the captain came back the next day with a packet of spaghetti for my mother."

Maria put her hand on Sir Winston's arm. "So you see, Sir Winston, in my small way I was part of your great victory."

The entire table was silent. And then Onassis started to clap. "What a heroine you are, Maria, offstage and on."

Maria lowered her gaze as if taking a curtain call.

"Don't you agree, Sir Winston?" Ari looked over at the statesman, who was emptying his champagne glass.

Churchill lifted his empty glass to Maria. "On behalf of the RAF, I must thank you for your service, Madame Callas. What a pity you weren't at Dunkirk."

Polite laughter rippled around the table.

Tina opened her blue eyes wide and said in her high, clear voice, "What an amazing story, Maria. It sounds like a scene from one of those operas where impossible things keep happening, but nobody seems to notice."

Her smile was warm, but Maria heard the skeptical undertone and bristled. It was true that she had made the story a little neater for dramatic effect, but that was all. They *had* sheltered a young British airman called Jimmy in their flat on Patission Street. He had a crush on Jackie, of course, but he knew enough about music to know that Maria was the talented one. He told her that when the war was over he would come and hear her sing in Covent Garden. But he had been killed a few months after his escape, a fact that she had not included in her story as it spoiled the ending. And when the soldiers came looking for Jimmy, he had already been gone for days. She had sung for them, but it had not been her idea. Litza had been the one to suggest that she might like to sing for their "guests." Maria had been reluctant, but her mother had made it impossible to refuse.

So she had sat down at the piano and had sung "Vissi d'arte," which had indeed brought tears to the eyes of the captain in charge of the search party. Later he had returned with a sausage and a packet of spaghetti, and Maria had sung for him again while her mother made dinner.

All she had done really was to compress the story into a more dramatic form, and Tina had no right to wrinkle her tiny little nose as if there was a bad smell.

Ari frowned at his wife and said, "Those were dramatic times during the war when strange things happened. Not all of us were lucky enough to spend those years at boarding school in America."

Tina's eyes were blue chips of ice, but she laughed merrily and said, "That is the remark of someone who has never been to a girl's boarding school. I think even Sir Winston would struggle to mediate between fifty feuding teenage girls."

Celia, Churchill's granddaughter, who had barely opened her mouth since she came on board, said in a loud, clear voice, "I quite agree. Girls my age are simply horrid. I would much rather drive a tank than be a prefect at my beastly school."

Her mother and grandmother looked at her in astonishment, but her grandfather chuckled. "Quite right too. I always say that my education was only interrupted by my schooling."

There was general laughter at this, and the moment of tension was forgotten. But Maria knew that a line had been crossed, that whatever there was between her and Ari was no longer their secret. She looked down the table to see how her husband had reacted, but he wore his usual expression of incomprehension. Maria wondered how it was possible that she could speak four languages fluently and her husband could barely parse a sentence in English. She could see that the other guests were not happy to sit next to him, and she wondered what it would be like to have a husband who was as socially adept as Onassis.

v

The *Christina* was on course for Greece via the Strait of Messina. Onassis decided not to stop in Genoa but to press on until they got to Capri and the Amalfi Coast.

That afternoon as they hugged the Tuscan shore, the passengers were gathered around the swimming pool. Tina was wearing a turquoise bikini that was chosen to set off her tan and immaculate figure. Lady Churchill was doing a stately breaststroke in the pool; Diana was asleep on a lounger; and Celia was languishing in the shade, clearly mortified by having to wear what looked like her regulation school swimsuit.

Maria, who remembered the agonies of adolescence, took pity on her. "Celia, I have brought too many bathing suits, and I wonder if any of them might fit you."

The girl looked up at her in surprise. "But . . . I mean, that's awfully kind, but wouldn't they be too grown-up?"

Maria smiled. "How old are you? Sixteen? That sounds quite grown-up to me."

Celia went with Maria apprehensively; she found the singer rather alarming. But she forgot her fear when she saw the amazing array of swimwear that Maria was inviting her to choose from. Maria urged her to try on a green bathing suit with a halter neckline and a bikini in blue-and-white polka dots. Celia put them on in Maria's bathroom and was amazed at how flattering they were. She had always been rather bashful about her breasts, but the swimsuit made her look as though breasts were meant to be displayed, not hidden.

"Can I see?" Maria's voice came through the door. Celia came out and shyly turned around in front of her.

"Well, that's much better. You don't want to cover up that lovely figure. God, what I would have given to have had a body like yours when I was your age."

Celia looked puzzled. "But you have a very good figure, Madame Callas."

"Now, yes, but I wasn't born with one. I had to work at it."

Celia was surprised. "That must have been awfully hard. Doesn't singing make you really hungry? I know I am always starving after choir at school, and when we did the *Pirates of Penzance*, I lived on cream buns."

Maria laughed. "Yes, it was awfully hard, but I wanted to look right."

Celia looked around the cabin and saw Alain's sketches of the cruise outfits that were taped to the dressing table mirror.

"Oh, how glamorous. I wish Mummy had something like this. She has very nice clothes, but she always gets something wrong somehow, like the wrong belt or funny shoes."

Maria, thinking of Diana Sandys's clothes, mentally agreed, but said, "Everyone knows that your mother is the daughter of Winston Churchill. They do not expect her to be a fashion plate. But when you are Maria Callas, the whole world expects you to look the part."

Maria sighed and Celia wondered whether she was meant to feel sorry for her.

When they went back on deck, Tina was the first to notice the swimsuit.

"That color looks terrific on you, Celia."

"Madame Callas gave it to me."

"You should have asked me—I have hundreds of bathing suits."

Celia could tell that Tina was annoyed.

Maria took off her caftan to reveal a white bikini. She lay down on her sun bed and called to Meneghini, "Tita, darling, can you come and do my back?"

Her husband, who had been sipping ginger tea in the shade, obediently went to where Maria was lying and poured out some of the bronzing oil she used onto her back, and started to rub it in.

Onassis, who had been talking to Churchill under the awning, came out on deck and stood watching Tita oil Maria's body and then her legs. Throwing the end of his cigar overboard, he started to take off his Hawaiian shirt. As he undid the buttons Maria's eyes widened. She had never seen such a hairy chest before, even in Greece. Ari caught her glance and he smiled.

"Are you coming in?"

Maria shook her head. "Not yet. I need to warm up first. Tita and I are battling over the air-conditioning. If there is one thing that sopranos hate more than other sopranos, it's air-conditioning."

Ari jumped into the water with a loud splash. "The water's lovely."

But before Maria could move, Tina was up on the diving board and executed a perfect swan dive into the pool, narrowly missing her husband.

☞

That evening Tina spoke to her husband as they were getting ready for dinner.

"I was thinking, Ari, that it might be nice to ask Reinaldo to join us in Naples. He is such good company, and we are a man down, not to mention Signor Meneghini being such a washout. Reinaldo would flirt with the little Churchill girl and be charming to her mother, and of course he would amuse me."

She looked at Ari, her little mouth pouting adorably.

But her husband shook his head. "No, Tina, not while the Churchills are on board. I don't want to embarrass them."

Ari was standing in his boxer shorts, looking at himself in the mirror as he decided which shirt to wear. He sucked in his stomach and threw back his shoulders.

Tina's retort was icy. "Don't you think you have done that already?"

Ari tore himself away from the mirror. "What are you talking about?"

"The way you behave around the great diva. But I suppose I should be grateful: at least she isn't one of my friends."

Tina had not been happy to come home to their estate on Long Island to find her friend Jeannie Rhinelander with her head between her husband's legs. She knew that Aristo had other women, and as she no longer found him sexually attractive, she didn't much care, but she did not want to be publicly embarrassed. Part of the advantage of the boat was that it was the place, until now, where Ari could be trusted to behave.

"Tina, you are being ridiculous. Maria and I have a lot in common. We are the only two people on this boat who started with nothing and have made something of ourselves."

"You think you have more in common with the warbler than with Churchill?" said Tina, opening her eyes wide.

"Sir Winston is the grandson of a duke. He was born an aristocrat. Your father is one of the biggest shipowners in Greece; even the Montague Brownes went to the right schools and know the best people; but Maria and I didn't have any of that. We had to make it on our own. So I enjoy her company."

Tina sighed. "Well, you are the only one who does, Ari. That story she told the other night about saving the airman as if she were some Resistance heroine was quite absurd. Everyone thought so."

Aristo picked up a white shirt and started to put it on. "I enjoy the fact that she has more to talk about than gossip and shopping. But let's not fight, Tina."

"Only if I can invite Reinaldo."

Onassis shrugged. "If you are discreet about it. I don't want the press to pick it up. These things are damaging to my reputation."

Tina looked sullen.

"And I can assure you that absolutely nothing untoward has happened between me and Maria."

"Oh, dear. Perhaps you are losing your touch. Or has your little problem come back?"

Ari ignored this and started tying a printed silk ascot round his neck.

"But I expect Maria's used to it. I can't believe her husband has much to offer in that department."

"Don't be spiteful, Tina. It will give you wrinkles," said Ari as he tucked a handkerchief in his pocket and went to the door.

On the deck below, Meneghini had been having a miserable afternoon. There was quite a swell now, and he was wretched. Now he longed more than anything to go back to Milan. He suggested to Maria that they leave the cruise when the boat docked at Naples.

Maria did not agree. "Tina Onassis would never forgive us for deserting her party. It would be incredibly rude."

Meneghini looked at her from where he was lying on the bed. "I am sure that she will understand that I am unwell."

"But I don't want to leave. It's not *my* fault that you are such a bad sailor."

Maria pulled up the zip of her dress with a sharp, angry tug.

Tita picked up the score of *Poliuto* that was lying on the bedside table. "Have you even looked at this, Maria? You are meant to be singing a new role in a few months. Is staying on this boat really more important than your next performance?"

Maria's hand shook as she painted on her eyeliner, and she had to wipe it off and start again.

"I am entitled to a holiday, Tita. I can't work all the time."

He stood behind her and put a hand on her shoulder, stroking her collarbone with his finger.

"Maria, *mia carissima*, you must cherish your voice while it is still here."

"Don't you think I know that?" Maria snapped.

"I am just trying to protect you. Have you forgotten what happened in Rome?"

Maria looked at him in the mirror.

"Just give me one more week, Battista, that's all I want."

At dinner Maria made her way to her usual place next to Churchill, but Aristo caught her arm before she could sit down.

"Tonight I am going to be selfish and have you all to myself with no other gentlemen to distract you," he said.

Maria saw Celia hovering at the end of the table and called to her to come and sit down next to her. Onassis would not have it all his own way.

She leaned over to Celia. "I want to hear all about your horrible school."

Celia blushed. "It's not so bad really. But there are lots of stupid rules, like having to wear a hat every time we go into the village. I think it's to make us look so hideous that we won't meet any boys."

Aristo leaned over. "And does it work?"

Celia blushed again.

Maria tapped his hand crossly. "Don't embarrass the poor girl. I am sure she has many admirers, with or without the hat."

Celia looked down at her plate.

"But you should be careful. How old are you? Sixteen? I married Tina when she was seventeen."

"Oh, I don't want to get married yet, Mr. Onassis."

Aristo finished his drink. He was getting bored with this conversation. "But why not? Every woman wants to marry a good provider who will look after her and the children."

Maria looked at him in surprise. "Do you really think that is all women want?"

Onassis shrugged. "Pretty much. But I admit there may be some exceptions." He looked directly at Maria.

Maria felt uncomfortable under that gaze; she wanted what he seemed to be offering, but she was also terrified. She decided to retreat.

"This cruise has been so delightful, but I worry that I am becoming something of a lotus-eater."

She saw a glimpse of gold as he smiled. "Why would you be afraid of that?"

"Well, I am singing in a new production soon and I really should go home to prepare."

Onassis leaned closer. "You know that the lotus-eaters were most likely eating opium? They were perfectly content in the present. But here you are, worrying about your next performance. It seems to me you need to eat more lotus, not less. But if you feel you really must go back, then I will arrange for one of my planes to take you anywhere you want."

Maria nodded and was about to reply when Onassis continued. "Yet I hope you will stay until we reach Asia Minor. I would like very much to show you Smyrna where I grew up, and then we are making a stop in Istanbul. The patriarch, the Orthodox pope, is an old friend and I promised him that I would bring you to his church for a blessing on your name day, which is on the fifteenth I think, the feast of the Blessed Mary."

Maria looked surprised. "You know my name day?"

Onassis shrugged. "I am Greek Orthodox too. We grew up with the same calendar. And that is why I know that you can't refuse, not if you want to go to heaven."

Maria crossed herself. "But my life will be hell on earth if I am not prepared when I go to the Met. My public is not forgiving."

Onassis gestured to the sea, which was Homerically wine-dark. "Do you know where we are right now?"

Maria shook her head.

"We are entering the Strait of Messina between the toe of Italy and the island of Sicily. On the Sicilian side, there is a whirlpool and on the Italian side—hidden rocks. Our ancestors called the rocks Scylla and the whirlpool Charybdis. Odysseus had to make a hard choice as he made his way through the strait. Which was the greater evil—the man-eating monster living in the rocks, or the whirlpool that destroyed everything it touched? You will have to plot your course very carefully, Maria."

He signaled to the waiter to fill everyone's glasses with champagne.

"To Scylla and Charybdis!"

Maria raised her glass. "But which are you, Aristo?"

Aristo shrugged and drained his champagne glass.

Maria hardly slept at all that night.

She should leave, of course she should, but if she did, it would mean ending the possibility that Onassis represented. She could go back to Milan and her rehearsal room, and tend to her talent, the tyrant that had ruled her for so long.

Or she could stay on board and find out what it was like to be kissed by a man who made the hairs on her arms stand up every time he touched her. She did not dare think further than a kiss; the sight of the hair on his chest by the swimming pool had been disturbing. It had been so long since she had seen another man's naked body. It had been so long since she had taken off her clothes in front of anyone but Meneghini's indifferent gaze. She bit her lip as she imagined being naked in front of Onassis. The thought of it made her twitch with desire. There was a week until her name day, a week to feel like this, a week to pretend that there was nothing else in the world but what was here right now. A week to be a lotus-eater.

VI

The *Christina* wound its way through the Greek islands and the Dardanelles to reach Izmir in Turkey (formerly Smyrna), where Onassis had been born and lived till he was sixteen.

That night Onassis recounted the story of how the Turks had massacred the Greeks of Smyrna in 1922.

"In those days, the town was a mixture of Greeks, Armenians, Turks, and Jews. My father, Socrates, was a merchant who was on very friendly terms with the Turkish community. My grandmother Gethsemane spoke only Turkish because her family had been in Asia Minor for so many generations. Even her Bible was in Turkish. There were more Greeks living in Smyrna then than in Athens.

"But the Greek army had been active in Asia Minor and my father heard from the American consul that the Turks were planning to retaliate by attacking Smyrna. He sent the women in my family—my stepmother, my sisters—away to Lesbos with gold sovereigns sewn into their underwear."

Onassis looked around the table. Everyone was listening intently except Tina who looked out to sea, as if she had heard this story many times before.

"The Turkish cavalry came the next day. They made the men kneel in the square and they took their scimitars and went like this"—Onassis made a dramatic gesture with his hand and Maria shuddered.

"I was on an errand for my father and I was trying to get home when I saw a Muslim mob enter the cathedral and set upon the Metropolitan Chrysostomos. They gouged out his eyeballs and then they cut off his nose, his ears, and finally his hands."

Aristo looked down at his own hands.

In the pause that followed Tina protested, "Really, Aristo, it's been a long day. Perhaps you should save the gruesome details for tomorrow. You don't want to give everybody nightmares."

Onassis looked up, his hooded brown eyes liquid. "Maybe you're right, Tina. I have lived with this horror for so long that sometimes I forget what it must sound like. To see this man of God cut to pieces is something I shall never forget."

The table was silent until Maria asked, "What happened to your father?"

"The Turks took him away to a camp. But he was luckier than my uncles. They were hanged in the main square and my aunt Maria, her husband, and their little girl took shelter in a church that the Turkish soldiers set alight." He stopped, looking out over the sea for a moment before continuing.

"I managed to convince the soldiers that I was too young to fight and to let me stay in our villa that they had requisitioned. They tolerated me because I could find them things like cigars and alcohol."

Onassis looked at Maria. "I find in life that if you make things comfortable for people, they will like you."

Tina yawned. "Well, right now I think everyone will like you a lot more if you let them go to bed, Ari."


## VII

Onassis looked uncharacteristically ill at ease as the tender drew up alongside the quay.

"This is the first time I have been here to Smyrna, since I left in 1922," he announced.

The cars were waiting for them. Onassis took the Churchills in the first car, and Tina took Maria and the Montague Brownes in the second. The tour started with the colonnaded white building where the young Onassis had gone to school.

"I was not the hardest worker in the class, but I was the most popular because I could always get hold of cigarettes."

Churchill flourished his cigar. "You have always had a way with tobacco, dear boy."

From the school they went to the house where Onassis had grown up. The white paintwork was faded, and the green shutters were hanging off their hinges. But in the ironwork of the gates, the initials of Socrates Onassis still wound their way across the entrance arch.

Aristo jumped out of the car, eager to have a look at his old home, but when he saw his father's initials he stopped and was silent. Maria could see the pain in his face as he ran his fingers over the Greek letters sigma and omega.

Tina, who was wearing a pink gingham strapless sundress with white pumps and a bow in her blond hair, looked about her with bemusement. "Such a funny little house. I thought your father was a successful merchant, Aristo?"

Onassis ignored her and pushed the gate, but it was locked. He turned and looked at the view of the harbor.

"I used to play here every evening. My father and his friends would smoke hookahs, and we would rush up and down these steps pretending to be . . ." He stopped and Maria thought that there were tears in his eyes.

Churchill must have seen something too, because he put a hand on his friend's shoulder and said, "I'm sorry I never met Mr. Onassis Senior, but take it from an old man, I know that he would have been damn proud of you."

Onassis brushed his eyes with the back of his hand and smiled at Churchill.

"He would have been very glad to know that I was coming here in such distinguished company." Onassis was looking at Churchill as he said this, but Maria thought that he raised his eyes to look to hers, just for a second.

At that moment all she wanted was to run toward him and kiss away his tears. His sadness had made him real suddenly, not an invincible wizard who could produce anything in his kingdom with a click of his fingers but a man who needed solace.

"It used to be so beautiful here. We had a pomegranate tree and so many figs. My grandmother always said that the figs from this garden were the sweetest she had ever tasted."

He started to walk back to the car, the rest of the party following. Maria caught up with Aristo.

"What happened to your grandmother? Did she escape?"

Onassis turned around, his eyes dark. "She refused to leave with my sisters, but when the fires started, my father persuaded her to get on a boat going to Greece. But the crew was Turkish and when they saw that she had money, they tried to rob her. My *haj neh* fought back, she was not a coward, but the effort was too much for her and she had a heart attack. The other passengers, the Greek ones, tried to save her, but it was too late. When they got to Athens, she was dead. She is buried in the cemetery at Piraeus. I always visit her there when I am in town. I have to speak to her in Turkish though, because her Greek is very bad."

He gave her a smile quite unlike his usual wolfish grin. It was the expression of a little boy who is trying to be brave after being stung.

Nonie Montague Browne, who was standing nearby, said, "Your grandmother sounds like a redoubtable lady."

"She was. My sisters sometimes complain that they never got the chance to go to college and have a proper education. But I always say to them that they have a degree from the University of Gethsemane, which is the best kind of degree to have."

"It's true—there is nothing like a Greek grandmother," said Maria.

Tina appeared impatient to be back on the boat in time for lunch. Onassis said that he had one more stop to make, and that anyone who wanted to go back should go with his wife. Churchill was clearly dying for a rest and a drink, so he went back with Clemmie and the girls. Maria found herself sitting next to Onassis again, with the Montague Brownes in the back.

Onassis drove the car up a winding road to a hilltop where there was the dilapidated ruin of a Greek church and an equally tumbledown cemetery. Onassis looked about him, confused, trying to get his bearings, and then he walked to a spot in the northwest corner shaded by a cypress tree, where the weeds had been trimmed and the headstone stood unencumbered. In Greek letters, the stone read "Penelope Onassis, beloved wife of Socrates and mother of Aristotle and Artemis."

Onassis crossed himself. "Poor Mama. She was ill in bed for much of my childhood, and I used to like to sit on her bed and talk to her. She had a gentle voice and such a sweet smile. My grandmother was very stern, but Mother was always sympathetic. I was so upset when my father married again. I couldn't understand it. I was still missing my mother so much. But he couldn't live without a woman, and six months later he found himself a new wife. Now I understand, but then . . ."

He shook his head, and Maria said, "Parents forget that children have feelings too."

"Sometimes I think that her death was the reason for my success. There is no doubt that if she had lived, she would have spoiled me rotten, as the English say. I was the only boy and she adored me. If she had lived, perhaps it would have been too hard to leave her side and make my way in the world."

He shrugged and Maria said, "What would you rather have?"

Aristo turned to look at her. "What do you mean?"

"Your success or being spoiled by your mother."

Aristo smiled. "Oh, that's easy. We always want what we can't have." He looked out to sea.

"I would exchange everything, even the *Christina*, for one more evening lying on my mother's bed, listening to her stories, and feeling her stroking my hair."

Maria was silent. She was picturing Ari as a little dark-eyed boy gazing up at his mother.

"What about you, Maria?"

"What about me?"

"Is there anything you would rather have instead of all your fame and success?"

Maria sighed. "There was a time when all I wanted was for my mother to love me properly. I realized a few years ago that was never going to happen, but the wish still remains—to be loved as Maria, not as Callas."

Onassis looked at her searchingly. "But I have seen you perform. Don't tell you weren't happy when the audience was applauding. I was watching you and I thought you looked ecstatic."

Maria smiled. "You have to remember that I am an actress as well as a singer."

"And you have to remember that I know something about women. That wasn't acting!"

"Not entirely. There is enormous pleasure in knowing that you have accomplished the task of singing to the best of your ability and knowing that the audience understands that. After what happened in Rome, it was a relief to know that I could still perform to my own satisfaction. But I think that I would give all that up to have a mother like yours, who adored me just as I was."

The *Christina*'s horn blared out over the water, startling them, and making the Montague Brownes, who had retreated to a tactful distance, come out of the shade.

"Sound like it's time for lunch," said Anthony.

Nonie stepped forward with a small bunch of wildflowers that she had picked, and gave them to Ari. "I thought perhaps you might like these for your mother's grave."

Onassis looked surprised, but he took them and put them at the foot of the small tombstone and, kneeling down, he kissed the earth.

"Goodbye, Mama."

Then he sprang to his feet with an agility surprising in a man in his fifties and, taking Maria by the elbow, he shepherded his party back to the car.

On the way back to the quay, Onassis drove past a house with blue shutters set back from the road and shaded by pomegranate trees. He slowed down and pointing to it, he said, "That was Fahrie's, where I got my real education."

Maria looked puzzled, until Ari continued. "Fahrie's was the finest brothel in Smyrna. Oh, the smell of the women there. The noise their silk stockings made when they crossed their legs."

Ari smacked his lips.

"My father took me there on my fifteenth birthday. He said that it was time I understood how the world worked."

He looked over to Maria and Nonie. "Forgive me, ladies. I hope you are not shocked."

Nonie shook her head, but Maria said solemnly, "I shall pray for your immortal soul."

Onassis looked taken aback, but when he saw the glint in Maria's eye he said, "I remember one old Turkish whore telling me, 'You know, kid, in the end, one way or another, all ladies do it for the money.' As I said, it was an education."

VIII

When Maria woke up the next day, the first thing she saw as she looked out of the window was the unmistakable profile of the Hagia Sophia. In the night they had crossed the Sea of Marmara and sailed up the Golden Horn to moor on the European side of the ancient city. In the bay directly ahead of them was a small island with a spherical building that Onassis said was where the sultan's concubines who no longer pleased their master were left to die.

"Or sometimes if they had misbehaved they were sewn into a sack and tipped off the cliff just there."

Churchill nodded his approval. "There are a number of women and men whom I would happily put in a sack. One of the great disadvantages of not being a sultan."

Onassis grinned. "Life would be so much simpler," he said with a sigh, "but these days we have to be civilized."

He looked across at Maria. "Do you agree?"

She thought for a moment. "I can think of at least two people I would like to have sewn up in a sack."

"But could you push them over the cliff?" asked Onassis.

"Easily," said Maria. "I am Greek, after all."

Tina, who was listening to this conversation with barely concealed impatience, clapped her hands. "Well, I am just as Greek as both of you, and I have no desire to put anyone in a sack or push them over a cliff, so you can't use that as an excuse for your homicidal impulses."

Onassis laughed. "Tina, you have never spent more than five minutes in Greece, you don't like Greek food, and you speak Greek with an English accent."

Tina flushed, but then she recovered her poise. "And when I speak English, people say I have a Greek accent, and in French an Italian one. I will never be at home anywhere, it seems."

That morning Onassis drove Maria and the Churchills around Istanbul in the open-topped Fiat that he kept on board for sightseeing trips. There had been no press when they started out, but by the time they reached Hagia Sophia, photographers had started to gather. Maria sighed and prepared to smile and pose, but Onassis ignored them and swept his party inside.

They stood inside the vast space that had been a church, then a mosque, and was now a museum. Maria was fascinated by how the sound traveled around the cavernous interior. She heard the echo created by the footsteps around her and wondered for a moment what it would be like to sing there.

She slipped her glasses out of her bag so that she could get a sharper view of the dome. Onassis touched her elbow and when she turned round, he looked shocked for a moment. "I've never seen you in glasses before."

Maria didn't need her glasses to perceive that he preferred her without. "I can hardly see without them."

"Then it will be my pleasure to guide you."

Maria took the glasses off and put them back in her bag.

⸺

After Hagia Sophia, Onassis took them back to the boat, so that they could change before seeing the patriarch.

Maria put on a black linen dress and draped the black mantilla she had bought in Portofino around her head. The lace made her feel like Tosca in the scene where she goes to see her lover in church. She took a breath; she had been waiting for this moment. It was like stepping onstage to sing a new role for the first time.

Meneghini came in as she was wrapping the mantilla around her face, and she saw that he understood that she was preparing for a performance.

"How are you feeling?"

Meneghini had not come on the tour of Istanbul.

"Much better. I have been making some phone calls while you were out. San Francisco want you to do *Norma*, and Covent Garden are offering *Tosca*. Deutsche Grammophon want you to record an album of arias as soon as possible. It was a very good morning."

Maria turned round. "I hope you didn't make any firm commitments, Tita."

"I agreed to the recording date—they want it urgently so they can release it for Christmas."

"I don't think I want to make a record of arias."

Meneghini looked wary. "But why not? Everybody does them now, and they sell very well. You have such a broad repertoire; it will be easy for you to prepare eight or ten pieces."

Maria stared at him as if he were in the back row of the stalls. "I am not everybody, and I don't care to pander to an audience who can't be bothered to listen to a whole opera."

Meneghini sighed. "But they are a very big record company, the best, and I said that you would be happy to do it."

"Then you will have to tell them that you made a mistake."

Maria picked up her handbag and made for the door. Meneghini followed her.

Maria saw him behind her on the stairs and hissed in Italian, "What are you doing?"

"Coming with you. As it is obviously important to you, I would like to be there."

"But you won't understand a word!"

Meneghini gave a rueful smile. "I am used to that, Maria."

The party to see the patriarch consisted of Maria and Tita, Onassis and Tina, the Montague Brownes, and the *Christina*'s captain, Kostas Anastiades, and the first mate.

The boat took them from the *Christina* to the Fener pier, a short walk from the Patriarchate and the church of St. George.

As Maria walked into the church, she could not shake the feeling of walking onstage. The fact that she, Tina, and Nonie were wearing lace mantillas made it even more like a production. There was a hush in the church that seemed to her like the pause after the conductor picks up his baton before he sets the musicians going. She crossed herself in the Orthodox way, right to left, the way she always did when standing in the wings waiting to go on. She lit a candle in front of the icon of the Virgin and Child and prayed, as ever, for her voice to be strong. Meneghini stood behind her, looking at his surroundings as a tourist might at the end of a long and boring day. Maria could see that he had his cigarette case in his hand. She nudged him sharply and told him to put it away.

"But there is so much incense in here—no one would ever notice."

When they had finished in the church, one of the priests showed them into the patriarch's private sanctum, which was lined with cedar wood panelling and bejewelled by icons. Patriarch Athenagoras stood at the other end of the room. He was over six foot and had a long gray beard that reached to his waist. He was dressed in black robes, and on his head was the *kalimafki*, the tall headdress draped with a long black train. Maria gasped at the majesty of his presence. Unlike the pope, who at the audience she had with him seemed dwarfed by his vestments, the patriarch looked like the voice of God.

"Will Aristotle Onassis and Maria Callas please step forward so that they may be blessed." His voice was deep and resonant. A basso profundo, like the Commendatore in *Don Giovanni*.

Maria felt weak as she stepped forward to kneel beside Aristo. The patriarch placed his spade-like hands on their heads, and he began to intone in Greek, "Heavenly Father, please bless these two sinners who have brought great glory to their homeland. One is the finest singer of her time, the other is a modern Odysseus, the most famous mariner of the modern world."

As he spoke Maria felt his blessing flow through her as if he was pouring warm oil on her head. It spread from his fingers all the way down her body. She felt soft and relaxed as if her insides were melting. Perhaps this was the breath of the Holy Spirit. She glanced over to Onassis, and he moved his little finger so that it touched hers, and Maria felt completely at peace.

"Please bathe them in the glory of your love and protect them from harm. In the name of the Father."

As the priest intoned his prayers over the couple, Meneghini, who was standing at the back with Montague Browne, began to sweat. He pulled his handkerchief out of his pocket and wiped his forehead with it. "Do you understand anything?" he whispered to Montague Browne.

"I'm afraid it's all Greek to me, old boy," Anthony whispered back.

"It looks like a wedding," Meneghini said sadly.

Meneghini knew that Maria had always blamed him for the fact that she did not have a "proper" Orthodox wedding. Whatever was happening in front of him now, he knew could be easily confused with a wedding in Maria's mind. She was perfectly still, which Meneghini found ominous. He had seen that kind of stillness only onstage, when she was completely submerged in a character. But whom was she playing now?

That evening Maria wore the most glamorous dress in her wardrobe, a black chiffon column that left one shoulder bare. Her only jewelry was a pair of emerald earrings that she had bought for herself in Milan.

Peering in the mirror, Maria did not feel the usual disappointment at how far her reflection was from the image in her head. She didn't want to look like the petite Tina with her perky nose and tiny frame; Tina would never look like a goddess.

As Maria went into the dining room, she saw that Ari, for a change, was wearing a dinner jacket, a white one that made his skin look very brown and his teeth very white. He beckoned to her to come and sit between him and Churchill.

"What a magnificent dress," he said as the waiter pulled out Maria's chair. "Don't you think, Sir Winston?"

Churchill looked at Maria gravely. "I am no expert on women's clothing, but the general effect is very striking. In fact, you look as if you're about to perform. Does that mean you are going to sing later?" he said.

"If you would like me to, Sir Winston, I would be honored."

Churchill put up his hands in protest. "Oh, I wouldn't dream of asking you, dear lady."

"Tonight we are going to watch *City Lights* after dinner," Tina said sharply from the other end of the table.

"I know it is one of your favorites," added Onassis.

"Yes, indeed. Do you know that I actually visited the set when he was making that film?" Churchill proceeded to tell an anecdote about his time in Hollywood that everyone listened to reverently.

There was caviar that night, but Maria found that she could not eat more than a mouthful. Onassis looked at her in surprise. "What has happened to your appetite, Maria? I ordered the caviar especially for you as it is your name day."

Maria shook her head. "I have seen and heard so much today. I think I am too full of experience."

Onassis muttered in Greek, "With no room for anything more?"

Maria looked at him, her lips parted. Since the blessing all her defenses had crumbled. She knew now why Norma had betrayed her people for a man, why Tosca had murdered Scarpia, why Violetta had chosen to die in poverty. They had been possessed by a feeling that so far she had only been able to imagine.

Onassis saw the look on her face and understood. Deftly he put his hand on her leg and stroked the inside of her thigh through the thin material of her dress. Maria knew how to keep her face impassive, but the touch of his fingers made her shudder.

She forced herself to bring her attention back to Churchill, who was still talking about Chaplin, but his words kept fading in and out as Onassis's fingers moved up her leg.

The dinner seemed to last forever, though Tina was very strict about keeping meals at no more than an hour. Maria ate almost nothing but found herself gulping down the cold champagne. At the end of the meal, the waiter brought in an ice cream cake and put it in front of Maria.

"For your name day, Maria. I know how much you like ice cream," Onassis said.

Maria did not trust herself to speak. Onassis handed her the knife.

"Quick! Cut it before it melts."

"You should make a wish," said Celia, who was eyeing the cake with interest.

Maria closed her eyes, and for the first time in her life her wish was nothing to do with her voice.

"There." She opened her eyes, and started to cut the cake.

All the ladies refused it except Celia.

Churchill accepted his slice but made no move to taste it. Maria could see the confection melting on his plate and she took a spoonful and held it up to his mouth.

"Oh, you really must try it, Sir Winston." Obediently Churchill opened his mouth and Maria fed him the ice cream cake until it had all gone.

"I can never resist a woman with a spoon," said Churchill when she had finished. "Reminds me of my first love, Nanny Everest."

⸗

When Maria got to the cinema, all the seats in the front row were taken. Onassis was sitting between his wife and Churchill. Maria went to sit in the row behind with Celia. Meneghini had gone to bed.

Afterward she wouldn't have been able to recount a single detail of the film: she was too busy looking at the back of Onassis's head to have any interest in Chaplin. At one point he put his arm on the back of Tina's seat and Maria thought for one awful moment that his hand was going to land on his wife's shoulder. But it remained on the chair.

The focus of Onassis's attention was Churchill; he was vigilant about filling up his glass and bringing out more cigars. As the lights went up at the end of the film, Churchill could be heard weeping. Clemmie put her hand on his shoulder.

"What would Nanny Everest say, crying your eyes out over a film. Come on, Winnie, let's get you to bed."

The Churchills accompanied by Onassis and Tina moved toward the staterooms.

Maria looked at the Montague Brownes. "I think I need some air."

"It was a bit sickly, wasn't it," said Anthony, "but the boss adores it. I expect we will get *Henry V* tomorrow—very keen on 'Once more unto the breach' is the boss."

Maria looked at him vaguely. As *Henry V* had never been made into an opera, she had very little idea what he was talking about.

She went to stand on the deck and looked out over the water. She could hear the call of the muezzin across the water and the tinkle of the bells on the local fishing boats and the occasional deep note of the ferry sirens as they went from one side of the Bosphorus to the other. It was a soundtrack of sorts, an overture to the drama ahead. She was alone on the stage, waiting for the man who she knew now would become her lover. Where was the music for that? From a radio in the staff quarters there was a burst of Greek folk song that was quickly silenced.

To keep herself from shaking she began to hum "Vissi d'arte," allowing the musical memory to flood through her. Maria's hum was louder than most, so she did not hear the footsteps behind her; it was only when she felt the breath on the back of her neck that she knew he had come for her. Turning around, she could see the gleam of his teeth.

"I've been waiting for this for so long." He put his finger to her lips and traced their outline, then he ran his hand down her throat past her collarbones to the space between her breasts.

"Not just tonight but all my life, Maria," Onassis said as he kissed the tops of her breasts. He looked up at her. "Plato says that originally we were all two halves of a perfect whole, but then the whole was divided and we were spun off as imperfect beings, constantly looking for our other half to feel complete."

He put his other hand on the small of her back and pulled her to him.

"You are my other half, Maria, and I have been looking for you all my life."

He kissed her with his surprisingly soft lips, gently at first and then harder as they both strained against each other. He slipped his fingers down the front of her dress and flicked her nipples, and then, pulling the dress aside, he put them one by one in his mouth. Maria squirmed with pleasure, but then a sudden noise made her start.

"Ari, you must stop. Someone will see us."

Ari smiled. "I know just the place."

He took her hand and walked along the deck to where the lifeboat was hanging in its cradle. He climbed up into it, and then he held out his hand to Maria.

"Come here."

His hands were warm and dry as he undid the zipper of her dress and let it fall to the bottom of the boat. Maria felt as if she were on fire. Reflexively she crossed her hands across her breasts, but he took her arms away gently and said, "Please. Let me look at you, Maria."

And then he put a tarpaulin on the bottom of the boat and made her lie down as he stroked her all over, kissing her toes, her fingertips, her nipples, her navel, the inside of her thighs, and finally her sex itself.

"Oh, Maria, you taste of caviar," he said as he parted her legs and began to flick her with his tongue. Maria tensed, this was something that had never happened before, but Ari took her hand and stroked it.

"Trust me, Maria, I know what I am doing."

Maria closed her eyes, and soon she forgot that she was lying in a lifeboat in the middle of the Bosphorus. She forgot about everything but the sensations that were flooding through her body; she felt as if she was about to sing the highest note she had ever sung, her body shaking with the effort and then suddenly it was over, her body relaxed and she was shuddering with pleasure.

She looked at Ari in wonder. How had he made that happen? He saw the expression on her face and grinned. "Was that your first time?" Maria nodded.

"I am honored," and he kissed her mouth and began to push inside her, and she clung to him with her long fingers digging into his back, pulling him deeper and deeper.

Afterward as they lay in the bottom of the lifeboat looking at the stars, Maria found herself smiling. Ari stroked her cheek. "What are you smiling about?"

"You, of course. I was thinking that I have spent half my life being possessed by passion onstage, but I never understood what it meant in real life."

"Because you were waiting for me, Maria."

He kissed her again, and then he sat up and started fumbling in the pile of clothes in the corner of the boat. Turning around, he dropped something small and shining between Maria's breasts.

"This is for you, *agapi mou*."

Maria picked it up and peered at it in the dim light; it was a bracelet with letters FMWLA picked out in diamonds. There was something familiar about it.

"For Maria with love Ari," he said, kissing her again.

Maria put it around her wrist, and then she remembered the bracelet that Tina had been wearing on the first day. An unwelcome thought struck her. "When did you have this made?"

Ari smiled down at her. "Do you really want to know?"

"Yes."

"After we went to Torcello and ate caviar. I have been carrying it around with me ever since."

Maria gasped. "But how could you be so sure?"

"Because, Maria, you may be the greatest singer in the world, but you are still a woman. And I knew that day that fate had meant us to be together like this."

She felt the heat in his gaze, but she pulled away in protest. "But I didn't know, not even when I decided to come on the cruise. It was only today when we knelt in front of the patriarch that I knew."

Ari laughed. "And who made that happen, Maria? Perhaps I know you better that you know yourself."

Maria buried her face in the hair on his chest, alive with a mixture of joy and doubt.

He began to kiss her again, his hand sliding across her breasts and down her belly to between her legs and very soon her doubts were forgotten as she realized she had no choice but to surrender.

"I've never felt like this before."

"Because you weren't with me, *agapi mou.*"

Maria realized that since they had been in the lifeboat, they had been speaking Greek.

"I feel like I have come home."

"That's because we come from the same place."

IX

She didn't appear until lunchtime the next day. Her radiant smile and the fact that she and Onassis were careful not look at each other made the union between them as obvious as if she had been wearing a scarlet *A* on her forehead.

Tina picked up the scent at once. After lunch she made a point of sitting next to Maria on the long sofa under the awning.

"What a charming bracelet. I believe I have one just like it."

Maria looked back at her defiantly.

Tina continued. "Of course, you have no idea how much these trinkets cost."

"I am not in the habit of asking the price of gifts."

Tina raised an eyebrow at the vehemence of Maria's tone. "Pity. Because you might decide the price is a little too high even for you."

"I don't know what you are talking about."

Tina smiled her well-bred smile. "Not yet, perhaps, but you will. You don't imagine that you and I are the only two women with bracelets like these? Ari must have some jeweler somewhere churning them out. I don't really care anymore—Ari can have as many women as he likes, so long as he doesn't humiliate me and remembers that I am his wife."

Maria looked at her with contempt. "From what I understand you are not exactly blameless yourself."

"Why do you think that I allowed Ari to invite you and your poor sap of a husband? As soon as we dock in Monte Carlo, Reinaldo is coming with us and some of my friends to Venice. And I can tell you that Reinaldo is much better company than Aristo"—she paused significantly—"in every way."

Maria stood up, but Tina caught her hand and made her sit down again. "I don't like you very much, Maria, and I am sure you feel the same about me, but I want to give you a word of advice. Ari can make you think that you are the most important person in the world. He will convince you that he is the only man who understands you. But as soon as the shine wears off, he gets bored and looks for something else. To put it in terms you will understand, Maria: Aristo is not Alfredo in *La traviata*, who swears undying love and means it. No, my husband is like the duke in *Rigoletto* who makes every woman think that they are his one true love."

Tina stood up to deliver her parting shot. "Remember, Aristo is Greek. The two things he cares about most are family and money. Whatever you think is going to happen, just remember that."

She walked off, not a hair out of place, her smile wide and welcoming as if she were hosting a reception for the queen of Romania.

Maria looked over to where Onassis was talking to Churchill and felt a glow of warmth steal over her. Tina's words had simply bounced off the cocoon that surrounded her. She had never felt happier, not even after her first standing ovation at La Scala. Tina was bound to be jealous even if she did have her own lover. Of course, Ari had other women, he was Greek after all, but then he had never met his other half. Until now. Maria knew that she was not some conquest, she was his equal: a Greek of humble origins who had made herself into a world-famous star but who, underneath, was like him—a simple soul.

She caught Aristo's eye for a moment. She could feel that he was as keenly aware of her presence as he was of hers. Crossing her legs, she wondered when they would be alone together. Now that he had touched her right at the core of her being, she couldn't wait for him to do it again.

Her reverie was interrupted by Celia, who wanted a makeup lesson. Maria spent an enjoyable half hour showing Celia how to angle the brush so that the line of black along her eyelid would end in a sharp point.

Celia did both eyes to her satisfaction and then turned to Maria and said, "Do you think it suits me?"

"Very much."

"Do you think it makes me look grown-up?"

"Definitely. But is there a reason why you want to look grown-up?"

Celia blushed. "Takis—you know, the little boy Alexander's tutor—has been teaching me how to water-ski and I really like him."

Maria nodded.

"But he thinks I am just a child, so I thought I would show him that I am quite grown-up really. Every time he looks at me, I feel like I am going to melt."

"Do you know lots of boys at home, Celia?"

"I suppose so, cousins and things, but they are all so English. None of them is like Takis."

Maria smiled. "Boys become men early in Greece. But be careful that he doesn't take any liberties."

"But that's exactly what I want him to do—take liberties."

Maria made a disapproving face. "I don't think your mother would approve."

"I don't care. I want to be like you, Madame Callas. Someone who does whatever they want and doesn't give a damn what other people think."

Maria looked at her in surprise. "What makes you think that I am like that?"

Celia replied earnestly, "But that's what everybody says about you, Madame Callas, that you always do whatever you want and you don't let anyone get in your way."

Maria shook her head. "And what do you think of me, Celia?"

Celia bent down and kissed her on the cheek. "I think you are the only person on this boat who notices that I exist."

⊐

That night they met by the lifeboat again. This time he was inside her at once, and she wrapped herself around him as if she would never let him go. He put everything else out of her head—all she could think of was his body against hers taking her to a new place.

Later when Ari lit a cigarette, she took it from him and put it to her lips.

"But you don't smoke," he said.

"It's different when it's your cigarette," she replied, inhaling the smoke and having to use all the muscles in her throat to stop herself coughing.

"Here, give it back to me—you shouldn't be smoking."

"I shouldn't be lying here with you, but here I am. You know, don't you, that this is the first time I have been unfaithful?"

"I am flattered," said Onassis, turning his head so that the smoke wouldn't blow in her face.

"I am surprised I don't feel guilty. But we didn't have an Orthodox wedding, so I suppose you could say that we were never married."

"And the patriarch did give us his blessing," said Onassis, smiling.

She kissed him. A few minutes later she said, "Tina knows about us. She told me this afternoon that you would play with me and then discard me for someone new."

Onassis laughed. "Tina is jealous because you are Maria Callas. Don't take any notice."

"I would have respected her more if she had scratched my eyes out."

"They don't teach that at Swiss finishing schools."

He leaned over her and looked into her eyes. "Has your husband said anything?"

Maria shook her head.

"Only one more day. And then, we will find somewhere more comfortable." He gestured at the lifeboat.

"You don't find this comfortable?" Maria said indignantly. "You are lying on the twentieth century's most important opera singer."

"I was thinking of you, *agapi mou.*" He stroked her hair. "I want to be like Odysseus and build you a bed around an olive tree, as he did for Penelope."

Maria closed her eyes in pleasure. "Where would you build it?"

"On one of the islands, maybe even Ithaka itself. Have you ever been there? It's very beautiful. Maybe I will buy it and we can eat spanakopita every night."

"Can I have a piano on the island?"

"Only if you promise to sing Greek songs."

"I shall learn some specially for you."

"I shall expect perfection."

"And you will have it."


x


The *Christina* reached Monte Carlo in the small hours. Maria and Tita left the boat at dawn. Maria decided to skip the goodbyes. But she left a note for Celia along with eyeliner, lipsticks, and powder. The note read: "Never forget how beautiful you are, with love from Maria Callas."

When the fifteen pieces of luggage had been loaded and they were in the back seat of the car that was taking them to Nice airport, Maria took a deep breath and told Tita that their marriage was over.

"When we get to Milan, you can go to the villa and I will stay in town."

Tita began to cry, big hiccupping sobs.

"And I no longer want you to manage me. I will make my own arrangements from now on."

Tita's tears stopped abruptly. "I am your husband, Maria. You can't just toss me aside."

Maria looked at Tita's pasty face and his trembling lip. "But I don't want to live with you anymore."

Tita tried to take her hand, but she wrenched it away.

"We should never have gone on that cruise. That . . . man has turned your head. But you should remember who made you, Maria. Do you really think that you would have any of this"—he gestured at the pile of monogrammed luggage—"if I hadn't supported you?"

Maria looked at him coldly. "Without me, you would still be making bricks and living with your mother."

The car pulled up outside the airport, and Maria could see that the photographers were waiting. She checked her reflection in the mirror of her compact and then she turned to Meneghini.

"It would be better if I went out alone. It will give you time to compose yourself."

Maria got out of the car and smiled politely at the waiting press.

"Madame Callas!"

"Maria!"

"Is it true that Mr. Onassis is going to build an opera house in Monte Carlo for you?"

She turned to the reporter. "I have no idea."

"Are you going to give up singing for a career in movies?"

"Did you sing 'God Save the Queen' for Sir Winston?"

"Are the rumors about you and Sir Winston true?"

Maria laughed in relief. "If the rumor is that I was lucky enough to spend time in the company of the man who saved my country from civil war, then yes."

"So Churchill isn't going to leave his wife?"

Maria shrugged. "He says that marrying the right woman was the best decision he ever made, so I think that is highly unlikely."

A voice came from the back of the press pack. "Do you think that you married the right man, Maria?"

Maria's smile vanished. "That's enough questions for now, gentlemen. I have a plane to catch."

On the airplane steps, as she turned to wave to the photographers, she knew that she should have answered the last question with something anodyne like, "Of course." But for all her years on the stage, she could not summon the ability to say it with any kind of conviction. She knew that the gossip mill would start to churn but she could no longer say in public that she had married the right man.

꒐

Bruna was waiting on the steps outside the Milan apartment. When she saw the car drive up, she opened her arms, and Maria fell into them. There was no need for words.

Later when Maria was sitting in front of her dressing table, she declared to Bruna, "Signor Meneghini and I are separating."

Bruna said nothing; she had guessed as much.

The telephone rang, and Bruna went to answer it, but Maria was there first. When she heard the voice on the other end of the phone, she began to talk in rapid Greek. Bruna looked at the way that Maria was curling a lock of hair around her finger and smiled. She had never seen her mistress look so soft or so happy. The phone call lasted for at least fifteen minutes and when Maria eventually put the phone down, her eyes were shining.

"Pack a small bag, Bruna, I am going back to Monaco for a few days. No public engagements, just private dinners. And make sure you put in something black and my pearls."

Bruna selected what she considered the most flattering of her mistress's extensive collection of peignoirs, feeling the satisfaction of knowing that for once these garments designed for seduction would be put to use. Signor Meneghini had only himself to blame for not giving his wife the kind of attention that she deserved. Bruna had not forgiven Meneghini for trying to persuade her the Christmas before that Madame had made a "mistake" in giving her a bonus of a hundred thousand lire.

"You know how she is, Bruna. I believe that she put the nought in the wrong place. She only meant to give you ten thousand lire, which is a perfectly generous gift."

He had put his hand out for the money. Bruna said that she had cashed the check, but would happily return the money to Madame if she asked her. Tita had lowered his hand. Bruna had never mentioned the incident to Maria.

She picked up a cocktail frock in matte black jersey and packed it together with the pearls and a pair of evening shoes with a low heel discreet enough not to exaggerate Onassis's lack of height.

The maid put the suitcase in the hall and went to run the bath that she knew that her mistress would remember that she wanted any minute now.

"Bruna, I think I will have a bath now, before I go to the airfield."

⤴

Onassis flew to Milan in his Piaggio to fetch her. Maria hated small planes, but with Ari she felt no fear. If the plane crashed at least they would die together.

"Thank you for coming to get me. I don't think I could have done it on my own."

"When you meet the love of your life, every minute matters, *agapi mou.*"

He held her hand as they took off, and then he told her in Greek that he had bought the biggest, most comfortable bed in France and put it in the suite at the Hôtel de Paris.

"And I don't intend to leave it for two days."

Maria felt herself trembling. "And what happens after two days?"

Ari's eyes went opaque for a moment. "The *Christina* is sailing to Venice."

Maria said nothing. She hated the thought of Ari being with Tina, but what mattered now was that he was here with her.

The bed was as magnificent as Ari had promised, and when they had finished enjoying its splendors, Maria fell asleep as she had as a child, instantly.

For breakfast there was caviar and silky scrambled eggs, and for lunch there were emeralds and rubies from Cartier.

Maria shivered as Onassis fastened the emerald necklace around her neck.

He led her over to the mirror; and as she looked at herself, he took away the towel she had been covering herself with so that she was naked.

"That's better," he said, fastening the emerald cuffs around her wrists.

Maria turned her head away, but he forced her to look at herself. The emerald pendant lay exactly below the dip in her collar bone. When she said this, Onassis grinned. "I leave nothing to chance, Maria. Please don't make me throw this one into the sea."

Maria turned around to face him. "You can't give these to me, Ari. It's too much."

"Who said anything about a gift? You get paid for singing, don't you?"

Maria nodded.

"So why shouldn't you get a few emeralds for fucking?" Maria glared at him. Ari laughed. "What's the matter? Would you rather have the rubies instead?"

Maria tore a sheet from the bed and furiously wrapped it around herself. "I get paid for doing my job. This"—she pointed to the bed—"is what I do for pleasure."

Onassis put up his hands in surrender. "Then wear the emeralds to make me happy, Maria. What's the point of having all this money if I can't spend it unwisely?"

Maria relented. "Will it really make you happy if I cover myself in emeralds?"

He nodded. "And even happier if that is all you are covered in."

Maria slowly let the sheet drop, and he pulled her onto the bed.

She was still wearing the necklace when he left to go back to the *Christina*.

"Will you wait for me here in Monaco?"

Maria shook her head. "I need to go back to Milan. Back to work. I am due to record *La gioconda*."

"The cruise won't take more than a week."

"Take as long as you like. I will be quite happy with my music."

"I could get a piano moved in here."

"And advertise to the whole world that you are sharing a suite with Maria Callas?"

Onassis pointed to where the *Christina* was anchored.

"If you stand on the balcony this evening, I will be able to see you from the boat."

Maria laughed. "Well, I won't be able to see you, unless I wear the glasses that you don't like."

He pulled her to him. "I want you to be there, Maria, where I can see you."

He paused and then said in a voice unlike his usual confident rumble, "My mother died one day when I was at school. My grandmother said goodbye to me on the morning of the day the Turks came to Smyrna and I never saw her again. I don't want you to disappear like that, not now that I have found you."

Maria stroked his hair as if he were a child and kissed his eyelids. "I won't disappear."

"How do I know that?"

"I told Tita that our marriage was over."

Ari looked at her in surprise. "Already?"

"I couldn't pretend anymore."

Ari looked wary. "How did he take it?"

"He is very upset, but he only has himself to blame. He has never cared for me really, only for my career. We never had this." Maria pressed herself against Ari.

"Then he is a fool, and deserves to lose you. Fancy being married to a woman like you and not spending every moment in bed."

He kissed the hollow between her collarbones. Maria arched her body toward him, but then they heard the unmistakable sound of the *Christina*'s siren. Reluctantly, Onassis pulled away from her.

"I must go. The Rainiers are coming for dinner and even though they are only Hollywood royalty, they get annoyed if they aren't the last to arrive."

He straightened the collar of his shirt in the mirror on the dressing table, and kissed Maria goodbye.

"Leave your light on at least, so that I can see you moving around."

⸗

After he'd gone, Maria telephoned Bruna and told her that she would be coming back tomorrow. When Maria asked her if she had seen Tita, the maid answered in a voice that sounded strained.

"Yes, madame."

"Is he there now?"

"Yes, madame."

"Don't tell him anything."

"Of course not."

"And I don't want him there when I get back."

"I understand, madame."

Maria felt the heaviness of Tita's resentment pressing on her even at this distance, but she would not let it spoil her mood. She put on the black lace peignoir and ordered room service, with a large order of French fries alongside her steak tartare, and then after one last look at the smudge of glittering lights in the harbor that she had worked out must be the *Christina*, she got back into the bed that had seen so much use that day and fell into a deep sleep.

# CHAPTER ELEVEN

# *Rear Window*

On the *Christina* later the same evening, Onassis was his usual charismatic self, although Princess Grace, who as the guest of honor was sitting next to him, teased him about the way he kept looking at the Hôtel de Paris.

"Are you expecting some kind of signal in code, Ari?"

"What do you mean?"

"Every time I look at you, you are gazing up at the windows of the penthouse of the Hôtel de Paris, as if you are waiting for some kind of revelation."

Onassis forced himself to concentrate. "Then I am a fool, because I have the most beautiful woman in France sitting next to me."

The former Grace Kelly raised one of the perfectly arched eyebrows that Alfred Hitchcock had gloried in and laughed her tinkly laugh.

"Oh, come off it, Ari. We know each other too well for that kind of talk. You have got someone stashed away there. You might as well tell me the whole story, because you know there are no secrets in Monaco."

Onassis glanced down the table to where Tina was sitting between Prince Rainier and Reinaldo Herrera. Reinaldo had his head very close to Tina and she was smiling.

Grace continued. "And don't use your wife as an excuse, because we both know that she is perfectly happy with her Venezuelan."

Ari shrugged. "There is no story, Grace, I promise you."

Grace's clear blue eyes narrowed. "What a pity. I was hoping that I might persuade you to build a proper opera house here. It's time Monaco had some culture."

Onassis tried not to react. Did Grace know about Maria or was her mention of the opera house just a coincidence?

"You don't call this gathering cultured?" Ari gestured down the table at Tina's friends, who all gleamed with the kind of expensive elegance that only a lifetime of privilege can bestow.

"I call them rich—there is a difference, you know. And none of them had to work for what they have." Onassis nodded.

"So what do you say to a real opera house? Monaco needs a center beyond the Casino. Somewhere else for the women to show off their jewelry."

She leaned forward, showing him the swell of her breasts.

"Talking of jewelry, there was a fine emerald set in Cartier last week that I was quite smitten with. But when I sent my lady-in-waiting to inquire about it, it had already gone."

Onassis shrugged. "I am sure Cartier can find you something just as good."

"I hope so. I was really taken by those emeralds, such a good green. But I have to say I am surprised that Tina isn't wearing them now, what with her green dress and all. But maybe you are saving them for a special occasion? A wedding anniversary perhaps?"

Onassis remembered where he had seen the look on Grace's face before. It was in that movie where the guy had been in a wheelchair with binoculars and she had been trying to help him solve the disappearance of the woman in the apartment opposite. He had not thought much of her acting in the movie, but now he realized as he saw the flush on her razor-sharp cheekbones and the gleam in her eye that it had been an entirely naturalistic performance of a rich, rather bored woman looking for excitement.

"Don't worry, Ari, I won't give away your little secret."

Grace put a fingertip to her mouth in a parody of secrecy. She said archly, "It can't be easy being married to a man like you."

Ari wanted more than anything to look back at the hotel windows for a glimpse of Maria, but he forced himself to concentrate on Grace, who, it seemed, was just a little drunk.

"Are you saying I am a bad husband?"

"Oh, Ari, there is no such thing—only an inattentive one."

Her eyes flickered toward Rainier and then back at him. He felt a slight pressure as her knee brushed against his underneath the table. The invitation was subtle but unmistakable.

"Something I am sure that you have no experience of," Ari said politely.

Grace took a gulp of her drink. "No, indeed. Rainier is most attentive. Just not to me."

Onassis sighed. Ever since Rainier had married the movie star, Ari had wondered how enduring the fairy-tale romance would be. Grace was quite a prize and if the pressure on his knee had happened a month earlier Ari would by now have been plotting exactly how he would take advantage of the situation. But now, when the ice queen of *High Society* was practically giving him the keys to her bedroom, he wasn't interested. Grace was beautiful, and he could see the wickedness underneath the porcelain skin, but at this moment she left him cold. The only woman he wanted was on the other side of the harbor.

His thoughts were interrupted by a hand stroking his thigh. He looked over at Grace who by now had the glassy look of someone who is trying to convince herself that she is not drunk.

He decided to use the only tactic open to him. He snatched the hand from his groin and, raising it to his lips, he kissed it.

"I think that the opera house is a wonderful idea, Your Serene Highness, and I would be happy to help you in any way I can."

It was an expensive way to resist a seduction.

Grace's eyelids flickered. "That is extremely generous of you, Ari, and I shall certainly be calling on you for all the help you can give me."

She raised her voice just a fraction. "Perhaps we could ask Maria Callas to give a gala performance on opening night? Wasn't she just with you on a cruise?"

Onassis looked at the angelic profile in front of him, wondering if she was taunting him.

But before he could answer, Tina piped up from her end of the table. "I am sure Ari would be happy to negotiate the fee. You always say that everyone has their price, don't you, darling?"

Ari looked at Tina with dislike. Twelve years ago, he married a teenager, thinking he would be able to mold her into the sort of wife he needed. But Tina just grew more difficult as she got older. She was quite adamant about not having another child. "It took me six months to get my figure back after Christina. I really don't want to have to go through all that again. And you know as well as I do that the more children we have, the less money they will inherit."

Onassis had protested that he was rich enough to take care of a whole regiment of children, but Tina would not relent. They still had sex occasionally, but for Onassis it was more a question of asserting his rights than actual desire. He thought of the way that Maria had clung to him last night. Not once in a dozen years of marriage had Tina ever wanted him like that.

He risked another glance across the harbor at the penthouse and was rewarded by the sight of Maria standing in the window, but he looked away quickly before Grace or Tina followed his gaze.

For the first time since he had acquired the *Christina*, he wanted very much to be somewhere else. The boat was his most cherished possession, but at this moment he felt completely indifferent to its splendors, to the well-trained dance of the stewards as they brought out the individual baked Alaskas that were always served when the Rainiers dined on board. He was bored of watching the well-bred pick delicately at their food and bored of listening to them talk about their tennis serves or their polo ponies.

At last Tina stood up and they all followed her on deck to where the swimming pool had been transformed into a dance floor, and a band from the Casino was playing the kind of music that you could dance to while holding a conversation. He could see Rainier was dancing with Tina, which meant that he should partner Grace; but to his relief Reinaldo had got in there first, and so he was able to lean against the rail and look out over the harbor at the hotel and smoke his cigar.

It was two a.m. before the Rainiers indicated that they wanted to go home, and Onassis summoned one of the three different tenders he kept for these parties, in order to confuse the press, and jumped down into it so that he could help Grace into the boat.

"Oh, Ari, there is no need for you to come back with us. I think we can find the way just fine."

Rainier's cigar glowed in the darkness. "Grace, you always say this, and Onassis always comes with us. Don't you know that we are his responsibility until we get to dry land?"

Behind him Onassis could hear the *Christina*'s engines starting up as they got ready to raise the anchor. They were due to sail to Venice for the festival. Tina had already ordered her costume for Elsa Maxwell's ball, where the dress code was to bring "something hideous." Tina was going to take a live eel in a string bag to offset her green sequined Dior gown.

"Although I could just go with you, Ari. But you are too rich for anyone to notice how ugly you are."

He could hear the band playing the twist, the new dance that Tina loved. She liked to show just how low she could go opposite the swivel-hipped Reinaldo.

He waited for the Rainiers to disappear inside their car, and then, instead of signaling to the sailor to take him back to the yacht, he unhitched the line from the bollard and threw it at the crewman and told him to go back to the *Christina*. Turning away from the harbor, Onassis started to walk toward the Hôtel de Paris.

# CHAPTER TWELVE

## *Fasten Your Seat Belts*

### MONACO, AUGUST 1959

Maria was in the kitchen in Patission Street, her mother was putting a plate of eggs in front of her, and she had just broken the skin of the yolk with her knife when she woke up to feel Ari breathing in the bed beside her.

"You came back," she cried, pressing herself against him.

"I couldn't see you any more from the boat," Ari said.

"I needed to sleep."

"And I needed to see you." He kissed her neck and started to stroke her thighs until she could think about nothing but his hand's progress.

When she went back to sleep, she curled her body around his. She wanted to make him feel safe.

⸗

Ari was standing on the balcony when she woke up. She put her arms round his neck, and he smiled at her.

"Are you looking for the *Christina*?" she asked.

"Oh, she will be halfway to Venice by now."

"Did you tell Tina that you weren't going?"

Ari shook his head. "She won't mind. Everyone on board is her friend, and she has Reinaldo to keep her amused. The only people who will miss me are the children. I promised to teach them how to play chess."

He looked out to sea. "Tina was raised by nannies and governesses—she sees nothing wrong with seeing her children once a day for ten minutes."

"If I had a child, I would never leave it to strangers to bring up," Maria said.

Ari looked at her. "Did you want one? A child, I mean."

"Of course. But my life is planned months, years in advance. I can't just stop and say now I am having a baby."

Ari gripped the rail of the balcony. "You know that if it weren't for the children, I would leave Tina, or I would buy her and Reinaldo a house in the south of France so that they can be together whenever they want."

Maria was amazed. "You would buy them a house?"

Ari shrugged. "No. Reinaldo can buy his own house—he has plenty of money, after all, and so does Tina. But I wouldn't mind, so long as I had you."

⌐

Ari went down to his office on the ground floor, and in his absence, Maria started to pack for the trip back to Milan.

The recording studio was booked in two day's time and she had work to do on the score. A recording was always easier than a live performance, but she hadn't practiced for weeks. She tried not to think about Ari and Tina. She knew from the moment that Onassis had kissed her on the deck of the *Christina* that her marriage was over, so why didn't he feel the same? For a moment she felt as vulnerable as if she were singing onstage and the orchestra had gone silent. She didn't want to sing alone, the mistress of a married man. The word "mistress" made her think of her mother screaming at her father about Alexandra Papajohn and reflexively she wrapped her arms around her body; but then she comforted herself with the fact that Ari had come back to her last night. He had left the boat, his wife, and his children to come back to her bed. Slowly she relaxed, as she remembered the pleasure last night of waking up in his arms.

⟆

She was folding up the black silk peignoir when Ari slipped his arm around her waist.

"And what do you think you are doing?"

"I have to go back to Milan."

"Then I will take you in the Piaggio."

Maria turned around. "Will you hold my hand all the way?"

"Will that make you feel safe?

She nodded.

"Then I will not let go for a second."

He was as good as his word, although it wasn't just Maria's hand that he held during the flight to Milan. Taking advantage of the fact that the pilot could not see behind him, Ari played with Maria's body while her rising excitement fought her fear. By the time the airplane began its descent, Maria was taut with longing. Even the small plane's bumpy landing could not extinguish her desire. As the plane slowed to a stop, Ari kissed her. "Shall I take you to your house or shall we find a hotel?"

"A hotel," Maria whispered.

Ari laughed. "Unless we find a convenient lifeboat on the way."

But just as they unbuckled their seat belts, the pilot turned round. "I'm sorry, Mr. Onassis, but there seems to be a crowd outside the terminal building. I think it might be the press."

Ari looked out of the cockpit window at the line of photographers on the ground below.

"Damn. Somebody must have tipped them off." He thought of Grace's knowing looks the night before.

Maria came to see what he was looking at. She groaned when she saw the press pack.

"How did they know we were flying together? We didn't even know until this morning."

Angrily, she pulled out her compact and started to apply her makeup. Onassis looked at her for a moment, and then turned to the pilot.

"How much fuel do we have left."

"About a quarter of a tank."

"Enough to keep us in the air for another thirty minutes?"

"Definitely, sir."

Ari turned to Maria. "If you get out now, I will take off again and then come and join you when these parasites have dispersed."

Maria finished applying her lipstick. "I hope that will be soon."

"Don't worry, I have no intention staying away from you a moment longer than I have to."

He kissed her carefully so as to not smudge her lipstick. "You look so beautiful, Maria."

⸙

Walking toward the terminal building, Maria was almost blinded by the flashbulbs. She fixed her smile and tried to look unconcerned as the mob surged in her direction.

"Madame Callas, do you want to give a statement on your separation from Signor Meneghini?"

"Is it true that you will be contesting custody of your poodles?"

"Signor Meneghini says that you have canceled all your singing engagements."

Maria's smile did not slip as she tapped her way across the tarmac in her Ferragamo heels. She wondered how the press knew about the separation, and she realized that it could only have come from Tita. She knew it was only a matter of time before her relationship with Onassis would become public knowledge.

She felt like Orpheus returning to earth from the underworld, knowing that she must look straight ahead and not turn round no matter what. She could see her car waiting for her; it was only ten feet away.

"Signor Meneghini says that your career is finished. Would you like to comment?"

Her body moved faster than her mind, and she whirled around to face the reporter. "The only career that is finished is that of Signor Meneghini as my manager."

The press swarmed toward her as she realized her mistake. She held up her hand in a commanding gesture that had served her well in the first act of *Norma* when she had to pacify her people.

"And that is all I have to say."

She was still trembling as she got to the house. As the car drew up, she saw Bruna standing in the window of her apartment. She was waving to her, but not smiling. The gesture was not a welcome but a warning.

She wasn't sure if the press had followed her from the airstrip, but she hurried up the steps to the main building just in case. The main door was open. She looked up and saw Tita standing at the top of the stairs.

For a man whose wife had just left him, Tita looked surprisingly dapper. He was wearing a biscuit-colored linen suit and had a red silk handkerchief in his breast pocket. He looked cared for and confident. Maria regarded him coldly. "What are you doing here?"

"Where have you been?" answered Meneghini.

Maria walked up the steps and pushed past him into the apartment. Bruna rushed forward to take her bags. Maria picked up Toy the poodle, who started to lick her face in delight at her return.

"I am waiting for an answer, Maria."

"And I am waiting for you to tell me what you are doing here. We agreed that you should stay in the villa."

"We didn't *agree* anything. You ordered me to go there," Tita said.

"Because I don't want to see you. Our marriage is over."

"Do you really think it is that simple? You can't erase me as if I never existed."

Maria put Toy down and turned to face him. "Why did you tell the press that my career was over?"

Tita laughed. "Because it's the truth. Do you really believe that you can carry on without me? You wouldn't even have a career if I hadn't picked you out of the chorus in Verona."

"I was never in the chorus!" said Maria furiously.

"You were a fat foreigner with bad Italian, no money, and an unfashionable voice. I paid for the lessons, the clothes. I taught you how to speak Italian without sounding like you were onstage and I stopped you from making enemies of everyone at the theater. Why do you think that your career took off in Italy and not in Athens or New York? Because I was there to make it happen."

He patted his chest as he said this, swelling with the sense of his own achievement.

"We both understand that you don't have much time left, Maria. Your voice is not what it was ten years ago, and everybody knows it. Yes, you are still Callas, and people will want to come and hear you sing; but you can't reach the high notes anymore and every time you fail onstage, it will make it more difficult for you to go out there the next time. How will you manage without me there to support you, to stand there in the wings, to calm your fears? Who else is going to do that for you? Aristotle Onassis, the world's richest man? Is he going to wait in your dressing room while you change your mind about whether you can perform? Is he going to talk round all the opera managers that you have insulted? Is he going to make sure that your piano is tuned and that your scores are arranged alphabetically? Is he going to hide the newspapers that dare to print less than flattering reviews? Is Aristotle Onassis really going to stand behind you and smile as he is introduced as Maria Callas's husband?"

Tita took the handkerchief out of his pocket and wiped his forehead, which was beginning to glisten with sweat.

"You think you are leaving me, Maria. But really you are leaving your career."

Maria lifted her right hand and delivered a slap to his glistening cheek. The flesh felt damp. Her words tumbled out in a torrent that gathered in momentum.

"Do you think that you are the reason that I am Maria Callas? You didn't give me my voice. Yes, I have been grateful to have you there in the wings, but do you imagine you are the only person who could do that job?"

Maria gestured toward the hall.

"Bruna is the one who really looks after me, and she costs me a lot less than you do."

Tita touched his slapped cheek gingerly. There was a little cut from Maria's ring. He saw the blood and sat down on the sofa. Maria saw the blood too, and she started to tremble.

When he spoke his voice was gentle. "You can be so cruel, Maria. And yet I don't believe that underneath you are the monster that you seem to be. I am prepared to forgive you for the way you have behaved. I understand that for you the attentions of a man like Onassis might be overwhelming. He is rich, powerful, and even I admit that he has some charm. But I am your husband, Maria, who you married under the eyes of God. I may not be able to give you emeralds"—Maria's hands felt for the necklace around her throat—"but I will never leave you."

His words sounded more like a threat than a promise.

This time when she spoke there was compassion in her voice. "I don't love you, Tita. I have affection for you, but what I feel for Ari is completely different. He is my soulmate—and now that Fate has brought us together, I don't want to live without him."

Tita grimaced at her words. "Fate has brought you together! You sound like a teenager. So where is your soulmate now? Is he really going to divorce Tina and marry you?"

Before Maria could reply the doorbell rang and Bruna went to open the door.

"Madame Callas and Signor Meneghini are in the drawing room, sir."

Onassis stood in the doorway. He took in the scene: Meneghini sitting on the sofa with blood on his cheek and Maria staring down at him like a vengeful goddess. He smiled, his teeth gleaming in his tanned face.

"I seem to have to come at an awkward moment."

Meneghini stood up. They were about the same size, but Onassis took up so much more space.

"I was asking Maria what your intentions are."

Onassis's smile grew broader. "How Victorian. Are you intending to horsewhip me?"

Maria recovered her voice. "I want you to leave now, Tita."

Tita shook his head. "Why should I? This is my house and I have a right to be here."

Onassis looked at him for a moment. Then he reached into the inside pocket of his jacket and took out his checkbook. "How much?"

Meneghini looked confused. "How much for what?"

"How much will it take to buy your share of this house? What it is worth—ten million lire? Suppose I write you a check for five million right now. You can go straight to the bank, and then buy yourself a little garçonnière a couple of streets away, find yourself some buxom companions, as I believe that is what you like, and everyone will be happy."

Meneghini pulled his shoulders back. "I am not for sale, Mr. Onassis."

With a sigh, Onassis put the checkbook back in his pocket. "I don't want to buy you, just your share of this apartment. For some reason I thought it would it easier for us all to behave like civilized human beings."

Tita shook his head. "Why should I be civilized? You are taking my wife away from me."

"Do you seriously think that I could take Maria anywhere that she didn't want to go?"

He flashed a smile at Maria. "Why don't we all have a drink and talk about it sensibly?"

He turned to Bruna, who was standing in the corridor transfixed.

"I believe you must be the famous Bruna. Do you think I could have a whiskey and soda; I am sure you know what the others drink."

He took his cigar case out of his jacket and offered one to Meneghini, who waved it away in disgust.

"You sure? I seem to remember you were very partial to my cigars on the boat."

Maria watched her husband trying to control himself in the face of Onassis's relentless geniality. Tita looked deflated: the linen suit was crumpled, the bluster and spite of a few moments ago had disappeared.

Onassis gave Bruna a beaming smile when she handed him his whiskey and soda. She gave Maria a glass of champagne, and Meneghini a vermouth.

Ari lifted his glass. "Here's to health, wealth, and happiness." He drained his glass and looked at Meneghini, whose glass was still full.

Ari sat down at one end of the sofa and, after a moment's hesitation, Maria sat at the other end. Meneghini did not move but remained standing in front of them.

"Are you sure you won't sit down?" Onassis said, in the solicitous tone of a perfect host.

Meneghini shook his head. "I will decide what I do in my own house."

Onassis shrugged and continued in the same reasonable tone, the voice of a man negotiating a tricky shipping contract. "All I am saying is that you could save yourself a fortune in legal bills, if you make a decision now about dividing your property. And if you keep it private, you will have the added benefit of making a lot of reporters very unhappy. Every newspaper in the world is going to want all the gory details, but why give them the satisfaction? Make an agreement now, stick to it, and everything will be forgotten in six months."

"But I have not agreed to the separation. Maria is still my wife."

Ari looked at Maria, and then back at Meneghini. "I don't think you can stop Maria leaving if she wants to, and my understanding is that she does."

Maria nodded. "Our marriage is over."

Onassis pointed at Meneghini. "So you have a choice—agree to part amicably and make the lawyers and the press miserable, or you can create a scandal that will cost you a fortune and put you both on the front pages for weeks."

Meneghini turned pale with anger. "I can see that it would make your life much easier if I did that, Mr. Onassis, but the only person I care about in this situation is my wife."

"Are you sure about that? How does it help Maria if you fight publicly over your assets? I am sure it can all be settled easily enough, provided you are discreet."

Maria could see that Meneghini was beginning to tremble.

"He is right, Tita. We don't want a public scandal. It will only make things more painful."

Meneghini swayed slightly and Maria wondered if he was going to faint, but he got control of himself and pointed at Onassis.

"I will ask you again, Mr. Onassis. Do you intend to marry Maria?"

Onassis blinked. "That is none of your business. I have come here to help Maria end her marriage with you. Maria has told me something of your situation, and I want to make it clear that I am prepared to make sure that you will not suffer financially."

Meneghini looked at Maria. "I thought you were a proud woman. Are you really prepared to let this man buy you from me like a whore?"

Onassis jumped up and grabbed Meneghini by the collar. "How dare you talk to Maria like that! If you weren't so old, I would knock you down."

He took Maria's hand and pulled her up. "Come on, there is nothing more to say here." He turned to Meneghini. "I am in love with Maria, and I am not going to give her up. But I won't force her to come with me."

He looked at Maria with burning eyes. "Will you come with me, Maria, or do you want to stay here with your husband?"

Maria took a step toward him, and he put his arm around her waist.

Meneghini made a sound halfway between a moan and a shout of protest, and he held out his hands to his wife. "But I will be so sad, Maria!"

Maria heard the anguish in his voice and for a moment she hesitated. He would be lost without her, she knew. She leaned forward and kissed him on the cheek, before following Onassis out of the room.

Bruna was standing in the corridor with Toy in her arms.

Maria took the dog and leaned down to whisper in Bruna's ear. "I'm not leaving you, Bruna."

Bruna nodded. "I know, madame."

# Act Three

# CHAPTER THIRTEEN

## *Skorpios*

IONIAN SEA, OCTOBER 1959

The water was still calm; and where it touched the shore, it was that vivid turquoise that Maria saw only in Greece. Even in October the sun was warm on her bare shoulders, and she was grateful for the breeze coming from the water as the *Christina* cruised along the coastline. They were sailing through the Ionian Islands on the western side of the Peloponnese.

"There it is, Maria."

Ari pointed over her shoulder to a rocky hump on the horizon. Maria pulled her glasses out of the pocket of her skirt to take a closer look.

"It is called Skorpios because of the way that the land curves back on itself, like the tail of a scorpion."

Maria peered at the island in front of her. The slopes were covered in olive and birch trees, silvery green against the brown of the earth and the gray of the rock.

"Does anybody live there?"

"Not now. Just a few goats. But they are only tenants." Maria laughed.

Onassis gestured as the boat passed the promontory at one end of the island and revealed a secluded bay.

"Look, it's a perfect natural harbor." He gestured to one of the deck-hands.

"Tell the captain to anchor here. I want to go ashore." He turned to Maria. "Shall we go and have a look?"

She went down to her stateroom to get her shoes and caught a glimpse herself in the mirror. Her skin was dark brown from the sun, and her hair was fuzzy from the humidity. She was wearing a white swimsuit under a linen caftan. She knew that Alain would throw up his hands in despair if he were to see her now—she was not looking like a diva and she was definitely rounder than the last time she had been in his studio. But she smiled back at her reflection, she looked exactly as she felt, ecstatically happy. The last few weeks with Ari had been the most joyful of her thirty-six years. Here on the *Christina*, they were together day and night, and she felt as if there were electricity rather than blood flowing through her veins. Onassis only had to touch her shoulder or graze her hand, and her body would flicker with desire. He told her she was insatiable, but she could not help herself: she wanted him all the time and she had to summon all her formidable willpower not to follow him around the boat like Toy the poodle. She had never experienced anything like this before. Onstage, of course, she had expressed every kind of passion: it was all there in the music. But now she didn't need music to tell her what to feel. Every time he gave her that piratical smile, she felt herself tremble.

She had sung only once since the affair with Onassis had started. The concert was in Bilbão, a rainy city in the north of Spain. She wanted to cancel, but she knew that if she did the rumors about her career being over would flare up. Tita had been playing the role of the injured husband with gusto. He had given a press conference where he had called her Medea and compared Onassis to Hitler. Maria had wanted to sue him for slander, but Ari had laughed it off. "He is making himself ridiculous; the only thing to do is ignore it."

But Meneghini's declaration of himself as the injured party had made it impossible for Maria and Onassis to go anywhere in public, and so they had retreated to the *Christina*. Onassis had offered to come with her to Bilbão, but Maria had refused. Of course, she wanted him to be there, but she knew instinctively he would come between her and the audience.

The concert had not been a success. As she walked onstage Maria knew she was too relaxed, that the tension she needed to perform at her best was not there. She had neglected her practice, but the real problem was that for the first time in her life, she faced an audience without really caring whether she won them over or not. Her singing was fine, she made all the notes, but the audience sensed that she was not giving them everything. There had been applause and bouquets but there had not been the stunned moment of silence when she finished singing that she was used to. The reviews had been tepid, some papers accusing her of choosing a lotus-eater's lifestyle with Onassis over her music. Maria did not react to the criticism. She knew they were right. She had been neglecting her music for Ari, but it had been a price worth paying.

The morning after the concert, she was sick. She blamed the seafood she had eaten the night before—"You must try our Galician clams, Madame Callas." But when Bruna had found her crouched over the toilet, throwing up, she had asked if Maria could remember the date of her last period.

Aristo was waiting for her on the deck. The sea between the boat and the shore was every shade from wine-dark to bright turquoise.

"Let's swim over, Ari. The boat can come and pick us up."

She didn't wait for him to answer but walked down to the stern and dived in.

When she came up for air, Aristo was beside her, slicing through the water with his streamlined crawl. She swam beside him, rejoicing in the buoyancy of the sea. It was still warm and so clear that Maria could see the yellow bulbs of the Mediterranean coral on the seabed.

Ari reached the strip of white sand before she did. He climbed out and stood on the beach, surveying his new kingdom.

It was very quiet apart from the lapping of the water and the bleats of the island's goats.

"What do you think?" Ari asked.

Maria kissed him. "I think it's completely perfect."

"I think the house should go up there on the ridge, so that you have the view of the sea from both sides of the house."

Maria looked to where he was pointing, a gap in the tree line. The house would have a spectacular view.

"And here on this beach, I will build the chapel." He looked around with satisfaction. "My grandmother Gethsemane would be very proud of me. My own chapel. And I will plant all the trees she loved around it."

Maria decided that there could be no better time to tell Aristo the secret that she had been keeping.

"I hope the chapel can be built quickly," she said.

Ari looked at her, trying to understand her meaning. And then he frowned. "Maria, we are both still married. . . . I think it is too early to plan a wedding."

Maria shook her head. "Not a wedding, a baptism."

Onassis went still.

"I am going to have a baby, Ari."

She put her head on his chest and she could hear his heart beating rapidly.

"A baby," he repeated in a flat voice.

Maria continued. "I always dreamed of having a child one day, but I never thought it would happen. And now here I am, with your baby inside me."

She sat down on a rock and gestured to Ari to sit next to her.

"We can call it Socrates after your father."

Aristo started to pat his pockets for cigarettes, but then, remembering he was wearing only his swimming trunks, he waved to the *Christina* to bring over the tender. It was only when the cigarettes had arrived, and he had one in his hand, that he replied. "Are you sure?"

Maria nodded. "It must have happened that first time in the lifeboat."

Ari sat down beside her. "This is going to be complicated, Maria."

She heard the reservation in his voice. "Aren't you pleased?" she asked.

"I am pleased for you, if this is what you want, but I didn't expect this."

"I didn't either. It is fate, Aristo."

He closed his eyes for a moment. "Have you told anybody else?"

Maria shook her head. "Of course not. Only Bruna knows."

"We have to keep it a secret, Maria. I don't know what Tina would do if she found out. Not to mention your husband. It will make everything so much worse."

Maria picked up a pebble and threw it into the water. This was not the conversation that she had imagined having. She didn't understand why Ari kept talking about problems when the fact that she was pregnant at all was a miracle.

He stubbed out his cigarette and put his arm around her, and, as if he could hear her thoughts, he said, "Remember that I already have two children, *agapi mou*. They are not happy about the split with Tina, and this will be even harder for them."

"Ari, you know that I will do everything I can to make your children happy. Especially Christina. She is very like I was at that age, an ugly duckling—but I could help her feel like a swan."

Ari squeezed her hand. "I think the best thing is if we find a house somewhere like Switzerland where you can have the baby in private. And then when things are easier, we can decide what to do."

Maria leaned against him. "I want this baby because it is ours."

Ari was silent for a moment, and then he lit another cigarette and grinned. "Suppose it has my voice and your eyesight?"

Maria laughed. "Or my legs and your hairy chest."

Ari put his hand on her thigh. "I like your sturdy peasant legs. Very much." He took her hand and pulled her to her feet. "Let's go and find an olive tree."

"But there are olive trees everywhere . . ."

"Not the kind of olive tree that I am thinking of," he said, scrambling up the rocky slope, pulling Maria after him. When they got to the top of the ridge, he pointed to a particularly sturdy tree that looked like it was a few hundred years old, left over from the time when the whole island was cultivated. Aristo patted its trunk approvingly. "This is the sort of tree that Odysseus chose to build a bed around."

He grinned. "Shall we christen it?"

He backed her up against the olive tree and started to pull her swimsuit down. She reached her arms over her head and held on to the branches as he kissed her breasts, her navel, and then her sex until she was begging him in Greek to fuck her, which he did with such vigor that in the evening she had welts on her shoulders where the bark of the tree had rubbed against her back. But at the time she felt no pain, only the pleasure that he gave her and the knowledge that he would build a house for her here one day.

"I'm so happy," she whispered as they lay next to each other on the hard ground, looking up at the sky through the canopy of leaves.

"Good."

"Are you really going to build a bed like Odysseus?"

"Of course. That means that you will have to be faithful to me for the next twenty years while I go away and fight the Trojans."

"I will always be faithful to you, Ari. You are the only man I will ever want."

"I should think so too."

As they picked their way back through the scrubby undergrowth to where the boat was waiting, Ari stopped and said, "Promise me you will keep it a secret."

He looked at her so seriously that Maria crossed herself as she said, "I promise not to tell anyone."

"Not even your mother."

Maria laughed. "I haven't spoken to her in six years."

Ari didn't smile. "And Bruna can be trusted?"

"Completely."

He thought for a moment, and then he said, "You must try to behave normally until you start showing. The best way to hide something is in plain sight. I will make sure that the doctors you see are discreet."

There was a briskness about this conversation that Maria had witnessed before only when she had overheard Onassis talking to his business associates—when his usual breezy geniality was replaced by this focused staccato.

"My stomach muscles are like iron from singing, so I shouldn't show for a few months."

He nodded. "That's good. And by then we will have everything arranged."

"Just think, one day our child will be playing on this beach."

But Onassis was already wading out to the tender.

Later that night as Maria lay in bed, waiting for Ari to finish his late-night business calls to America, she pictured the chapel he would build on Skorpios, a simple building painted white and blue with a small bell tower. He had not yet proposed marriage, but then they were both still married to other people. Divorce was illegal in Italy, yet Maria knew that there were ways round these things, and she trusted Ari to make the impossible happen. It was a pity her child would most likely be born out of wedlock, but a miracle could not be delayed. God had created this baby and so it could hardly be a sin to have it. She understood why Aristo wanted to keep everything secret; she thought of what her mother would say if she found out that Maria was having an illegitimate child and she shuddered. When Litza had been asked by reporters what she thought of the breakup of Maria's marriage she had said that "Maria has left her husband, just like she left me, without a word or a backward glance. She is a monster who thinks only of herself."

§

MEXICO CITY, SEPTEMBER 1950

*Maria asked Litza to come on tour in South America as her companion while Tita attended to business in Verona.*

*In those days Maria still thought that there was a way to make her mother happy. In Buenos Aires she bought Litza a gold watch, and in Rio a crocodile-skin handbag. In Mexico City, when Litza announced that she could not face another New York winter without a fur coat, Maria had asked the concierge to recommend a furrier, and they had been driven to a small boutique in the Polanco district.*

*The weather outside was warm and both women were wearing summer dresses, but inside the fur shop it was cool and smelled of camphor. The vendeuse was a Viennese woman who had settled in Mexico City after the war. She recognized Maria instantly and was enchanted to have the great diva and her mother in her humble shop. A maid was sent out for suitable refreshment, and Kaffee und Kuchen were brought out with great ceremony. The vendeuse said that she had the privilege of hearing Maria sing Tosca at the opera house and it had taken her back to her youth in Vienna when she would go to the opera two or even three times a week.*

*Then with exquisite manners she turned to Litza and said that she must be very proud although she could hardly believe that Madame was old enough to have a grown-up daughter. If she had seen them in the street, she would have taken them for sisters.*

*Litza smiled at the compliment, and began her familiar refrain. "When I first heard Maria sing, I knew that I had to do everything to make her talent come to life. It was not easy, but a mother must sacrifice herself to make her daughter's dreams come true."*

*The vendeuse nodded. "We mothers would do anything for our children."*

*"I remember going hungry during the war so that Maria could eat."*

*Maria's legs felt heavy. They swelled up in the heat, and she looked resentfully at her mother's sharply etched anklebones, and said impatiently, "I think you should try something on, Mama. I must be back in the theater in a few hours."*

*The vendeuse got the hint and came back with a selection of furs.*

*Litza was entranced by her reflection in the mirror, her face framed by fox, sable, mink, even ocelot. She twirled and pouted as the vendeuse exclaimed over Litza's model proportions.*

*"It will be impossible for you to choose, I think, gnädige Frau, you look sehr schön in all these models."*

*Maria looked at her watch. Her legs were really swollen now, and she wanted to go to the theater so that she could put them up before the performance. She looked at her mother and said firmly, "I think you should take the mink coat with the dolman sleeves."*

*Litza screwed her face up. "It's beautiful, but what about the astrakhan trimmed with fox," slipping on the coat in question and holding the collar up to her face like a silent film star.*

*Maria realized that there was only one way to get out of the shop. "Fine, we will take both coats."*

*The vendeuse clapped her hands together. "Oh, gnädige Frau, you are indeed fortunate to have a daughter who is as generous as she is talented."*

*Maria nodded modestly and looked over at her mother, hoping to see some reflection of the vendeuse's sentiments. But Litza was not looking grateful or even pleased; she was looking at a white fox stole and running it through her fingers.*

She looked at Maria with reproach. "Don't you think that this would look beautiful on Jackie? She has such a fine neck and shoulders. And it doesn't seem fair that you should have so many nice things, when your sister has to make do with your castoffs."

Maria felt the blood rising to her face. "The castoffs were from Dior!"

Her mother shrugged. "But there is such a difference between secondhand and having something new." She held up the stole. "This is just right for Jackie."

Maria felt something snap inside her head. It was suddenly clear to her that nothing she could do for her mother would be enough. Maria could give her all the furs, the hotel suites, the champagne and couture, but nothing would ever make up for the fact that Maria was the famous one, not Litza. Maria had spent her whole life feeling the burden of her mother's sacrifice, the meals not eaten, the years spent in war-torn Athens, so that Maria could pursue her career; but now in this room that smelled of mothballs she understood her mother would never be satisfied to be the mother of the diva: she wanted to be center stage herself. And to make it worse, here Maria was buying Litza not one but two fur coats, and all her mother could think about was Jackie.

Jackie with her slim ankles, her blond hair, and ready smile, who had made nothing of her life, who had not struggled to become great, but was still, despite everything, her mother's favorite. Maria felt unwelcome tears coming to her eyes. She got to her feet, and speaking Greek so that the vendeuse would not understand she spoke to her mother. "Jackie can buy her own furs."

Litza frowned. "How can you say that? You have everything—fame, a husband, and plenty of money—but poor Jackie lives in Athens working as a secretary for a man who won't marry her. It wouldn't hurt you to share a little of your success with her."

Maria took a step closer to her mother and looking directly into her eyes she said, "You think I have everything? I tell you one thing I have never had, and that is a mother who really loved me. You have always liked Jackie better, always."

Litza put up her hands in protest. "Have you lost your mind, Maria? When I think of all that I sacrificed so that you could be a singer. Everything in my life came second—my husband, even Jackie—so that you could succeed."

*Maria would not allow herself to cry; she didn't want to blunt the edge of her fury.*

*"You wanted me to succeed because you had failed to do anything with your life. And now you want all the credit. But it is my talent and my determination that has taken me to where I am today. My success is my own."*

*Litza stepped forward as if she was going to slap her daughter, and the vendeuse, who had been watching the argument without understanding a word but nevertheless following every nuance, interposed herself.*

*"Allow me to get you a glass of water, madame." The distraction was enough, Litza let her arm drop.*

*Maria picked up her handbag and her gloves. "I brought you on this trip to try to make you love me, but I realize now that nothing I can do will ever be enough."*

*Litza's face twisted with fury. "You brought me with you, Maria, because you were too mean to pay for a maid. But did I complain about having to wash your underwear which was black from all the makeup you wore for Aida? No, I have done nothing but try to make your life easier, and this is how you repay me."*

*The vendeuse returned holding the glass of water.*

*Maria turned to her. "Please send the bill to my hotel, for everything except the fox stole."*

*"If Madame Callas would care to wait, I can pack it up for you."*

*Maria shook her head. "I am going to the opera house right away." She turned to look at her mother, hoping to see something, but there was nothing there except resentment.*

*"Goodbye, Mama."*

*Her mother turned her face away from her, and Maria walked out of the shop.*

⸎

That scene had been nine years ago, and she hadn't seen or spoken to her mother since. If only she could leave Tita so easily, but she knew that he would do everything he could to make their parting as difficult as possible. She wondered if he regretted turning down the money Aristo had offered. As Ari had said, it would all be so much easier if they behaved like civilized human beings.

She heard Ari open the door that led from his study to their bed-room; and when she looked up, he was smiling.

"It's done!"

"What's done?"

"Skorpios. It's mine."

Maria got out of bed to embrace him. "That's wonderful."

"All the shipping families have their own islands, but Skorpios will be the best. I can't wait to tell the children." But then he frowned. "Tina will do everything she can to stop them coming."

Maria stroked his cheek. "But you are their father, Ari, and besides soon there will be another child."

Ari was silent for a moment, and then he said in a neutral voice, "I suppose there is no doubt that the child is mine."

Maria sat down abruptly on the bed. "Of course not! Do you think that I am the kind of woman who would pass off one's man's child as another's?"

Onassis shook his head. "No, but it happened so quickly, I had to ask. Such things have been known."

Maria stood up and gripped him by the shoulders. "But I am not that kind of woman. I don't want your money or your boat or even your island. I just want to be with you. Remember that whatever happens, I will never lie to you."

Aristo picked up her hand and kissed it. "Forgive me, *agapi mou*. Not every woman is as honest as you."

Maria softened. "Tell me about all your plans for Skorpios. Will there be a studio apart from the main house where I can practice? I like to sing loudly even when I am rehearsing."

Onassis smiled. "That can be arranged; perhaps we should build a recording studio as well. I don't want you going away all the time."

Maria kissed him. "Everything will be different when I have a baby."

Onassis pressed the bell beside the bed. When the purser came, he ordered a bottle of Dom Pérignon and some caviar.

"But I have gone to bed," Maria protested.

"It is never too late to celebrate," said Ari.

When the champagne arrived, the glass dark with condensation, the coupes equally cold, Onassis dismissed the purser and opened the bottle with a gleeful pop. He poured both of them a glass and then raised his in a toast. "To Skorpios."

Maria waited for him to mention the other cause for celebration, but he was already touching her glass with his own.

"To Skorpios and the baby," she said, trying to meet Ari's eye.

# CHAPTER FOURTEEN

## Samson and Delilah

MILAN, NOVEMBER 1959

On their last night on the *Christina*, Maria was brushing her hair in front of the dressing table mirror. Aristo came in and she offered him the brush. When he looked surprised, she said, "It feels so nice to have someone else do it."

He started to pull the hairbrush through her dark hair, which came to well below her shoulder blades. After a few strokes he stopped and stood back looking at her in the mirror.

"Why don't you get it cut? It's old-fashioned to have long hair, like a Greek grandmother."

Now it was Maria's turn to look surprised. She was proud of her hair.

"I have always had it long."

"All the more reason to cut it. Surprise the world."

"Don't you think I have done that already?"

Aristo shrugged. "New man, new haircut. Makes sense to me."

"You really think I should cut it?"

"Definitely. I think it would make you look younger and more modern."

"But I thought you liked it," Maria couldn't help saying.

"I do, but I don't want you to look like an old peasant."

Maria reached for his hand. "If you want me to cut my hair then I will. You know that all I want is to make you happy."

Aristo looked at her in the mirror. "Is that really all you want?"

Maria nodded.

Aristo put a hand on her shoulder. "Then maybe you should think about a . . . termination. It is such bad timing for both of us. We could try again when things are less complicated; but if you have a baby now there will be such a scandal. I am thinking of you, Maria. Imagine what it will mean for your career."

Maria looked at him in dawning horror as his words sank in. She shook her head violently. "I won't do it, Ari. You said that it was fate that brought us together. I say it is fate that has given me a child. If you don't want our baby, I will bring it up myself, but I won't murder it because it is an inconvenience."

Onassis put up his hands in protest. "Don't be so melodramatic. How far along are you? About nine weeks? I believe it is a very simple procedure."

Maria put her hands over her ears. "I don't want to hear any more."

Ari shrugged. "If that's how you feel, then of course I will support you. I just wanted to be sure that you know what you are doing."

"I know exactly what I am doing. I am going to have our baby."

She glared at him with such fury that he stepped back, putting up his hands as if she were pointing a gun at him.

"I'm sorry, Maria. I don't want to upset you. Of course, you must do what you want, and in so many ways I want to have a baby with you. I just wish it didn't have to be now."

Maria said nothing. For the first time since they had slept together in the lifeboat, she began to wonder if she had made a mistake.

Aristo saw the change in her face, and he realized that he had pushed her too far. "Forgive me for not understanding how much this baby means to you."

He put his arms around her, but she stood rigid as a statue.

"Please, Maria, tell me you forgive me."

She didn't move.

"I'm a businessman, Maria. I have to look at things from every angle. I can't help it. But I can admit when I am wrong."

There was an urgency in his voice that she couldn't ignore. Slowly she began to melt against him. "A baby is not a business deal, Ari."

"I know, *agapi mou*. Forgive me for talking like an American."

He kissed her neck and put his hands around her waist. "How can I make you forget this conversation? Would you like to go dancing? We could hop over to Athens in the Piaggio?"

She pulled back to look at him. How could he be talking about dancing? Aristo's smile faded, and he fell to his knees before her.

"I forgot that your patron saint is the Virgin Mary, blessed among women. Of course, you cannot give up your baby—it is your birthright, your destiny. Forgive me, Maria, I beg you."

Maria waited for a moment, the time it would take her to pick up the knife in the second act of *Tosca* in order to stab Scarpia through the heart. Could she forgive him? For a moment she had felt as if she were standing on quicksand.

"Please."

Maria put her long white hands on his head and pulled her to him, pressing his head against the place where the baby was growing. He pulled up her nightgown and began to kiss her stomach.

"I'm sorry, little one. You deserve a better father. But you have a tiger for a mother."

Then he started to kiss the inside of her thighs and Maria began to lose her sense of grievance. He knew how to make her forget everything else. She thought she had loved Meneghini in the early days; she had enjoyed lying next to him in bed and feeling the warmth of his body and the hand that was always ready to hold hers. But now she realized that had been comfort, not love. What she felt for Onassis was something she had only experienced in opera. She understood now why Gilda would willingly take the place of the Duke her lover and offer herself up to Sparafucile's dagger in *Rigoletto*. She too would lay down her life for Onassis. The only thing she wouldn't sacrifice was their child.

Later, while she was lying in his arms, he asked her to sing something for him, and she started humming a Greek folk song that her father used to serenade her with in Washington Heights. Even though she tried to sing pianissimo, when she opened her mouth, all the glass in the cabin started to rattle.

Aristo began to laugh. "Oh, Maria, what a force you are. I don't think you will be singing any lullabies."

"For the baby, I will do anything but it will be hard. I need to make a noise to feel powerful."

"You don't need to sing to be powerful, *agapi mou*." His voice was soft, just the right pitch to send a baby to sleep.

⸺

It had been hard to leave him, but he had to sort out the situation with Tina, who had filed for divorce. And she had a performance of *Medea* in Dallas. On the plane to America, she had found an enormous bunch of red roses on the seat next to her. The note said in Greek, "For my Maria, from her Ari."

The Dallas performance was a triumph. Even though the sets were mediocre and the costumes a disaster, she knew that she had never acted better. Her voice had been there when she needed it; but when she was in full flow, she knew that her voice could have failed and no one would have noticed, as the audience was mesmerized by Medea's dilemma: Should she kill her children to revenge herself on their father for whom she had betrayed her country?

But she had been forced to cancel the final two performances to go to court with Meneghini. He had tried to take everything of course, but the judge had rejected his claims to her royalties and had given her the house in Milan and all her jewelry.

The victory over Meneghini had made her even more determined to please Onassis. So now she was sitting in the hairdresser's chair, ordering her stylist, Fredo, to cut her hair short.

He could not disguise his dismay. "But madame has such beautiful hair."

"It makes me look old. Short hair is younger and fresher."

The hairdresser looked mournful. "Maybe on someone else, but you are la Divina, madame. You don't need to look young or fresh; you are yourself and nobody else."

Maria put up her hand. "I have decided to do it, Fredo, and, believe me, I have a good reason."

Fredo had spent his life listening to women in love, so he caught her meaning instantly. "In that case, Madame Callas, I shall do as you ask. But no haircut can make you more beautiful than you already are."

Maria blew him a kiss in the mirror.

But as Fredo picked up the scissors, Maria closed her eyes. There was a superstitious part of her that felt like Samson. Was she surrendering more than her hair?

She opened her eyes only when Fredo had finished with the hair dryer.

"*Allora!*" he said and she looked in shock at the woman in front of her. Her hair just touched her shoulders in a bouffant bob. Shocked, she realized that apart from the color, it was exactly the sort of hairstyle favored by Tina Onassis.

She gasped and Fredo touched her shoulder. "Do you recognize yourself?"

"Not really, but I think it looks very chic."

Which was true. Apart from her height and her presence, short-haired Maria was no longer instantly Callas, she was a woman of fashion. Exactly the sort of woman one might expect to see on the arm of Aristotle Onassis.

But when Bruna opened the door of the apartment and saw her, the maid burst into tears. "Oh, madame, what have you done?"

## CHAPTER FIFTEEN

# *Ash Wednesday*

### MILAN, MARCH 1960

Everything was white when she opened her eyes, white and pure and peaceful. But then she heard Bruna's voice calling her and saw the round face crumpled with sadness.

"Oh, madame," and Maria felt something wet fall on her cheek. She had seen Bruna cry only once before, after she cut her hair. What had happened now?

And then she felt a wave of desolation as she understood the reason for Bruna's tears.

She had been shut up in the apartment for weeks. By Christmas there was no hiding her pregnancy, and although she could disguise the bump under her mink, the moment she took it off, her condition was obvious. So she had lived in seclusion, with only Bruna for company and a call from Aristo every evening to look forward to.

He had left to take the Churchills on a cruise in the Caribbean. Maria hated being apart from him, but she was relieved that he was not there to see her body changing. She didn't mind the new fullness in her breasts, but her ankles were so swollen that she could not bear to look at them. The weight she had gained with the pregnancy reminded her of the early days in Verona when she had weighed 220 pounds. As the weeks went by, she needed less and less water to immerse herself in the bath; and as she lumbered from room to room in her apartment she marveled that she had ever been able to move around onstage carrying so much weight.

Music was her consolation during the midwinter darkness. When Aristo was there, it was hard to practice, but now he was gone she fell back into her former habits—and would sit at her piano for hours. She had forgotten how much pleasure she found in singing just for herself. It was a joy to run through her repertoire without the knot of fear that she had lived with every day since that terrible night in Rome. In those weeks her only audience was herself and of course the baby, who would kick vigorously as she sang.

Bruna had been instructed to tell everyone that Maria had a chest infection and had been ordered by her doctor to rest. That didn't stop friends, and once Meneghini, from coming to the apartment. But Bruna was a human Cerberus, and they were all dispatched. When Maria had heard Meneghini's voice at the door, she had been tempted to stand in front of him, belly first, to show him exactly what Aristo had given her.

But she knew the satisfaction that would bring would not make up for the scandal, and of course the possibility that Tita would claim the child as his own. When she finished her practice she listened to her own recordings and wrote letters. Elvira had written to her after the affair with Onassis became tabloid fodder to say that she knew that Maria would leave her husband only for a man she loved deeply, "and if you have found that kind of passion, dear Maria, then I am happy for you. The stage should not be the only place where you are loved."

It was at the end of Carnevale that she felt the first pain. She dismissed it at first—she was not due for another six weeks. But as she lay in her bed, listening to the sounds of the revelers in the streets and the fireworks exploding, the pain returned, and she asked Bruna to call her doctor. An hour later she was in an operating theater.

⸗

The doctor had a kind face.

"We did everything possible, but the infant's lungs were not developed enough to breathe independently."

Maria looked up at him. "Did he cry?"

The doctor shook his head. "No, he did not take a breath."

"I would like to see him."

The doctor looked doubtful. "I wouldn't advise it, Madame Callas. You have had a major operation, and you need to recover."

But Maria's gaze did not waver.

A nun with the Ash Wednesday cross on her forehead brought in a blanket-wrapped bundle. Maria put out her arms to take it, but the nun kept it out of her reach, allowing her only a glimpse of the dead baby. Maria could not believe the perfection of the tiny face, the eyes closed against the light he would never see. She touched the cheek with her finger: it was cool, not yet cold. She closed her eyes for a moment, and when she opened them her baby was gone.

॥

When she spoke to Aristo that night, she told him that their son looked just like his father, and she heard him make a noise which sounded very like a sob.

"I will be there as soon as I can, *agapi mou*," he said. "I don't want you to be alone."

She started to cry then, and Bruna took the phone away. Outside the bells were ringing for the beginning of Lent.

॥

Aristo was there a week later, his pockets full of diamonds.

"Tribute for you, my darling," as he covered her lap with gems.

Then he lay down on the bed next to her and asked her to tell him everything.

"I want to feel every detail."

Maria told him about the baby kicking when she sang, about the fireworks exploding outside in the street when the pain had started, the cross on the nun's forehead, the tiny face, and the eyes that would never open.

Aristo listened intently. When she had finished, he crossed himself, left to right. "Where is he buried?"

"Bruna knows. I wasn't able to—" She caught her breath.

"I will go, for both of us," Ari said.

He held her as she wept that night and told her that as soon as she was feeling better, he would take her to the Greek islands on the *Christina* and she would recover her strength. Maria felt the warmth of his body next to hers, and the strength of his warm, dry hands as they stroked her hair.

When she was back in her apartment, Ari told her that Tina had been persuaded to pursue a no-fault divorce, which meant that the whole thing would be over in a month.

"Of course she told the press that she didn't want any money. But that isn't true. Her lawyer alone cost one million dollars. Can you imagine."

Maria said nothing. It occurred to her that if the baby had gone to term, Ari could have married her before it was born.

She remembered Meneghini's curse on them both, and she bit her lip. Then she thought of all the jewelry that Tita had given her, and how he has asked for most of it back when they split, even though, as it turned out, he had paid for it using her money. She would not let herself be cursed by a man like that.

Still there were times when she would wake up in a sweat, convinced that the baby's death was a punishment for breaking her marriage vows. Ari was with her one night when this vision had come upon her, and he had tried to make sense of her words as she clung to him shaking with dread.

"No, no, Maria. Don't think that way. You and I were meant to be together."

"Then why did the baby die?"

He was silent for a moment.

"Perhaps it just wasn't meant to be. Maybe God wants us to be lovers, not parents."

Maria looked at him uncomprehendingly.

"Think of how often we made love when you were pregnant. Remember that time on Skorpios, against the olive tree? When Tina was pregnant, I didn't go near her but you . . . I couldn't keep my hands off you. Perhaps we aren't meant to have both."

Maria went rigid in his arms. "You think that was why the baby . . ."

"I don't know, Maria," he said, a touch of exasperation in his voice. "I just wonder if lovers and children are really compatible."

This idea haunted Maria. She understood that the death of the baby was somehow her fault. She had sung in too many operas to believe that such a tragedy could happen randomly. Had she been punished for loving Onassis too much? For sharing her body with him and the baby? It made awful sense to her.

And she could see that while Ari felt her grief, he did not share her sense of loss. He wanted her as a woman, as a lover, but not as a mother or even, she was beginning to think, as a wife. He took little interest in Maria's attempts to divorce Meneghini. The only way she could legally end the marriage in Italy was through an annulment, and that would be almost impossible without Tita's cooperation. When she attempted to discuss the difficulties of her situation with Ari, he always advised her to leave it for a while.

"Meneghini will calm down, and when he does we can make it worth his while to play ball. No self-respecting man will want to play the deserted husband forever. Leave it a few months. He will meet someone else and then he will look at everything differently. And what's the hurry. Aren't we happy just as we are?"

Maria could not deny that they were happy. Despite her grief, she felt cocooned in Onassis's world. He loved her, he wanted her, he whispered to her in Greek, and she felt closer to him than anyone in her life. But she did not want to be his mistress—she wanted to be his wife. When she tried to talk to Ari about this, he would shrug and say, "Maria, my love, isn't it enough that we are together? Remember that if we were married, I might be tempted to find myself a mistress."

# CHAPTER SIXTEEN

## *The Green-Eyed Monster*

MONTE CARLO, MAY 1960

When the Rainiers had asked them for dinner at the palace, Maria had been delighted by the invitation as it made her feel that despite the scandal she and Onassis were now accepted as a couple in society. This was the first time they were attending an event together. But from the moment they sat down to dinner Maria found herself trying not to notice what was happening at the other end of the table where Aristo was flirting with Princess Grace, judging by the eddies of silvery laughter coming from the former film star.

Maria was being monopolized by Prince Rainier, Grace's husband, who knew nothing about opera but was interested in using Maria to burnish the reputation of his principality. He kept asking her when she planned to return to the stage and when she would sing in Monte Carlo. For a moment Maria missed having Tita to soak up all these questions.

It did not help that Elsa was also at the dinner. Maria had not met her since their encounter at the Hôtel de Paris swimming pool just before the famous cruise. Elsa had been outspoken in the press about Callas's outrageous behavior in coming between Onassis and his "charming wife, Tina," and Maria could not forgive her treachery. Nowhere in those press comments was it reported that she had been the person to introduce Maria to Onassis and that, as Maria now knew, she had been paid handsomely to do so. Her awareness of Elsa's beady stare made Maria doubly careful to conceal the frisson of jealousy she felt every time she heard Grace give one of her rich-girl laughs and rest her hand on Onassis's arm.

She tried to reassure herself that Ari was only being polite by flirting with the princess, but there was a part of her that wanted every molecule of his charm to be her property.

There was another couple at the dinner, also a prince and princess, but they were not actual royalty like the Grimaldis. Prince Stash Radziwill was one of many Polish princes who had chosen to retain the title despite giving up his Polish citizenship. His wife, Lee, was American, an East Coast society girl who was so thin and chic that even Grace looked a little matronly in comparison. She said very little until the conversation turned to American politics. It turned out that her sister, Jackie, was married to the Democratic presidential candidate. Rainier asked her whether she thought her brother-in-law, Senator Kennedy, would prevail against the Republican nominee, Richard Nixon, in the upcoming election.

Lee Radziwill smiled and in her soft voice said, "Well, I am quite sure that American women will be voting for Jack. He is handsome, charming, and rich, and Nixon is none of those things."

Grace nodded. "And it would be a great thing to have a Catholic president."

"Even if his father was a bootlegger," said Ari.

Lee Radziwill looked annoyed. "Well, I guess all great fortunes have murky origins. I have heard rumors that you started life as a cigarette smuggler, Mr. Onassis."

Ari grinned. "You are very well informed, Princess Radziwill. I did indeed start my career with some speculation in tobacco, but on the other hand I am not running for office."

Maria felt the hairs on her arms stand up. She had heard that tone in Ari's voice before, that combination of challenge and seduction. It was the tone he had used with her at their first meeting in Venice. She could not see Lee Radziwill from where she was sitting, but she could see Elsa, and from her face Elsa had sensed something too.

After dinner Maria watched Onassis as everyone went out onto the terrace for coffee.

He talked almost exclusively to the men, but when he broke away to greet Elsa, Maria noticed that they both looked over to where the skinny American princess was standing, self-consciously silhouetted against the lights of the harbor, smoking a cigarette.

"No one is safe with women like her around."

Maria turned round in surprise to Princess Grace narrowing her eyes at Lee Radziwill.

"Women like her?"

Grace nodded, and something about the gesture made Maria realize that her hostess was not entirely sober.

"Women who do nothing but buy clothes and look for a richer husband than the one they already have."

Maria felt the knot in her stomach turn. Had Grace seen the flicker between Ari and Lee? But then Rainier joined Lee on the terrace , and as he bent to light her cigarette, she laughed and put her hand on the prince's arm. Grace went on to say tartly, "Women who have done nothing with their lives except marry and decorate. At least you and I, Maria, are women in our own right. I have an Oscar and you are a great singer. But what is that so-called princess? Just a woman with a famous sister who dresses well and who laughs at men's jokes."

Grace turned her back on Lee and looked directly at Maria.

"Rainier didn't want to invite you tonight, but I insisted. I like Tina all right, but she is just like our friend over there: a woman born to look good at the head of a table. But you have done more with your life than rattle about the Med on a yacht."

She put her hand on Maria's arm. "Promise me you won't stop singing, Maria. Aristo isn't worth it; no man is."

She swayed slightly. "I thought that I would go on acting after I married. It's not like there is anything serious for me to do here, apart from the children and parties like this. But Rainier won't hear of it. Hitch offered me a million dollars to be in a movie, a million dollars! Rainier said that if I went, I couldn't come back. So now I'm an extra while he canoodles with the likes of Princess Lee Radziwill."

Maria tried to soothe her. "But Ari says that you have done great things for Monaco, that you have made it glamorous."

"Excuse me, but that is BS. All I have done is smile and wave and have a couple of kids. I'm an actress, a great screen actress, and the only role I will play now is the devoted consort of a tin-pot prince."

Grace's voice was growing louder, and Maria saw Rainier look up in alarm. To her relief she heard Onassis's voice. "I told Maria all about your famous tapestries, Grace. I was hoping you could show them to us."

Grace laughed at this obvious ploy to get her inside and away from Rainier and Lee. "I blame you, Aristotle Onassis, for my predicament. It was you that thought Monaco needed a movie star princess. If you hadn't egged him on, Rainier would have stayed with his mistress and been quite happy."

Ari took the princess by the elbow and skillfully coaxed her inside. "I would have married you myself, Grace, if I had been free. Any man would, including Rainier."

He deposited Grace on a sofa and signaled to a woman, who Maria realized must be a lady-in-waiting, to bring coffee.

"Would you really have married me, Ari?" Grace said, looking up at him with liquid blue eyes.

"Of course!" said Ari, making a bow.

The lady-in-waiting came bustling over with the coffee and stood over Grace to make sure that she drank it.

Maria looked out onto the terrace and saw that Rainier and Lee were still talking, their heads just a little too close together.

"I'm just going to say goodbye to Rainier, and then we'll go." Ari moved out onto the balcony, and Maria watched him interrupt the tête-à-tête.

"I guess you didn't have much acquaintance with the green-eyed monster when you were with poor Meneghini." Elsa had appeared out of nowhere.

Maria bristled at her words. "I don't know what you are talking about, Elsa. All I know is that as usual you have very strong opinions on things that are none of your business."

"When will you understand that everything you do is my business? You may not care for me, but I will never stop loving you, Maria."

In her eagerness to escape, Maria almost ran out onto the terrace.

Knowing that Elsa was watching her, Maria approached the group by the balustrade with her most prima donna smile. "Such a lovely evening, sir," she said to Rainier.

She turned to Lee. "I don't think we have been properly introduced. I am Maria Callas."

She held out one of her long white hands to Lee, who took it gingerly. "Oh, I am a great admirer of yours, Madame Callas. I was just telling Aristo here that I saw you sing Norma at the Met, and do you know what he told me?" She paused to blink with calculated slowness. "He said that he had never seen you in an opera."

Lee looked around her, her eyes wide. "I mean, it's like dating Marilyn Monroe without having seen any of her movies."

Maria's smile did not waver. "But I feel fortunate that Ari knows that singing is only one of my talents."

She touched Onassis's arm and to her relief he took the hint, and he made his goodbyes.

＝

On the tender going back to the *Christina*, Maria asked him, "Would you really have married Grace Kelly?"

Ari laughed. "Of course not. Sure, I would have fucked her if she was up for it, but marry her? No way."

Maria watched as he drew on his cigar. "Women like Grace want constant adoration. That can work for a mistress but not for a wife."

"Grace said that you arranged the marriage between her and Rainier."

"I did. Rainier needed an heir—otherwise Monaco would have become part of France, and all my investments would have been lost in taxation. I knew that Grace would give him a son."

"That's a wife's job," said Maria sadly, but Ari seemed not to hear.

"Rainier must have been the only man in France who wasn't in love with Grace Kelly."

"But you brought them together."

"He got a son, and she got to be a princess. How long do you think she could have gone on being a Hollywood star—five, maybe ten years max. This way she retires gracefully, and the public is left wanting more."

"But she is a brilliant actress."

"Maybe, but she is a mother now, she has other priorities."

Maria had no answer to that. "What did you think of the other princess?"

"Jackie Kennedy's sister? I heard that she slept with Jack Kennedy to get even with Jackie for marrying a future president."

"That's horrible."

Ari's teeth showed white in the moonlight. "You don't think that your sister would sleep with me if she thought it would annoy you? Why don't you invite her for a cruise on the *Christina* and see what happens."

She could hear him laughing in the darkness, and she dug her elbow into his ribs.

"You know I'm right, Maria. But, don't worry—I have no intention of going near your sister. I have one Callas woman, the best one, and that is quite enough for me."

He put his arm around her shoulders and drew her close and kissed her hard on the lips. Before she could stop herself, her body responded, and she was kissing him back. Their embrace was so passionate that they didn't notice that the tender had reached the *Christina*. When Maria opened her eyes, she saw that the crew had disappeared.

Onassis laughed. "What about it, Maria? Shall we christen the dinghy for old times' sake? The crew are so discreet they have all crept off to bed."

Maria kissed him again, and she banished Elsa, Grace, and the skinny Lee Radziwill from her mind. Feeling Ari's desire for her made the knot in her stomach dissolve and they made love in the tender as passionately as they had that first night in the lifeboat.

# CHAPTER SEVENTEEN

# *Norma*

EPIDAURUS, GREECE, AUGUST 1961

There had been talk of rain, but Maria had lit a candle in the tiny chapel on the road up to the ancient amphitheater. She had prayed and it seemed that God had listened. It was the perfect summer night, clear and starry and with a light breeze.

When the idea of performing *Norma* at Epidaurus had first been raised, Maria had been hesitant. She was enjoying her new life on the *Christina*, sailing round the islands and only occasionally giving a concert or making a recording.

Maria relaxed her rigorous self-discipline to stay up late drinking with Ari; and while she didn't smoke herself, she loved the smell of his cigars. It felt good to lie in the sun and swim in the sea, to drink ouzo in little tavernas on the coast, and not to be worrying about her next performance.

The last time she had been on board, Princess Grace had scolded her for not practicing. "You can still use your gift, Maria. You aren't a prisoner like me."

Maria would have shrugged it off, but Onassis had scolded her too when he heard about the offer to sing at the ancient amphitheater at Epidaurus.

"You can't say no, Maria. It is the oldest theater in the world, the cradle of our civilization. Think what it will mean for you, a Greek, to sing there. And think what it will mean for Greece if Maria Callas sings at Epidaurus."

Maria finally agreed when Onassis offered to throw an opening night party on the *Christina*.

"I will go on a cruise around the Cyclades while you are rehearsing and come back for the first night. It will be a party that no one will want to miss. We will ask the prime minister as well as the Grimaldis, the Agnellis, and all the usual crowd."

Maria was thrilled at his use of the word "we," as if they were really husband and wife. Apart from a wedding, there could be no more public acknowledgment of their relationship than this party.

So she clapped her hands with excitement and began to practice in earnest.

⌐

Maria had said goodbye to Ari in Athens a month ago and had plunged into an intensive period of rehearsal. The last two weeks had been in the amphitheater itself. And, as there was no hotel nearby, she had moved into the local museum, using the director's office as a bedroom and dressing room.

She endured the discomfort: sleeping in the stifling museum, forgoing her nightly bath, and the rigors of getting her voice back into shape, secure in the knowledge that she was proving her worth to Ari. As the rehearsals continued, Maria began to rediscover the joy of fully entering a role, and she knew that even if she had to stretch to reach the top C, her performance was as good if not better than it had ever been. The passion she had found with Ari had made her a better Norma.

Norma had broken her sacred vows to serve her people and her goddess when she fell in love with Pollione, and Maria felt that now she fully understood what it meant to sacrifice one's vocation for love, for hadn't she left her music for Onassis? Like Norma, she had been compelled to follow her heart, and, like Norma, she knew what she had sacrificed for love. It had never really felt as if she could have both, but as she rehearsed, she wondered if that was right. Perhaps there was room for passion in her repertoire, that the feeling that fulfilled her as a person could enrich her as an artist. Did she really have to choose between art and life? With Tita there had been no competition: their life together had been all about her voice.

But with Aristo it was different. Part of her wanted to be his woman and nothing else, but there was another part that wanted to be a diva again, to share her unique gift with an adoring audience. If the baby had lived, then things would have been different—she would have been happy to devote herself to a child, but in the absence of one?

She began to warm up for the performance, starting with arpeggios and then moving on to scales, exercising the muscles around her mouth and throat as she moved through the vowel sounds. Every rehearsal, every performance always started like this; and while in the early days in Venice she had been able to skip a few stages without it having an impact on her voice, nowadays she was rigorous about making sure that she exercised every part of her vocal range. She hit a top B-flat almost without noticing as she sped through the scales. It occurred to her that singing was a lot like sex: if you were relaxed and enjoying it, then everything came easily; but when you were worried about the result, then every muscle seemed to work against you.

She stopped for a moment to get a glass of water. At the window she looked out over the bay to see if the *Christina* had arrived. She thought she could make out the familiar shape steaming across water, and she thought longingly of the long bath she would have that night in her stateroom. She picked up a pair of binoculars that belonged to the museum director to take a closer look.

She wore contact lenses now, at Ari's insistence, and she was able to focus on the yacht. To her great relief she could make out the blue-and-white flag of Greece and shape of the lifeboat where she and Ari had found each other. She was about to put the binoculars down when she saw a flash of white on the upper deck. She looked closer and saw that it was a woman in a long white evening dress. She adjusted the focus of the binoculars to magnify the image, but the figure was too far away to be identified, although Maria could see from her posture that she was smoking.

Something about the woman's pose jogged Maria's memory; but then she saw the stage manager signaling to her that there were only thirty minutes till the start time (there was no curtain at Epidaurus), and she banished all thoughts from her mind except the performance ahead.

In the makeshift dressing room, she decided to take out her contact lenses. It would put her off, she thought, to be able to see the audience clearly. She had never sung with her lenses in, and there was too much at stake to start now.

There was a knock at the door and the stage manager came in, carrying a huge bunch of red roses. Maria tore open the envelope, thinking they must be from Ari, but the writing was in Italian not Greek: *Per la Divina, con amore, Franco.*

She was happy that Franco would be there tonight, but all the same she couldn't help feel a shadow of disappointment.

Bruna came to take the flowers away, and as she did so she pressed Maria's hand. "I am so looking forward to hearing you sing again, madame."

Maria saw that Bruna's eyes were full of tears.

♩

Maria made her way through the corridors of the museum, past headless figures of goddesses, until she found herself at the foot of the theater. She stopped for a moment and listened to the hum of the audience. The three-thousand-year-old auditorium was famous for its perfect acoustics: everyone could hear everything. Maria heard the rumor of anticipation, the hard and soft syllables of her name ricocheting around the stadium: "Callas, Callas," and the sibilant hiss of "Onassis, Onassis." But here in Greece, that noise was not one of disapproval. Here, Maria was not Onassis's mistress but his rightful consort; in their homeland the two Golden Greeks were a celestial couple who transcended earthly morality.

Her father was in the audience that night and she wondered if she could hear his laugh. She had introduced him to Onassis when they were in Athens, and the two men had hit it off immediately. They had sat in a café on Syntagma Square, drinking brandy and smoking cigars and making jokes about the passersby. Meneghini had always disapproved of Maria's father, nervous perhaps that he might have financial claims on his daughter. But Ari had treated George like an equal.

They both laughed at the same kind of smutty joke. And George, of course, never chastised him about the fact that his daughter was living in sin. Indeed, he never stopped boasting about his daughter's relationship with Onassis.

Karamanlis, the prime minister of Greece, was in the audience with his wife. From the opera world, there was Ghiringhelli, who had gotten over his fury with Callas, and Elvira de Hidalgo. The only fly in the ointment was the presence of Elsa. Grace had telephoned to say that Elsa had threatened to drown herself in the bay if she wasn't invited.

The dress rehearsal had been in front of an audience of local people who had been bussed in from the villages in the surrounding countryside. Most of them had never seen an opera before but they were enchanted by the spectacle of their national heroine singing for them, even if it was in a foreign language.

Tonight's audience would not be so easy to win over. Tonight, she would be facing people who were waiting to calibrate this Norma against her previous performances, who would be listening to every note, not as music but as a test.

She began the usual prayers as she stood backstage listening to the overture, gripping Bruna's hand. She heard the chorus announcing her entrance and, crossing herself three times, she glided onto the stage.

From the moment she opened her mouth to sing she felt the magic of the occasion, the perfect stillness of the night air, the star-studded sky; and when she came to sing the aria to the moon goddess, "Casta diva," a perfect crescent moon appeared on the horizon as if summoned by the music. She forgot the technical difficulties that the score presented and lost herself in the moment. Tonight, she was singing for Greece, for the glittering audience, but she was really singing for Ari. She wanted him to be transported by her music, to fall under her spell. And so, she sang as she had never sung before—every note was there, but, more than that, there was a purpose to every note that could not be ignored.

After she had led the lover who had betrayed her onto the funeral pyre to die together, and the orchestra had played the final chords, there was complete silence in the amphitheater. Then the applause came like a thunderclap, charging the air with electricity. Maria lost count of how many times she was called back onstage. Normally she knew exactly how many curtain calls she made and even the relative decibel counts of the applause, but tonight it was different. Tonight, it was not about the adoration of the audience, although that had made her feel buoyant, it was about Onassis witnessing her triumph.

But unlike Tita, Onassis was not standing in the wings, and she could not distinguish him in the blur that was the audience. For a moment she felt untethered, unsure of why she was there and what she was doing. Then the surge of applause rose again, and she turned to face the audience, reaching out her hands in gratitude.

There was a car to take her down to the harbor to the after-party on the yacht. Maria had changed into a chiffon chiton dress in the black that Ari preferred.

George Callas whistled when she stepped into the car. "I don't think I have ever seen you look so beautiful."

Maria kissed him on both cheeks. "Have you seen Ari?"

Her father shrugged. "Not yet, but, Maria, you will never guess who I was sitting next to."

Maria wondered where Ari could have been sitting if George hadn't seen him. "I don't know. Who were you sitting next to?"

"Princess Grace of Monaco! And she guessed that I was your father and said that I must be very proud to have such a talented daughter. She could not have been more friendly, and she introduced me to Karamanlis, who said that you were a credit to Greece. I didn't like to remind him that you are an American citizen because you were born there."

Maria was looking over his shoulder for Onassis. Where could he be? He must have gone straight back to the yacht after the performance to make sure that everything was ready for the party. She felt a surge of love for him.

Then her father had caught her by the arm, and said, "Maria, I have a surprise for you."

Standing by the car was a blond woman wearing a blue dress in last year's fashion. Maria rocked backward for a moment, thinking that it was Litza, but as she focused, she saw that it was not her mother but her sister, Jackie.

"*Kallispera*, Maria," said Jackie softly.

Maria looked at her sister closely. She was—what?—forty-two, and there were some signs of age and disappointment on her face, but she was still slim and, despite her slightly dated clothes, elegant. For a moment Maria felt all the resentment of her early years boiling in her stomach: How could her father have brought Jackie here to spoil her evening? To take the attention away from her? But then she noticed that there were dark roots showing where Jackie parted her hair, and she felt a twinge of pity.

She stretched her hands out in her most divaesque gesture. "Jackie!"

Her sister stepped forward and kissed her shyly on both cheeks.

"You look so different," Jackie said. "If I hadn't recognized your voice, I wouldn't have known it was you."

"Well, you look just the same, Jackie."

There was a moment of silence. Then Maria motioned for them all to get in the car. "I don't want to be late for my own party."

She looked at Jackie as they drove down the hill to the harbor. "I can find you something more suitable to wear, Jackie. We are the same size now, although of course you are a little shorter."

"Thank you, Maria. I didn't realize that this would be such a glamorous occasion."

George Callas broke in swiftly. "Tonight is a double celebration. Maria has made history by singing at Epidaurus and at last I am able to put my arms round both my beautiful daughters."

Both women laughed and kissed him on the cheek; and the atmosphere was civil as they traveled on the tender to the *Christina*, until George, who clearly had had a few drinks in the interval, said, "Maria, did you know that your sister has also become a singer? She gave a concert in New York that was well received. Who knows—one day I might be here in Epidaurus to watch Jackie."

Jackie gave an embarrassed laugh. "Oh, Papa, I would never be able to sing in an opera."

"No, you wouldn't," said Maria crisply. "To sing a role like Norma on a stage takes a lifetime of practice and dedication. Concerts, where you have time to prepare the songs and to make sure that they are all in the right key, are one thing, but to perform in an opera house is no job for an amateur."

George took both his daughters' hands. "But I tell you, Jackie was really good. What a shame she didn't get lessons when you did, Maria. Think how happy your mother would be to have two famous singers in the family."

Maria moved her hand away from her father's grasp. "Papa, I know you mean well, but while Jackie may have a good voice, she does not have a great talent; otherwise it would have surfaced just as mine did. And I am quite sure that Mama would have exploited it just as ruthlessly as she did mine."

To the relief of everyone on board, the tender finally pulled up to the stern of the *Christina* and the sisters and their father were helped aboard by the ship's crew.

Maria turned to Bruna, who had come with them in the tender. "Bruna, can you take my sister to my cabin and see if there is something she wants to wear."

Maria turned to Jackie. "Do borrow any jewels that you like, but make sure you leave them behind when you go. The dress you can keep."

Jackie said nothing but followed Bruna down the stairs leading to Maria's stateroom.

George turned to Maria. "Why did you have to be so hard on her, Maria? You have everything and she has so little. Why don't you encourage her if she wants to sing? She is hardly a threat to you."

Maria took a deep breath. Everything her father said was true, but he could not understand what it had been like to be the ugly duckling while Jackie had always been a swan, and to know that however hard she practiced, whatever roles she sang, their mother would always, always look at Jackie with love and at Maria with calculation.

"Perhaps if you had been there, Papa, when we were in Athens, then you would understand." Then she relented. "But I am grateful that you brought her tonight; it has been too long. Will you wait for her here, while I find Ari?"

Maria kissed her father, who looked at her mournfully. The women in his life were only constant in their disappointment with him.

There was a wave of applause as Maria walked onto the main deck, which was already full of guests. She smiled her acknowledgment, but her eyes were searching the room for Ari. She hadn't seen him for a month and all she wanted at that moment was to fall into his arms. She wished she could put on her glasses so that she could see better, but she did not want to be wearing them when she was reunited with Ari.

Maria was being congratulated by Princess Grace and the Greek prime minister when Aristo appeared as if from nowhere and put his arm around her waist. "Maria, *agapi mou*, I hear you were a triumph," and he kissed her on the lips.

Maria looked at him in disbelief, but Grace was the one to speak. "You didn't see her?"

Onassis shrugged. "I had so much to do here to get ready for this." He gestured to the festoons of lights that were hanging round the deck.

Karamanlis nodded. "I am sure everybody is grateful for this magnificent party, but I am sorry if it meant you could not attend one of the greatest performances I have ever seen." He made a little bow toward Maria.

Maria had recovered herself enough to acknowledge his praise with one of her graceful hand gestures.

Grace gave Onassis a cool look. "You need to get someone else to organize your parties, Ari, so that you can hear Maria sing." She put her hand on her chest as if swearing an oath. "You know that one day we will all be forgotten, but Maria Callas will be immortal."

Onassis took Maria's hand and kissed it. "I just wanted your party to be a success. Will you forgive me?"

Maria wanted to scream that she had been singing for him and for him alone, but she nodded and smiled. "I am singing again on Friday. I will make sure you get a seat, Ari."

When Grace and Karamanlis moved on, she and Ari were alone together for a second, and she took his hand. "I was singing for you, Ari. Why didn't you come?"

Ari touched her cheek. "I was scared, Maria."

Maria looked at him, bewildered.

"In case you couldn't do it." He shrugged. "I didn't want to see you humiliated."

"You thought that I was going to be humiliated?"

"Let's say the thought crossed my mind. You haven't seemed that interested in music lately."

"You should have had more faith in me. I wanted you to see me triumph."

Ari laughed. "I didn't need to be there to see that. All anyone can talk about is how magnificent you were."

He shepherded Maria through the crowd like a queen, clearly enjoying the praise that was being heaped on her. Maria introduced him to Elvira, and was pleased when he kissed the old lady's hand saying gallantly, "The famous Elvira de Hidalgo who taught Maria everything she knows."

Elvira blushed. "I did my best, but there are some things you can't teach and Maria was lucky enough to have those already."

She turned to Maria. "You were exceptional tonight."

Ari went over to chastise the waiters for not filling glasses quickly enough, and Elvira leaned in and whispered into her former pupil's ear, "Unmarried life seems to agree with you." Maria smiled, and Elvira squeezed her hand. "It was a great performance."

A shadow passed over Maria's face; she was still recovering from Onassis's words about not wanting to see her fail.

"I don't know how many I have left, Elvira."

Elvira looked at her with compassion. "Nobody knows, Maria." She touched her arm. "But it is always better to stop before you find out."

"Are you saying I should retire now?"

"After tonight's performance? Of course not."

"So how long have I got?"

Elvira sighed. "You will know, Maria, when the time comes."

"Madame de Hidalgo!" Jackie, now wearing a green chiffon gown of Maria's, embraced the older woman.

"I hear you too are a singer now, Jackie."

Jackie looked at the floor. "I gave a couple of concerts, but really it was Mama's idea, and it seemed to make her happy." She shrugged and looked at Maria with appeal in her eyes.

"But nothing will make Mama happy, Jackie. Surely you know that by now?" Maria said briskly.

"At least I try, Maria."

Elvira put up her hands. "I can see that you two have much to talk about," and she slipped away.

Maria was about to answer Jackie when Ari appeared with Elsa in tow.

"Aren't you going to introduce me, Maria?"

"This is my sister, Jackie. Jackie, this is Aristotle Onassis and Elsa Maxwell."

"Older or younger sister?" asked Elsa.

"Older," said Maria shortly, "by six years."

"Welcome to the *Christina*, Jackie," said Ari. "Let me get you a drink." He snapped his fingers at a waiter.

"Thank you, Mr. Onassis. I am very glad to meet you."

"Call me Ari, please." He waved over a waiter who had a silver tray with canapés.

"Here, Jackie, have one of these. If you are anything like your sister, you like caviar."

Jackie took one of the blinis. "How delicious."

"Have another one."

Jackie shook her head.

"Not greedy like Maria, eh? She would eat all of these if I didn't stop her."

Elsa looked at the scene with her bright malicious eyes. "I hear that your mother is writing a book about you, Maria."

Maria froze.

"Oh, I didn't mean to shock you, Maria. I assumed that you knew."

Maria turned to Jackie. "Did you know about this."

Jackie looked uncomfortable. "She mentioned something about writing a book, but I didn't think she would actually do it. Her English isn't good enough."

"Oh, that won't be a problem if she has a good enough story to tell," said Elsa. "The publisher will find someone to turn it into decent prose."

Onassis waved his hand impatiently. "I'll find out how much she is being paid, and then I will offer her double not to publish."

Maria looked at him seriously. "Please, Ari, you will do no such thing.

If my mother thinks that she can exploit our relationship for money, she will never stop."

Jackie twisted unhappily. "She really is quite badly off, Maria. It would make such a difference if you could send her money every month so that she can stop working in that shop."

Maria could not stop herself from replying. "Why should she stop working? She is only fifty-five. I work, you work, Ari works, even Elsa here works. Why should my mother be a lady of leisure just because her daughter is famous?"

Elsa took out a little notebook from her evening bag. "You don't mind if I quote you on that, do you, Maria?"

Onassis took the book out of her hand and threw it in the sea. "Now, Elsa, you know better than that."

There was a cough from a couple behind them, and Karamanlis appeared with his wife.

"I would like to say a few words if you will give me permission, Onassis."

"I would be delighted." Onassis led the prime minister to the gantry where he could address the crowds on the deck below.

Karamanlis, an imposing figure with tuft-like eyebrows, gestured for silence, and gradually the cocktail party chatter subsided.

"My friends, a politician cannot let a moment like this pass without making a speech. First, I must thank two of my country's most distinguished representatives: Aristotle Onassis and Maria Callas."

Maria was listening and not listening to the prime minister's speech. She could tell from the moment he opened his mouth that he was someone who very much enjoyed the sound of his own voice and that he might be up there for some time. Ari, though, was watching the prime minister intently.

Her gaze wandered over to where most of the guests were standing on the other side of the deck. She had put her lenses back in, so she had the novel experience of being able to see reasonably well. She smiled at Franco and his friend, the designer Renzo Mongiardino, but then her smile faded as she saw a woman in a white dress standing just behind Renzo. It was the same woman she had seen earlier. Now she remembered where she had seen that silhouette before, against the balustrade of the Grimaldi Palace terrace, smoking a cigarette. Her skin looked even more tanned against the white dress that left one shoulder bare, and the slit in the skirt exposed a slim brown thigh. It was the first lady's sister, the American princess, Lee Radziwill.

With the clarity that only jealousy can bring, Maria realized that her engagement at Epidaurus had suited Ari very well. While Maria had been busy rehearsing, Onassis had been cruising around the Cyclades with the Radziwills.

Karamanlis was still talking. "Maria Callas may have been born in New York, but we Greeks know that in her heart she is one of us, and it is her Greek sense of theater that makes her the greatest opera singer of her generation, perhaps of all time. It is a great honor to hear her sing here in Epidaurus, the cradle of our Greek civilization."

Everyone was looking at Maria now, apart from Lee Radziwill, who was looking at Ari.

Another jealous insight pierced Maria's heart: Ari had missed the performance so that he could stay on the yacht with Lee. Despite the warmth of the night, Maria shivered. All that talk from Ari about not wanting to see her fail was just a way to make her feel so insecure that she wouldn't argue with him.

Karamanlis's speech finished at last. Maria gripped her arms tightly to stop herself from lashing out. She had to content herself with imagining drawing her fingernails down Lee's lean brown leg and across those high cheekbones.

Her murderous thoughts were interrupted by a touch on her arm. "Maria, I have come to say goodbye." Her sister looked up at her, anxiously smoothing the green chiffon of her skirt. "Are you sure that I can have this?"

"Of course. It looks good on you."

"You have so many lovely clothes."

"I have worked hard for them."

Maria's face was hard, but Jackie persevered. "You know when you first came onstage, I almost didn't recognize you. It is hard to believe that you and I once shared a bedroom in Patission Street, and now you are the most glamorous woman in Greece, living on a yacht with a millionaire."

Maria sighed. "Are you happy, Jackie, with your life? Are you still living with Milton?"

Jackie nodded. "But he is not well. He has a cancer; I don't know whether he will live much longer."

"I am sorry. So, you look after him, and he still won't marry you?"

Jackie looked sad. "I am afraid that Milton is more afraid of his family than of me leaving him. And I still love him, so I stick around, even though I know that I should really move on."

Maria noticed the tiny lines around her sister's eyes. "You never wanted to have children?"

"Of course, but not as the mistress, and now"—Jackie shrugged gracefully—"it's too late." She turned to Maria. "It was quite something to see you tonight. I had no idea that you had become so . . . so magnificent. Of course, your singing has always been wonderful, but now you have caught up with your voice somehow."

Jackie took her sister's hand. "I suppose what I am trying to say is that I am proud of you, Mary Anne Kalogeropoulou."

Maria looked her in the eyes. "Thank you. But you know, Jackie, whatever it may look like, it is not easy to be me. Like you, I am now with a man who may never marry me, and, like you, I love him so much I cannot leave him. I do not know how much longer I can go on singing. Yes, I have the dramatic skills but my voice . . . cannot be relied upon forever. And then where will I be? A has-been soprano without a ring on her finger."

Jackie gave her a half smile. "That's one thing that hasn't changed about you, Maria. You always loved to exaggerate. You will never be a has-been—you will always be Maria Callas, whether you are singing or not."

⸗

When at the end of the evening, Maria and Ari were alone together in their stateroom, they looked at each other warily for a moment like two boxers sizing up their opponent's swing and then they fell upon each other savagely, making love with a violence that felt ancient in its ferocity. Onassis pushed Maria facedown on the bed and he started to push into her from behind, ignoring her gasp of surprise and pain. When he had finished, he turned over and looked at her, his dark eyes unreadable. "You may be a great singer, but here I can do whatever I want to you." Maria knew that she should protest, tell him that she was not his possession, but she felt curiously passive, drained of all emotion. All she could think of were the twiglike limbs of the American princess. Had she been here in this bed or had Ari taken her to the lifeboat? Or perhaps he hadn't fucked her yet but was still waiting for the right moment.

"You didn't tell me that the Radziwills were on the cruise."

Onassis smiled. "They nearly weren't. Garbo was meant to come but she canceled, and they are the kind of Eurotrash that will accept an invitation at the last minute. My guess is that the princess has very expensive tastes, and poor Stash is realizing he can't afford her."

He said this so naturally that she wondered if she had been imagining things.

"But I wish I hadn't asked them because all Lee could talk about was American politics."

He sounded quite sincere as he said this, and the force of Maria's anger began to shrivel. She said lightly, "She didn't seem like a person who was particularly interested in politics."

"Oh, she isn't, but because of her sister she takes a personal interest. I think she imagines herself becoming a fixture in the White House."

Maria put her hand to Aristo's cheek. "I have missed you so much, you know."

"And I you."

He bent over and kissed her gently. "And I will be there on Friday to hear you sing."

Maria nodded and pulled him to her.

## CHAPTER EIGHTEEN

# "L'amour Est un Oiseau Rebelle"

NEW YORK, MAY 19, 1962

Her first instinct was to say no. She didn't want to go to New York; she didn't want to see Lee Radziwill or her sister, the first lady. But when Aristo heard that the Democratic committee organizing JFK's forty-fifth birthday party fundraiser at Madison Square Garden had invited her to be the headline act, he insisted that she accept.

"Are you crazy, Maria? It will be the biggest event of the year. Everyone will be there—how can you possibly refuse?"

"But I like being here on the yacht with you, Ari."

"What's the point of that famous voice of yours, if you don't use it? And I will be going to that concert whether you sing or not."

Maria accepted the invitation that afternoon. The organizer of the committee suggested that she should choose something to perform that would suit the venue and the occasion. Maria had asked rather acidly if they wanted her to sing "Happy Birthday," and the woman on the other end of the phone had laughed nervously. "Oh no, Madame Callas, we already have someone to sing that. We want you to sing something operatic."

"Does the president have a favorite opera?"

"Well, I really don't know. I think the first lady is the musical one."

Maria closed her eyes. "Perhaps I should sing something from *Carmen.*"

"Oh yes"—the woman sounded relieved—"that would be perfect. Everybody loves *Carmen.*"

Maria bit her lip. Everyone did love *Carmen*, which made it difficult to sing past people's preconceptions.

She had tried to explain this to Ari, but he had dismissed her fears. "Look, Maria, they booked you because they wanted to look classy and you are the opera singer that everyone has heard of. No one is going to know whether you are singing well or badly—they just want to be able to tell their friends that they heard the great Maria Callas sing at Madison Square Garden on the president's birthday."

She had gone to Milan to have a dress made for the concert. Alain and she had gone back and forth about the sort of thing she should wear.

Alain had shown her one sketch, a mermaid dress in red, and Maria had torn it up in fury.

"Just because I am singing Carmen doesn't mean I want to dress like a Spanish whore."

Ari had told Maria that he had heard that Marilyn Monroe would also be performing at the concert. Maria wanted to make the distinction between a serious artist and a blond movie star.

"They have asked her to sing on the same bill as me! If Ari wasn't so desperate for me to do it, I would pull out now."

Alain tried to soothe her; he came up with a dress that was the antithesis of something Marilyn might wear, full skirted with a tight bodice, a square neckline and long sleeves. It had a faintly Renaissance look to it, and the material echoed the shape, being a richly patterned moiré silk, magenta poppies on an emerald background. It gave her the look of a Spanish infanta in a Velázquez painting. It was a serious dress, one that made it clear that the wearer was there to give a performance, not an act.

On the day that Maria had her final fitting, she got a call from her sister.

"It's Mama," said Jackie, sounding tearful. "She has taken an overdose. She is in Lenox Hill Hospital."

Maria's voice was cold. "What do you expect me to do about it, Jackie?"

"Aren't you going to New York to sing at the president's concert? You could go and see her. I can't leave Athens because Milton is dying, and it's you that she wants to see anyway."

Maria let out a long breath. "To be honest, I wish the overdose had worked."

She had to hold the phone away from her ear, as she heard the anguished gasp from her sister.

〜

When Maria phoned Ari to tell him about her mother's suicide attempt, he was pragmatic. "You will have to see her, Maria."

"It's blackmail."

"But it won't look good for you if the press finds out that you have snubbed her."

"I don't care about the press," she said defiantly.

"You know that's not true."

"I can't see her, Ari. You don't know how much she made me suffer."

There was a sigh at the other end of the phone. "Then give her the money, Maria. Otherwise, she will go on doing this."

"But why should I spend the money I have worked so hard for on her?"

Onassis sounded impatient. "Because she is your mother, Maria, and you have an obligation to her whether you like it or not. Just do it."

So, with great reluctance, on the day before she flew to New York, she made arrangements to pay her mother two hundred dollars a month. It made her feel better to think that she was following Aristo's advice. In her head she convinced herself that she was doing this for her lover, not her mother.

〜

When she arrived at Madison Square Garden for the run-through, Maria's heart sank. The arena was festooned with balloons and every balcony was swagged with banners celebrating the president's birthday and the Democratic party. Although the organizers of the gala had been at pains to tell her that she was headlining the event, when she was taken to her dressing room, it was not the one nearest the stage—that she realized had been reserved for Marilyn Monroe.

When she complained about this to Onassis, who had come to wish her luck, he shrugged. "She's a movie star, and you are just a diva. If you want to be that kind of famous, make a movie."

"You don't think I am famous enough?"

Onassis shrugged. "I'm not the one complaining about my dressing room."

They were in Maria's suite at the Plaza. Onassis was staying on the other side of Fifth Avenue in the apartment he kept at the Pierre Hotel. Maria had wanted to stay with him, but Onassis had said that he didn't think it would be respectful to the president if they became the story by sharing a hotel suite. And he had mollified Maria by making sure that she had been assigned the penthouse suite at the Plaza.

She went to change into her dress. Bruna held open the net petticoats for her to step into, and then she pulled the dress over her head. As she did it up, Bruna tutted.

"What's the matter, Bruna?"

"Madame has lost weight; the dress is loose on you. You should be careful; it is not good for you to be too thin."

Maria saw the concern in the other woman's face and, as she looked at herself in the mirror, she could see that Bruna was right: her cheekbones were more angular than normal and the bodice looked deflated.

But her reverie was interrupted by Ari who had grown tired of waiting. "Turn around so I can see you," he ordered. Maria turned around.

Onassis looked her up and down. "Well, no one is going to mistake you for a movie star in that dress," he said.

Maria felt her stomach knot. "I know you like me in black, Ari, but I can't wear it onstage. I have to wear something that will catch the light, especially in a huge space like that."

Ari frowned, and Maria started to wonder if she had anything else she could wear—she didn't want to go onstage wearing a dress that Ari hated.

Then Ari put his hand in the pocket of his suit and pulled out a red leather box, which he held out to Maria.

"Well, this should help you stand out."

The light from her dressing table hit the box as she opened it, and Maria was dazzled by the diamonds inside.

"Oh, Ari, I don't know what to say."

She held them up around her neck, and Bruna rushed forward to fasten the triple-strand diamond choker.

Ari nodded his approval. "Now you look like a million dollars." He grinned. "Literally."

She stepped forward and flung her arms around him. Bruna slipped out of the room.

"Oh, darling, I don't know how to thank you."

Onassis whispered in her ear, "I can think of a way."

"But we don't have time, I have to be at the theater in ten minutes."

He put his hand on her shoulders, trying to push her to her knees, but she resisted. "No, darling, not like that, not before a performance."

Feeling his mounting frustration, she let him push her against the desk, and enter her from behind, her dress billowing in front of her like a flowery pool. His hands closing around the diamonds on her neck.

Afterward he said, "I wonder if Marilyn is doing the same for JFK?"

Maria looked at him in amazement. "You mean they . . ."

"Surely you knew?"

Maria shook her head.

"That's why the first lady won't be at the concert."

There was a knock at the door and Bruna came in to tell Maria that the car was waiting. As Maria stood in the elevator, she lifted her hands to her throat to feel the diamonds and tried not to think about how Ari knew that the first lady wouldn't be at the concert. He must have been talking to Lee.

⇋

The traffic was snarled around the Garden, and Maria worried that she would be late for the first time in her life. But she arrived just as the beginners bell was ringing. She had just sat down to retouch her makeup when the director, Richard Adler, burst in. "Oh, thank God you're here, Madame Callas."

"I'm sorry—the traffic was terrible."

"I hope you don't mind but we might have to ask you to sing 'Happy Birthday,' if Marilyn doesn't show. No one can get hold of her."

Maria extended a hand in a gracious gesture of assent. "I hope I can remember the words."

He looked at her in horror, and then, realizing that she was joking, he gave her a thin smile. "You can't imagine how difficult this has been to organize. I wish everyone was as easy to deal with as you."

Maria laughed. "You must be the first director in the world to say that."

Adler hurried off and Maria started to fill in the black wings around her eyes. She could see Bruna watching her in the background.

"What do you think of my necklace, Bruna?"

Bruna nodded. "It is magnificent, madame." But Bruna's voice was flat.

Maria noticed at once. "What's wrong, Bruna?"

"Nothing, madame."

Maria was about to press her when a huge roar, which announced the arrival of the president, went up from the audience. Then the orchestra started to play the specially composed birthday overture.

The lineup for the concert was unlike any that Maria had appeared in before. The evening was hosted by Peter Lawford, the president's brother-in-law, and the acts included Ella Fitzgerald, Henry Fonda, and Peggy Lee.

Maria's was the only classical performance. She understood why Ari had wanted her to be on the bill—he was fascinated by Hollywood—but it was galling that he didn't understand the difference between talent and celebrity. She couldn't help feeling that her currency was being debased by appearing in this company.

But her opinion changed as she stood in the wings listening to Ella Fitzgerald singing "Summertime." She realized that Fitzgerald was her equal as an artist and Maria couldn't help envying the other woman's phrasing and her longevity. She must be at least six years older than Maria, and yet her voice was in peak condition.

Fitzgerald was followed by Henry Fonda, reading out something patriotic, and then there was a military band.

Maria went back to her dressing room; she was the first act after the interval. She had insisted on that: it made the evening less like a variety show. There were gales of laughter coming from the audience as they watched Danny Kaye. Maria started to do her warm-up exercises; moving up and down the scales through all the vowels of the alphabet. She was halfway through E-flat major, when the door was pushed open by a blond woman in high heels who appeared to be naked.

"Oh, I am sorry to disturb you"—the voice was soft and whispery—"but I wondered if you had any ice. I have all the fixings for a martini, except the ice." She held up a cocktail shaker.

Maria looked closer and saw that the woman was in fact wearing a flesh-colored dress that clung to her like a second skin and was embellished with sparkling beads at every relevant point.

Bruna opened the icebox and started to fill the bucket.

The blonde smiled at her. "Oh, that is so kind of you. I just need a bit of a boost." She held out her hand. "I'm Marilyn, by the way, and you must be Maria Callas."

Maria took the small soft hand that felt as fragile as Marilyn's voice.

"Are you nervous, Maria? I am," said Marilyn, as she dropped cubes of ice into the shaker.

"I am always nervous before a performance," Maria answered.

"That is so surprising. I have heard you sing, and you seemed fearless."

Maria showed her surprise. "You've heard me sing?"

Marilyn giggled, "I know—Right, you don't expect someone like me to go to the opera.... I went to *La traviata* at the Met. I watched you die onstage, and I swear I saw the lights go out in your eyes. It was incredible. I mean everyone knows you have a wonderful voice, but you are a great actress too." And Marilyn bestowed on Maria her sweetest smile.

"Thank you, Miss Monroe."

"Oh, call me Marilyn, I don't feel like a 'miss' tonight." She winked and did a little shimmy that made all the beads on her frock sparkle. "What do you think of the dress."

Maria picked her words carefully. "It is very ... glamorous."

Marilyn gave another little shake. "It's too much, right? But the DNC booked Marilyn Monroe, the world's favorite piece of ass, and, boy, is that what they are going to get."

She picked up two glasses from the tray on top of Maria's icebox. "Do you mind? I hate to drink alone."

She held the cocktail bullet firmly and shook it back and forth vigorously. She poured an inch of oily frosted liquid into each glass.

Maria took the glass, even though she never drank before a performance. But she was transfixed by Marilyn. She had met many movie stars—Marlene Dietrich and Elizabeth Taylor were almost friends—but Marilyn was different.

Even though she must be one of the most famous women in the world, there was no trace of that in her manner. On the contrary, she seemed to be looking for approval.

"Bottoms up," said Marilyn, taking an adult swig of her martini.

Maria took a cautious sip of her drink, and then put it down. "If I drink that, I won't be able to remember the words."

Marilyn took another swig. "I need all the help I can get. I am not really a singer, you know."

Maria smiled at her. "Do you want to warm up with me?"

Marilyn swayed slightly. "That would be just swell."

Maria took her through some of the simple arpeggio drills and was touched by the breathy sweetness of the other woman's voice. It didn't have much force, but it was in tune and was an instrument that Marilyn clearly knew how to use.

"I'm not really meant to be here," said Marilyn. "I'm in the middle of a movie, but when the president calls, you can't really say no."

"Did you want to?" asked Maria.

For the first time, Marilyn looked down. "No, I wanted to come. Big-time."

And when she looked up again, Maria recognized the look in her eyes. She had seen it before. There was a photo of her and Onassis on the *Christina*, and she had been looking at Aristo with just the same intensity.

Maria hesitated. "I hear that the first lady has another engagement."

This time Marilyn's smile was knowing. "Well, this is the president's night, after all."

She touched Maria's hand. "Is there someone you are singing for?"

Maria nodded.

Marilyn opened her lovely eyes wide. "He is going to be very proud of you tonight, Maria."

There was a great clattering as the dancers from the Jerome Robbins troupe ran past the doorway. The vibration made the beads on Marilyn's bosom jingle. Marilyn started to laugh and Maria joined in.

"Beads and skin, that's all this dress is," said Marilyn.

The interval bell rang, and Marilyn stood up. "You're on next, aren't you?"

Maria nodded, impressed that, though Marilyn was clearly quite drunk, she could remember the set order.

Marilyn wobbled to the door. "See you on the other side, Maria." And she was gone.

ᔍ

Later, Maria watched Marilyn's performance from the wings: the sashay to the podium, the audience's gasp as she dropped the white fox stole she was wearing and for a moment it looked as though she was naked. On another woman the dress would have looked indecent, but on Marilyn it looked divine, as if she were Venus herself. As she sang, or rather breathed, "Happy birthday, Mr. President," there was a great stillness in the audience. It was a stillness that was familiar to Maria. The audience knew that they were seeing a great performance that, like all great performances, came from the heart. It was not often that Maria was upstaged, but tonight it was breathy-voiced Marilyn who stole the show. Maria was surprised to find that she did not mind. There was nothing to envy there. Maria understood that Marilyn was desperately in love and that it was an affair that could not end happily. Before she met Onassis, she would have found the spectacle of a woman so publicly displaying her desire for a married man shocking, but now her world had changed and she quite understood why a woman would want to bare her soul to the world in front of the man she loved.

At the party afterward in a paneled apartment high above Fifth Avenue Maria and Marilyn posed for pictures. The movie star had clearly finished off the shaker of martinis, and she was too obviously waiting for the arrival of JFK. When Onassis came over to congratulate them, Marilyn looked at him with big eyes. "I hope you know how lucky you are, Mr. Onassis."

Onassis gave her his most wolfish smile. "I know that I am talking to the two most beautiful women in America."

Marilyn blinked and then shook her head. "You had the greatest singer in the world singing her heart out for you. That's what I call luck, don't you?" bestowing on him her sleepy smile.

Ari looked uncomfortable, but before he could reply the Secret Service men came into the room and Marilyn was swept up in the crowd that surged toward the president and his brother.

Ari looked after Marilyn and shrugged. "Just as well the first lady had another engagement, don't you think?"

Maria was watching Marilyn smiling up at the president as they shook hands like strangers.

"I feel sorry for her," said Maria.

"For Jackie Kennedy?"

"No, for Marilyn. She is so much in love, and she is never going to find happiness with him."

Onassis laughed unkindly. "A woman like that knows what she is getting into when the president makes a pass."

Maria looked at Marilyn swaying in front of JFK and his brother, her blond hairpiece slightly askew. "I don't think any woman knows what she is getting into when she falls in love, Ari."

Maria wanted to leave the party then, but Ari told her that it would be considered rude to go before the president did. So she mingled with other performers, who sadly didn't include Ella Fitzgerald. She was talking to Jack Benny and failing to laugh at his jokes when she was aware of a small baleful presence at her elbow.

"Hello, Maria," said Elsa.

Maria nodded in greeting and Jack Benny took his chance to escape.

"How does it feel to sing Carmen in front of a president?"

"It was a great honor."

"Are you going to sing mezzo from now on?" Elsa asked with a knowing smile.

"Not at all. I am going to be singing Tosca soon at Covent Garden." This was not strictly true; Maria had been hesitating about signing the contract for *Tosca* with Zeffirelli directing, but the look on Elsa's face had made the decision for her.

"Oh well, that is something to look forward to," said Elsa.

"It will be such a pleasure to work with Franco again." Maria inclined her head regally.

"Interesting that neither the first lady or her sister were at the concert, don't you think?" Elsa's eyes flickered.

Maria understood the implication behind Elsa's remark but kept her face neutral. "If you say so, Elsa."

"I can quite understand why Jackie didn't want to hear the *maîtresse-en-titre* making love to the president onstage, but I am surprised at Lee; she is so fond of her brother-in-law."

Elsa looked at Maria expectantly.

To her relief, Maria saw Dr. Krim, the hostess, standing behind Elsa.

"Madame Callas, the president would like to thank you for your performance tonight."

Maria followed her to where Kennedy was standing with his brother.

"Such a pleasure to hear you sing, Madame Callas. I can't thank you enough," said the president.

Maria put her right hand on her heart in the graceful gesture that she used to acknowledge applause.

"It was an honor, Mr. President. But I am forced to admit that mine was not the most memorable performance of the night."

In heels she was the same height as Kennedy and she looked him straight in the eye as she spoke.

Kennedy's grin didn't falter. "My actual birthday isn't for ten days, but I already feel that I have been celebrated enough."

The president moved on, and Maria looked over to where Marilyn was standing surrounded by members of the Kennedy entourage. One of Kennedy's brothers-in-law had an arm around her waist, which was clearly a protective measure, as the actress looked as though she might be about to fall over.

The presidential party finally left, taking Marilyn with them, and Maria caught the other woman's eye as she was corralled toward the door. She looked utterly lost.

# CHAPTER NINETEEN

# *Those Whom the Gods Love . . .*

IONIAN SEA, AUGUST 1962

Two months later Maria woke up to headlines announcing that Marilyn Monroe was dead. Maria felt cold even though it was August in Greece. It was horrible to think of that shining fragile creature being snuffed out. The newspaper report said that she had died at home, and Maria wondered if she had taken her own life. She crossed herself reflexively and looked out over the Mediterranean with tears in her eyes.

Aristo walked on deck after his morning swim and gave Maria a salty kiss.

"What's the matter?"

Maria gestured toward the newspaper headline.

Onassis sighed and he too made the sign of the cross.

"She was only thirty-six, Ari. What a waste."

He shrugged. "In a few years, she would have lost her looks and then where would she be? Better to go when you are still at the top of the tree."

Maria looked at him in horror. "How can you be so callous?"

Ari said in Greek, "Those whom the gods love die young."

Maria was silent. It occurred to her that they very rarely spoke Greek together anymore.

Ari went on in English. "The first lady must be happy. Maybe the president will get another baby."

Maria got up. "Why are you being so cynical. You know I liked Marilyn," she said accusingly.

"You met her once for thirty minutes, Maria," replied Onassis without emphasis.

"But she made a big impression on me. We had a lot in common." Maria thought of Marilyn asking her whom she was singing for.

"You had nothing in common with Monroe, apart from being a great piece of ass, of course."

"Don't be disgusting. And, anyway, how do you know? Did you sleep with her?"

Ari winked at her. "Let's say I have it on good authority. I think Miss Monroe was a more willing partner than Mrs. Kennedy."

Maria turned away, hating him in that moment.

"What I don't understand, Maria, is how you can be so upset about a woman you hardly know and yet when your own mother tries to kill herself you don't bat an eyelid."

"It's completely different. My mother didn't want to die. She just wanted attention. You've never met her; you don't know what she's like." Maria spat the words out.

Ari went on talking in an annoyingly calm voice. "Oh, I think I have a pretty good idea."

Maria narrowed her eyes. "What's that supposed to mean?"

He shrugged. "I'll let you figure that out while I go and take a shower."

Maria watched him walk up to the steps to the master cabin and disappear.

The *Christina* was moored off Meganissi in the Ionian Sea. She looked over at Skorpios, where she could see that work was beginning on the chapel at the beach. Ari spent most of the day on the island, chivvying the workers and planting trees. He worked shirtless and his back was the color of the *Christina*'s teak fittings. He was quite happy to work all day in the hot sun, but Maria had felt faint after twenty minutes, much to Ari's delight.

"You aren't from true peasant stock like me."

Maria resented the island for taking Ari away from her during the day and for making him so tired that when he came back, he would fall asleep without touching her.

She knew that she should go back to Milan and start practicing again. She had a recording of *Medea* coming up, and there was the Zeffirelli production of *Tosca* to prepare for. She knew that the smart thing to do would be to leave; but every time she resolved to tell Bruna to pack the bags, Ari would give her that grin, or kiss her on the neck in passing, and she would ask herself why she was in such a hurry.

She decided to go when his children came at the end of the week. They were always rude to her, and Ari never reproached them. She had tried so hard to make them like her, especially Christina, but it was clear that they blamed her for the breakup of their parents' marriage. She knew that behind her back they called the singer *Kolou*, or fat arse. Maria had attempted to explain that sometimes things happened that were beyond your control, but they had looked at her with sullen, closed faces. Maria knew that they were dead set against the idea of her marrying their father and that they still dreamed that their parents would reunite. Maria had hoped the children might change their attitude when Tina married the Marquis of Blandford, the son of the Duke of Marlborough and a relation of Winston Churchill, but it had made no difference at all.

Tina's wedding had thrown Ari into an uncharacteristic sulk. Maria overheard him shouting on the phone one day. "Who told you to marry that Englishman with no chin? Everyone knows he's a drunk with no money. You should never have left me, Tina. You don't know how to look after yourself."

Maria had gone into the bedroom and slammed the door. But Ari had been cheerful at dinner, and she decided that to say anything would be pointless. She wasn't jealous of Ari's feelings for Tina; the only thing she coveted was her wedding ring.

She hoped that Tina's wedding might prompt Onassis to propose, but he still stuck to his argument that they were perfectly happy as they were. "Why do you want to marry me? You are Maria Callas. The whole world knows who you are. Why do you want to be anything else?" There were times when Maria almost agreed. But since Lee Radziwill had begun to hover at the edges of her vision, she wanted something more.

She remembered Tina's words to her on the yacht—comparing Ari to the Duke in *Rigoletto*, swearing undying love to one woman after another.

Ari came back on deck, wearing a polo shirt and white trousers, looking pleased with himself.

He put his hand on her shoulder. "What are you going to do today, *agapi mou*?" Their earlier spat had evidently been forgotten.

"Practicing. I am meant to be recording in a couple of weeks."

"Where?"

"In Paris."

Ari sighed. "You know how I hate it when you go away."

Maria took her hand in his. "Do you want me to cancel?"

Ari shook his head. "No, you should go, and maybe I can join you there later. You should stay at the Paris apartment."

"Thank you, darling."

"Have you thought any more about the film?" Ari asked. "I told Carl that if you were no good, I will pick up the tab."

Maria was surprised. "But that would cost a fortune."

Ari shrugged. "I think you should be on-screen, and I am happy to put my money where my mouth is."

The film was an adaptation of *The Guns of Navarone* that was being produced by Ari's friend Carl Foreman. There was a cameo part for a Greek actress and Ari had suggested to Maria that it would be the perfect start to her film career.

But Maria was not at all sure that she wanted a film career. A film of an opera was one thing; but she knew nothing about acting for the screen, and she wanted to do something only if she knew she could do it well. Ari didn't understand her hesitation. To him there was no difference between an opera about a nineteenth-century courtesan and a twentieth-century thriller about Greek partisans. He couldn't understand why Maria wouldn't leap at the opportunity to be in a Hollywood movie.

"I don't know, Ari. I am nearly forty. You thought poor Marilyn was over-the-hill and she was only thirty-six."

Ari shrugged. "You are playing a Greek partisan, Maria. No one is asking you to be sexy."

Maria laughed sardonically. "That's a relief."

Ari looked at her in exasperation. "I don't understand you, Maria. One minute you say that you are too old, but when I say it doesn't matter how you look, you are offended. I am only trying to help you."

"Ari, can't you understand that I am a great singer, maybe the greatest singer in the world. Why would I want to do anything else?"

But Aristo was walking away, putting his hand up to say that he wasn't listening.

Maria went to her stateroom and told Bruna to start packing. "We are going to Milan and then Paris."

"And do you know when we will be coming back, madame?"

Maria shook her head.

# CHAPTER TWENTY

## *Poor Butterfly*

PARIS, OCTOBER 1962

The recording had gone better than she had expected. Medea was a demanding role but she had felt happy with her performance. Singing in a recording studio was never as satisfying as singing before an audience, but now she understood so much better the jealousy that had driven Medea. Giuseppe Di Stefano, who had sung Jason with her many times before, almost fell over when they sang their first duet.

"You have never sung it like that before, Maria. I was frightened."

Maria smiled. "Jason should be frightened of Medea."

"But I am frightened of you, Maria. I thought you really wanted to kill me."

"I am sure it has done you good to be frightened of a soprano, as it is usually the other way round."

The other female singers in the recording studio's greenroom smiled at that remark. Di Stefano was notorious for taking liberties with attractive young singers onstage when they had no way of retaliating.

Onassis had rung the night before to say that he would be joining her the following day. Maria had gone to Alexandre to have her hair done. She kept her hair short as Ari preferred it, but sometimes she would try to twist her hair around her hands, as she used to do when she was rehearsing; and when she found nothing, there would be a pang of regret.

Maria had brought a few clothes with her, and she decided to wear a black jersey sheath that she knew Ari liked and the necklace he had given her on the night of JFK's birthday fundraiser.

After she had done her eye makeup, she went into Ari's study to retrieve her necklace. She had put it there for safekeeping because it was not something she would wear on the yacht, and the security of her house in Milan could not compare to Ari's apartment on Avenue Foch.

Although she didn't know the combination, she had watched Ari open it enough times to guess that it was set to some combination of the day and year that he was born. The first combination she tried didn't work, and she wondered whether she should wait for Ari. But she wanted to be wearing the necklace when he arrived.

She fiddled with the combination again, but this time she tried the number of Ari's saint's day instead of the day of his birth, and the lock released with a satisfying click.

Maria saw the box with her necklace immediately, sitting on top of a couple of files. She was about to close the safe when she saw that there was another Cartier case that had slipped down behind the files.

She picked it up and, after a moment's hesitation, opened it. She recognized the contents at once. It was a bracelet exactly like the one she was wearing at that moment, a simple gold bangle with five letters picked out in diamonds. She didn't have to peer at the diamonds to know what letters they were. They would be the same as the ones on her bracelet, except that one letter would have been changed. Instead of *M* for Maria there would be an *L* for Lee.

She suddenly felt cold. She felt around to see if there was anything else in the box. Tucked into the velvet lining, she found a slip of paper on which Ari had written, "Plato believed that all souls consisted of two halves that have been separated and are trying to find each other again. I have found my other half in you, Ari."

Maria crumpled the note and tore it into tiny pieces. She put the box back into the safe and turned the combination lock. She took the diamond necklace and put it around her neck. It really was a beautiful piece.

The bracelet was a shock, but she had always known that she wasn't the first woman to be given one. She had after all seen the same one on Tina's matchstick of a wrist on the *Christina*. Finding the note was much worse, not just because he had used the same words but because she realized there had been nothing special about that night for him. Ari didn't believe she was the other half of his soul: that was just a line he used to seduce all his women. Worse still was the thought that Ari had not yet had Lee, that he was just waiting for the right moment and had made all the necessary preparations, just as he had waited for her.

The tragedy was that the twin soul line would be wasted on someone who would not appreciate it. Maria had been around enough women like Lee, raised to marry money, to know that their hearts were never touched. That's why they always liked opera so much: it gave them a chance to see how the other half suffers.

Maria felt absolutely calm as she went into Ari's bathroom and opened the cabinet. She had remembered correctly: there was a large bottle of sleeping tablets on the top shelf. She took down the bottle and, walking into the drawing room, she went over to the cocktail cabinet and decided to make herself a drink. Remembering Marilyn and her cocktail shaker, she decided on a martini. She rang the bell for the maid and asked her to bring a bucket of ice. When the maid returned, Maria told her that she was not to be disturbed that evening.

"Even if Mr. Onassis calls, you tell him that I have gone out," she told the maid. The maid looked worried, so Maria took a fifty-franc note out of her handbag and gave it to her.

Bruna was in Milan.

Maria had never made a dry martini but she knew that it consisted of gin and vermouth. She poured a generous quantity of both into the cocktail shaker, added the ice, and then shook it up and down as she had seen Marilyn do in the dressing room at Madison Square Garden. She poured a generous amount into a tumbler and remembered just in time to add an olive.

Then she walked over to the gramophone, and after a moment's hesitation she put on the recording of *Madama Butterfly* that she had made seven years ago. Sitting down on the sofa she sipped her martini as she listened to the first act. When the recording reached "Un bel dì," Maria opened the bottle that she had taken from Ari's bathroom and poured the pills into her palm and started to swig them down with gulps of martini.

By the time Butterfly was singing her final aria, Maria was slipping into unconsciousness. She could hear her voice hitting each note perfectly as she closed her eyes.

⸺

When she opened them again, she was in a hospital, choking on a tube that had been forced down her throat. She tried to take it out but found that her arms were being held back by a nun in a white habit. Finally, a nurse pulled the tube out of her throat and an impatient-looking doctor with a stethoscope round his neck poked at her eyelids and took her pulse.

"You have had a lucky escape, madame. Another half an hour and it would have been too late. It is dangerous to mix alcohol and sleeping pills in this way; you must promise me that you will be more careful in future." Maria tried to speak, but no sound would come out. She felt a surge of panic, but the doctor said, "Don't worry—it is just the effect of having a tube stuck down your throat. It will pass in a day or two. There shouldn't be any lasting damage."

He patted her hand and left the room. Maria tried to pull her thoughts together. All she could remember was the sound of her own voice effortlessly claiming that top B-flat. Then the door opened, and Ari was there in front of her.

"Oh, Maria, thank God."

He bent down to kiss her, and his cheeks were wet. "When I came back and found you on the sofa, I thought you were dead."

Maria's state of sleepy calm vanished. Suddenly and horribly she remembered why she had been lying unconscious on the sofa.

Ari was stroking her cheek. "What were you doing, *agapi mou?* There was a shaker full of gin and some sleeping pills. What am I meant to think?"

Maria tried to speak again, but she could only manage a rasp. "I didn't want to go on without you."

Ari looked at her in surprise. "What do you mean?"

Maria sighed; it hurt so much to talk. "I found the bracelet for Lee."

Onassis blinked. "What are you talking about?"

Maria whispered, "In your safe."

His eyes slid away from her for a second, and then came back to hold hers. "Maria, that means nothing. I had it made ages ago."

Maria said nothing. She was remembering the note.

"I am sorry if you thought it meant something, but, Maria, you must know that I would never leave you. We are always going to be together, you and I, it is fated."

Maria tried to smile, but then he took her hand. "Whatever happens, you and I can't be divided: we are two halves of the same soul."

Maria closed her eyes. The nun came over and suggested to Onassis that he should let Madame sleep.

When he had gone, Maria tried to put everything together in her head and failed. It had been so clear to her earlier, after she found the bracelet—Ari was in love with someone else, just as he had been in love with her; and she could not bear the idea of life without him, and so she planned to sleep forever. But now he didn't sound as if he was in love with Lee, and she had never seen him cry before. Could she have misjudged him? Had she, like Othello, given the bracelet and the note a significance that it didn't deserve? Her thoughts were all jumbled; all she could think about were Ari's tears and him saying that he would never leave her.

Had she really meant to kill herself? All she could remember was wanting to close her eyes and not wake up. Now, though, she was happy to be alive: Ari had been crying for her.

⇌

She left the hospital two days later by a back entrance, wearing sunglasses and a headscarf. Ari had been very careful to keep any mention of Maria's "episode" out of the press.

The night before she was discharged, the impatient doctor, who had warned her about mixing pills with alcohol, had come to examine her.

After checking her pulse and blood pressure and listening to her chest, he looked at her sternly. "When you first came in, I did not recognize you. But later the nurse told me your name. Eight years ago, I was in Milan, listening to you sing *La traviata*. I shall never forget how you made me, a doctor, believe that you were dying of consumption and the tears I cried then. Real tears, madame, even though I see death every day."

Maria put her hand to her chest in the gesture she always used for receiving tributes and gave him a wistful smile. "You are too kind, doctor."

But the doctor did not smile back. "I am a scientist, madame, so I choose my words carefully." He paused. "Please listen to me. You are a great artist who can transform the lives of people like me. So you must not play games with your own life, Madame Callas. I do not know what was in your heart when you were swallowing sleeping pills with gin, but I know that it was a reckless thing to do. A few minutes later, or a couple more pills, and I would be one of the millions of people mourning your untimely death. I cannot let you leave here without telling you that what you are doing is selfish. You must not deprive ordinary people like me of the joy that your music brings us, because of a moment's unhappiness."

Maria looked into the doctor's reproachful eyes. "Haven't you ever wanted to go to sleep and never wake up?"

He nodded. "Of course, but I also know that there are people who need me—my family, my friends, and my patients who would suffer if I was not there to take care of them. Therefore, I put aside my desire to sleep. And you must do the same, because, while I can be replaced—thankfully the world is full of good doctors—there is only one Maria Callas."

Maria's eyes filled with tears. "But my voice will not last forever, doctor."

"Nothing lasts forever, madame, but a talent such as yours will find another way to express itself, I have no doubt."

Maria lowered her eyes. "Have you ever been in love, doctor?"

He shrugged. "Of course. More than once. But love is like la grippe: once the fever subsides, the body recovers."

Maria did not reply.

"You think that I do not understand the strength of your feeling, and perhaps I don't, but I know the people who really want to kill themselves usually succeed. I don't want you to die by mistake, madame, when you have so much more to do. I must warn you that the variation in your heartbeat is most uneven, and I am worried that your heart is not altogether healthy."

She sat up in alarm. "Are you saying that I am sick? Is it serious?"

The doctor smiled. "Not if you take care of yourself."

Maria sank back on the bed. "I don't want to die of a heart attack."

He took her hand. "Good. I hope you will remember my words, madame."

Maria nodded. "I will. I really am glad to be alive."

She was thinking about this conversation as she sat in the back of the limousine that was taking her back to Avenue Foch. When she got to the apartment, Bruna opened the door, her face white with worry and concern. "Oh, madame, Mr. Onassis rang me, and I came right away. But he said that I shouldn't come to the hospital in case I was recognized."

She hugged Maria fiercely.

"Now come and lie down, and I will make you a special tisane."

Maria followed her obediently into the bedroom. She lay down and allowed Bruna to fuss over her.

"But why didn't you send for me, madame? Why did you stay here in Paris alone?"

"I don't know. I thought that if Ari was coming, then I didn't need you to come all the way from Milan."

Bruna looked at her sternly. "I know that you love Mr. Onassis, madame, and so I say nothing against him"—her face was straining with the effort of not speaking her mind—"but you need other people around you, people like me who will always put you first."

Maria raised a hand in protest. "But Ari loves me, Bruna. When he came to see me in the hospital, he was crying."

Bruna pursed her lips. "But who was he crying for, madame?"

Maria looked at her in surprise. "For me—who else?"

"But, madame, can you imagine the scandal if you had, God forbid, died in Mr. Onassis's apartment?"

Maria shook her head. "I can't believe you would say such a thing, Bruna. He was crying because he realized how unhappy I have been and how close he came to losing me."

Bruna didn't flinch. "I know you don't like me to say it, madame, but Mr. Onassis does not treat you with the respect you deserve."

"Surely that is for me to decide, Bruna," said Maria softly.

The maid realized she had gone too far, and she bowed her head. "Madame."

Five minutes later Ari was at Maria's side with the pistachio ice cream that she loved and a small box from Cartier. She ate the ice cream first and then she looked at the box, her heart in her mouth. Could it be a ring?

It was a pair of earrings, diamond notes on ruby staves.

"I told them to give me the opening bars of one of your hit songs."

Maria saw that the notes were the opening of "O mio babbino caro," and she hummed the notes for Ari.

"Thank you, darling. I don't deserve these at all."

She fastened them in her ears and asked Ari to bring her the hand mirror so that she could see how they looked. The earrings were heavy and awkwardly shaped, but she smiled at herself in rapture. The residue of her conversation with Bruna was erased. These earrings were for her and no one else; they would not be awarded to other women; they were destined only for Maria Callas.

She kissed Ari tenderly. "I should have trusted you, Ari. I am sorry."

CHAPTER TWENTY-ONE

# *"Vissi d'Arte"*

SKORPIOS, AUGUST 1963

Zeffirelli had been phoning Maria every day to persuade her to commit to the production of *Tosca* at Covent Garden. She had agreed to do it the year before, but she had been skittish about firming up a date. The truth was that she didn't dare to leave Ari. Even though he had been contrite after her discovery of the bracelet, she felt more secure when she was at his side.

At the end of August, Maria had been in bed with Ari on the *Christina* when the phone rang in the small hours. Ari answered the phone at once—he was a very light sleeper—and Maria knew from the sound of his voice that the caller was Lee.

Ari got up and took the call in his study next to the bedroom. He didn't close the door, so Maria could hear him talking in low tones. "I am sorry to hear that." There was a pause. "Of course, anything." Another pause. "Tell her that the *Christina* is at her disposal. The weather will still be good, and she can go anywhere she wants."

Maria heard him chuckle. "I will keep out of the way if that makes it easier."

There was a mumble that Maria couldn't decipher and then Ari put the phone down.

She pretended to be sleepy when Ari came back into the bedroom.

Ari lay down next to her and Maria put her head against his shoulder.

"I thought I heard a phone ringing in my dream."

"It was Lee calling from the White House. She says that her sister is very depressed because of the baby dying, and she thinks a cruise on the *Christina* might help her recover."

"And you agree?

"Maria, I have been on an FBI watch list for years. Bobby Kennedy thinks because I'm Greek I must be a crook. So, if the first lady of the United States, Bobby's sister-in-law, thinks that a cruise on the *Christina* might be of use to her, I am not going to argue."

Maria said softly, "So it's a business decision?"

Ari sighed. "I think that you of all people should be sympathetic to the first lady, Maria. She had a son who died at birth."

Maria flinched. "Of course I am. It's not the first lady I am worried about."

Onassis switched out the light and pulled her to him. "Don't be jealous, Maria. You know you are the only woman I love," and he started to kiss her neck in a way that he knew she liked. She didn't relent immediately, but as he started to whisper in her ear how much he wanted her and what he would like to do, the specter of Lee Radziwill began to fade, and all she could think of was where Ari would put his hand next.

The first lady's name was not mentioned by either of them for the next couple of weeks. Ari would fly to Athens from the yacht, which was anchored near Skorpios, every morning in his Piaggio and come back in the late afternoon. Maria would rise late and swim before going to her piano. She would practice for a few hours and then spend the rest of the afternoon getting ready for Aristo's return. Sometimes he would bring guests back from Athens for dinner, but mostly they were alone, which suited Maria very well.

When Franco called about *Tosca*, she would prevaricate, until one day he stopped her mid-excuse and said, "I want you to play Tosca, Maria, but if you are going to fuck me around, because you don't want to leave your boyfriend, then I will have to find somebody else. I know Renata would kill to work with me."

"You can't ask that virgin to play Floria Tosca," scoffed Maria.

"I will have to if you don't make a decision, Maria. And you should remember that absence makes the heart grow fonder. Your Ari fell in love with a diva, not a Greek hausfrau who has his slippers and his martini waiting when he comes home."

Maria had put the phone down. Franco didn't understand her relationship with Ari. Ari didn't love her because she was a diva, he loved her because she was a Greek woman who knew how to take care of her man. Tina had always been more interested in socializing than being a wife, and she had been unfaithful to Ari. Maria made sure that Ari put a sweater on when the cool breezes started up in the evenings, and to order dinners from the chef that she knew he would like. She listened to his stories, even the ones she had heard many times, and laughed in the right places. She would coax him out of his occasional dark moods and remind him of everything he had achieved. And at night she would give herself to him without reserve, telling him what a vigorous lover he was. Even when they fought, they would usually make up in bed, all the bitterness erased by their lovemaking.

Onassis had been angry when she had finally turned down the part in *The Guns of Navarone*. "I get up every day of my life to win," he shouted at her, adding, "I don't know why you bother to get up at all."

Hurtful as his words had been, the hurt had dissolved that night in bed.

But those words came back to her when, halfway through September, he told her that the first lady had accepted his invitation to come on a cruise and would be arriving with the Radziwills and Franklin Roosevelt Jr., the commerce undersecretary, and his wife at the beginning of October.

"So you should go back to Milan next week, Maria," he said casually.

Maria looked at him, frozen in surprise. She had heard nothing more about the cruise since the night of the phone call and she had assumed that the president had vetoed his wife's going on a cruise on a yacht belonging to a man on the FBI watch list. But now it was a reality, and she was to be banished.

"Oh, don't look like that, Maria. This is the first lady's cruise."

Maria hated the way that Ari said "first lady" with such relish.

"I have told her that I am going to keep out of their way entirely, have all my meals separately, and so forth, so that she can relax totally. So, you see it wouldn't work if you were there too."

"I thought Mrs. Kennedy was fond of music. I could sing for her," Maria replied.

Onassis smiled. "Maria, I had to beg you to sing for Winston Churchill. You told me then that you were not an 'entertainer.' Besides, Mrs. Kennedy is a Catholic and she might be offended by the fact that you are my mistress."

Maria was about to retort that the first lady clearly didn't object to the fact that Ari was sleeping with her sister, but then held her tongue.

If the first lady was anything like Lee, she would be a woman whose major talent was to marry well and then spend her husband's money with panache. Maria had nothing in common with women like that, women with no direction beyond finding a man to finance their lifestyle.

She might dress well, and decorate the White House elegantly, but that was hardly a career. Jackie Kennedy and her sister had never had to do battle with an audience, unlike Maria Callas.

Maria made her face bland.

"Actually it works out rather well. For months Zeffirelli has been begging me to sing *Tosca* at Covent Garden. I have been putting him off because we have been so happy here, but I will call him now and spare the first lady any embarrassment."

She walked away before he could reply.

Franco cackled with satisfaction when she made the call. "I knew that threatening you with Renata would tempt you from your lotus-eating stupor. But now you will really have to work, Maria. I want this *Tosca* to be a sensation."

"No one works harder than me, Franco. You know that."

"Well, I hope that is still true now that you are a *poule de luxe*. We won't be able to stop for caviar."

Maria laughed and relaxed a little. She realized that she was looking forward to the rehearsals.

With Callas confirmed as Tosca, Covent Garden had given Franco the go-ahead to create a completely new production. He was obsessed with creating Tosca through her costumes—a light carefree muslin in the first act where Tosca goes to see her lover, and then a dramatic red velvet empire line dress with a long gold stole for the scene where she offers herself to the villain Scarpia to save Mario's life.

She was in London for a costume fitting when she saw a newspaper picture of Onassis leading Jackie Kennedy by the hand through the streets of Smyrna. She showed it to Franco.

"That was me four years ago, being led around his childhood haunts."

Franco was busy adjusting the drape of the train that hung down from her shoulders. "Well, at least you know that he is quite safe with her. There would be six Secret Service agents with guns at his head if he so much as laid a hand on the first lady."

"She looks very happy."

"Perhaps she really likes caviar," said Franco as he pinned some gold lace to her shoulder.

"Yes, that works." He turned to the costume maker, who was arranging different kinds of metallic lace on the cutting table. "But it needs to be ruffled like this, so that she looks like a magnificent cockatoo, or do I mean porcupine?"

He squinted at Maria's profile in the mirror.

"She wanted to go on the cruise because she was depressed after losing her baby. She doesn't look depressed to me."

"Well, clearly the woman likes luxury and Ari is providing it. Put it out of your head, Maria. You are about to be the best Tosca the world has ever seen."

⟿

A week later there was another set of pictures, this time in *Paris Match*. The two sisters were standing on the deck of the *Christina*, laughing, Jackie wearing a white headscarf and wide sunglasses, Lee pushing her hair out of her eyes with one fragile arm. Maria's eyes went straight to the arm. Around the wrist was the bracelet she had found a year ago in Ari's safe.

She threw the magazine on the ground. Hearing the noise, and the sound of her mistress swearing, Bruna came in. She saw the magazine and picked it up. She noticed the bracelet at once.

They were in the drawing room of Maria's suite in the Savoy. The Thames was gray outside the window, and there was an autumn mist rising off the water. The contrast with the sunny Mediterranean could not have been starker.

"It's time to leave for the rehearsal, madame."

Maria looked at her watch. Bruna was right, of course. There was no time to ring Ari, and anyway what was the point? If he wanted to fuck that stick insect, then there was nothing she could do. He had rung her only last night to tell her how much he was missing her and looking forward to seeing her again. He had sounded so genuine. He probably did miss her; she didn't imagine that the first lady and the princess were going to make sure that he had a sweater when it got cold and that the chef was making spanakopita.

As she walked out of the hotel and up the hill that led to the opera house, she found to her own surprise that although she was angry, and hurt, she did not feel despair. She was not even tempted to cancel the rehearsal. In fact, she was looking forward to it. The anger would help her in the act two scene with Scarpia. And the pain would all be there in "Vissi d'arte," the soprano anthem: "I lived for art, I lived for love."

As Maria rehearsed that scene with Tito Gobbi, she found herself imagining Scarpia as a bad Onassis, the part of him that she felt most frightened by. Franco was delighted by the shift.

"Yes, that is perfect. You hate him but also you want him."

He walked around the two of them, and he turned to Maria. "When he takes your hands like this"—he held her hands apart over her head—"I think you are struggling, but are you struggling with Scarpia or with yourself? Does your body want one thing and your mind another? When you stab him, who are you stabbing? Are you stabbing Scarpia or your-self?"

He looked at Maria intently and could see that she understood perfectly.

"Sometimes love and hate are so narrowly entwined that it is impossible to tear them apart. Don't you think, Maria?"

Maria glared at him, but she knew he was right.

"This scene is so erotic: here Tosca is not singing about love with a ridiculous tenor, she is fighting the strength of her own desires."

Maria could feel Franco's eyes on her. He thought he was being clever by playing on her feelings for Onassis.

Perhaps he was. She had never played Tosca like this before, but she now realized that it was all there in the music. She had sung the role so many times. During the war she had sung it every other night for a month, and then she had been a frothy Floria Tosca, head over heels in love with Mario and determined to save him from the wicked Scarpia. But now she knew that Mario was just a diversion; the interesting relationship was between Tosca and Scarpia. He had coveted her from afar and now he was using his power over Mario to possess her. The difference was that Maria now saw that Tosca was attracted and repelled by Scarpia in equal measure.

She would resist him, of course, but there was a thread pulling her toward him, the longing to be possessed, to be dominated. She had never seen it before, but now she could feel Tosca tearing herself apart.

As Scarpia raised her arms high above her head, instead of bowing away from his, she arched her body toward him, so that they were almost touching.

Franco clapped his hands. "*Brava.* That is exactly it. Does she want to kill him or fuck him?—that is what the audience must be thinking."

The rehearsals went on through November, with Maria feeling more and more bound up in the Tosca she was creating. The production was going to open on New Year's Day and Franco had told Maria that he was going to lock her into her hotel suite on New Year's Eve: "So that no one can tempt you into losing your voice in a nightclub."

Maria laughed. "I will never make that mistake again."

Franco wagged his finger at her. "But you are playing Tosca now, a woman who is quite capable of self-destruction. I want you to do that onstage only. Do you understand?"

Maria nodded. She was exhausted after a day rehearsing the stabbing scene with Gobbi and she wanted nothing more than to go back to the Savoy and sink into a hot bath.

Coming out of the stage door, she sensed that something had happened. The small knot of fans who were always there at the end of the day were now too busy talking among themselves to crowd around her as they usually did. One of them, a young man in his early twenties, who liked to bring her violets, had red eyes from crying.

Maria knew that she should stop and ask what was wrong, but she took the opportunity to slip past them and out into Wellington Street. It was dark now and she was pretty sure that no one would recognize her in the headscarf that she had knotted under her chin and the glasses she wore to rehearsal; it was such a relief not to have to fiddle about with those wretched contact lenses. There were some compensations for being apart from Ari. It was beginning to drizzle and Maria wished she had brought an umbrella. But the Savoy was only minutes away. The streets were quiet. There was none of the bustle and excitement that she usually encountered at this time: people trudging home from work jostling with theatergoers dressed to the nines, ready for a night out.

As she walked along the Savoy forecourt, the commissionaire did not call out "Evening, Madame Callas," as he normally did, but held the door open in silence.

Maria went past the American Bar, and even in there it was quiet. When she got to her suite, Bruna was waiting for her with tea and honey and a hot bath. Maria stopped wondering about the strange atmosphere as she sank back into the fragrant water and closed her eyes.

The phone rang in the early hours of the morning. Maria was groggy from the sleeping pill she had taken, and it took her a minute or two to understand what Ari was saying. He seemed to be telling her that he had been invited to the White House.

Maria tried to make sense of it. "But why do you have to go today? Why is there such a hurry?"

There was a pause. "Is it possible you don't know? President Kennedy was shot in Dallas yesterday."

Maria crossed herself instinctively. "Is he dead?"

"Yes. Jackie was sitting next to him when he was shot."

Maria gasped. "How terrible."

"She only agreed to go to Dallas because she had been on the *Christina* for so long. There are pictures of her covered in her husband's blood. What a tragedy."

Maria said nothing; she was still trying to take it all in.

"So I am flying to Washington today, and will stay for the funeral. I am surprised to be asked, but Lee said that Jackie insisted."

Maria almost asked him if his decision to go was a business one but decided to stay silent.

"But I will be back in Paris for your birthday, *agapi mou*."

"I will be waiting for you, Aristo."

Maria tried to go back to sleep after her conversation with Aristo, but it was useless.

All she could think about was the tragedy of Kennedy's death, mixed with unease that Ari was now so indispensable to the sisters that he had been summoned to the White House. All the press around the first lady's trip on the *Christina* had been disapproving. There was a feeling that America's queen was debasing herself by consorting with the Golden Greek, as the American press called him. She wondered if it had been Jackie who had insisted on summoning Aristo to the White House, or whether the order had been engineered by Lee. She had recognized the excitement in Ari's voice and knew that to be at the funeral of an American president at the invitation of the first lady seemed like a great prize to the former cigarette smuggler. She was always surprised how much Ari relished these signs that he was accepted, as he said, "in the best circles."

Perhaps this honor would allow Aristo to relax a little, and next summer he would not cram the boat with people he thought might give him more social cachet. Ever since Tina had become the Marchioness of Blandford, Ari had been inviting aristocrats of every description to prove that he was just as well connected. Maria had joked that it was a great pity for Ari that titles only came with husbands, not wives. In the year that followed Tina's ennoblement, Maria thought he would have married anyone who would have made him a duke.

Maria was comforted by the thought that whatever Ari's motives for going to the White House, the one thing that would not be in the cards was his affair with Lee. Mrs. Kennedy must be unaware of the relationship between her sister and Aristo or she would not have invited him to stay.

When Franco heard that Ari was staying in the White House, he laughed. "I thought you were the one who liked to be center stage, Maria."

They watched the coverage of the funeral together on the television in Maria's suite.

Franco was impressed by the dignity of the grieving widow. Maria spent her whole time trying to catch a glimpse of Aristo or Lee. Both cried when Kennedy's three-year-old son saluted as his father's coffin went past.

"I wonder what Mrs. Kennedy will do now," Franco said. "She is one of the most famous women in the world, but now she doesn't have a role."

"She has her children, Franco."

"I wonder how much money the Kennedys will give her. She has expensive tastes, I hear."

Maria slapped him on the wrist. "Stop it. The poor woman has just seen her husband killed. She is not going to be thinking about money."

Franco murmured, "A woman like that is always thinking about money."

∫

There was a break from rehearsal in December and Maria went back to Paris to see Ari.

She had not seen him now for two months, which was the longest time they had been apart since their relationship began. Maria was trembling with anticipation as the taxi turned in on Avenue Foch. She was determined to banish the thought of the bracelet hanging from the princess's wrist. If he was really in love with Lee, Maria thought that she would know from the moment he touched her.

But Onassis wanted her as much as he always had. Within minutes of her arrival he had pushed against her against the Biedermeier sofa and was pulling up her skirt. They made love urgently, and Maria could not decide whose need was greater. When it was over, Ari looked at her wrist. "You are not wearing your bracelet."

Maria paused, and then said lightly, "It felt too much like a badge of office."

"What's that supposed to mean?"

"There was a photograph of Lee Radziwill wearing the bracelet I found in your safe. I wonder if she knows how many women you have given bracelets to."

Ari laughed. "She wouldn't care, so long as hers was more expensive."

Maria did not smile back. Aristo gave her a slap on the bottom.

"Don't give me that face, Maria. I was curious, that's all. She means nothing."

He took her to dinner at Maxim's on her birthday. They settled into their usual table in the corner. They came here so often that Ari used to joke that the red velvet–covered banquettes had taken on the shape of their behinds.

Neither of them bothered to order. They always had the same thing: caviar followed by steak tartare for Maria and chateaubriand for Ari. After the caviar and the shots of iced vodka that went with it, Ari took out a box from his pocket. The box was small; and Maria, as always, felt a flutter of hope about the contents. But as she picked up the box it rattled, and she knew that whatever was inside, it wasn't a ring. She opened it and inside was a golden key on a tag which said, "For MC with undying love from AO." She looked up at Ari.

"Is this the key to your heart?"

He grinned. "You have that already, Maria. This is even more exclusive. It's the key to an apartment on Avenue Georges Mandel. You love Paris, and I thought it was time that you had your own place."

Maria summoned up a suitably grateful smile. "Oh, Ari, I don't know what to say."

"I think you will like it. It's in the *Seizième* just round the corner from Avenue Foch. We can wave to each other, almost."

"It sounds perfect."

"And the building fees will go through my company, so you don't have to worry about that."

"You think of everything, Ari." She squeezed his hand under the table.

"But I can't accept."

Ari leaned back. He gestured to the waiter to bring him a cigar. "Why on earth not?"

"Because I am not a kept woman. I may be your mistress, but you know that I always pay my own way."

Maria looked him straight in the eyes. What she said was true. Although she spent a lot of time on the *Christina*, where Onassis paid for everything, she was careful to pay for her clothes, her furs, Bruna, even the flights she took on Olympic Airways, which he owned.

"But that is precisely why I am giving you the apartment. You didn't ask me to do it, and I respect that. But it is crazy that you should have to stay in a hotel when the children come to Paris."

Usually when she was in Paris, Maria stayed with Ari on Avenue Foch. Once she had moved to the Ritz because Christina, Ari's daughter, had come to stay, and Aristo had thought that it would be easier if Maria was not in residence. Maria had agreed; Christina was becoming more hostile and unfriendly, not less, and Maria had no desire to fight her for Ari's attention. But she couldn't help wondering if that was really why Ari wanted her to have her own apartment. Was it because he wanted more freedom to see other women? Was this in fact a farewell gift, a reward for services rendered? A way to pension her off?

She stroked his thigh, and, summoning all her courage, she whispered in his ear, "Ari, you are so generous, but you won't give me the one thing I really want."

He took the cigar out of his mouth and blew a perfect smoke ring. "There you go."

Maria broke up the ring with her hand. "Very funny," she said bitterly.

Onassis nuzzled the side of her neck. "*Agapi mou*, don't be angry. You know I would marry you if it were possible. But the children would crucify me and then let's remember that you are still married. Perhaps in a few years when things are calmer."

She didn't respond to his caresses.

"We have a good life, Maria. We are together because we want to be, not because a priest has given us permission."

Maria knew that it was pointless to pursue the subject. She had no leverage. Perhaps she could have gotten him to marry her when they first met, if their child had lived, but now?

The one thing she knew about Ari was that he wanted to get something out of every deal and what would marriage to her bring him? He already took her devotion for granted.

She touched Ari's cheek with her hand. "Every Greek woman wants to marry her man, Ari. You know that."

"But you are hardly an ordinary Greek woman, Maria."

"Even Greek divas want husbands, Ari."

"You know I would want my wife to be at my side every moment. You would have to give up singing."

Maria smiled. "I would do that in a heartbeat if that is what you wanted."

Onassis looked around. "Think what your fans would say if they could hear you."

Maria made a face. "You think that I care about them compared to you, Ari?"

Onassis shrugged. "A good shopkeeper doesn't disparage his customers, Maria."

Part of her wanted to walk out of the restaurant right now. But she knew that if she did, she would not be able to resist looking back to see if Ari was following.

"You are comparing me to a grocer?"

He smiled. "That whistle in your throat is what you sell to people who want to buy it. My father sold tobacco in Smyrna; you sell your pipes in opera houses around the world. I don't see that it is so very different."

Maria could not resist rising to the bait. "But I was chosen by God to be given this voice. Anyone can sell tobacco, but no one else can sing like me."

Ari gripped her hand. "You think it's easy to sell tobacco in a town like Smyrna, where even the street rats are trying to make a deal? Do you think it was easy for me to become the richest Greek in the world, for a *Tourkospouros* to becomes the friend of Winston Churchill?"

Maria winced as his hand closed around her fingers. "Ari, don't squeeze my hand like that—you are hurting me."

There was a cough behind them, and the room lights dimmed as one of the waiters brought a birthday cake complete with forty candles, and the whole restaurant joined in the chorus of "Happy Birthday." Even Ari sang, and he smiled as Maria leaned forward to blow out the candles. One puff from those powerful lungs, and all the candles were immediately extinguished.

She started to cut the cake, and Maurice Chevalier, who had been sitting at the table opposite, came over to wish her happy birthday. He was followed by the Duke and Duchess of Windsor, who had just arrived, and who were pressed by Onassis to join them for a coupe. The duke, wearing a rose velvet dinner jacket, chattered happily to Onassis while the duchess scrutinized Maria's jewelry.

"What unusual earrings." Maria was wearing the musical earrings Ari had given her after her overdose.

"Ari designed them for me."

The duchess opened her eyes wide. "Did he now? I had no idea Mr. Onassis was so talented." She raised one penciled eyebrow.

"Are they meant to represent something?"

Maria nodded. "The opening bars of 'O mio babbino caro.'"

"Well, isn't that just darling," said the duchess, clasping her surprisingly large hands together. "Were they your birthday present?"

Maria shook her head. "No, he gave them to me on another occasion," and she bit her lip remembering the pleasure they had given her then.

The duke was discussing the Kennedy funeral with Onassis. "I thought they brought it off awfully well. Not too much pomp and circumstance, but serious and moving as a republican funeral should be."

Ari nodded. "It was like a Greek tragedy. With Mrs. Kennedy grieving for her husband like Andromache for Hector."

The duchess turned her much-lifted face with its wide gash of a mouth and looked at Ari; and ignoring his last remark she said in her harsh voice, "Such a good-looking couple, and she, of course, is really chic. So unusual in the wife of an American politician. In France of course they know that a well-dressed woman is always an asset."

Maria saw Ari's face and for a second their eyes met in total accord. They were both thinking how nice it would be to be alone on the yacht, instead of having to listen to the vapid chatter of the ex-king and the woman he had given up his throne for.

Ari gestured toward the cake. "Would you like to try some of Maria's birthday cake? The chef makes it with ice cream because he knows that is Maria's only weakness."

The duke looked longingly at the cake with his huge round eyes, like a small boy in a sweet shop, but the duchess pinched him quite hard on the arm. "Oh, you are kindness itself, but the duke and I haven't eaten yet."

She took her husband's elbow in a tight grip and marched him off to the other side of the restaurant.

Onassis was the first to laugh and Maria couldn't stop herself joining in. There was nothing like a reminder of their shared Greekness to bring them together.

"Come on," said Onassis, when Maria had eaten the two forkfuls of cake that she allowed herself.

"Where?" asked Maria.

"To Avenue Georges Mandel. I think you should at least look at what you are turning down."

The apartment was on a wide street lined with chestnut trees. The car pulled up outside number 36 and Ari jumped out and rang the bell for the concierge.

The apartment was on the second floor. It was dark when Ari pushed open the door, but Maria could see the light from the streetlamps pooling on the parquet floor through the line of floor-to-ceiling windows. She always complained to Ari that the apartment on Avenue Foch was gloomy, but this room faced south and would get light all day long. Despite her reservations, she knew that the apartment was perfect. She would put the piano in the corner facing the fireplace, so that she could look out of the window as she sang.

Onassis turned on the lights, and she could see elegant moldings on the high ceiling. She walked on through the apartment, entering each room in darkness until Onassis switched on the lights.

There was a dining room, a corner room that she could use as a study, a bedroom for her, a guest bedroom, and a kitchen with another room for Bruna. It was exactly the sort of place that she might have picked for herself. Whatever his motives, Ari had been thoughtful in his choice.

Even though he ignored her most fervent wish, he understood her well enough to find an apartment where she instantly felt at home.

When the tour was over, Maria turned to Ari, who was looking at her like a child giving his mother a drawing. She knew that she should refuse the gift. Accepting the apartment was an admission that she accepted the status quo, but she also felt that in choosing this place, he had shown how much he understood her. The notion that he had thought so deeply about how to please her made the rock of resentment inside her dissolve.

"Well? Do you like it? There were so many apartments, but I thought this was the right one for you."

His face was uncertain, until Maria smiled. "It is so right, Ari, that I feel it would be churlish to refuse such a thoughtful gift."

She threw her arms around him and kissed him.

"Will you allow me to come and visit you sometimes?" Ari asked.

"Maybe," said Maria, "as a reward for good behavior."

"What about bad behavior?" asked Ari as he pushed her against the wall between the floor-length windows and started to pull up her skirt.

"I reserve judgment," gasped Maria as his fingers found their way inside her.

The parquet floor was hard, but Maria didn't care. It had been a long time since they had made love anywhere but a bed. Making love in an empty apartment reminded her of the lifeboat; they were in a world of their own desire.

As Ari lit a cigarette, he turned to her and said casually, "The thing is, I don't make a very good husband, Maria. I would be unfaithful."

Maria laughed, "You are unfaithful to me now."

"Maybe, but the point is that I always come back. Now you know that is because my love for you is so strong that I cannot live without you. But if you were my wife, it would be different. I would return because after one expensive divorce I have no intention of having another. Surely it is better for us to be together because we want to be, that the ties between us are of love, not money."

Maria considered this. There was some truth in what he said. He had treated Tina like his possession, not his equal. He had not seemed to mind when she was openly unfaithful to him with Reinaldo, but he had been furious when she had left him. Maria thought it was probably the first independent decision that Tina had made in their marriage, and Ari had not expected it. He did not consider his wife as an independent entity. Whereas Maria was free to leave him at any time, and, unlikely though that was, perhaps it was a strategic advantage. Yes, she would like to have the status of being Mrs. Onassis—how pleasing it would be to prove wrong all the people who doubted his intentions toward her and to find a second act in being the wife of the Golden Greek—but she knew that the status was no substitute for Ari himself. And knowing Ari as she did, she found it hard to imagine him marrying someone else, unless of course the queen of England suddenly became available. He would only marry someone who had something that he couldn't buy, and it was hard to imagine who that woman might be.

"At least I can practice here without you complaining about the noise," Maria said.

# CHAPTER TWENTY-TWO

## *Curtain*

COVENT GARDEN, LONDON, NEW YEAR'S DAY, 1964

The queue around the opera house had started forming on Boxing Day. By the day of the performance, it stretched all the way along Floral Street and around the Piazza. It was bitterly cold, but the fans had come prepared with sleeping bags and thermoses, and their spirits had been lifted when they caught a glimpse of their idol arriving for the dress rehearsal.

The diva had been gracious and had stopped to sign autographs, smiling as she told them not to get pneumonia. "I won't be able to sing for you in the hospital."

One young man at the head of the queue had knelt in front of her and had kissed her hand. "I would die happy if I had heard you sing Tosca, Madame Callas."

This moment was captured by one of the television crews that hovered outside Covent Garden, hoping to get a glimpse of Callas, and was shown on the evening news. Maria asked the house manager to make sure that the young man got a ticket. She did not want his early death on her conscience.

The dress rehearsal was a fever dream. Maria had performed Tosca more times than she could remember. She had sung it at the Athens

Conservatoire, for Italian soldiers in Patission Street, and in opera houses around the world, but she knew this was the first time she really understood Floria Tosca. In the past she had always found the moment when Floria becomes jealous when she sees that her lover, Cavaradossi, is painting another woman farfetched, but now she understood exactly where the music was taking her. Tosca's jealousy turned out to be groundless, but Onassis was betraying her, and anything she was able to imagine would most likely be true. Onstage though, Ari's betrayal was a gift: there was no difficulty in summoning the pain she needed. She was playing herself, an opera singer, a diva, tormented by her feelings.

In the second act she wore the empire-line dress in red velvet with gold fillets in her hair, a gold lace stole, and long gloves that buttoned at the wrist. It was the perfect costume, one suitable for the diva she was playing and for the diva she was. As she began to sing the duet with Scarpia, where she asks him what it will take to save her lover's life, she could sense the heat in her performance building, and she felt as if she would explode when she hurled the word "*quanto*" ("how much") at Scarpia.

But instead of singing, Scarpia rushed toward her and, snatching the stole out of her hands, he threw it over her head and started to pat her head firmly with his hands. The conductor silenced the orchestra.

She tried to pull away, but he held her there, batting at her head, until finally he stopped.

She was about to shout at him for ruining her performance when he said, "Your head, Maria, was on fire."

And he held up the remains of the long curly black hairpiece that hung down her back. The sweet smell of singed hair filled her nostrils. She understood that she must have gone too close to one of the lighted candelabra on the table and her wig had caught fire without her realizing.

"Your hands! Are they all right?"

The baritone nodded, and she put her head on his shoulder. "*Grazie*, I was somewhere else."

Gobbi smiled. "I know, *cara*. You were getting ready to stab me."

She heard Franco's voice from the auditorium. "Do you want to stop, Maria?"

She shook her head and nodded to the conductor to start again.

Franco burst into her dressing room as she was taking off her makeup.

"Maria, you crazy genius. Didn't you smell your hair burning?"

He shook his head and then he kissed her roughly on both cheeks, undeterred by the cold cream and greasepaint.

"No opera is worth killing yourself for, darling. And if you are going to burn yourself alive, save it for the first night so that the audience gets its money's worth."

He winked at Maria, whose eyes were huge and dark.

"I had no idea, Franco."

Franco put his hands on her shoulders. "You must be careful, Maria."

He looked around the dressing room, which was full of red roses that in January must have cost a small fortune. He picked up a flower and held it to his nose, discarding it with disgust when he discovered that it had no smell.

"Is Ari coming to the opening?" Franco couldn't keep the disapproval out of his voice.

"I hope so." Maria's voice was flat.

"If Onassis misses the chance to hear you give the performance of your career, then he definitely doesn't deserve you."

Maria wiped a streak of cold cream from her face. "He gave me an apartment in the *Seizième* for my birthday."

Franco spread out his hands. "If I were in his shoes, I would give you Versailles and still I would feel that I hadn't done enough. He is a philistine, Maria; he doesn't understand that you are a great artist and your Tosca will be the one by which all Toscas are judged."

"You thought it went well tonight?"

Franco caught her eye in the mirror. It was easy to forget how vulnerable Maria was and how much she needed reassurance.

"You know it did, *cara*. The only performance that will surpass it is the one you will give on the opening night."

Maria nodded obediently.

"Now go home and go to bed and I will come and have breakfast with you tomorrow."

〜

Maria put up the collar of her silver fox coat as the doorkeeper opened the stage door, but it was not enough to fool the crowds that were gathered outside hoping to catch a glimpse of her.

"Madame Callas."

"Maria!"

The voices surged around her, the hands reaching out with photographs and autograph books. It was the last thing she wanted after a performance, yet she looked at the eager faces fondly. Floria Tosca would have stopped to sign the books of her fans, and she would too. So she smiled and signed until the stage doorkeeper came out and shooed the fans away.

In her suite there was another monstrous bouquet of red roses in the sitting room and on the table a box from Wartski, the jeweler in St. James's. She hesitated before opening the box. If Ari had sent her a gift already, he must be feeling guilty about something.

Inside the box was a brooch made of flowers and butterflies that trembled on tiny springs. It reminded her of the piece she had worn in *Turandot* that had vibrated every time she moved her head, but that had been made of tin, and this was made of white gold and diamonds.

It was exquisite, the sort of thing that would have been worn by a Russian archduchess.

But its beauty meant that it was more than a good luck present, she thought. There was a card inside the box.

The message was written in Greek. "Forever and always, your Ari." She knew that meant he wasn't coming.

〜

The day of the performance she woke early and felt the constriction in her throat immediately. She opened her mouth, and no sound came out. She pressed the bell and Bruna came running in. Maria pointed to her throat, and Bruna touched her hand to Maria's forehead and looked grave.

"I think you have a temperature, madame. Shall I send for the doctor?"

Maria nodded and whispered to tell Franco to call the understudy. Then she turned her face to the wall in despair. The doctor came and gave her a shot of $B_{12}$, several aspirins, and an anesthetic throat spray. Maria tried to sit up, but she felt too dizzy.

"Your blood pressure is very low." The doctor looked at her with compassion. "I can't say whether you have an infection or if your body is reacting to the stress of your upcoming performance. I suggest that you try to relax and see if anything improves. Of course, it's very easy to tell a patient to relax but much harder to do it."

"Do you think I can sing tonight?"

The doctor shook his head. "I'm afraid I am the wrong person to ask, Madame Callas, as I have tickets for tonight's performance."

The phone rang, Bruna picked it up. Maria knew from the expression on her face that it was Onassis on the other end.

She reached out her hand to take it.

"*Agapi mou*, are you looking forward to the show?"

"I have a fever. I don't think I can sing."

She heard the wet rattle as Ari took a puff of his cigar.

"Well, that is a pity, Maria, as I have come a long way."

Maria felt her heart beat faster. "You are in London?"

"I am just on my way from the airport. Did you get my present?"

"It's beautiful," she croaked, "but even better is knowing that you are here."

"Of course I am here. But you must sing."

Maria closed her eyes. "I will sing for you, Ari."

"Good. I will see you after the show. I want to meet Princess Margaret."

Maria felt the tightness in her chest dissolving.

⸺

Franco came to wish her luck in her dressing room. "Are you feeling better, *carissima*?"

She looked at him in the mirror. He looked very handsome in his dinner jacket.

"I think so, but, Franco . . . I am scared."

He put his hands on her shoulders and squeezed them.

"Of course you are. That is why you will be a great Tosca tonight."

Maria was silent. It was not stage fright she was feeling but the intimation that she would not be on a stage much longer. This would be the last time that she would open a new production with Franco. The golden coins were nearly spent. So tonight would be a beginning and an ending. But knowing that Ari would be there made it less painful. She had another life beyond the stage that would still be there when she stopped singing. But tonight, if it were a swan song, would be a magnificent one. Tosca was a part that demanded an actress, not a vocal acrobat; and while she was no longer sure of her high Cs, she knew how to play Floria Tosca.

"Just try to not set fire to your wig." Franco smiled. Maria smiled back.

"And remember this is Covent Garden, not La Scala. If you miss a note or two, no one will notice."

"I will notice, Franco!" Maria looked horrified.

"Which is why you are la Divina. You could be singing to an audience that was stone-deaf, and still you would be worried about the wrong notes."

Maria turned to look at him. "Ari rang me this morning. He is going to be there tonight—he came back specially."

Franco tapped her on the shoulder. "No wonder you have made a miraculous recovery."

He kissed her lightly on the cheek, so as not to disturb her makeup, then left.

The beginners bell sounded, and Maria started her vocal exercises as Bruna and the dresser helped her into her act one costume.

As she worked her way through the arpeggios, she wondered idly where Ari would be sitting. Knowing him, he would have wangled his way into the Royal Box and would be whispering into the ear of Princess Margaret. Perhaps even now he was inviting her for a cruise on the *Christina*. Maria sang the last arpeggio and felt her voice slip on the high C.

She tried again, clenching her stomach muscles to push her voice higher. This time she got the note, but the tone was shrill. Her heart began to beat rapidly, and she took a deep breath to calm herself. She tried to remember what Elvira had taught her: "See past the note and it will

not seem so daunting. You are making music, not climbing a mountain."
Maria made her shoulders relax and tried again; this time she scaled
the top C with ease. If Ari had come to hear her sing, then he would be
rewarded.

⊐

In the foyer a TV reporter was talking to a middle-aged couple who had
queued for twenty-four hours for a place in the gods, the seats right at
the top of the opera house.

"Do you think you will be able to see anything?" the reporter asked.

The man held up a pair of binoculars. "That's why I brought these.
And I will be able to hear her well enough."

"Have you queued like this before?"

The couple shook their heads. "But we have all Callas's recordings,
and we didn't want to go to our graves without seeing the real thing, and
this may be the last chance we get."

"Are you worried that there might be a problem tonight? Madame
Callas has a reputation for not fulfilling her engagements."

"No point in worrying over something like that. I reckon singing
is like everything else," the man said, putting his arm round his wife's
shoulders. "You've got to be in the mood. Isn't that right, Joan."

Joan gave her husband a nudge. "Stop that, Eric—we're on television.
Anyway, I know everything is going to be all right."

"How can you be sure?"

"Because I read the leaves this morning and they never lie."

⊐

Maria stood in the wings as Cavaradossi and Angelotti his revolutionary
friend sang. They were both in magnificent voice, but Maria could feel
the anticipation of the audience. It was waiting for her. Would Callas
appear, and when she did, how would she sound? All her performances
were battles but this would be the bloodiest. Tonight she had not just to
win but to conquer. There could be no second chance.

She heard the theme from the orchestra that signaled her entry and she crossed herself three times, and then another time for luck, and picked up the basket of flowers that Floria Tosca had just bought in the Campo de' Fiori and, banishing every thought from her head except the thoughts of a diva going to meet her lover, she sang "Mario, Mario" from the wings and then stepped lightly onstage.

The applause was thunderous with joy and relief. Callas was there in front of them, looking like a goddess. Some singers might have stopped to acknowledge the audience's excitement, but Maria was Tosca, intent on the man she loved. The conductor signaled to the orchestra to slow down until the applause faded.

As she knelt before the altar with her flowers, singing of her plans for the evening, she knew that the audience was relaxing and paying total attention. No coughs, no rustling, it was just Tosca and her Mario and two thousand others listening in the dark. As Cavaradossi protested that the only eyes he loved were dark and furious like hers, she sang the line, "You who can make any woman love you," thinking of the bracelet in the safe in Avenue Foch.

Maria hardly knew how she got through the grimy corridors to her dressing room. The dresser and Bruna knew not to say a word as they got her into costume for the second act. As she got ready to go back onstage, she looked for the Madonna that had always lived in her dressing room, and then remembered that Meneghini had kept it out of spite. The box containing Onassis's diamond brooch was on the table, as she was planning to wear it to the after-party. She opened it and, touching one of the diamond flowers, set its petals trembling, filling the grimy dressing room with pinpoints of light. *"Vissi d'arte, vissi d'amore"* thought Maria as she made her way back to the wings. For thirty-five years she had lived only for art, and now she lived for love, but which did she need more?

The somber velvet drapery, heavy furniture, and shadowy lighting of Scarpia's room gave the set the feel of a luxurious torture chamber. Scarpia was resplendent in the costume of the ancien régime, with powdered wig, gold brocade waistcoat, satin breeches, and silver-buckled shoes with heels that made him loom over Tosca. As they tangled with each other, Maria as Tosca felt the familiar push and pull of repulsion and desire. She hated Scarpia; she wanted to save the man she really loved, Cavaradossi. She would do anything for the man she loved, even give herself to Scarpia. When Scarpia came up behind her and spread out her arms as if he were crucifying her, she was Christlike in her submission. But as she sang "Vissi d'arte" she knew that the battle she was fighting was not whether she should submit to Scarpia but with the pleasure she felt in anticipating that submission.

Singing the great aria, she knew that the tears in her eyes were being reflected in the darkness. She was singing an elegy onstage to her own career. Like Tosca, she was singing for something greater than herself; she could see the end in sight. The audience understood and could not look away.

After he signed the letter that guaranteed her lover's release, Scarpia came toward her with a wolfish smile, one that she had seen so many times before on the *Christina*. She could pretend to cower, to be horrified at what lay ahead, or she could take arms against the author of her misfortunes. The knife lay on the table that was laid with a meal for two, plastic caviar and fizzy water disguised as Dom Pérignon. As Scarpia came toward her, his arms outstretched, ready to claim his prize, she picked up the knife and plunged it into his chest. He staggered away and she pursued him, holding the dagger like a spear, standing over him, ordering him to die. And then finally Scarpia went still, and Maria remembered she was Floria Tosca and she fluttered about the stage gathering her belongings, her stole, her reticule, the gloves that she had taken off so provocatively; and just as she was about to blow the candles out, she hesitated. She picked up two candlesticks and placed them to the left and right of the body. Then she took the crucifix from the desk and put it gingerly on Scarpia's chest, shrinking away from him as if she feared him still.

She did not sing a note in those last five minutes, but the audience was completely rapt, understanding every nuance of her emotions from her face and body. As the curtain came down there was a cathedral-like stillness, and then an eruption of sound that felt like a blessing to Maria.

She took her curtain call with Renato Cioni, who played Cavaradossi, and Tito Gobbi as Scarpia, standing between them, holding their hands with outstretched arms. She was grateful for their presence; if they had not been there, she might have fainted. Maria smiled as if her face would split while the fans threw flowers onto the stage, and as Gobbi kissed her hand. Everyone knew that they had seen something that night which could never be repeated.

Franco had to fight his way into Maria's dressing room after the performance. Maria was hemmed in by the flock of well-wishers, who were vying with one another to find the right superlative. Maria looked a little dazed, as if she had been brought round from an anesthetic. Franco shouldered his way past a minor royal, a newspaper proprietor, and a theatrical knight to get to her.

He didn't say anything, he just knelt at her feet, took her hand and kissed it.

"You were even better than I imagined in my wildest dreams, *carissima*. There will never be another Tosca like you."

He saw that Maria's eyes were full of tears. And he understood—how could he not?—why she was crying. This perfect performance, this great artistic triumph that would never be rivaled, meant that she would now always be looking backward. Her acting skills would still be there, but the voice would slowly shred until it became just an echo of its former glory.

He said, "You know, *cara*, the best moment for me was the last five minutes of the second act, when you placed the candles around Scarpia—what a piece of acting. You didn't sing a note, but no one could look away."

"Perhaps I should make a silent movie," she said, trying to smile. Then the door opened, and she looked up in hope.

Franco knew whom she was looking for, but he knew that Onassis would not be walking through the door.

# CHAPTER TWENTY-THREE

## *Encore*

The phone was ringing. Maria opened her eyes; it was morning. She heard Bruna answer the phone.

*"Un momento, signore."*

Maria felt a wave of mingled relief and regret. Whomever Bruna was talking to in Italian, it wasn't Ari. Of course, it wasn't Ari. He was on his honeymoon with the Widow.

Bruna came in and plugged in the bedside telephone. "Signor Pasolini, madame."

Maria sat up in bed. The first time she had met the famous Italian director Pier Paolo Pasolini, he had declared his undying love, and she had been charmed. She knew, of course, that, like Franco, he was not interested in women sexually, but even so she felt a frisson in his company. Ever since they had met, he had been imploring her to make a film with him. He had seen her playing Tosca at Covent Garden years ago and after that he had suggested that she could play Medea in his film of the Euripedes play.

Maria had been amazed. "You don't want me to sing?"

"No, I just want you to act." But so far it had been just a fantasy, an excuse for them to chatter on the phone. Maria had been flattered that he thought her acting good enough to sustain a nonsinging role.

Pasolini was breathless with excitement. "I am sorry. Maria, I should have called you before about that terrible wedding, but I have been busy finding the money for our film. And now I have it."

Maria felt her heart pound.

"So are you ready, Maria? To play Medea, a woman who has been abandoned by her lover and decides to avenge her wrongs?"

"I have some experience in that area."

Pasolini laughed. "This film will be your revenge, Maria. You will be so good that the world will wonder how anyone could be crazy enough to leave you."

"Maybe."

"Definitely! Please say you will do it, Maria."

Maria lay in bed, considering Pasolini's offer. The thought of acting in a film was terrifying. There would be no audience to win over, no music to guide her. She didn't know if she could act without a score. But terrifying though the prospect of acting on the screen was, it was less scary than going onstage and singing badly. There were still so many offers to sing at opera houses all over the world, but Maria knew that there weren't enough golden coins left for a full opera, so reluctantly she refused them all. She still recorded and gave concerts, but she missed the excitement that came from submerging herself in a role. After a lifetime of playing other people, the role of Maria Callas was hard to inhabit.

She got out of bed and called to Bruna.

"Pasolini wants me to play Medea in a movie. Not singing, just acting. Filming for two months in Turkey. In Cappadocia."

Bruna saw that her mistress looked really awake for the first time since the wedding.

"I've heard that Cappadocia is beautiful."

"But very remote."

Maria started to pace up and down the room. Bruna picked up the clothes Maria had thrown on the floor the night before.

"I don't know, Bruna. I don't know anything anymore."

Bruna took her mistress's elbow and guided her to the telephone in the sitting room.

"Why don't you ring Signor Zeffirelli? He has been calling every day, you know."

Maria picked up the telephone. "Do you think I should do it, Bruna?"

Bruna shrugged. "I think that it would be good to go somewhere new, madame. You spend too much time looking out of the window."

"Like Penelope waiting for Odysseus," said Maria.

She gazed at the telephone in her hand, as if guessing why she was holding it. She wondered where Ari was now, what he was doing. Bruna's voice cut into her thoughts.

"You were going to phone Mr. Zeffirelli, madame?"

She was going to tell Bruna to go away and leave her alone, but then she remembered the photo she had seen of the happy couple after their wedding on Skorpios. Ari had been wearing sunglasses and the bride had an air of bewilderment on her plate-shaped face. But it wasn't Jackie, with the ridiculous bow in her hair like a little girl at a birthday party, that had caught her eye but the building in the background. The simple blue-and-white chapel she had always dreamed of being married in.

She felt a stab of anger. Bruna was right: she could not spend the rest of her life looking out the window like Butterfly waiting for her Pinkerton to return. She started to dial.

⸺

Franco came over that afternoon.

"I'm jealous as hell, of course, but I think you should do it. You are Medea," he pronounced, leaning against the veined marble fireplace.

Maria shook her head. "I don't know, Franco. I am too old, and I don't know that I will photograph well."

Franco waved his hand at the many framed photographs of Callas that were lined up on the piano. "That is absurd."

Maria hesitated and then she said, "And if I go away, he won't know where to find me."

Franco sighed. "Maria. He has just married another woman."

"I know. But I still love him."

Franco sat down beside her. He took her hand and clasped it tightly.

"*Carissima,* I have to tell you something that will make you angry, but you must not be angry with me. Do you promise?"

Maria nodded.

"Remember the first night of *Tosca*? Four years ago?"

Maria opened her eyes wide. "Of course."

"Onassis phoned you that morning to tell you that he would be there at the performance, didn't he?"

"Yes. He was in the car coming from the airport. But then there was some crisis and he had to go to Athens. He phoned me the next day to apologize. I was upset, of course—I so wanted him to be there—but in the end, it was such a triumph it didn't matter."

Franco put his hand on his heart. "Maria, when I heard that morning that you had woken up with a fever and a sore throat, I did the only thing I could think of. I called Ari."

Maria looked at him without understanding. "What do you mean?"

Franco spoke urgently. "I knew that you needed a reason to sing and someone to triumph over—Lee or Jackie, it doesn't matter, he was involved with them both—but you needed to show him and them that you were not some geisha looking for a rich protector but a great artist, a genius. You wanted to show him what he was playing with. Am I right?"

She shrugged. "Maybe. I don't know."

"But I do, Maria. You needed him to be there in order to sing the greatest Tosca there has ever been. You were sick that morning because you knew he wasn't going to come. Is that right?"

"Perhaps," Maria said.

Franco squeezed her hand in his. He spoke quickly as if trying to rid himself of a burden. "So I found him, don't ask me how, and I told him that unless he came to the performance I would kill him. He was not impressed, but when I told him that I would tell the press that he was trying to seduce America's widowed queen barely six weeks after her husband had been murdered, then he started to listen."

Maria's eyes were huge. "You mean that even then, he was with . . . her?"

"Even then, Maria. When he phoned you, he was in New York, not London."

Maria began to shake with anger. "You made him lie to me?"

Franco caught the hand that was about to slap him.

"He took no persuading, *carissima*. But I knew that your performance was the most important thing. No one who heard you sing Tosca that night would disagree."

Maria said nothing. There was nothing she could say. Franco had done the right thing for Callas, but had it been the right thing for Maria? If he had told her then that Ari was trying to seduce Jackie, would she have believed him? But did Franco have the right to decide for her?

"Why are you telling me now?"

"I couldn't tell you then, because he came to see you two days later, and I could see how happy you were. Why would I spoil it for you? He was so proud that you were famous again, and I thought perhaps that would be enough. But I have to tell you now, Maria, because I suspect that one day soon he will come back, begging you to forgive him. And perhaps you will, perhaps you won't, but I want you to know everything."

She nodded slowly. "He does love me, you know."

"I know, I know. But you have sung in enough operas to know that love is not enough. Don't end like the characters you sing—dying for love in the third act. Make your own ending, *carissima*. I beg you."

# Final Curtain

# CHAPTER TWENTY-FOUR

LATER THAT DAY

That evening Maria stood on the balcony, watching the streetlights come on one by one. She was trying to make sense of what Franco had told her. Ari had been courting Jackie not for the last six months but for the last four years. Clearly the Widow had played her hand more adroitly than Maria had done. But managing men was Jackie's talent, not hers. Maria knew that after the first encounter in the lifeboat of the *Christina* there could be no question of playing a game, of manipulating the situation. She had willingly surrendered.

And even now she did not regret her capitulation. Without Ari she would not have known what it was like to love someone so much that she cared for his happiness more than her own. She had sensed almost from the beginning that he would never be hers completely, but then she had her music. Her affair with Ari had meant that her last performances were the best she had ever given. Even his infidelity had added a layer of experience that had not been there before. Her voice was fading, but she had done so much more with what she had left. It might not be perfection, but it was truthful.

Maria knew that she would not always see so clearly. There would be times when the clench of betrayal would overwhelm her. But she would not throw herself from the ramparts. Franco was right. She needed to find her own ending.

Turning her back on the street, she contemplated the piano standing in the corner of the room. Quickly, before she could change her mind, she opened the lid. As she sat down she noticed that her fingertips were gray with dust.

It took a long time to warm up, but Maria waited until she could feel the spring come back into her voice before she launched into "L'amour est un oiseau rebelle" from *Carmen*. She had not sung a note since news of the wedding, and as she poured herself into the melody she could feel the vibrations right at her core. To follow the music—that was the thing.

Maria was so caught up in her practice that she didn't hear the doorbell ring, so Bruna's touch on her shoulder made her jump. How could Bruna of all people have interrupted her? But then she caught sight of the maid's face.

"He is here, madame. Shall I let him in?"

Maria hesitated for a moment and then nodded. Bruna looked at her. "Are you sure, madame?"

Maria nodded again.

Ari's hands were on her shoulders before she could step back. His smell, the mix of vetiver and the foxy sheen of his skin, made her tremble with longing.

"Oh Maria, do you know how much I have missed you? Do you know how much I need you?"

Maria shuddered. There was nothing she wanted more than to let him take her there and then and to feel his desire for her obliterate all the pain of the last weeks. But before her body could dissolve into his, she pushed herself away from him.

"That was a short honeymoon," she said.

Ari shrugged, and Maria could see that the shadows under his eyes were even darker than normal. For a moment he looked old, as if all the juice had been squeezed out of him. But then he smiled and Maria could see him reviving as he looked at her.

"What can I say? I made a terrible mistake, Maria. It was hubris . . . I thought if I married her I would be invincible: every door would be open, every deal would go through." He spread his hands wide.

Maria twisted a lock of hair around her finger. In the last six weeks it had grown long enough to do that. She would never cut it again.

"Why are you here, Ari?"

"Because I need you, Maria. You make me feel safe." His voice faltered. "I never told you this but when I would wake up in the night and I could hear you breathing next to me I felt like a little boy again lying down on the bed next to my mother when she took her afternoon nap."

Maria's eyes widened in surprise—he had never mentioned his mother since that day in the cemetery in Smyrna. She wanted to put her arms around him, to trace away the purple shadows under his eyes, to take him by the hand into the kitchen and make him a plate of strapatsada—she could see that he had lost weight.

She stood motionless; a lifetime onstage had taught her how to take her time, and to conceal her racing thoughts. Her hands were ready to fly open, to pull him against her, when she saw a movement in the hall behind Ari. Reflected in the Venetian mirror was Bruna's face.

Maria looked back at Ari, and this time she saw the impatient curve of his mouth, and the glitter in his black eyes.

"What a pity you didn't think of that before you married Mrs. Kennedy."

Ari scanned her face.

"Don't you think I know that?" He leaned toward her. "I came here tonight because I want to make things right again. I can't live without you and I don't think you can live without me."

Maria looked over his shoulder, but Bruna had disappeared. She took a deep breath from her diaphragm as if she were about to sing.

"You're too late, Ari."

The silence lay between them until Ari blinked. "Another man? I don't believe it."

Maria shook her head.

"No, that's not the reason."

"Then how can it be too late? It can never be too late for us, Maria. Remember, we are twin souls."

Maria remembered.

"Not anymore. You see, Ari, you don't make *me* feel safe. Whatever you say now, I know that there will always be something shiny out there, out of reach, something that you just have to have. I was that something once." She paused and then took another breath.

"I used to blame them, those sisters with their little-girl voices and their skinny arms, but now I know better. You pursued them, just as you pursued me. Lee was too easy for you, but the widow, she was a challenge, I think you had her in your sights since she invited you to her husband's funeral."

Maria pressed one hand to her chest, a gesture she had used in *Traviata* when Violetta tells Alfredo that she doesn't love him anymore.

"You weren't thinking of your mother when you were sleeping next to me, you were thinking of her, the president's widow!"

Ari tried to interrupt her but Maria would not stop. "And now that you have her, and the whole world has seen you get married, now that the *Tourkospouros* arriviste has secured the ultimate trophy, you find that she is no longer interesting. Maybe she doesn't try to please you like I did. She doesn't bring you your favorite sweater on a cold night, or make the eggs the way you like them, maybe you don't like fucking a skeleton, who knows? I don't care. Yes, I loved you, maybe I still do, but whatever it is you are offering I don't want it."

Ari put his hand in his pocket and pulled out a small red box. As he opened it, Maria looked away but not before she saw a flash of green.

"Not even this, Maria?"

He had given her so many jewels, but never a ring. For a moment she imagined him slipping it onto her finger. She could feel the tears coming, but she fought them down. She had not cried that night in Rome, and she would not now. Instead she raised her arm, a gesture she had used onstage as Norma, and pointed to the door.

"Please go. Bruna will show you out."

Ari clicked the box shut and put it in his pocket. He looked up at her and gave the wolfish smile she had first seen that night in Venice.

"If that's what you want, Maria. But you know, don't you, that I'll be back?"

Maria was silent. He stepped forward and before she could turn away, kissed her lightly on the lips.

When she opened her eyes he was gone, Bruna standing in the hall, a smile on her face.

"*Brava*, madame."

That night she woke up drenched in sweat. She stumbled toward the windows and stepped out onto the balcony, sighing with relief as the cold air hit her skin.

She was turning to go inside when she heard someone whistle. A red circle glowed in the darkness. She thought she could smell the cigar smoke. And then the familiar voice rich with desire.

"Maria, *agapi mou*."

She could not make out his face, only a pale oval under the moonlight. But she knew that he would be grinning, confident that after everything Maria would still be waiting for her Ari.

Maria stepped inside, shut the window, and drew the curtains.

# ACKNOWLEDGMENTS

I have wanted to write this book for a long time, but it was Charles Spicer, the editor at St. Martin's who inherited me from our mutual friend Hope Dellon, who coaxed it from me with such skill and tact. I am very grateful to have been passed into such talented hands. And I must congratulate Hannah Pierdolla for her composure in the teeth of rogue formatting. Thanks to John Karle and to Brant Janeway and Amelia Beckerman and the rest of the team for making *Diva* a reality. Bravo to Ervin Serrano for the glorious cover. As always I am lucky to be in the orbit of my interstellar agent and incomparable Caroline Michel and her satellites at PFD.

Maria Callas would not have taken the shape she did in my head without the insight and unwavering eye of Jasper Conran, and I will never forget a memorable tour of the costume department of La Scala with the brilliant Patrick Kinmonth. I couldn't have written this book without taking singing lessons with my very own diva, Josephine Goddard, who discovered my high F sharp. Nicoletta Simborowski has taught me all the Italian I know and many other things besides. Huge thanks to the story wizards Rebecca Keane and Damien Timmer and for the psychological insights of my dear friend Janet Reibstein. I have to thank the Morocco Bound crew, particularly Stephen and Jenni, for giving me a bird's-eye view of Skorpios, and to the Greek national treasure Victoria Hislop for teaching me some Greek terms of endearment. Sailing around Skorpios was the fun part; the rest was wrestling with my laptop in the London library while looking out at the people who weren't writing about divas cavorting in St. James's Square. There is no better place to write, and I couldn't have kept going without the support and encouragement of fellow members Jordan Waller, Ellie Keel, Max Gill, and Isabelle Dupuy. I need a lot of reassurance when writing, and I am lucky to have the best friends in the world—Shane, Emma, and Joanna, thank you. My daughters, Ottilie and Lydia, have lived through the writing of this novel and are the reason I wanted to write about a woman who never doubts her talent. The reason I have the confidence to write is because my father, Richard, reads every word I write and always tells me it is wonderful. My undying gratitude as ever to my husband, who luckily loves to listen to Maria Callas as much as I do.